Redemption

FREDERICK TURNER

Redemption

Harcourt, Inc.

Orlando   Austin   New York   San Diego   Toronto   London

www.HarcourtBooks.com

This is a work of fiction. Though it draws on aspects of New Orleans
history in the early years of the last century, it does so with a very free hand.
The characters and incidents are thus the author's own inventions and
are not intended to represent actual figures and events.

Library of Congress Cataloging-in-Publication Data
Turner, Frederick W., 1937–
Redemption/Frederick Turner.—1st ed.
p.   cm.
1. Police—Louisiana—New Orleans—Fiction.   2. Prostitutes—Fiction.
3. Organized crime—Fiction.   I. Title.
PS3620.U765R43 2006
813'.54—dc22   2006009241
ISBN-13: 978-0-15-101470-5   ISBN-10: 0-15-101470-1

Text set in Sabon
Designed by Cathy Riggs

Printed in the United States of America

First edition
A C E G I K J H F D B

For Steel Bokhof

Contents

Humanity, thou strong thing, I worship thee,
not in the laureled victor, but in this vanquished one.

—HERMAN MELVILLE, *The Encantadas*

Redemption

I. Fast-Mail

After so many years it seemed too late for hope—he'd never really get used to it. For Francis Muldoon, coming out at this hour, everything felt confused and out of place, as if, mysteriously, he found himself not on the porch of his cottage but instead somewhere on a shuttered passageway running between dream and the waking world of wharves, steamers, and the broad bend of the great river that flowed at the foot of his street.

The light helped him a little but not much. A late winter evening fell fast over the sooty roofs of the city. The last ferry across to Gretna was only an ancient smoke smudge against a mauve-gray sky, and as he watched it broke apart into rags and filaments and then was absorbed into the abiding haze that hung shroud-like over land raised a few precarious inches above the river that raced towards its delta. Searching in his time-grooved ways for bearings, he rolled his tongue along his upper lip as if tasting the outer edge of the night he would inhabit—and tasted instead the scrim of tooth powder he hadn't quite gotten off the black bristles of his moustache. He raked them with his fingertips, then tasted again. Behind him in the other half of the double cottage he heard the weary rattle of pans from the rearward kitchen as his sister Maureen set about supper for her two girls, and above this there ran a piping complaint from one of them.

Up and down Washington Street lamplight began to seep from between the sun-blistered shutters of other cottages, catching edges of the furious decorations of their façades—the carved fans and furbelows of the carpenter's jigsaw, the scrollwork of the lintels, the gingerbread icing of the eaves. Beyond the high, darkening bulk of the Double X Brewery down on Tchoupitoulas he could just make out portions of the steamers from Liverpool and Antwerp, Bordeaux and Genoa, moored at the Stuyvesant Docks whose broad wharves lay below street level, their chafed plankings open to sun and rain, the iron wheels of wagons and carts, and the bright, battered shoes of mules and horses.

With feet wide-planted on his porch Muldoon reached into the inside pocket of his suit coat for a cheroot, his hand sliding across the harness of his shoulder holster. He allowed himself six cigars a night and wouldn't smoke half of this first one; more than anything else these preliminary puffs were another of the ways he sought his bearings. Beyond the brief flare of the match he spotted Rob Scanlan trudging up the shallow slope towards home, jacket flung over shoulder and held there by spatulate thumb, and some paces behind Scanlan a small gaggle of men swinging lunch pails with Frank Behan in their midst and talking so loudly Muldoon knew he'd stopped at the dago's down on Washington and Chippewa. Shortly, he knew, there would be fireworks at the Behans', unless Frank made still another stop at the Black Rose on Magazine, in which case the fireworks would be delayed. As the men passed, one raised his eyes to the ruddy-faced fellow who stood smoking on his porch above them and nodded shortly in acknowledgement. Muldoon responded by touching his hat rim, then watched their backs, bent with fatigue, as they plodded through the mud and oyster shells of Washington towards home—wife, kids, supper, the sagging rack of the too-narrow bed that might well be shared with the youngest child. And then tomorrow as he himself came homeward in the morning light he would encounter some of them again, bound out for another day down at the docks, or at the bag factory, the paint plant whose fumes seared your nostrils when you walked past it, the scrap-iron dealer's with the rusty welter of its yard like a manifestation of the lives they lived: random, heavy, sharp-edged with ordinary peril.

When they were well up the street and Mrs. Seavoy had silently passed on the far side, bent beneath her bundle of laundry, Muldoon carefully stubbed out the cheroot on the porch railing, swept the ashes down into the tiny flowerbed Maureen kept, and checked the cigar to make certain it was dead out before replacing it in his suit coat pocket. The figures of other workingmen were visible down below the Chippewa corner, but no one was near the cottage now. Muldoon tugged at the skirts of his coat, took a deep inhale, and went carefully down the twelve steps to the street, the left foot leading and then the right one drawing even with it, its toe dropping suddenly, helplessly, until the heel hit and corrected the misstep. When he stood on the street he turned left with an almost military air and limped at a good rate down to the levee on Tchoupitoulas, still leading with that left foot, the right coming along behind, its toe dropping into the mud, the heel hitting, then taking the weight of the stride, the walker's shoulders squared and his head up under his hard-crowned bowler.

He passed below the last of the cottages to where the commercial buildings took over, beginning with the long, low stretch of the bag factory where once he'd worked and across from it the dago's at Chippewa, its doors off and the drinkers a dark clot at the bar. Two whiskey-roughened hoots sounded as he waded through the odor of sawdust, spilled beer, and stale urine that lay across that portion of the street like a permanent and pestiferous fog. Then the Double X on his right and behind it, on Tchoupitoulas, Cooper Smith's Stevedoring, opposite which the streetcar stopped. He could hear its rattle before it emerged out of the gathering gloom, swaying along its grooves past Toledano Street and Pleasant on its way to Downtown. When it drew up, he swung aboard with one hand, bringing his right foot deftly up while Martin Whitelaw worked the gears, jamming the car forward. "Mr. Muldoon," Martin Whitelaw said, taking his nickel. "Evening, Martin," Muldoon came back, taking his seat in the sparsely occupied car.

At Decatur he changed for the Canal Street line up to Basin where he swung off with the same athletic grace he'd boarded with, disguising for just that moment the old wound he carried. Then the car rattled and swayed on its way out to the cemeteries, leaving him where his work was, where he lived his life. He went over the railroad tracks and passed the long passenger shed that extended for blocks down the Line, then turned on Basin and crossed the invisible barrier separating the District from the rest of the world.

Inside it there was a muffled beat like a sullen pulse; there was the winking of a hundred lights, sequins on the tawdry gown of night; and a low moaning like that of a creature alive and trapped and that wanted to pull you into its snaky grasp. It was early, just the first moments of what in here was daybreak, but already there were some stray notes aloft, the first tinkles from the piano professors who played the painted uprights in the whorehouse parlors; some horn toots from the opened doors of the cabarets; the first *ping-ping* of the cheap .22 rifles the customers fired in Charlie Marcet's shooting gallery; the opening burst of liquor-oiled laughter—backwash of a dirty joke— from Milton Kelly's Terminal Saloon. And beneath these first moments of daybreak in the District, these cock-crows, there was something else, a current of sound lower down than the notes of instruments, more continuous than the bibulous bursts of laughter, heavier than the reports of the rifles and the thud of the bullets hitting the slowly moving train of lead elephants in the shooting gallery. Something that wailed with an irremediable and endless despair and that commenced at the moment when the sun sank behind the oven vaults with their crosses, their crucified Christs, in St. Louis Cemetery Number 2, turning tombs that were by day a leprous white into inky outlines against the last scarlet and brass of the suddenly sunless sky. It was the weedy, rank chorus arising from the violated throats of the colored whores, hundreds of them, singing snatches of the blues from the doorways of the cribs that lined Iberville and Bienville and Conti, all the way to St. Louis Number 2, and all the way down Robertson and Villere, Marais, Liberty, and Franklin to St. Louis Number 1 at the end of the Line. For some reason the white women of the cribs rarely sang, though if the blues were the expression of sadness, Muldoon supposed they too had their reasons to moan.

Only at this daybreak moment was it possible to distinguish any of the words. And as the penile wand of the clock rose through the dark hours and then drooped towards dawn, the blue chorus became buried beneath the roar from the saloons and cabarets; the gassy gargle of primitive autos; the still more primitive bellows of the drunken johns reeling along the banquettes, their seminal loads long since emptied into one worn crack or another and nothing left to do now with the dregs of night except to descend yet more deeply into the darkening well of drunkenness. Now, though, Muldoon could pick out some few words, tatters of lines even, sung by the women who stood at the thresholds of the cribs—bed, washbasin, tiny coal stove: *Doan you leave me here. If I was a bird Papa. Blues all in my bed. Six feet in the clay. . . .*

He knew a few of the singers by sight and even fewer by the names they went by, though the personnel changed every few months—even more frequently among the colored—as the women got sick and couldn't work, or were marked or even murdered by their pimps or customers, or simply wore out and so could no longer afford the rent of a crib and were reduced to turning stray tricks in an alley for a dime. Walking these streets therefore felt a bit like running a gauntlet, having to make your way through all these women and the blues the colored ones sang—*You just getting ready for some cypress grove*—some of them whipping up the hems of their short dresses as you passed; some fingering themselves, simulating the breathless passion that could be yours for a buck; some calling out their specialty—*Up my ass, Papa, what's your hurry now?* Some would snatch the hat off a man's head if he strayed within arm's reach, and once he went up the two steps to the crib door it was a resolute fellow who got out with his belt still buckled. And there was also the hazard of those washbasins, swimming with suds and spent semen, that the women would empty from the top step, swinging them in a practiced, professional arc, the stuff sloshing across the banquettes, drooling down into the street, so that even during a dry spell there was always a gummy mud that stuck to your soles like sin itself. On his nightly errands through those streets Muldoon made sure to walk well away from the banquettes, only approaching a crib when he was sure it was safe to do so.

For the most part he was all but invisible to the women who looked right past his limping passage through their midst, knowing him for what he was: not a customer but instead the gimp who collected the crib keys at the end of night down at Toro's Saloon. And just as they looked past him, their eyes searching dully for the live john who might be following in his wake, so he too looked through them, their hopeless hope, the visible wreckage of their lives, the swift certainty of their nameless and unremarked deaths. They were numbers, street addresses, to whom only occasionally was some provisional name attached. And he was there among them as a faceless feature of their world, on a mission for his boss, Tom Anderson—an overdue rent, lost key, chimney fire in an overstuffed stove, the report of a fracas.

He'd learned the trick of not really seeing them years back, even before he'd become what Tom Anderson liked to call his "man about town." Back then he'd been a rookie cop on the city's force, a job Anderson had also gotten him. His beat was the District where the hazards were so high the cops always patrolled in pairs and at certain times in threes but where the rewards—bribes—were commensurately substantial.

Right from the outset, Captain Porteous had made it clear that his work would be impossible if he didn't learn to overlook much of what went on within the District's municipally mandated boundaries. They sat in the captain's office, its walls covered with engravings of heroes of the force, especially the martyred chief, Hennessey, murdered by the Black Hand. If the whores weren't actually out on the banquettes physically accosting pedestrians, Porteous instructed him, "then y'all just walk on by, walk on by." And as for what went on behind the doors of the cribs, that was none of his business short of serious mayhem or outright murder. "Now them fancy places on Basin," the captain continued, "they have their own men in there to keep things right, so unless you're asked in there, you just give em the go-by. Plenty of other things to occupy you without you put your oar in where it aint needed." He'd winked then at the kid sitting across from him in his spanking new uniform with its double rows of brass buttons, a kid he was obliged to treat with a certain deference because he had Tom Anderson's stamp of approval.

Muldoon had known something of the District before this, and, of course, he had known of Tom Anderson. Everybody in the city did. But until he began walking his beat he hadn't understood just how much of the District the man controlled. And shortly he was to hear that Captain Porteous and Anderson held regular consultations on the best ways to keep the District running at maximum profit for landlords, madams, pimps, and politicians, right down to the rawest rookie on the beat who on the last of the month could count on a cash lagniappe wrapped in a handkerchief and left on the doorsill of a house by the grateful madam or pimp and the girls who worked there.

"Here's the straight shot, lad," Captain Porteous had said in summation, making his points by tapping the desk blotter with an upended pencil. "We run things down here just the way City Hall wants. Plenty for everybody long's things're done right. We don't stand for freelancing outside the limits— that's on the Uptown side of Canal and above Claiborne and past Number 1. Then, no kids. Easiest way to bring trouble for everybody is to let em run loose in here after dark. When you have the day shift, them shoeshine kids is okay, them and the newsies and the messengers and the little girls that carry hats and such to the houses. But come six, out they go, ever one. You see em, you run em.

"Now, the little niggers, you can understand their hustle. But, it's truly surprisin how many little white boys'll try to sneak in here to get a look at the women. After dark, there are even some who'll hang around the cabarets and dance places to listen to the music—can you beat it?" He laughed shortly and shook his big head. "Anyways, they all go. And the fallin-down drunks, they go, too. Man can't stand up, in the wagon he goes." Captain Porteous hadn't had any business experience before he got to know Tom Anderson, but he had a certain shrewdness and had absorbed a few important principles from Anderson, among which was the importance of appearances. Falling-down drunks and bodies lying in the street were unsightly and scared off sporting gentlemen down in the District for a night's entertainment. So, the drunks were to be collared and carted to jail until they sobered up or made the nominal bail—unless they were prominent persons or the sons of such, in which case when they were brought to the station arrangements were made for them to be collected.

As for the rest of it—the women who picked the pockets of their customers, then deftly handed off the wallet or watch to an associate; the drunks hooked into an alley and quickly rolled; the whores beaten or marked by their pimps and the ones who overdosed on morphine or cocaine; the steel-armed strongmen who cruised the streets, marking the flush sports for a pick, then followed them out beyond the hectic, winking lights, the bleat of the horns, to some dark spot—none of this, Captain Porteous gave him to understand, was his business or that of any other cop in the District. And back then there had indeed been plenty of times when he'd looked the other way, walking along with his partner, talking easily enough of other things while right behind them some form of mayhem went forward to a conclusion he'd been coached not to witness.

He recalled with a certain vividness a particularly outrageous bit of behavior on which he'd turned his back as bidden. It was Carnival, and some drunken sports from Tulane had taken a crib woman named Bang-Zang out onto Robertson, tied her to a lamppost with their cravats, and stuffed a couple of firecrackers up her vagina. While officer Muldoon and his partner had stood by laughing and Bang-Zang had cried and begged, the sports had made a broad show of lighting the salutes. Finally, corporal Flaherty had quit laughing long enough to tell the boys they'd better not follow through with their little joke, and then the blue coats had gone on, leaving Bang-Zang to the mercy of her high-spirited tormentors.

Muldoon couldn't now remember what had happened to Bang-Zang, though he thought the sports hadn't made good on their threat because he'd have heard about it if they had. But he couldn't recall ever seeing the woman around after that. Maybe she'd simply moved her business out of the District to some other area college sports would be afraid to enter, Back O' Town, maybe.

As for the kids, back then they'd been a kind of specialty of his because he was the only officer in the District—and probably on the whole force—fast enough to run them down. There were, as Captain Porteous had pointed out, those who had practical reasons for being in the District during daylight hours: the newsies, waving finger-smudged copies of the *States-Item* or the *Picayune*; the shoeshine boys with their small, square boxes and tins of wax, the rags they popped to let the customers know how expert they were; the messenger kids—boys and girls both—who carried notes or verbal instructions to and from the houses on Basin and the cabarets and dance halls and who also went out for packets of morphine and coke and brought them back to the women within the heavy-curtained houses. Most of the little girls worked for milliners and dress-makers outside the District, respectable retailers who knew the fallen women of the houses for the important customers they were. Muldoon never had the least trouble with the girls. They liked the handsome cop with the ruddy smile and black, bris-tling moustache, who every now and then might treat them to a praline from a nearby street-seller.

Even the boys, tougher types, had a distant respect for him, based on his speed, his reputation as a one-time champion runner from the Irish Channel where some of them hailed from as well. But they kept their distance because even the af-fable Fast-Mail Muldoon, as everyone knew him, had limits to his patience, and when he caught sight of a chronic offender after the six o'clock bell, he'd give chase and catch him, too, as he skidded around a corner, dodged into an alley, or flung him-self high against the boards of a fence, hoping to get over it. Then he'd give them a cut or two on the legs with the straps of his billy, yelling at them, "I told y'all—stay the hell outta here now!" Yet even at this Fast-Mail Muldoon hadn't been nearly as severe as some of his fellow officers who would just as soon break a boy's leg with their sticks if they were lucky enough to catch him. But even the tough cases, he thought, had been okay, nuisances at worst, and in the back of his mind he har-bored some old amusement tinged with affection when he re-called those chases, which often enough began with his partner saying to him quickly, "There he goes again!" and then give out with that old cry of the crowds back when he'd raced for St. Alphonsus, "Fast-Mail—sic em!"

But that had been another lifetime when he'd walked these very streets whole and unmaimed and where now he was known not for his speed but for his toe-dropping gait—just another one of the District's warped and misshapen crew, like the one he could see just ahead of him now, shuffling past the Terminal Saloon: a woman bent beneath a high cushion of burlap sacking across which was suspended a long stave polished by years of sweaty usage. From either end of it hung tin buckets, their bottoms hammered concave to increase their capacity.

"Zozo," he said to her, smiling. "Business good?"

"Oh, Monsieur Fast-Mail," Zozo wheezed, squinting her weather-blackened face under the low bind of her turban and shifting her shoulders beneath her sacking, "these whores, they taken my dust so fast. I done made two-three trips to fill these up," nodding at her buckets, "an two-three yestiddy." She turned her turbaned head in a short arc, looking nowhere in particular but comprehending all of the District in one glance. "They tink something happen."

"What might that be, you think?"

But Zozo merely shook her head at his question and then made that same motion with her head. She worked the District from noon to evening selling brick dust to the crib women who mixed it with their own urine and scrubbed their steps with it to ward off the bad luck that they knew from bitter experience hung over their lives like the city's shroud of soot. When he'd been on the force Muldoon had been told by a fellow patrolman that this was a voodoo practice and that most of the women, white as well as colored, believed in voodoo while professing to be Catholic. Voodoo was bosh, he knew, just another weird feature of this separate world of which he was himself so much a part. But down here you occasionally still heard someone speaking of Marie Laveau as though she were still alive—which would make her well over a hundred since his father had told him they were telling tales of the old voodoo queen as far back as the War Between the States.

He stepped carefully down off the banquette to let Zozo pass by on her slow, steady progress towards where Bayou St. John snaked into the city's outskirts. Beyond lay a small settlement where she lived. Out there, past the swamp and before the lake, some squatters lived in cypress board shacks fortified with cane stalks, scrap wood, palmetto thatching, and mud: street peddlers like Zozo, trappers, a few outlaws, Blind Albert, the street corner singer. As a boy with his father he'd seen it once from afar, the shacks leaning at crazy angles, blue scarves of smoke drifting from the cook fires, and the hollow carry of the barking of the squatters' gaunt curs.

He watched her for a moment, then crossed Iberville. Here a pale lemon light rained down on him from a grand electric sign hung catercorner above the entrance to Tom Anderson's Saloon and Chop House. ANDERSON it read simply. Above it from the building's third story hung a smaller sign, also in lights: THE ANNEX. This was the District's heart and nerve center, where Tom Anderson held court, entertained visiting celebrities, dispensed his justice from which no appeal was even conceivable, and issued edicts, and all in a quiet-voiced, smooth, and almost languorous manner that might have been mistaken for sleepy but was not. It was instead the calculated behavior of a man of immense and mostly sub-rosa power and influence; a man who amidst a world of raw, violent emotions immediately expressed never did anything on impulse.

Passing between the posts supporting the grand sign, Muldoon entered the barroom that stretched a full city block from Basin all the way back to Franklin. It was brilliantly, almost blindingly lit by a hundred bulbs embedded in the high, stuccoed ceiling. Equally impressive in its own way was the bar itself, a darkly gleaming mahogany expanse with snowy towels hanging from its lip at regular intervals and beneath these, shining brass spittoons sitting squatly on the white-and-brown tiled floor. But among these competing marvels what most drew your eye once you had adjusted to the brilliance of the lights was the structure behind the bar: a breakfront of monarchical proportions that must have taken a forest of cherry trees to fashion, its dark brown density broken by fat pillars supporting seven arches within which were set beveled mirrors reflecting the faces, hats, cravats, stiff collars, and suit-coated shoulders of politicians, pimps, pool hustlers, cotton and sugar factors, shipping executives, once-prominent boxers and jockeys, racing touts, professional gamblers, visiting vaudevillians, operatic tenors: the sporting gentry for whom Tom Anderson's was a clubhouse, secluded and safely removed from the workaday world and within which they enjoyed the special freedoms of that greater sporting world, international in scope, that lay beyond the purview of wives and lawmakers, ministers, and all self-appointed makers of moral codes. Here they talked politics and business in ways they couldn't in any other setting, discussing the inside dope on public affairs and what kind of money might be changing hands to affect the results. They talked odds; the gossip of back-room ward meetings; outlawed bare-knuckle bouts held on barges downriver; dog fights and cocking mains; billiards; hunting, guns, and dogs; horses past and present and how a particular race had really been won. And of course they talked women. They talked about famous ones whose pictures were in the papers—actresses of the stage and the new motion pictures. They spoke of those locally well-known, performers at the French Opera House and the cabarets of the District. They talked with magnanimous masculinity of women's sizes and shapes, of the variety of ways in which love could come. They told stories about women, and with the artful delivery of the punch line slapped one another fraternally on the back. They noted the awful predicaments a man might find himself in because of women. They never referred directly to the reason they were all gathered down here—the working women of Tom Anderson's domain and the services they nightly dispensed.

So, they talked freely. They drank. They smoked, chewed tobacco, spat. They ate the chops and steaks and shellfish of Tom Anderson's well-run restaurant. Behind the gleaming bar twelve white-jacketed bartenders saw to their needs, pretended not to hear any of the talk except when specifically asked for an opinion, and wiped the mahogany surface clean when they adjourned to the dining tables or left for the houses along Basin. Long-aproned waiters with black bowties moved among the tables bearing serving trays balanced on their flattened palms, and at the end of the bar a man named Canovan lounged discreetly, talking with the head waiter or a bartender but really awaiting the approach of Tom Anderson with some well-known or simply well-heeled guest in tow. The gentleman, Tom Anderson would confide to Canovan, was desirous of female companionship, and would Canovan accommodate him please. Beyond the door Canovan guarded lay the stairs to that Annex the sign outside obliquely advertised, five rooms, each with its high-priced occupant and supervised by Gertrude Dix, Tom Anderson's current mistress and sagacious business partner.

"Evenin, Fast-Mail," said Okey-Poke, the head bartender, as Muldoon stepped to the bar and rested his game foot on the brass rail. Okey-Poke gave the bar a swipe with his towel, though it hardly needed it.

"Okey," said Muldoon, pulling the partly smoked cheroot from his coat and inspecting it briefly. Okey-Poke leaned towards him with a lighted match. Muldoon drew in, exhaled a small blue cloud, and nodded his thanks. "Give Billy a jingle to let him know I'm here, will you?" he said then.

Billy was Billy Brundy, Tom Anderson's second-in-command—some said third, after Gertrude Dix. His office was upstairs where he oversaw Anderson's far-flung interests, wrote and edited the little newsletter about District doings, and saw to updated editions of *Sporting Life* and *Hell-O,* pamphlets that were handed out free to the city's visitors, telling them what was available in the District, with undisguised emphasis on Tom Anderson's establishments. Brundy was a tall, lank man in his late forties with a peculiar yellow cast to his clean-shaven face as if in permanent recovery from jaundice or some other liver complaint. He'd been a sailor earlier in life and carried with him yet the salty speech of his times working boats in the Caribbean and as far down as Brazil. Somehow along the way Brundy had cobbled together something of an education to go along with his sailor's swearing and an odd gift for mimicry. He had some Spanish and a few phrases of Portuguese. He could talk about books, the stage, and geography as the occasion demanded, and do so politely enough when Tom Anderson had some important guest on hand.

"T.A.'s entertaining in the Quarter," Billy Brundy announced when he joined Muldoon near Canovan's station at the end of the bar, "but there's a couple of things he wants you to see to." Muldoon nodded once, then nodded yet again at the waiter approaching with the cup of coffee he'd asked for. He took a preliminary sip while Billy Brundy polished his rimless spectacles with a handkerchief. Another waiter approached Brundy with a question on his whiskered face, but Brundy turned his back on him, replaced his glasses, and pushed them into position with his index finger. T.A., Brundy now told him, wanted word taken down to Toro's and over to the Astoria that the cops would be cracking down on saloons that were selling whiskey on a beer-and-wine license. Neither of these spots had a telephone hook-up, and so it fell to Muldoon to deliver the word.

"They hit that dago joint out on Claiborne just this afternoon," Brundy reported, "and another one in Chinatown last night. The mayor has had a hair up his hole about this for some time now, and until it stops ticklin him T.A. wants everybody toeing the line."

Muldoon nodded, sipping. Rumors of strict enforcement of the grandly ignored Tillinghast Law had been circulating down here since the end of last year, but recently Tom Anderson had gotten word out of City Hall that it would definitely be enforced before the end of January.

"And the other thing is this," Billy Brundy said, turning to face the room and squinting into the brilliant lighting. "He wants you to drop by the Tuxedo tonight and have a gander at that new beer garden they set up out back. They got a singer back there and some fucky-doo sort of group—band or whatnot. He wants a report on it, the whole set-up." He paused, thinking, the hovering waiter still poised near him, but not too near. "I guess that's about it for right now." Anderson would be back around midnight, and so if there were any further instructions, Muldoon would likely have them from T.A. himself. Then Brundy turned, brushing wordlessly past the waiter. Muldoon finished his coffee and then turned himself, threading his way through the slowly filling room, and went out into the night to begin his rounds as Tom Anderson's man about town, his roving troubleshooter: reliable, steady, performing his varied tasks with an almost machine-like thoroughness and regularity; night after night, dusk into dawn, moving with his limping gate through the garish, sex-slimed streets of Anderson's domain, beginning with his arrival at the Annex, as the head-quarters was popularly known, and ending at Toro's at dawn when he collected the crib keys from the played-out women, their faces ashen with effort and streaked with the dried sweat of anonymous and forgotten johns. More than twelve years of this during which time he'd missed only four days: two days laid up with influenza; and those two after he'd been slashed in the hand while breaking up a fight at Toro's. Tom Anderson regarded him as the most reliable employee he had. "He don't have much ambition," Anderson once told Billy Brundy, "but that aint the worst thing you can say about a man. You wind him up like a watch, and away he goes, round and round the spots. Come sun-up, he's about to run down, but he collects those keys, all right, and goes home to bed. Sleeps sound, never any problems with him. Reports in on the dot every night. Best thing I ever did, giving him that job. Wish we had a dozen like him."

"Best thing for him, too, considering," Billy Brundy came back.

Tonight as he did every night, Muldoon began his rounds just next door at Hilma Burt's, quiet at this hour, not all of the girls even downstairs yet and the ones who were chatting in a corner of the parlor with Tony Jackson, the resident piano professor. A lone customer, a portly old gent of sober suit, was buying champagne for Jackson and the girls, though Jackson's drink really was rye. He'd drink just about anything though and had already had several bumpers when Muldoon came in and removed his hat.

Jackson's presence, Muldoon well knew, was something of a problem for Hilma Burt, who prized decorum so highly. Not that Tony couldn't handle his drinks—he could—but because Jackson's reputation as an entertainer was so large he drew men to the house solely to listen to him speed through the rags and sing anything from light opera to gut-bucket blues in his high, vibratoless tenor voice. This went against house rules: the professor was only part of the come-on, not the feature attraction. That lay upstairs in Hilma Burt's lavishly done boudoirs. And if a guest was finally reminded of his obligations yet still refused to pick out a woman and retire with her, Hilma would ask him to leave. Most would, but occasionally there would be a bit of trouble at Hilma's—a "singularly well-run establishment where a gentleman may find refined company amongst Miss Burt's bevy of beauties," as Billy Brundy put it in *Sporting Life*. Last year during Carnival Geoff Pippen, the bouncer, had been stabbed in the stomach in such an incident, though not fatally. Tom Anderson had replaced him with two Cuban brothers, Ricardo and Santos Villalta, the latter doubling as Muldoon's driver when errands took him out of the District. Several times Hilma had told Anderson Tony Jackson wasn't worth the risk his presence in the house entailed. Tom Anderson thought otherwise. The way Tony went after the bottle, he reasoned to Hilma, he couldn't last that much longer anyway, and they might as well capitalize while they could on his popularity. So Tony stayed.

There would be no trouble with the old gent in the corner at least, and when Hilma Burt swept into the parlor it was clear she was comfortable with the situation.

"Evening, Miss Burt," Muldoon said, toying with his bowler.

"Good evening, Fast-Mail. Won't you sit a spell?" She herself took a seat on the divan and made room for him to join her at a decorous distance. Across the parlor Tony Jackson said something that made the girls laugh and the old gent giggle and then slowly rose, smoothing his starched shirtfront. He sat down at the white-painted upright, and presently music bloomed beneath his dark, slender fingers, something as ornate and dusky as the rooms upstairs. The old gent clasped his pudgy hands in pleasure. Hilma Burt leaned towards Muldoon and said under the notes, "He's one of Tony's fairy friends. Harmless." Muldoon nodded.

Hilma Burt had once been a mistress of Tom Anderson's, his third it was said, and still enjoyed some special regard. No other madam had two bouncers on her premises, though it was true Santos had other duties, and no other house was so carefully, constantly monitored, Tom Anderson making it clear to Muldoon that whatever Miss Burt wanted, he was to get it, and if he couldn't get it—champagne, more sloe gin, new rollers for the carpet sweeper, a piano tuner—he was to notify Tom Anderson immediately. But tonight there was nothing she was in need of just now, and after he'd sat a polite spell, refusing coffee and a glass of the champagne the girls were drinking on the old gent, he said goodbye to Miss Burt and said he'd look in later when he came for Santos.

Then he was out again on Basin, walking down the Line in the continuation of his routine, though there were always variations of it, and in a place as unpredictable and hazardous as the District there could scarcely be a real routine in any form. Even for the women in these houses, taking on one john after another, night after night—medicinal wash, inspection of the penis, splay of the thighs, the john's quick clutch of come—even this couldn't really be a routine. Always there was at least a potential threat up there in those dim rooms, always something that could go suddenly, badly wrong, some strange, demented demand whispered at the last moment: Would she wear a blindfold? Allow herself to be tied to the bedstead? Let him mount her wearing a dagger? And the house wasn't really doing its job if the john went up there sober, either. That was what the parlor and the professor were for—the drinks, exorbitantly priced. Most of the customers arrived with drinks already under their belts anyway: for courage, the shallow assumption of sexual suavity, coarse bravado. So, Muldoon had his routine, all right, a certain repetitive order to his errands, but every night danger in one form or another threatened to wreck it. Once in a while, riding homeward in morning's gray streaks or in the blinding slash of high summer's sun—slumped and swaying in the trolley that trundled back up Tchoupitoulas, the docks already active with the first cries, shouts, boat horns hooting in the smoke-blued air—then he might fumble towards the formulation of a thought about the night just passed: that it had passed without incident or injury to himself, his own small routine preserved intact for another night to come, that was in fact already on its way. But most of the time on those homeward sways he was simply too tired to think about anything except staying awake for his stop.

And he'd been very lucky so far, he knew. He'd seen the nightly, inevitable fist fights, shoving matches, challenges hurled; the knives pulled, razors flicked open with a dexterity that would have made a magician marvel. And there'd been that time when Boar Hog Robertson shot it out with Buss Pickett at the Astoria while he'd stood there breezing with the bartender and then from the open door had heard the *pop-pop!* of Buss Pickett's little pistol and the answering *wow-wow!* of Boar Hog's big .44. But he hadn't had to do anything because both men had run off in opposite directions, unscathed. He'd had to pull his own pistol a few times but had never fired it at a man. He'd clubbed a man with it, though, and that was when he'd gotten the hand wound, a clean scar running at a diagonal across his palm. He'd only been on his new job a few months when he'd rushed in to break up a fight at the Perdido, and a long-armed roustabout had wheeled on him, drawing a dark-bladed dirk from his boot and slashing at him. But he'd kept coming and somehow with his other hand had cleared his pistol from its holster and cracked the man on the temple with it, the gun discharging harmlessly at the ceiling when he'd involuntarily squeezed its trigger. Then he'd been on top of the roustabout, hammering at him with the pistol until the man had lain senseless. But even here he'd been lucky because the dirk hadn't cut any muscle, and the word quickly got around that Tom Anderson's new man, the one with the suit and the limp, had some fight in him, all right. For a fellow in his situation the reputation was essential, though in hiring him Anderson had made it clear he wasn't doing so for Muldoon's muscle. "We have plenty of fellows who do that sort of work," Anderson had told him, a fatherly hand on Muldoon's shoulder. "Billy will give you a pistol to carry, but I want you to be, well, my 'man about town,' if you like. I want you to visit around, see the shape of things. I want you to report to me just how you see things runnin, what needs fixin." The way things were supposed to run in the cauldron that was the District was at a steady, rolling boil, one that kept the customers coming but that never bubbled over the cauldron's black, encrusted rim.

He went past the French House, run by two lesbians, where they specialized in oral sex with exotic preliminaries if you wanted to pay for them. Then the Little Annex, another Anderson operation at which he would stop later on. Lizette Smith ran it for Anderson. She had once been one of his women, and some said he still paid her an occasional visit. But these days her chief service to him was her professional, competent supervision of the high-priced women made available to visiting bigwigs for whom the Annex was a bit too public.

Then Bessie Browne's, once an Anderson operation but no longer, one half of a large house catering to working men and where Muldoon himself often ended his nights. Bessie was a petite, brown-eyed woman, careful, soft-spoken, and one of the few madams who apparently had never had any sexual involvement with Tom Anderson. She was Muldoon's best friend in the District, or anywhere else in the city, for that matter, and the only one down here who called him Francis. Her place was a reflection of her personality and demeanor, quiet, clean, and serving a solid breakfast in its dining room during the final hours of business. In the mornings before he went down to Toro's to collect the crib keys Muldoon might pay a visit upstairs, then have breakfast with Bessie in the kitchen. There was a woman there he felt comfortable with who claimed to be the half-caste daughter of a planter in Martinique and who could be depended on to take her time with Tom Anderson's handsome, quiet man.

"Why you aven't got a woman, my andsome fellow, hah?" Octavia would teasingly ask him when they were together in her room. "Why you go to they putas, hah?" Then a languorous smile like palm fronds slowly stirring in an island breeze, while she shimmied her gown down her high-yellow body with its cocoa-colored nipples and neat pubic triangle. "But since you here,"—broader smile now, like island sun—"you know Octavia do her best to make er fellow appy." Then she'd be at his belt, undoing it with both hands but her left hand doing a bit more with his risen member. Then the quick check, holding his penis in both hands and twisting its head so that it yawned open like a fish out of water. "You clean, my fellow. No gleets for Octavia. I like that, I like that, ah, yes." And finally, to the narrow bed that creaked with usage and crackled with whatever Bessie Browne used for mattress filling.

Afterwards, he'd be down in the kitchen with Bessie, sitting at a small corner table while the girls worked at breakfast and washed the grimy glasses of the spent night. Bessie liked her coffee heavily laced with chicory and cream that was so fresh from the dairy out in Chalmette that sometimes while they waited for one of the girls to bring them another pot the milkman would barge into the kitchen with his wire cases in either hand and deposit that morning's cream on the counter along with the milk and eggs and butter.

In winter the light beyond the wavy glass of the windows was a weary gray-black that while they sat there sipping would grow thinner, more weary yet, the night growing tired of itself. While he was served his eggs, sausage, and red beans along with the thick, hot slice of French bread he used to sop up the last of the yolks and bean liquor the bit of sky he could see would turn a dull, tarnished gray. In spring the light became a flat nacre, and as spring folded into summer the nacre became tinged by blue until in high summer it was sure-enough morning when he left Bessie's and walked on to Toro's.

Bessie Browne's sat next to the Arlington with its signature cupola atop its four stories. Once, it had been the pleasure palace of Josie Arlington, Tom Anderson's second mistress, but Josie was long gone from these premises. Some said syphilis. Others pointed to the fire a few years back that had gutted much of the building and from which Josie herself had barely escaped. Whatever had happened to her, Tom Anderson owned it now, and the madam was Edith Simms, calm, almost saturnine at times, but attentive to every aspect of the business. Anderson got complaints once in a while that customers had found Miss Simms frosty. For the most part she was courteous enough if aloof, and she was a real friend to her women, to whom she gave expert business advice. "I learned this trade from bottom to top, honey," she'd tell some newcomer. "There isn't a trick in the bag that I don't know."

The only problem Muldoon ever had to handle at the Arlington was maintenance. Despite the dollars Tom Anderson had put into rebuilding it after the fire, there remained problems with the wiring and the new indoor plumbing. Muldoon often found himself charged with carrying back to Tom Anderson Edith Simms's tartly correct oral messages about what new problem there was or else a note written on the Arlington's creamy stationery with its sepia drawing of the building's famed cupola: "Tom—girls lights don't work on 3rd. Can't we get someone who can fix this?—E."

Muldoon rarely exchanged more than simple greetings and farewells with Edith Simms, who sat in a sort of subdued regalness on a divan in the parlor corner, surrounded by dark-hued and tasseled pillows. Once, though, out of nowhere as it seemed to him, she invited him to have a cup of tea with her. It was gunpowder from Chinatown, she told him when it was brought, and had a smoky flavor she was fond of. Then they sat sipping and unspeaking while the professor, Sammy Davis, ran through some rags on the upright, the girls expressing delight and amazement at his speed-fingering and some of them even seeming to mean it, though they heard Sammy nightly and knew every one of his tricks and showy runs. Then while the girls called for the customers to reward Sammy with some champagne, Edith Simms had asked Muldoon about the fire at the French Market that morning and whether he'd seen how much damage had been done. He hadn't been over there, he told her, but up at the Annex he'd been told it was more smoke—from the stacks of sugar cane—than real damage, but by the time he'd finished this brief report he was getting the feeling that Edith Simms had already lost whatever interest she might have had in him and the subject. He gulped down the rest of the smoky tea and guessed he'd be shoving along to Toro's. She raised her slow eyes from her cup. "I pity you, mister, having to call at that spot every night," she said. "I've never been in there, but just the looks of it is plenty enough for me." She made a small grimace of distaste.

He didn't like going into Toro's that much himself. It was a rough place, filled with men from the river and the woods: screwmen and stevedores, roustabouts, tugboat crews, and turpentine mill hands, their faces and necks black-scabbed with ancient sap. A few years ago Tom Anderson and Ed Mochez had bought out the owner, Frank Toro, but as far as he knew neither one had set foot in it since. Tom Anderson never visited his other establishments; he had Muldoon to do that for him. And as for Ed Mochez, who owned a hundred suits, if he was anywhere in the District it was at a corner table with his back to the wall of Milton Kelly's Terminal Saloon or else at the French House, which he owned. But Toro's remained a very popular place, catering to those who patronized the cribs and couldn't afford the French House or the Arlington. The new owners kept Frank Toro and his family on, and along with the cheap drinks they served up sandwiches, red beans and rice, and Mrs. Toro's thick gumbo.

Lately, a ragged group of white kids had been gathering outside Toro's in the afternoons and entertaining the drinkers who stood on the banquette with their growlers of beer; the kids played homemade instruments fashioned from cigar boxes, parts of beer cases, bailing wire, and broom handles and went by crazy names like Family Haircut, Laundry, and Warmed-Over Gravy. The only problem with them was when they hid out after the six o'clock bell, dodging around the District streets, playing a tune here and there, scooping up the flung coins from the rough men, then running on to some other likely location. And strictly speaking, this was the cops' problem, not Muldoon's. But Tom Anderson and Captain Boyle of the force promoted a kind of Three Musketeers idea of District governance—one for all—and so Muldoon felt obliged to pass along information on the kids when he spotted them after hours: "Frank, Len, them crazy kids was up at Abadie's a few minutes ago." Last week he'd dissuaded patrolman Danny Leavitt from destroying one of the kids' instruments when it had been dropped in flight. Leavitt was about to stomp it into splinters when some obscure inner prompting caused Muldoon to pick the thing out of the mud—this poor contraption of saw-wood, nails, and horsehair strings. "Ah, what the hell, Danny," he'd said, setting the thing carefully against a post. Leavitt said he thought such leniency simply encouraged the little turds; he had a chronically sore back and hated chasing them. Later that same night, passing the place again, Muldoon saw it smashed and soundless and felt a small stab of sadness.

The muscle in Toro's was in the sleek shape of Alto North, a silent man carrying the valuable reputation of a ready and nerveless killer and said to have served time for a murder he had committed while still a boy. Rumor credited him with at least two other homicides for which he hadn't been arrested, and in the loud, jostling room that was Toro's with its hairy, sweaty crowd no one wanted to tangle with Alto North who carried a .44 tucked into his waistband and was known to be handy with a razor. In his own way North operated on something of the same principle as Muldoon had when he'd been a cop: he overlooked the things that didn't appear threatening to the boisterous operation of the place, but when matters verged on violence, then North would sign to Frank Toro or his son, Lorenzo, and silently, smoothly insinuate himself into the midst of a moiling group, just as if he'd been there all along. He'd say something into a reddened ear, maybe making a knowing wag of his head, his hands held out a little from his sides; and then usually the knot of tension would begin to loosen when the men saw who was there among them. Or, if some of the hotheads were strangers, boatmen from up north, cypress mill hands from way out in the swamps, a regular would say, "Hey, man, that's Alto North. You don't want no part of what Alto's bringin, man."

Other than such tense, sotto voce remarks Muldoon didn't think he'd ever seen North speaking with anyone in Toro's. Certainly he'd never said anything to Muldoon. Nobody seemed to know anything more about him than his murderous reputation, not even his race. Some said he might even be a *passé-blanc,* a mixed-blood passing for white. His face was as smooth, as unreadable as alabaster, but an alabaster with a faint cast to it. Nor could anyone estimate his age. There were no lines around his cold-as-ashes eyes nor around the small, silent mouth. But it was there—the mouth—that Alto North carried an advertisement of his trade: a deep scar running in a short half-moon towards the corner of his mouth where it curled sharply upward, as if some nameless assailant, slashing with knife or razor, had had one last instant to leave his artistic signature on North before North had put him away. In the crepuscular air of the saloon the scar could give the stranger the impression that North was smiling.

Muldoon never made that mistake. He didn't like looking at North, but that was the second thing he always did when he entered the long room with its low ceiling and few splintered tables. First, he caught the eye of Frank Toro or Lorenzo, and then after he'd found a place at the bar he turned around to spot Alto North, who he knew had marked him the moment

he'd come through the doorway. And if in that instant when
he'd picked out North, sitting alone perhaps in a chair tilted
against a wall, North happened to glance at him, then
Muldoon's underwear felt suddenly prickly against his torso
and loins, and he had a sensation of deep cold down through
his thorax, as if he'd just taken a gulp of well water.
Involuntarily, he'd shoot his cuffs then and give a quick nudge
with the inside of his elbow to the pistol inside his coat.

The Astoria Café on Rampart was probably a rougher
place than Toro's, and the Perdido almost as rough. But somehow it was always Toro's he thought of when he'd go down to
the Stuyvesant Docks on his Monday off to fire a few rounds
of target practice from the downriver end, aiming at bobbing
bottles in the brown, soupy flow, the bloated bodies of cats
and dogs. But hitting dead things at your leisure, he well knew,
wasn't really much like what he might be called upon to do at
Toro's. And as he stood there, firing at the drifting, dodging
targets, he knew it wasn't the roughnecks, the roustabouts he
had in mind as potential, desperate adversaries. It was instead
the specter of Alto North, a man, presumably, on his side.

Tonight thus far was a tranquil one at Toro's, the room
half-empty, the drinkers only one row deep at the bar and talking quietly enough in twos and threes, and instead of the over-
powering odors of tobacco and beer and old sweat you could
actually smell the kitchen where Mrs. Toro and her sister
toiled over the stove and its pots of beans and rice and gumbo.
When Muldoon had found a space at the bar Frank Toro
brought him a mug of coffee with a spoon in it though there
was neither cream nor sugar available. Alto North was
nowhere to be seen.

"Where is everybody?" Muldoon asked, stirring the dark
brew.

"S'what I like to know," Frank Toro muttered. "This quiet all along?"

Muldoon nodded. "Pretty much." Together they glanced around the room at the men in their caps and collarless shirts, their rumpled coats and shapeless trousers, their muddy boots and high, scuffed brogans. Near them stood a somber, middle-aged man holding a glass of beer and staring into it as if asking it some kind of question. Frank Toro took him in, glanced at Muldoon and shrugged. In here you might get almost anybody, though this fellow did look as if he'd wandered off his wonted path.

"Frank," Muldoon said, leaning forward and lowering his voice slightly, "Billy Brundy wants everybody to know the cops're crackin down right now on selling whiskey on a beer-and-wine license. Yesterday they hit a place in Chinatown, and this afternoon they hit a spot on Claiborne."

"I heard that," Frank Toro said. He took a swipe at the bar with a bit of ragged toweling. "Poor dago"—referring to the owner of the Claiborne saloon—"he don't got friends."

"Not the right ones, anyways."

Frank Toro nodded and sniffed. "I hear you," he said, then rapped the bar twice in quick succession and moved off towards a customer who had shoved his glass forward with a calloused, dirty hand.

"Nuther," the man mumbled. Frank Toro took the glass and put it in place under the tap. As he drew the beer he glanced back at Muldoon, confirming his understanding, and then Muldoon nodded back and was out again into the night, passing the Countess's and then the Studio where they held the sex circuses in which a naked pubescent girl straddled a trick pony while the animal mounted the girl's mother.

Strictly speaking, there wasn't any reason for him to walk on farther than Toro's since Tom Anderson owned nothing more on Basin. But he liked to drop by the firehouse if his cousin Denny was on duty, as he was tonight. He'd have a smoke with Denny and a few of the others, the group standing on the board apron in front of the station's broad doors with the two steam pumpers gleaming darkly within and the coach dogs lying watchfully in wait. On these occasions they talked sports mostly, with brief forays into women and local politics. Now that spring was in the offing they talked baseball. The Pelicans would be training out at the grounds on Carollton against Detroit and Cleveland. Wahoo Sam Crawford, the Tigers' slugger, was a hold-out one of the men said, and would train with the Pelicans until he signed. "If he does that," Muldoon's cousin said, "I'll make the trip out, sure. He's like to bust them fences, he's that strong." Denny Christopher spit a brown gob of tobacco juice onto the boards of the apron.

Once Muldoon had known most of the men of this company, but there had been some turnover recently and two of the group gathered tonight were younger fellows he hardly knew at all. What they knew of him, he thought, was probably only that he was Denny Christopher's cousin and did something for Tom Anderson. So he thought little of it when one of them asked him what he thought of the police force converting from horses to motors. "They got what they call these *motorcycles* now," the man said. "You seen em?" Denny Christopher shifted his feet, looked sharply at the man, then spat again. Muldoon looked out on the darkened street as if one of the new machines might just then be putt-putting into view. But there was only a solitary figure, a working man by his clothes, slouching slowly in the direction of St. Louis Number 1. A feather waved jauntily from his hatband, placed there by the whore he'd just done business with, warning all her colleagues not to waste their attentions on a john who was definitely done for the night.

"I haven't talked to anybody over there in a while," Muldoon answered carefully as his cousin continued his fidgeting and spitting, "but to see how them things can rip right along, seems like they make sense, don't it? Quick as they are, they could squeeze through traffic where a wagon or even a horse couldn't. Course, you'd have to be able to get off em right quick, and I don't know how you'd do that. A horse you can train to stop and stand still."

Horses turned the group back to the spring meeting out at the fairgrounds, and after an upcoming feature race had been handicapped Muldoon wished the men a quiet, safe night, and they wished him the same. He turned back the way he'd come, heading for the 102 Ranch on Franklin in the block behind Basin, walking through one of the long, blue corridors of lament though now some of the women had disappeared behind the coffin-lid doors of the cribs, and the coal smoke from their tiny stoves lay so thick you could make it out even in the settled, Stygian gloom of night.

It had been a rainy winter right to its very end, and there was a clammy chill to the air, making him glad he had on his stout wool suit. Still, there were knots of drinkers standing about on the banquette in front of the 102 and across Franklin in front of the Tuxedo. Somebody over there on a cornet was whinnying like a horse, and laughter eddied like smoke into the street. The Parker brothers had a good crowd in there for this early. Damned good. Tom Anderson's partner in the 102, Billy Phillips, would be in a foul humor about that.

In all the years he had known him, Muldoon couldn't recall Anderson ever expressing concern about business competition, and why should he? The District wasn't known as "Anderson County" for nothing, and so when the newcomers, Harry and Charley Parker, had made Charlie Marcet an offer

on his second shooting gallery across from the 102 Tom
Anderson had merely shrugged and given his approval to
Marcet. "When they first come to Charlie, well, then he comes
straight to T.A. and says he wants to sell," Okey-Poke had told
Muldoon some weeks ago in the Annex. He was polishing
glasses behind the bar and building them into glistening pyramids within one of the mirrored arches. "He tells T.A. the
money's good, real good, and we know Charlie's gotten to
where he don't feel that much like runnin the two places no
more. So T.A. tells Charlie it's fine to sell, long's all they got in
mind is runnin the gallery same as ever. Gentleman's agreement." Okey-Poke paused in his polishing to raise his eyes just
a little. "Look what we got now." What they had was direct
competition for the 102, because what the brothers had
done—and with astonishing swiftness, too—was to knock the
old gallery into a big boisterous saloon with bar, dance hall,
and now a new beer garden out in back. "Billy's really hot,"
Okey-Poke had told Muldoon. "Phillips, I mean. But T.A., he
don't say much. Only, he says to Billy, 'Let's just eat their
lunch, Billy. We'll eat their lunch.'"

"Sounds like him," Muldoon had answered.

"Don't it, though?" Okey-Poke had come back with a
leathery smile. "Don't it just. And you know what, Fast-Mail?
That's just what he'll do: he'll eat the Parkers' lunch by
Independence Day." He slapped the surface of the bar once.
"By Independence Day. I'll put a tenner down on that."

Muldoon had smiled. "Not here, Okey."

Lately, though, there had been indications that it might
take a bit longer than that to drive the Parkers out of business
and that Tom Anderson himself had come to that realization.
Just tonight Billy Brundy had relayed Anderson's interest in
what the new beer garden looked like. And then there had

been the business of the Tuxedo's new sign, so big and brilliant it created a lemon-colored fog that cast all the neighboring establishments into a dingy obscurity. Heinrich Brothers had built it, and the word was that Harry Parker had told old man Heinrich he didn't care what it cost as long as it was bigger and brighter than the ones Heinrich had built for the Annex. It certainly was all of that.

Inside the 102 the crowd did look a trifle off and oddly quiet as if the new spot across Franklin were somehow leeching the life out of it. But Muldoon thought he might be under the influence of Billy Phillips's relentlessly bad mood—in evidence once again tonight with Phillips manhandling a cocktail shaker so violently it was alarming the man who'd ordered the drink. Phillips's youthful face was a strange, bloodless white and his mouth curled in a sneer as he told the customer that "those New York bastards better watch their step. We know how to handle foreigners—" But Muldoon didn't hear the rest of it, moving as quickly as he could towards the end of the bar where he'd spotted the wide blocky frame of Jimmie Enright. Enright's perfectly spherical head bobbed with energetic emphasis while he told a waiter precisely how he wanted something done.

Jimmie Enright's presence here was another indication that Tom Anderson had become a bit concerned about the Parker brothers, because for many years Enright had managed the Annex until the new sign had blazed into being. The day afterwards Tom Anderson had ordered Enright to move down to the 102 to help Billy Phillips put the place into what Anderson had called apple-pie order. The move had angered both Enright and Phillips, Enright because the Annex was the center of action and he had himself had a broad hand in making it so. Everybody knew genial, bluff Jimmie Enright, and he knew everybody who was anybody. But here, though it was hardly more than a block behind the Annex, was the Sahara to Jimmie, a banishment, nor had Tom Anderson given him much to hope for in the way of reprieve. When Jimmie had asked how long he might be down at the 102, Tom Anderson had merely made one of his inscrutable faces that gave away nothing yet—somehow—managed to silently insinuate that you were in his best confidence and said, "Long as it takes, Jimmie, long as it takes."

And as for Billy Phillips, Tom Anderson's move had made him feel, so he told someone, more like some sort of punk rather than a real partner. He'd installed his boyhood friend, Artie Spellman, as his manager, but now he'd been forced to tell Artie that just for the time being Tom Anderson wanted Jimmie in here and meanwhile maybe Artie ought to hang around Jimmie and pick up a few expert tips. As Muldoon drew up behind Jimmie he caught a glimpse of the displaced Spellman hovering indecisively in the middle distance.

"Welcome to the desert," Jimmie Enright said sourly when he'd finished with the waiter. "How's things back in civilization?" His small black eyes glittered with an anger he made no effort to hide. Muldoon smiled and clapped Jimmie lightly on a broad, sloping shoulder.

"Not as bad as that, is it Jimmie?" He looked about the room as he spoke. It was fitted out in the same style as the bar of the Annex, though hardly on that grand, glad scale, and no one saw that as clearly as its new manager. "Crowd's not too bad for this early."

Jimmie Enright glanced at the half-empty tables and booths, the row of drinkers at the bar where Billy Phillips and two others served up the drinks, almost as if he were contemptuous of those customers who were in there. "Come on,

Jimmie," Muldoon continued, giving him another soft shoulder pat, "let me buy you one."

Jimmie shrugged his powerful shoulders. "Well, what the fuck," he said in a tone between complaint and question but allowing himself to be turned towards the bar. "I.W. Harper," he said shortly to the bartender who hustled down when he spotted Enright waiting. Jimmie took a big swallow from the Old Fashioned glass, blinked his eyes once, then focused on Muldoon. "You see T.A. up there tonight?"

Muldoon shook his head. "He's entertaining in the Quarter. Billy told me."

Jimmie Enright made a muffled grunt and shook his head. "I just wish he'd tell me *somethin*," he said finally. "You know, like how long am I gonna be down here." He fished in his pants pocket for something, then went to his vest. "That wouldn't be too much, seems like, long as him and me been together." He found the desired item, a small piece of paper folded several times, flipped it open with his thumb and stubby forefinger, looked at it quickly, then replaced it. He took another, smaller swallow of the whiskey and tossed his cannonball head in Billy Phillips's direction. "And *he* aint helpin make it any easier—talkin all the time about what goes on over there." He made another head toss in the general direction of the brilliant place across Franklin. "It aint good business to be talkin about another place with your customers—makes em feel funny bein in *your* spot. It's like spreadin somethin. Pretty soon, they want to see for themselves, and you've kind of *sent* em. Not good business. I told him that second night I was in here. But he don't listen. Got a head on him like wood." He knocked his own with his knuckles and twirled the Old Fashioned glass with one hand. "You been over there since they opened the beer garden in back?"

"Not yet. Billy Brundy told me tonight he wants me to look in. They got a singer back there, I guess."

"They say she's a looker—big tits, eyes, everything," Jimmie Enright said in that same sour tone, as though the rumor had the new singer ugly instead of attractive.

"Better not let Billy hear that," Muldoon said, but Billy Phillips had moved off to the other end of the bar where he was lighting a customer's cigar.

"Aagh," said Jimmie Enright as if clearing something foul from his throat. He finished the glass and pushed it across the smooth surface of the bar with a flick of his fingers, wiping his mouth with the back of his hand. Muldoon reached for his wallet. "Forget it," Jimmie said. "You come by later, you can buy one."

"Deal," Muldoon said, his face in another ruddy smile. "It's a deal." He tugged at the skirts of his coat. "Need anything? Stocks and such all okay?"

Jimmie Enright didn't answer. "This all coulda been handled from up there," he said jerking his head backwards towards the Annex, its famous lights and life. "What they need here is *good will,* you know, like what I built up at the Annex. You can't just order that. It's gotta be *built.* Which takes time, and the way he's going at it, I'll be a fuckin *stiff* before things are the way T.A. wants." He made another head gesture in the direction of Billy Phillips.

A man approached and took Jimmie Enright's elbow. "Jimmie!" he bellowed. "Remember me from the Annex?"

Jimmie worked his face into the semblance of a smile. "Sure thing, sport. Meet my friend, Fast-Mail Muldoon— champeen runner." Muldoon was already turning to leave but stopped as the man in his loud-checked suit stuck out his hand. Muldoon shook it.

"Be sure to tell me later about them things," Enright called after him, making a broad pantomime of a woman's breasts. The check-suited man guffawed knowingly, and Muldoon nodded, then stepped out into the night with the lemon fog of the Tuxedo's lights all around and gleaming dully on the greasy cobbles of the street.

On the opposite side he moved carefully through the drinkers outside the doors and those gathered just within. A man with a cloth cap set at an angle above a big hawk nose and hollow cheeks gave him a hard stare as he entered looking for a space at the long bar. If he'd known where it was, he'd have headed straight for the beer garden, but the old shooting gallery had been so transmogrified he recognized nothing and knew it wouldn't do to go blundering about in here and quite possibly open the wrong door. He felt the eyes of the hawk-nosed man boring into his back as he wedged between two drinkers and put a hand on the bar. Turning back to face the crowded room he found the man almost at his elbow, but this time his eyes were set straight ahead as though he'd never marked Muldoon's entrance. Muldoon watched him swing through an open doorway at the end of the bar, hurrying somewhere under the rakish cap.

"What'll it be?" a voice said behind him: a bartender was planted opposite him, his hands on the intervening surface. The middle fingers wore thick brass rings that were dulled with nicks and scratches.

"Double X, if you got it," Muldoon answered.

"We got it all right," the bartender came back and stepped around another barman to the row of pulls. He yanked down needlessly hard on one of them and the beer came spewing white into the waiting mug. When he slammed it in front of Muldoon it was half head. Whatever else the man was,

Muldoon knew he was no bartender. He waited for the beer to calm, watching the movement in the room, the booths crowded, the cabaret girls with their hands full, and the noise level inching up and up. The Parkers had a good crowd in here, all right. When a clump of men came past him and disappeared through the same doorway as the hawk-nosed man Muldoon made up his mind to follow them and found himself in a dim corridor that led past a closed door and then the entrance to the dance hall. From the hall a man he recognized as the cornetist King Keppard was sitting with his band on a low stage, looking out on the room with his sleepy cafe-au-lait face and absently fingering the valves of his instrument.

At the corridor's end swinging half-doors opened out onto the beer garden that was surrounded on three sides by a high latticed fence. Grouped around a raised platform partly covered by a bit of roof were twenty captain's tables that had plainly once done duty in firehalls. A big potbellied stove stood in what to Muldoon seemed a hazardous proximity to the platform, and it was stoked and humming, shedding its heat on the near tables that were all occupied. In the smoky air a string of tiny lights like valiant stars was festooned along the edge of the roof above the platform, and coming towards him through the tables was the hawk-nosed man with a clutch of full mugs in either hand.

"Beer for you, mister?" the man asked as he brushed by Muldoon who had found an empty table halfway back towards the fence. The man set the mugs down on the table behind where four men leaned at different angles in the middle stages of drunkenness. Their talk was the loud, oath-spattered sort Muldoon was completely familiar with, and he wouldn't have noticed it had he not just then become aware of a girl and a mandolin accompanist stepping out onto the little platform.

In the smoky air it was hard to judge her age, but she had more than a kid's composure, he thought, as she faced the tables. The sodden sports behind Muldoon became aware of her too and hollered out their uncouth encouragement. "Show us yer tits, little gal!" one of them bellowed. Whether she understood what occasioned the gust of laughter that blew towards her on this remark, she showed no sign, looking steadily enough out beyond the tables and waiting for her accompanist to signal he was ready. When he rippled an introductory chord she brought her hands together and kept them gently clasped at her waist as she sang "Moonlight Bay," which was popular just now, though not in the District, her voice thin but clear and tuneful.

The men at the table behind greeted the sentimental song with sniggers as did some others. A bored restlessness rustled among the tables, and Muldoon heard someone let go with a raspberry—*fffffttt*—a wet, farting noise that caused him an inward wince as he gazed at the girl's pale, oval face and heavy eyebrows. This, he now knew, was going to be very rough for her, and he wondered what the Parker brothers had led her to expect when they took her on. Wherever she had been before, whatever the winding road that had brought her here to this beer garden, he doubted she'd ever been in a place like the District, and still she'd showed up for work again tonight, and that took guts.

She got through "Moonlight Bay," said something to the mandolin player, and while the restless rustle continued, she brought her hands together again and sang "A Bird in a Gilded Cage." By the time she'd sung a dozen other numbers, almost all of them similarly sentimental, some of the men had pointedly walked out, others had turned their attentions away from the platform, and the drunks behind Muldoon were bawling for another round.

"Fer Chrissake!" one of them said to the hawk-nosed man when he brought the dripping mugs, "git some damn dame back here what knows how to give a man some kind of good time. This here dame—." But he was interrupted by a companion.

"She can't sing fer shit," he growled. "Can she maybe fuck?"

There was a long pause before the hawk-nosed man answered, and it was impressive enough in its duration to tempt Muldoon to turn around, but he restrained himself, waiting, keeping his eyes on the girl as she and the mandolin player left the platform.

"Listen, friend," the hawk-nosed man said finally, "she's here to sing and nothin but."

"Aahh, horseshit," the first speaker came back.

"You don't like her style," the voice came back, low, level, and with something heavy, leaden in the middle of it, "you're free to move along—you and your friends. The management likes her style, see. She'll be here tomorrow night, and the night after." He moved past Muldoon then, glancing briefly at the almost full mug Muldoon was trifling with. When he was well out of earshot the first speaker said grimly, "Tomorrow night, suck on my cock, cock-sucker," and his companions supported this show of bravado by slamming their mugs on the slippery tabletop.

He'd seen enough to make a full report to Billy Brundy, and Muldoon arose and went past the humming stove that smelled as if the Parkers might be burning creosote ties. It made him think there was a kind of thrown-together, jerry-rigged quality to the whole operation, evidence of the speed with which the Parkers had gone to work once they'd bought out Charlie Marcet: they must have had all this in mind, right from the start, and he would tell Billy Brundy that, too. It looked as if they'd scooped up the tables at some sort of sale, knocked the platform together, bucked up the cross-ties, and hired the girl before anybody had an idea that they were welching on their gentleman's agreement with Tom Anderson. At the same time, you had to admit that so far they were getting away with it: the crowd in the bar had been sizeable, and passing by the dance hall again he saw there was a fair group in there, moving uncertainly to King Keppard's raggy numbers. And then there was the sign out front that put the 102 and all the adjacent places in the shade.

Suddenly a side door in the hallway was flung outward in his face, forcing him to swiftly alter stride and land on the game foot. It gave under him, and he lurched headlong, helplessly forward into the arms of the girl who had rushed out into the corridor. For some seconds man and woman stumbled backwards in an accidental embrace, her arms about him, his face buried in her bosom, before the door stopped them, though still she continued to clutch him while he struggled to regain his balance. As he came upright at last he saw her eyes, wide with alarm as he jerked away from her, his lips burning from their intimate contact with that very part of her that Jimmie Enright had jokingly instructed him to report on. And what was worse yet was that all this had been witnessed by a man standing in the room out of which the girl had just come, his lips drawn back in what was either a smile or a snarl, or both. It was one of the Parker brothers, which one Muldoon didn't know.

"Oh, m'Gawd, Miss," he stammered, his brick-red face now a still deeper shade, his hands held halfway towards her in ineffectual compromise between mortification and an offer of assistance. Her eyes that had been steely with alarm now began to soften towards dove-gray with his words, and she raised a hand to her lips, the fingers a little parted. Still slightly crouched, hands yet held in a gestural no-man's land between imploration and silent offer, he could see the lips begin to soften as well towards the faint suggestion of a smile. Still holding the one hand over her mouth, she reached behind her and firmly swung the door shut on the watching man within, leaving them alone in the corridor with the single bulb shedding its dingy light on them. "M'Gawd, Miss," he repeated, the blood hammering his temples. "I didn't mean any harm. It's just this—" She stopped him with a gesture of her own, bringing her hand away from her mouth and turning it, palm outward in his direction where she made a little fluttering motion.

"It's all right," she said. "But are you?" She glanced down at his bowler that had flown from his head in their collision. He followed her glance, snatched up the hat, and ran his fingers around and around its brim while she waited. Finally, he had the presence to nod, Yes.

She made a half-turn away from him, tucking and smoothing her shirtwaist, and when she turned back her smile was a bit more definite. "I shouldn't have thrown the door open like that," she said. "It must have just missed you. I'm so sorry."

"No, no," he said, his temples still hammering. "Wasn't really watchin my step." He stopped, groping for further words. "I'm sorry I...startled you that way."

"Well then," she smiled back, "I guess there's no harm done: we were both startled, and we're both sorry." She extended her hand, and he grabbed it, pumping it vigorously, gratefully. There was a moment's full stop before she turned and walked with straight shoulders down the corridor and into the smoky warren of the barroom. Muldoon followed, watching her move with a confident grace to the service station at the end of the bar where she stopped to say something to one of the waiters. Shouldering past her in the crowd he caught a glimpse of the nape of her neck, suddenly exposed and defenseless-looking as she bent her head to hear what the waiter was saying in response. He was thinking how out of place she seemed in the Tuxedo—or anywhere in the District, for that matter—when he spotted the hawk-nosed man directly in his path. As Muldoon maneuvered past him the man raked his gaze over him a last time, and then Muldoon was out into the street, the light of the huge sign showering his head and shoulders with its brazen challenge.

His first hours of sleep were always the best, after he'd hung his suit on the back stoop to air; washed his face, neck, arms, and hands in the hottest water he could stand; then tumbled into bed in the silent, shuttered cottage. Swiftly then, he tumbled further into an exhausted blackness.

If that had been all, then his boss and patron would have been accurate enough in what he'd observed to Billy Brundy about Fast-Mail Muldoon: here was a regular, clock-like man, one who got wound up each evening for his rounds, ran down towards dawn, then went home to an untroubled sleep. Here was an utterly reliable fellow, unambitious, who never asked the why of anything, seemed uninterested in the why—and not much interested in the what of the District, either: the what he nightly limped through, dragging that foot, without doing anything more and never anything less than his scrupulous duty, which was to fetch and fix, collect the keys, and to report the changing phenomena of Anderson's operations with an accuracy that had a curious neutrality to it, as if Muldoon really was more machine—coil, spring, hammer, bell—than man. These were the traits that made him just about perfect from his employer's point of view, since one of Anderson's besetting problems was that of hirelings who were gradually seduced by the District's attractions and began to behave more like customers than employees. Tom Anderson knew, of course, that his man often topped off his night with one of the women at Bessie Browne's. But this almost sedate indulgence was virtually the only point where Muldoon's personal conduct made contact with the life of the District. He rarely had more than a social beer or two during the long nights. He never gambled at cards or dice. If it hadn't been for the woman at Bessie Browne's, Tom Anderson thought, Fast-Mail Muldoon would have been inhuman.

But as for the man himself, had he known of Tom Anderson's characterization of his life, his dreamlessly untroubled sleep, he would have given a decade off his allotted span if only it were true. And without a second's thought he would also have happily embraced the image of himself as an unambitious plodder, a mere cog in Tom Anderson's machine, if he could have such serenity. Instead of which he often had only those first few hours of real sleep and these the grudging, almost accidental gift of sheer somatic need. But then the waking world, the world of consciousness and conscience as well began to reach through like the slits of daylight that found their ways between the shutters and sills of the cottage, forcing their steadily lengthening lines into the darkness until they lay like bars across his bedroom. Sometimes it was the light that awakened him, especially in high summer. Sometimes it was a sound: the cry of the itinerant knife-sharpener; a tinker with hurdy-gurdy and monkey; the old praline woman who now had her teenaged granddaughter in tow to carry the candies to the doorstep, though the kid couldn't make change; the warning whistle of a neighborhood thug; the laryngitic rasp of the tethered bulldog in the yard behind. Or it could be nothing, neither light nor sound. Only something inside him that rent the patchwork veil of sleep and sentenced him to remembrance, dragged helplessly back to that hot July night in 1900, to the dark wood house on Saratoga and the great Robert Charles riot.

Nor did it make any difference what stratagems of escape he tried. Scenes recalled out of his Channel childhood. A train trip he'd once made to the western parishes with his father. Recollections of his career as a record-setting runner: of particular races won; the look of the track behind the buildings of St. Alphonsus. The time he'd shot at the payroll bandits outside the bag factory. Whatever he tried, he was never able to outrun the memory of that night and the high, bleak building in Uptown, windowless in front and with a wing-like annex at the rear connecting it to the house next door and forming the end of a chicken run that for him proved a kind of coffin where life as he'd known it ended and another half-life—shadowy, limping, lived out in darkness—commenced.

Everything ought to have felt shiny in that first spring of the new century—grasses, flowers, time itself. Yet it was as if the old century didn't want to let the new one start off fresh but wished instead to keep it back with the 1800s and their mired, unresolved matters. But few in New Orleans allowed themselves to see that. Their eyes were filled with the future, its grand prospects as well as some of its challenges. That stifling summer they hadn't wanted to see that the brooding past was about to explode into the unfledged present in the shape of a gigantic race riot.

There had been signs, though. On that all agreed in the smoking aftermath when they were plain enough to read.

For one thing, there had been those citizens who were warning that the city's Negro problem was getting more severe by the month and that something must soon be done to curtail the darkies' freedoms before they took over New Orleans and went where they pleased and when. These same citizens also noted that while whites elsewhere in the South—Mississippi, Georgia—had been voicing similar concerns, New Orleans had a greater concentration of Negroes within its limits than any place in the entire region. Just this spring there had been a horrifying act of Negro savagery in Newnan, Georgia, that ought to have awakened the city to its own peril: a black in that town had waylaid, raped, and then beheaded the twelve-year-old daughter of Newnan's leading citizen. He had hidden the head in the woods, hoping to conceal the identity of his victim, but they'd found it and found the monster himself. Then they had burned him alive, cut his heart into slivers, and sent them to the governors of Georgia, Mississippi, and Louisiana. Was this not a sign of the times?

Colonel Hearsey of the New Orleans *States-Item* thought so. In one editorial after another he told his readers that race war was inevitable and that the sooner whites faced up to this fact, the better prepared they would be when it came. The Colonel was a hero of the War Between the States, had seen slaughter up close, and knew its awful realities. Still, he said, bloodshed must come, and the outcome could not be in doubt: the extermination of the black race in America.

Against this rising tide of white public opinion there had been a sullen sort of black backwash, a surliness bordering on insubordination, where butlers moved about their daily tasks with a stubborn slowness, maids made perfunctory swipes with dust rags, and waterfront workers and mill hands slouched along with a lazy languor. An old conjure man, Paris Green, long absent from the city and presumed dead, was seen again in the city's streets in a swallow-tailed coat and wearing a necklace of alligator teeth. Old Green refused to answer directly when spoken to by curious whites but only muttered darkly about *vodun* matters.

In early June drums were heard one night, somewhere near the Vieux Carré, and reported to the police. Yet when the officers tried to find the source of the commotion nobody could agree on the direction. Sounds in the city had always had a mysterious, sourceless ubiquity, seeming to have no true home but to come instead from far away, even long ago, as if originating on some placeless, non-quotidian plane. Finally, the drumbeats were traced to Beauregard Square. But the old dancing ground of the slaves where before the war they had beaten barrels with beef bones and raised savage chants in tongues now unknown lay silent with only the serpentine arms of the oaks there as reminders of Damballa, the snake god of the long-vanished rites.

A few days thereafter a big voodoo gathering was reported out at Bayou St. John near Spanish Fort, and there was more drumming there. That at least was indisputable. But witnesses also reported the apparition of Marie Laveau, and that made senior officers laugh since they knew the old voodoo queen was long dead and even the daughter who had reigned in her stead hadn't been seen in years and was said to be bedridden behind the shutters of a tiny cottage on St. Peter. But a contemporary voodoo woman, Madame Papaloos, had pronounced so ominous a forecast of some huge trouble that a white man who had gone to her for love medicine reported this to his alderman.

In those endless, hot days there had also been more and more of the leaflets advertising passage to Liberia for the city's blacks. Handed to workmen on their weary ways homeward at dusk; to aproned women crying okra and pralines along the bowered streets of the Garden District; distributed in sheaves in the rough-and-ready black bars of Uptown; collecting in drifts on stoops and doorsteps along the waterfront; blowing loose in vagrant gusts of wind that momentarily dispelled the heat: these were the productions of the International Organization for Repatriation & Migration urging Negroes to begin depositing funds in the organization's coffers to secure passage back to the homeland. And if that had been all there was to the leaflets, that might have been fine with those whites who read only the bold lettering at the top—PASSAGE TO LIBERIA! After all, for those who had become convinced the Negro problem was intolerable, migration was a far less drastic solution than the race war the Colonel called for in the *States-Item*. Besides, only those Negroes provident enough to save money could take advantage of the organization's offer, while the servile and stupid remnant could be easily enough controlled while they performed their menial tasks.

But the body of the text was quite another matter because it claimed that migration was the only recourse the Negro had. Black men and black women would never get an even break in America, the text claimed, and especially not in the South, where night riders were on the rampage, lynchings an increasingly common phenomenon, and the national government afraid to protect the rights of those it had fought to liberate but had now abandoned to the hoodlum vengeance of the defeated Confederates. These were incendiary statements, and so patrolmen were ordered to do what they could to discourage distribution of the leaflets. "Tell them niggers to move along when you see em standin on the corners and passin that crap around," went the order. "You see a stack of them things anywhere, you be sure you pick em up and dump em somewheres."

On the first day of the new month, a morning gray and heavy as sodden flannel, a patrolman down at the French Market tried to arrest the notorious Negro thug known as Sheep-Eye for pistol-whipping a stevedore in a gambling dispute.

"I'll take that pistol," William Josselyn had said, reaching for it. He was a supernumerary officer and more than a head shorter than his huge, presumptive prisoner. "And then I'm takin you to the station for beating this here man," Josselyn said, glancing down at Sheep-Eye's victim who was on hands and knees on the cobblestones and staining them with his blood.

"Yo white ass aint tough enough to take me nowhere, man," Sheep-Eye came back, his heavy face making a sardonic leer and his milky eye rolling in its socket.

Patrolman Josselyn stepped quickly behind his man, grabbing the belt under Sheep-Eye's box-back coat, and Sheep-Eye, who had already tucked the pistol into his waistband, now looked back and down over one massive shoulder, and then began to run, picking up speed along the wharf with Josselyn hitched to him and afraid to let go. Sheep-Eye just kept going, ignoring the officer's order to stop, his back and shoulders humping right along and Josselyn beginning to lose his balance and clinging to his prisoner now without any pretense of making an arrest but out of sheer self-preservation, his hand still hooked to Sheep-Eye's belt and unable either to disengage it or to put on the brakes. Then Josselyn went down, and his helmet flew away, and still Sheep-Eye kept going with Josselyn bumping along behind and getting more and more torn up in the process—bloody, muddy, disgraced—until Sheep-Eye had made a full circuit of the market and come back to the site of his arrest where he shook off the cop like a rhino might a jackal. Then he opened his mouth with its missing molars and laughed, not a happy laugh now nor even a sardonic one but a laugh full of blood and menace. And the others there, the ones who'd been in the cotch game Sheep-Eye had busted up with his pistol, some of whom hated him and all of whom feared him, looked down at the bloody, beaten cop, and they laughed as well. To the green grocers, the fishmongers, the butchers and praline makers, the bakers, the owner of the coffee stand with its polished pewter pots of powdered sugar, the cringing, ragged form of supernumerary patrolman Josselyn was a bad sign.

So, when the emergency call for reinforcements came in to Muldoon's station some days thereafter, maybe they shouldn't have been surprised, because if you had put all of these pieces together—the drums, the gathering out on the bayou, the leaflets, poor old Josselyn—they might have made up a something. But nobody on the force had done this. Certainly not Muldoon himself, a rookie cop, and not inclined in those days to reflection. He recognized this habit of mind in others, well enough, chiefly in the Redemptionist brothers at St. Alphonsus who talked of history, philosophy, and meditation. But it hadn't been in his nature to look back. That was fatal, he thought, to being a runner. You had to look *ahead,* because if you turned to look back, you lost a certain physical equilibrium and also a kind of equipoise, and in that very backward-glancing instant someone might be right there, ready to take advantage of your subtly altered stride, your loss of clear, forward-looking vision. And, hell, if even the older heads hadn't put the pieces together, how should he have been able to when the captain had him called off the corner and ordered him into a wagon that went clanging off towards Uptown, all of them carrying extra ammunition, and Rebollet and Mix with shotguns?

When they had arrived at the scene they saw that this was no ordinary disturbance, though even then they didn't understand that here on Saratoga was the culmination of all those signs, portents, the fulfillment of the forecast of Madame Papaloos. At that point it looked like a very ugly situation that they were there to contain before it got any worse: two and possibly three officers injured, an unknown number of assailants cornered in a house, and an angry crowd of whites in the street.

That the assailants were Negroes was certain, members of that very troublemaking organization offering passage to Liberia. This had been reported by the original officer who had come upon what he described as a big buck insolently sitting on the steps of a white man's home. The officer had ordered him to move on. The buck never moved, though, only replied that he could sit anywhere he liked and would. He was holding a sheaf of papers in his lap, the officer said, and suspecting these might be the offensive leaflets being handed out around the city, he ordered the buck to hand them over. It was at this point that real trouble began.

"I goes to collar him," the officer had breathlessly reported from the nearest callbox, "and then he pulls on me and fires. He misses, thank God, but I don't, but I can't tell where I hit him cause the light's wrong, y'know. And just then, here comes another buck out of the alley, and they run off together, and I seen the big one with the pistol—I seen him kinda-like grab his shoulder. And he sure as hell dropped them papers right quick, and when I come up to em—the papers, I mean—I see a splash of blood across em, so I know I got him somewheres. I give chase, but I lost em, and so here I am, corner of Franklin and Delachase, and they gotta be somewheres right in this here neighborhood."

They were there all right, tracked by blood splashes to the house on Saratoga outside of which the whites now were massed. Little Henline tried to force the wagon through the crowd but couldn't, the men boiling up around it on all sides and a few of them grabbing at the horses' bridles and hollering for the officers to do something. At that point an officer had emerged out of the mass, and after they'd pulled him in he told them of the two men down—shot stone dead, he reported, by high-powered rifle fire from the house's second story. And he thought yet a third officer must be down, a man named Coakley, because after he'd crawled around the corner of the house into the chicken run, searching for a side entrance, they'd heard another shot and then nothing further from Coakley.

Little Henline kept on trying to urge the horses ahead, but they balked and reared, wild-eyed and frothing, and so the reinforcements had to stand there in the wagon, watching as the crowd built towards the proportions and mentality of a mob and parts of it began to break off as men ran home for hunting rifles, shotguns, even knives and clubs and old sabers from the war. And as they ran they spread the news that the niggers had risen up and were killing the whites. There were attacks then on Negroes in adjacent areas like the edges of the Channel and the Garden District. Along Canal gangs of whites began pulling Negroes from the trolleys and beating them. The precinct stations began to receive the first reports of deaths.

He could never forget the look of that mass of men. But even more, he couldn't forget the smell, the feeling of them. It was like being surrounded and almost inundated by a thousand swollen bags of boiling blood. And he'd thought fleetingly then of the hazard of hitting one of those bags with his nightstick and setting off a flood in which all of them would be drowned. All these years later, lying in his twisted bedclothes in the bars of midday light, he could smell the mob, feel it bubbling in his ears, taste it in his teeth, and sometimes he'd bolt from bed, panting and wiping at his face, thinking it must be covered with blood. But it was only fear's sweat.

But he had swung his stick after all, full force on a fat, bald head beneath him and then had leapt into the space where the man had gone down, like a sailor leaping from the imperiled deck of a ship. And then the others had followed his lead, leaping over the sides of the wagon and fighting towards tall Captain Porteous whose helmet they could see sticking out above the moiling mass. When they reached him at last he began shouting down into their faces, his own face plump and white as cooked pork. Two men were dead, he told them and a third trapped in the chicken run around the corner of the building; they must see to him directly.

But first there was the question of strategy, and here they had to contend with the crowd as much as with the black assassins. They could dig in for a siege, keep peppering the house with gunfire, and outlast the enemy, yet with this hellish crowd building by the minute it wasn't likely the people would stand for that and would take matters into their own hands. Maybe they were on the verge of that already, in which case many more lives would be lost, both from hostile fire and from those who would be accidentally shot by their own neighbors—or even trampled to death. Then there'd be hell to pay at headquarters and city hall. Or, they could burn the bastards out, but the house was connected to the next by that annex, and the whole block was made up of close-set wooden structures that would likely go if this house did, and who knew where that might end? Captain Porteous stopped shouting, jammed his helmet tighter on his head, and leaned down to say something in the ear of the officer next to him, but nobody else could possibly hear it.

Porteous took a quick visual inventory of the newly arrived reinforcements and jabbed a long, pale forefinger at Muldoon. "Muldoon!" he shouted. Muldoon was shoved forward in the blue-coated huddle, and when he was almost touching the captain's broad chest Porteous roared down at him from so close Muldoon could smell the dinner the captain had been enjoying in his office when the call came in. "Muldoon! There are men up there"—jerking his head up and back—"firin on us with high-powered rifles. We don't know how many, but several, anyways. As soon as we can get some men over there"—pointing to the adjacent house connected by the annex—"to give you cover, you will crawl around this here corner and rescue Patrolman Coakley who's lyin there bad hurt."

Then Captain Porteous formed six men into a wedge, their nightsticks and pistols drawn, and Rebollet and Mix in the middle of it with their shotguns at high port, and at his command the unit charged, slugging its way into the mob, disappearing into it. Meanwhile Muldoon waited for their covering fire to commence.

It was, he thought, a long time in coming. There was no fire coming from the house and hadn't been since Coakley had crawled around the corner and along the plankings that were raised a few inches above the chicken run. So the shot that had likely disabled him had been the last one from the house. But surely more could be expected as Muldoon made his preparations for the rescue—stripping off his belt and nightstick, removing his helmet, snapping open his pistol and checking its load. As he was snapping it shut again there came the heavy shock of a shotgun blast, delivered so close to him he felt its concussive wave. It had come from the mob, and as if it had been a sort of signal, their bellowings reached a new intensity, and a raw-throated voice rose above them all.

"Well, what'n *the* hell y'all waitin on?! Get *the* hell in there and get those black bastards!"

Instantly the burden was taken up by others: *Go in there! Get em! Blue-bellied cowards! What we payin y'all for? To stand around with yer thumbs up yer ass?! Y'all give us yer rifles, and by Jesus, we'll fetch them niggers ourselves! Shame on you, Michael Porteous! I never till now took you for a yellow cur! You don't dare show your face in the Channel after this, Michael!*

As the abuse thundered down on them Muldoon noticed Captain Porteous regarding him with a searching fixity, as if somehow he were responsible for this situation, as if the safety of the unit—and maybe the honor of the city's force, too—depended on his rescue of Coakley. He finished his tightening and trimming gestures, then crouched, tense and waiting like a runner on his mark, looking to Captain Porteous for the word that would send him off into the run.

It was at this point in his relivings of that night that he might be lucky enough to make a brief imaginative escape. Because while he had awaited Porteous's command someone in the crowd had recognized him as he stood there, bareheaded in the torchlights. "Muldoon!" the man had shouted. "You, Fast-Mail Muldoon!" Muldoon kept his eyes on the captain. But then another voice joined in, calling his name and adding to it: "Fast-Mail—*sic em!*" It was the old cry of the crowds that had gathered to see him set those quarter-mile records at St. Alphonsus and anchor the mile relay team that won the state championship one year. And so instead of watching himself ordered at last into the coffin-like gloom of the run and hugging the wall as he inched forward, he was allowed a glimpse of himself as he'd been back in those high school years when, flush-faced, his black hair flaring from his temples, he'd flashed past other crowds, admiring ones, towards victory. He would envision then that mile relay team and himself taking the baton from Jimmy Dunnegan or maybe one of the Mayne brothers who always gave him a good, solid hand-off, planting it in the palm of his back-reaching hand.

And then he'd hear the crowd's humorous, affectionate, admiring cry, "Fast-Mail—*sic em!*" and hear as well the cheering laugh that came right behind it. He'd take off then, baton grasped tightly, the mincing, timing stride of the transfer lengthening into the longer flow of the quarter-miler, and in that old-time instant he'd take in the whole field and instantly understand what it was he needed to do. Whatever the situation, whether it was a clear track or there were other runners ahead, the cinder path looked virginal to him, awaiting only his spikes, and he felt he didn't truly touch those cinders but passed just above them.

In those days he was incapable of considering anything less than victory, because in those days there wasn't anyone who could pull up on Fast-Mail Muldoon. And so, even if the way ahead were marred by the sight of a heaving torso, the gleaming spikes of a rival, he always believed he could catch him. Almost always he did so, knowing they heard him coming, knowing they knew he'd hooked them, sometimes catching them sneaking a backward glance over a despairing shoulder—fatal—and then he drawing up, drawing even, drawing past, making it appear so effortless it crushed the last reserves of wind from their bursting lungs.

He remembered once being surprised, shocked even, after he'd taken the hand-off from Rusty Mayne and looking ahead had seen victory shiningly in wait, that there had come out of the corner of his eye a something that wasn't even a shadow. And then, suddenly, there'd been this kid, right there on his elbow, long black hair, cheeks bellowing, in-out, sallow face drawn with desire and effort, eyes straight ahead. Later, when it was all over and he was talking about it with his buddies on a corner in the Channel, he'd said, "Man, I'm telling you that was like somebody puttin a torch up my rear, seein that kid there!" And they'd all laughed, standing there at Camp and Third, admiring him, reliving with him that brilliant burst he'd put on, and of course the sallow-faced kid hadn't been able to stay with him, had fallen back.

Then, a few years later and after Tom Anderson had gotten him on the force, he'd encountered the kid again and they'd become friends in a remote way. He'd been walking along Decatur across from the French Market, picking his teeth after his breakfast at Madame Begué's and had spotted the sallow-faced kid, staring at him from the street-front window of a bakery he must have passed a hundred times. They recognized each other: he, red-faced, still growing into his full moustache, belt, brass buttons, billy; and the other, the second-placer, engulfed by steam, dusted with flour, Dominic the baker's son. Thereafter, when he took his breakfast at Madame Begué's he made it a point to walk down Decatur towards the mint, and if he saw Dominic in the window, he'd wave and flash his wide, ruddy smile, and once in a while Dominic would come out onto the banquette beneath the long, uneven warp of the tin overhang, and they'd stand together, talking horse racing or weather, looking across at the market stacked with everything from pineapples to the gleaming mounds of fish that would begin to dull towards noon, the vendors positioned under the ponderous arches of the arcade, and maybe a cop standing watch over a few Negro inmates from the parish prison who pretended to sweep at the steadily mounting refuse with long-strawed brooms.

Yet if he was lucky enough to make this momentary escape into recollections of running, it could only be that—momentary—and then the very cry that had made these possible— "Fast-Mail—*sic em!*"—would pull him irresistibly back to that moment on Saratoga when he'd heard it, and had heard as well the opening salvo from his colleagues across the chicken run. Then he was fated to watch himself ordered into action by Captain Porteous who had stood tall and stout against the boards of the house, pointing the way around its corner and into the coffin-shaped enclosure where Coakley lay.

And he'd gone, of course, and without, as best he could recall, any hesitation. It had never occurred to him not to go, nor even to ask Captain Porteous what he was to do if he should find that Coakley was dead. That would come to him much later, when he lay in Charity Hospital, bound in mountainous bandages from waist to the mid-thigh of his right leg; when the consequences of his thoughtless alacrity began to take shape for him like objects coalescing out of a blank and shapeless fog; when he could begin to see that his life would never be the same, that he wouldn't ever be the same man, not to himself, not to others: *then* he had wondered why he hadn't thought to ask Porteous for fuller instructions.

But by the same token, there was no doubt that the reason why Porteous had so speedily chosen him for the mission was this very readiness to act, this alacrity, athleticism, a kind of handsome recklessness of style. That had been his way on the track, and it had been the reason why Tom Anderson had remembered him later when once again he'd drawn attention to himself for an exploit as a guard at the Mente Bag Factory on Tchoupitoulas. There on a soft spring afternoon in '99 he'd shot it out with three men who'd tried to take the company payroll satchel.

He'd taken no particular notice of the three who'd been lounging against the railings on the river side of the street, waiting for old Agee to arrive with the payroll and the guard Milliron along with him, Agee stumping along on his wooden leg, his badge of bravery from the Wilderness in '64. When

Agee and Milliron had cut across the street in front of the loungers towards the factory entrance where he'd stood, the men had whipped out pistols and dropped Agee in the street and wounded Milliron in the leg so that he dropped his own pistol and went down on one knee. And Muldoon had still been standing there at the entrance, smiling, a bit vacant, completely relaxed, and anticipating only some banter with Agee. But when he saw Agee go down, still clutching the leather-strapped satchel, he'd jumped into the street, flung aside the skirt of his coat, and pulled his .38, standing there, bold, uncovered, outmanned, shooting at the bandits across no more than twenty feet of dirt. They'd fired back, but nobody had hit anybody in the exchange. Then the bandits had fled without the satchel, two down the street and the third, the one Muldoon thought might have dropped Agee, leaping the railings and running along the wharf below. Then Muldoon had flung his pistol into the dirt and to the delight of the onlookers had given chase, catching the bandit and drilling him into the wharf with a flying tackle that broke off the man's upper front teeth. Down at the station house the bandit had continued his awful screeching from his broken teeth, until they'd found a dust rag and stuffed it into his mouth so that all he could manage was a muffled moan.

The incident had made all the papers—"The Further Adventures of Fast-Mail Muldoon"—and Tom Anderson had sent a man to see him, telling him Mr. Anderson would like to meet such a hero, which was how he'd come to leave the factory for the force where, so Tom Anderson explained, the pay was only marginally better but the side benefits of a beat in the District substantial.

And so, when Captain Porteous had looked at his available personnel in front of the house on Saratoga, maybe it was inevitable his eye should immediately find Muldoon and send him into the chicken run, crawling on knees and elbows along the narrow walkway.

He hadn't crawled very far before he had made out the sprawled form of Coakley, face down in the dirt, one leg on the plankings of the walk, and one hand, white, motionless, its palm pitifully upturned as though at the last moment the patrolman had been asking a mute mercy from his assailants. A few flickers from the mob's torches and bull's-eye lanterns threw scattered gleams into the run as he crawled yet closer to Coakley, and when he had stopped a little more than five feet from the body an orange ray had flashed across the leg, making it seem as if it had moved.

"Coakley," he'd called out, but his voice, he discovered, was so dry it was little more than a croak. He tried again, swallowing a couple of times. "Coakley! Can you hear me, man? Make a sign, man, and I'll get you out of here!" Something like a minute passed while he stared, and then the same orange ray found the body. "Give me a sign, Coakley—anything!" His eyes burned through the gloom as if they too had been torches, and just then it did look as if Coakley had made a sign by moving the foot that lay on the plankings.

Muldoon lay there, hugging the wall, staring at the foot, trying to recall precisely what Captain Porteous had said to him. He'd ordered him to rescue Coakley, but had he also ordered him to court certain death from above only to retrieve a corpse?

How long he remained against the wall he could never determine, and through the intervening years he swung back and forth in his estimates between only a few minutes to nearly an hour. Meanwhile, the roar of the mob in the street was like something solid and unchanging that had been going on forever, and he'd found himself wondering why the gunmen in the house weren't firing on the civilians, many of whom had made themselves targets by holding aloft those torches and lanterns. Maybe they wanted only to kill policemen, but he thought if the Negroes should begin to fire on the mob, then he might dart out, determine if Coakley were alive, and if so drag him back to the slender safety of the wall. He had just made up his mind to call to Coakley once again when the guns of his covering fire blazed again from across the run, and he knew they had commenced in the expectation that even then he must be maneuvering into position for the rescue.

He gathered his elbows beneath him, his pistol gripped in his right hand, tensed his legs to push off—and couldn't move. For the first time in his life his legs had failed him. It was like childhood's nightmare where the ogre was chasing you and you couldn't make your legs go because they were stuck in something—sand or mud or water. He tried again and, failing, tasted something overpoweringly metallic on the leather slab that used to be his tongue. Paralyzed, he lay there, hearing the covering fire and between the reports the solid wall of noise from the mob. High above him a window was shattered by a shot and dark shards of glass came showering down into the run, one of them breaking across Coakley's leg. He tried to burrow yet more deeply into the wall, shrinking from the shower, dazedly wondering where that invincible courage of his boyhood had gone, the kind that had stood him so splendidly in stead on the track, the kind that apparently had been once again in evidence in the incident at the bag factory.

Privately, though, he had never regarded that as so many others had. His actions out on Tchoupitoulas, he thought, had little to do with courage or bravery or coolness under fire. The thing was simply that he'd had a genuine affection for old Agee, had known him since childhood, and knew that Agee had once been a runner himself, but that had been before the war and the Wilderness where a fragment of a tree, transformed by a cannonball into a high-velocity missile, had sheered through his calf. Eventually, they'd had to take the leg off above the knee, and then no more running for Agee but hobbling through life as a cripple. So, when he'd seen the poor fellow shot from behind like a dog, why, he hadn't thought about himself, about duty, about courage—any of those things. He'd just gotten so angry about the injustice of the thing that he'd pulled out that pistol they'd given him and blazed away with it. When he'd missed with all four shots and seen the bandits escaping, he'd thrown it aside and collared one of them anyway.

That didn't make him a hero in his own view, which was how they'd treated him down at the station house, everybody hollering for him, pounding his back, holding high the precious leather-strapped satchel like a trophy he'd won. It was just like the old days when he'd been setting those records and collecting the medals and little trophies his mother kept on the parlor shelf next to the colored portrait of the Holy Father. And then they'd taken him to the Black Rose on Magazine where they bought him beer and sang to him. And he could never forget that Lou-Anne had come in with a few of her girl-friends, her hair lustrous under the lights of the bar it was against the law for ladies to enter, but nobody paid that any mind, not on a night like this, not in the Channel. And when she'd entered, her chestnut hair with its copper highlights shining like that, she'd shot him a look and made a gesture with her chin and shoulder—kind of tucking her chin behind her shoulder, sheltering part of her face—and he'd felt his belly tighten and his member move against his fly, and it seemed it was taking her forever to get through the throng. Then there she was, in front of him with her giggling retinue of girlfriends, and the throng closed in behind them, blocking any possibility of retreat, but she didn't seem to want one anyway. Face-to-face at last, there'd been that moment of natural embarrassment, the red hero and the lustrous-haired girl everybody knew he was stuck on—but so were a lot of other guys in the Black Rose that night. There were hot hands on his back then, pushing him towards her and a high carrying sound of acclaim (for him and for her as well) and a good-humored hilarity at this public situation that in its celebratory openness appeared to amount to some sort of declaration. The press behind them both was relentless, and the hero and the girl were moved—shoved really—inexorably towards each other until they were almost touching, and now they were laughing, too. Then Lou-Anne made another ineffable gesture, one that was a beguiling, enigmatic mixture of assent and regal resignation as well, and cocked her head at an angle, flinging her shining hair, and raised her round arms to encircle his blazing neck, and then with a movement that was demure and something else as well that reached back before manners and courtship even, kissed him fully, softly, pliantly on the mouth, and the roar in the Black Rose was like the beating of blood in his ears. . . .

And here was another crowd, urging him forward, demanding he move forward, and the beating of the blood he was aware of then was not his own but instead came from the mob on Saratoga: those boiling bags of blood that thirsted for still more blood, for black blood, and his blood, too, if that's what it would take to get the nigger killers out of the house. He thought again of old Agee, hobbling through his days on his splintering stump, the horrible way he had to twist his torso in a half-circle to bring that maimed leg around for another painful pace. Seeing that, he saw himself, trying to get

Lou-Anne to the altar on one leg, saw them on their wedding night and he unbuckling some ghastly leather contraption.

A shout had come from across the run, bringing him back to the hellish present. "Muldoon!" He thought it might have been Rebollet but couldn't be sure. In the dense gloom and flickers he could just make out a long eddy of gun smoke drifting lazily out of the house where Rebollet and the others were. "Muldoon!" the shout came again. But instead of answering it he found to his dumb amazement that he was moving at last, that his legs were working, that he had left the wall of the house and was inching out into the run. But it was as if he were watching somebody else do this, that it wasn't he who was doing the moving, but another man who was being *pulled* towards Coakley, by some combination of duty and duty's dark, obverse side, shame. Afterward, this volitionless movement was one of the central mysteries of the entire experience, though in his helpless returns to that moment he had plenty of occasions to inspect it, prying with the restless fingers of thought at the Gordian knot, attempting to pull one true strand from the dark tangle and be able to call its name.

He had just reached for Coakley's foot in its heavy black brogan when he heard the *crack* of the rifle from high up behind him, and in that same instant the slug kicked up dirt in front of his face and a pebble bit into his right eyebrow. "*Coakley!*" he screamed, feeling the blood from his wound suddenly wet on his cheek. He flung his pistol away, grabbing at his eye, his other hand still clutching the foot. He thought he might have screamed Coakley's name once more, but maybe it wasn't his name or any name but only the nameless sound of terror.

He didn't hear the next report of the rifle, because just then the officers opened up again, several guns speaking at once, and under them the thunderous blast of a shotgun. But he knew he would remember always—what he thought in fact would be his final memory of life—the sensation of being nailed into the earth by a molten spear shot from a great height behind him.

That was the end of the Robert Charles riot for him and the beginning of the rest of his life, the slowly, steadily lengthening stretch of years in which he efficiently functioned as Tom Anderson's "man about town," while his every other step proclaimed his dishonor.

And there was plenty of that—dishonor—to go around in the aftermath of the riot when it came out that the gang of assassins that had paralyzed a great city had numbered exactly one, Robert Charles, who had stood off the city's police force for days. The editorialists and reporters were an avenging horde, led by Colonel Hearsey. They wrote of the unmistakable omens ignored; of the craven cowardice of the police, beginning with officer Cecil Trenchard, who had originally encountered Charles but was then seen running *away* from him, not after him; of officers Rebollet and Mix, cowering in the house adjacent to Charles's rickety redoubt, and firing blindly rather than exposing themselves to risk; of officer Muldoon, ordered to rescue his fellow officer but instead attempting an escape and wounded, ignominiously, in the posterior—the coward's eternal brand. And all the while, the smoke was still rising from the blackened shells of houses on Saratoga and Liberty and Franklin; from threadbare Negro businesses torched by whites in the Uptown area; from a Negro orphanage that suffered a kindred fate; and from the charred bodies of Negroes who had been trapped in their homes by fires and who preferred that death to the mercies of the whites gathered outside, urging them to jump to safety.

In the morgues of Charity Hospital and Touro Infirmary the corpses of Negro victims of the riot lay cold as ashes and as gray. Many would remain unclaimed, their relations afraid to venture forth to claim them. Sheep-Eye, his no-color orb closed in death and at last only a big nigger on the wrong trolley at the wrong time, lay with three other stiffs in a cart parked in the alley behind Parish Prison, awaiting transport to a pauper's grave. Madame Papaloos was refusing to see any white clients, even those she had ministered to for years. Paris Green had once again vanished. The drums were silent.

But all was not silence and death in Uptown, for there were the beginnings of the legend of Bad Robert Charles, rising at first in whispers, like smoke, then becoming bolder, more vocal, expressive, taking on color and form: tales of his marksmanship, of how many policemen he'd dropped; ridicule of the patently false story the authorities put out about Robert Charles's death at the hands of the police, when everybody knew he had escaped, wounded it was true, but alive. There was a ballad as well, replete with scabrous references to the police and the mayor. It didn't name Francis Muldoon, but there was a stanza that could only have referred to him:

A-rresting officer, doan give me none o yo sass.
A-rresting officer, doan give me none o yo sass.
Or Bad Robert Charles put a bullet up yo ass.

Which wasn't precisely where Robert Charles had put the .30-.30 slug, but for the purposes of defamation and end-rhyme it was close enough.

Some said "Bad Robert Charles" had been composed by Blind Albert. Whether that was so or not, Blind Albert was certainly the one who popularized it, singing it on street corners with his guitar in Uptown, Back-O-Town, and in the District.

Then some of the whorehouse professors like Sammy Davis, Tony Jackson, and Game Kid picked it up. One night, though, when Blind Albert was singing for stray nickels on the Basin and Villere corner someone brought him a double I.W. Harper from a nearby saloon, and he answered a request for "Bad Robert Charles." Just then a couple of those "a-rresting" officers happened along, snatched Blind Albert's guitar from him, and broke it against a telephone pole. "Here's one for your black ass!" an officer said, giving Blind Albert a boot right there. The story got around that it might not be too healthy to sing about Robert Charles for a while, and so the professors would play the tune but not sing the words.

Muldoon himself never heard the song, at least not knowingly. By the time he was back in circulation it had become but another part of the blues, a song without words. When it had been current and popular among the blacks and the sporting world he'd been laid up in Charity Hospital, bandaged, swathed with dressings, and not much interested in anything, least of all a song. Then one morning he had looked up through the haze of his unfocused eyes toward the globular bulbs of a ceiling that seemed to him hundreds of feet high, and there was Dr. Bigges, white of hair and beard, holding out for his inspection what looked like a pebble. It was the slug, deformed by what the doctor thought must have been a deflection off a primary object before its subsequent passage through Muldoon's right buttock. In that passage, Dr. Bigges explained with inclined head and a series of brief gestures with it, the bullet had pretty severely damaged the sciatic nerve.

"A few inches to the right, it would have maybe given you a fairly superficial wound—right here—" and Bigges patted the fat of his own buttock. "A few inches the other way—" He paused, rolling the dark little lump between thumb and forefinger. "Then no family life for you, Mr. Muldoon." He was therefore a lucky man, Dr. Bigges wanted him to understand. Bigges had been an orderly in the War Between the States and had seen injuries of this sort that were badly disabling; his wasn't. He'd have to learn to live with a limp, though, because the affected muscle controlled certain functions of the foot. He wouldn't have the range of sensations in that foot he'd formerly had, nor would he have the control he was used to.

Muldoon listened passively to some of this, his mind drifting about like a rudderless boat. When he came back to Bigges the doctor was telling him a cane at first might be a good thing, just until he became accustomed to how the foot behaved. But then, he said, it would be for the best if he learned to walk unaided.

"Won't do at all to baby yourself with this, son," he said. "My experience with these matters tells me that the man that stands right up to his disability—whatever it may be—that man will make the best adjustment." There came a lengthy pause; Bigges seemed to be considering something. "They tell me you were a pretty fair country runner once," he said. "That right?"

"I guess I was," Muldoon responded at last, gazing up at the doctor seraphically surrounded by the high, dim globed lights. His voice surprised him a little with its lack of volume, its tentative timbre. He seemed not to have spoken in a very long time.

"Well," Bigges said, "you use that same kind of grit, and you should get along fine. My judgment there." He leaned forward and placed the twisted lump on the bedside table. In its asymmetry it quickly fell over. Bigges picked it up and handed it to Muldoon.

"Here. You may want a souvenir."

His family visited him, all except his mother, who was too undone by the whole business and couldn't bear the sight of her son lying in a hospital bed with that unmentionable wound. One or two friends from the Channel dropped by at the end of the day but were plainly embarrassed, and after shifting from one foot to the other had left, promising to return another time. Lou-Anne didn't come.

One day he was surprised by the arrival of Beverly Henline, the sister of little Henline who'd driven the wagon that night. She had her two-year-old daughter with her. He'd been up on crutches for several days by that point and was just coming back down the ward, swinging himself forward and now and again venturing a tentative touch of the right foot to the dull gray floorboards they scrubbed down early every morning with a solution so pungent it made his eyes and nostrils smart. Then he saw her standing at the end of his cot and stopped short, his foot raised. She saw him, too, and they stared at each other across an imponderable distance, he feeling naked in his issue pajamas and robe. He made a brief, fluttering gesture with the fingers of both hands, the palms still resting on the handles of the crutches, as though trying to wordlessly explain what these things were and how he happened to be holding onto them. Beverly Henline smiled slightly and nodded, signing that she understood. Still, he didn't move, and they continued to regard each other, the little girl beginning to twist and swing on her mother's arm. Finally, seeing he wasn't going to advance further, she'd come slowly up the aisle between the white-sheeted, paint-chipped cots, some with silent figures in them watching this pantomime with vague interest. When she had closed the distance she stopped, still wearing that small smile that had become a little fixed now in his silence, his one-footed arrest.

"Well," she brought out, "how you coming along, Fast-Mail?"

"Pretty good," he said, glancing down at the crutches in another wordless attempt at explanation. "Be off these shortly, then I can go home."

"Yes, that'll be grand, won't it. Hospital can get a body down so."

He nodded. "Some days it does get kinda boresome." He tried out a smile and thought he saw in her eyes what a wretched counterfeit of his hearty grin of long ago it must be. He dropped it, and with it silence fell, only the sound of someone in the long, echoing room mumbling something and beyond that the clank of bedpans and ironware pitchers in the corridor where two orderlies exchanged a joke and laughed.

The little girl began to ask something of her mother who now looked down at her, whispering a placating response. Then she looked at him with her sad, small eyes, the smile tucked away now, put back in that velvet-lined box of sadness where she kept a few other usable effects like the equally sad, wanly warm smiles she gave her daughter, seeing in the small face the likeness of the father who had left town rather than face along with her the disgrace of this product of their unsanctified coupling.

Beverly said she was certain he would get well quick, him being so strong and lively a fellow and all. She'd come back another day and hoped that when she did she would find he'd tossed aside the crutches and was getting around fine. But unlike the others who promised the same, Beverly did come back, twice, in fact.

The second time happened to be his last day in the hospital. Outside a rearward portion of the grim pile there lay a tiny oval of beaten grass and a gravel walk encircling it. Three or four stunted palmettos dropped dispirited fronds over a couple of rusted iron benches that patients and visitors might use when hospital personnel weren't on them, smoking and laughing during their breaks. He'd taken to walking around and around the oval, the protuberant black tip of his cane punching the gravel as he leaned on it, experimenting with holding the cane in one hand or the other, using different grips, weight shifts, trying to train the heel to take the weight of the stride before the helpless drop of the toes.

Then Beverly was there once again, and they found a place on one of the benches which they had to share with a mother and her son, badly scalded on his neck and back by a steamer's boiler explosion. In any other situation he was able to imagine this enforced close proximity to a polite woman he didn't know well might have made him uncomfortable. Around the women of the District though he'd usually been at his ease. His father had introduced him to them when he'd turned twenty. He'd been a regular customer ever since and found their company alluring in a way he couldn't define, for certainly it was perfunctory enough. But you didn't have to pretend anything with the women of the District, and so in that sense you were relieved of all social obligations.

This was different—or would have been before his wounding—sitting so close to Beverly that when they exchanged an infrequent glance at each other their faces almost touched. Somehow, though, it didn't matter that much to him, the ruined man and the disgraced woman almost flung into each other's company by misfortune, and Beverly's little girl sitting at their feet, rolling handfuls of gravel through her gray fingers. There was something almost relaxing about it all: what else could there be for either of them to lose? And so when she asked what he thought he might do when he was ready to go back to work he found himself sharing a note that had been hand delivered a few days earlier by a man named Jimmie Enright.

Its thick, creamy folds betrayed numerous unfoldings and re-foldings, but she overlooked this evidence, opening it directly and reading the vigorous, clear script:

Francis,
  "Bad break there lad — & trusting in yr full &
speedy recovery — When yr on yr feet again drop in &
see me — I may have something that will suit you —
    — Thos. Anderson

And he had eventually done just that, though not until several months had passed and he'd learned to get about without the cane, learned a good bit about what the foot couldn't do. And he was learning, too, about other, new realities he would have to live with just like his limp: the evident embarrassment of all those in the Channel who'd known him and had basked in his reflected fame but who now didn't know how to greet him, even in a few instances whether to shake his hand or to keep on walking when they spotted him across the street, grotesquely reduced by his gimping gait. *This* was their Fast-Mail?

He avoided the Black Rose, partly out of his own embarrassment and partly to spare others theirs. When he wanted a beer, which was rarely, he went down to the dago's on Chippewa where a rougher, heterogeneous lot got drunk in the afternoons and nobody cared who the hell he was or how he'd come by that tilting limp. They all had their own disfigurements to live with. But he had little money to spend on beer and had never been much of a drinker anyway. A lot of his time he spent down at the Stuyvesant Docks, not walking, just sitting silently, surrounded by all that life: the great booming ships moored; the shouts of the stevedores, sailors, straw bosses; the teams of mules hauling the high-piled wagons or standing in the autumnal glare, tossing their bridled heads to ward away the flies.

There came a day down there when he was suddenly roused from his moody reveries by a shift of the wind into the north. The temperature dropped, and the skies took on a steely edge. He thought of Tom Anderson's note, gathering its thin coating of dust on the bureau of the room he had in the back of his brother Kevin's house, and then he rose, deciding to go down that very day to see Tom Anderson.

He hadn't been back to the District since the riot, and it came as a shock to find, stepping carefully down from the car, how sharply he'd missed it. In the two-dollar parlor places on Iberville he used to frequent they'd be getting their first customer about now, and he'd be pressed to feed coins to the player piano and buy the girls a quart of wine. Then shortly—very shortly—that man would be on his way upstairs where his chosen girl would have his pants down in a hurry and his member in her hands, inspecting it. Standing still on Basin, his mind went back to that preliminary business: the strong, utterly unmistakable smell of those purple drops the girl would sprinkle into the basin of warm water; the mixture of the arousing and the soothing as the girl washed you and dried you with a soft washrag from the pile of them on the little washstand. Then she'd have you on top of her, and if she knew her business well, she'd bring you within a minute or two at most. And even though there'd been that inevitable sense of deflation afterwards—the whole thing over so swiftly—still there'd also been some dark, romantic tinge to it that saved it for him. Limping towards the Annex, he recalled his excitement in these streets when he'd be so eager to get to the parlor house he'd chosen for the evening that sometimes he'd actually run down Iberville. It was all he really knew of romance.

Plainly, he was never going to know of it with Lou-Anne, who was said to be keeping steady company these days with Jerry Flynn.

Tom Anderson wasn't at the Annex, but Jimmie Enright said he was expected soon enough and that Muldoon should stick around. An hour later Anderson arrived, turning all heads just as a king might in his appearance for a levee: tall, broad-shouldered, his strawberry blond hair waving back from his florid temples and making a striking contrast with his blond moustache. Anderson had then only a hint of that prosperous portliness that later would be one more distinguishing characteristic. Still, he cut so fine and conspicuous a figure advancing through the room that to the watching Muldoon it seemed he would be instantaneously identifiable as the most prestigious person in the place even if you had no idea who he was.

But of course everyone did know it was Tom Anderson, and he had many hands to shake, backs to pat, confidential asides to make, his glowing, pomaded head inclined at just the angle to convince his listener of the moment that there was no one on earth whose friendship he valued more highly. So it was some time before he intersected with Jimmie Enright and still later when he arrived at last at the small table where Muldoon sat waiting.

And there began what Muldoon came to regard as his after-life, for it was on that evening that Tom Anderson had laid out the job he hoped Muldoon would take, a job, so he said, he thought Muldoon might be uniquely equipped to handle, and wouldn't he kindly give it his most serious consideration? Muldoon had said he would and three days thereafter had met with Billy Brundy in his office on the second floor of the Annex where Brundy began the patient if profane process of his education in the complex webbing of Tom Anderson's kingdom. Now, more than twelve years later, Muldoon thought he might understand more about the night-to-night realities of the cribs, houses, saloons, and tonks than anyone in Tom Anderson's organization—more than Billy Brundy himself.

For the first several years no one in his family asked what it was he was doing for Anderson. They knew he worked six nights a week and wore a collar and tie, something no Muldoon was ever known to have done. Then, early one Sunday afternoon his father had asked him out for a beer at the Black Rose, and in the course of their conversation they had arrived at an understanding. In answer to his father's question about what it was he was doing for Anderson, Muldoon replied that it was mostly a matter of seeing that things ran smoothly at Anderson's various establishments. He himself, he explained, was rarely called upon to do anything physical in the way of keeping order, though he did carry a pistol in a shoulder holster. "Mr. Anderson has plenty of men," he told his father, "who do that sort of thing for him."

"Well, look here, Francis," Thomas Muldoon said then. "I don't think we ever need to get too clear to your mother about Anderson's businesses or what all you have to do. What I'll tell her is that you're a special constable of a sort and wear one of these to work." He straightened his son's tie, though it didn't need it. "That'll be enough for her—and it's enough for me, too. I don't want to know more." He took a sip of his beer and glanced down the bar at a row of familiar faces. When he turned back to his son his eyes were red-rimmed and moist. Francis had been his hero, too. "Her heart was bust because of that." He flicked a glance at Muldoon's foot. He took a deep breath and straightened his shoulders. "So, now we understand each other: a special constable it is."

Somewhere along this stretch of years Muldoon had come to another sort of understanding, though this one was gradual: he discovered how fully he had become just what Tom Anderson had wanted him to be—his man about town. For not only was he Anderson's eyes and ears every night, his quiet, clockwork collector of keys, but he was also wholly dependent on Tom Anderson's largesse in virtually every aspect of his life. Anderson owned the cottage he shared with his widowed sister Maureen and her two little girls. Anderson sent him to his personal tailor for his suits and paid for them as well, telling Muldoon it was worth it because a well-turned-out man was a walking advertisement for his employer. Tom Anderson had also gotten him to invest a portion of his salary in Anderson's Record Oil Refining Company, which had resulted in a tidy sum in Muldoon's savings account. He knew of no Muldoon who had ever been able to save anything, but Tom Anderson, he found, was a big proponent of saving.

"Spend money," Anderson had once advised him, tapping the Annex's gleaming bar top with the hardened stub of his right forefinger. "Spend money, Fast-Mail. It makes men feel good to see you do it." He made a short pause for effect, then in a slightly lower tone added, "But always remember to save a little more than you spend." He winked and patted Muldoon's shoulder twice. "That way you'll have enough put by so's they won't have to get up a collection when it's time to send you off."

For a time it seemed Anderson was even going to sponsor and oversee his private life as well, because when Muldoon had eventually married Beverly Henline, Anderson had hired the hall and the musicians and would have supplied the liquor and food, too, except Muldoon had said his father and the Henlines had already made those arrangements. As a Channel man himself, Tom Anderson immediately drew back, respecting the hard-swept pride of his own kind.

But then, several months thereafter, Muldoon had gone to Anderson to tell him that he had unwittingly given his bride a case of gonorrhea and that she had gone back to her family, taking her daughter with her. So once again, Anderson had taken charge, sending Muldoon to the city's best specialist for treatment and commiserating with him in a fatherly fashion, telling him most sporting men got it one time or another. It was too bad, he said, that the Missus was so unforgiving about it.

About the only significant aspect of his daily life, therefore, that Muldoon thought might be substantially his own was his choice in whores, and even here he reflected that if on a given night he happened to choose a house other than Bessie Browne's, the chances were that Tom Anderson had a financial interest in that house or its inmates. He wondered once whether this might be his reason for frequenting Bessie's—some small show of independence.

For the most part, though, he had easily enough accepted the terms required by his work. He lived far better than anyone he knew in the Channel. He had mastered a demanding and dangerous job. He had some money in the bank whereas he didn't think many of his neighbors did. And all this starting from the most disadvantageous, handicapped situation he could imagine: a disgraced, informally cashiered ex-cop, physically unfit for any work he could realistically aspire to. For that was precisely his situation on that late September afternoon on the Stuyvesant Docks, wondering what the hell he could do with the dregs of his life. There was, he'd thought then, staring off across the river towards Gretna, an awful lot of years to kill.

II. Tom Anderson

In the world in which he moved but hadn't created Tom Anderson was not regarded as a violent man. Quite the opposite. This, among many other things, set him apart and instilled something bordering on awe in his rough-handed and often low-witted associates to whom it was second nature to strike first. Anderson used violence only when necessary, the way a blacksmith might a cold chisel. Yet in the making of his character many of the same conditions that produced the violent, impetuous men and women who surrounded him produced in him an individual of singularly careful calculation.

The ninth of eleven children of a Channel couple, he was early pushed out into the streets the year after Appomattox and forced to find ways to get along in a world where no one cared how old you were. In those lawless and chaotic days he ran errands, then began to carry stove wood for a Cajun carter who would take a swing at him at odd moments that had nothing to do with his performance. Still, working for old Asfaux was not without its unintended compensations, because after enough reddened ears and skull knots, he learned he must always be on guard, anticipating a sudden assault. So, while still a boy, he became a characteristically wary man.

His apprenticeship with Asfaux came to an end one afternoon when he had just finished delivering and stacking wood in the cellar of a saloon while Asfaux waited in the wagon. When Tommy Anderson dragged himself up into his seat next to Asfaux, the man leaned close and breathed into his face. "Lezzy leetle turd you are," Asfaux said with a menacing slowness. "One day I must keel you." His black eyes glinted like chips of cheap glass in the walnut-colored seams of his patched and ancient face. The boy didn't show up for work the next day, and for a few days thereafter he made himself scarce. Sometime later he saw Asfaux on the street, but the man appeared not to recognize him.

He got work as a newspaper boy, a trade with its own hazards. But he consistently avoided confrontations with the scrappy kids—Irish, Italians, some Germans—though he was already bigger than many of them two or three years older. His size and steady manner bought him some natural deference, but more importantly it bought him time that he used to begin figuring the angles to his work, the way a billiards player must if he aspires to be anything more than a half-hand big shot playing for nickels at some corner saloon. He learned soon enough there was additional money to be made as what was called a "steerer," one who served as a guide to sporting men looking for a good time. He continued to sell his papers, but he also formed a kind of partnership with a whore: she issued him a pack of playing cards, and when he'd successfully steered a customer to her room, he signed the card—"T.A."—and the man took it up with him, for which the woman gave the boy a small cut. He was thirteen.

Another angle a sharp newsie could play was keeping his

eyes and ears open for the cops. This was tricky, however. Already he had one foot planted in the city's underworld, and being detected talking to the cops might well result in his permanent banishment from that world he knew held greater promise for him than the grinding life of manual labor that loomed as the obvious alternative. So, he had to learn patience and prudence, when it was safe to tell a copper about a drunk he saw being rolled in a nearby alley; a strong-arm man stalking his unsuspecting mark through the dim streets of dawn; a burglar casing a spot. Some of the time the officers would flip him a coin. But what was more important, he thought, was that he stood in well with them, and that might produce a more substantial payoff somewhere down the line.

At the same time, it was equally important to stand well with the underworld element, and this could require an almost instant calculation of the odds as well as the angles of any situation.

An incident out of his newspaper days stayed with him. He'd sold out his stack and was idling along St. Claude late one morning when he happened to glance into an alley near the intersection with Kerlerec and was immediately horrified he had. Because what he'd beheld in that glance was Chicken Dick, a gigantic black outlaw of whom he was so afraid that if he saw Dick walking towards him, he always crossed the street. Chicken Dick had another man up against the side of Fauria's Grocery & Pool Hall, and in the instant that Tommy Anderson's glance found him was delivering a knife thrust with the full force of his frame, slamming the blade home so hard that even Dick had to brace his legs and yank to disengage it. The man had screamed then, a high, warbling sound, and Chicken Dick seemed as if he was about to deliver another thrust, the blade black with arterial blood, but then he'd looked away from his victim to find the newsboy, frozen to the dirt of the street, and their eyes met. Dick's blazed with a fixed, feral flame, and then his mouth parted slightly and the boy had seen a bit of his upper teeth as Dick gave him a grotesque parody of a smile. Then the hand, still holding the knife's smoking blade, had come up level, and Dick had pointed it at him, holding it steady, unwavering in summons and threat and prediction, and then had run towards a shed at the end of the alley beyond which stretched a high board fence.

Even as he did so, Tommy Anderson heard the shrill, piping alarm of a copper's whistle and watched Chicken Dick disappear into the shed. Then Dick's victim had reeled out of the alley and onto the banquette, clutching at his heavy black vest that already was soaking. So were his striped pants as far down as the mid-thigh, so that Dick must have connected with the abdominal aorta.

Then here at last came the copper, his whistle bubbling in his mouth, nightstick held high, dodging between drays, pedestrians, loungers, until he reached the victim who by this time had sat heavily down on the edge of the banquette, still holding himself together. Then, as though he had only been waiting for the arrival of the copper, for permission perhaps, he had tumbled into the dirt, coughed once, and died.

And it had been then, at that precise imperiled instant, that he, Tommy Anderson, had been forced to a decision. For whereas he had already learned that it might sometime pay off to stand well with the coppers, now to be an informer might well cost him his very life. In pointing the murder weapon at him Chicken Dick was marking him for future extinction if he should say what he'd witnessed and point out to the panting policeman the shed Dick had run into. Because it could very well be that the shed had a window in back just as it had in front, in which case Dick might already have made his escape.

More likely though, he was still in there, watching to see what the kid would do, hidden behind a stack of wood, some randomly piled crates, a broken hame: crouched, monstrous, armed, a glaring gimlet eye watching in the blackness—unwinking, unforgiving as God or the Devil.

Or maybe Dick watched from the other side of the fence, peering between the slats, and if Tommy Anderson were to point the direction Dick had gone and the copper had given futile pursuit, what would his life then be worth? Chicken Dick or any of his outlaw associates could pick him off just about any day they chose. Marked for death, he would hardly be protected by this pudding-faced fellow perspiring in his heavy blue serge coat or by any of his colleagues.

So, he'd pointed quickly, decisively the other way, across Kerlerec, towards the Quarter. "Ya sure of that?" the copper rasped. And he'd said, "Yeah, sure," his blue eyes big with earnest excitement.

Late that afternoon, back in the Channel, he heard the casual talk at Dunaway's Saloon & Oyster House of a killing on St. Claude as he swept up the sawdust, tobacco plugs, and cigarette papers, the broom's soiled, stubby bristles making viscous smears of phlegm and tobacco juice along the boards. But he said nothing, mulling the matter in his mind until he had come to its meaning for him, which he wouldn't have called its moral but which amounted to the same thing: that if a poor kid like him were skillful enough, he might be able to play off both sides against each other and maybe come out a little ahead in the end.

And there was one other thing here, buried, as it were, in the frightening situation into which his idle eye had accidentally thrust him. It lay in the contrast between the giant black outlaw and the panting policeman whose name he later learned was Krug. Whatever the specific morality of that situation— and, yes, surely it was wrong to take a life like that—there was something you had to admire about men like Chicken Dick: they took their chances—cards, cockfighting, burglary, strong- arm stuff. He'd heard that Chicken Dick had even wrestled a bear for money once, at Rice's Café, and the bear had crushed his ribs before they clubbed it into submission and dragged Dick off. But the coppers on the beat, the supers in the station houses, the fat-necked men in City Hall whose well-oiled jowls left half-moons on their cravats: the one thing you could count on from them was that they *wouldn't* take chances, not if there was any way they could help it. None of them would ever wrestle a bear, not without having fixed the fight by drugging the beast beforehand or some such stealthy stratagem. There- fore, while you had to learn from them, how they rigged as much of life as they could, you couldn't truly admire them like you could Chicken Dick and his kind.

Tom Anderson subsequently built his life on the model of those who took only calculated risks and avoided even these if a surer thing could be arranged. But there was in him, he knew, a warm spot for those—men and women both—who took their chances, took them mainly because they really had no other choice. But took them. And he had spent his life artfully poised between these camps: living off the life of the District with its desperate women and men; employing them, going to bed with them; sharing something of his proceeds with them; listening to their inevitably, predictably sad little stories that all ended the same way, and that he, God-like, could even early on predict; taking care of a few of them when they'd been used up; in an occasional instance disposing of them when they'd become like distempered dogs. And there had been times, too, when he'd been moved to buy one of them a decent burial.

At the same time he dined, hobnobbed, and politicked with the safe, ostensibly sober men of judgment. They couldn't have him to their homes, it was true. But even truer was the fact that the superintendents, the senators, shipping executives, restaurateurs, and Rotarians all knew Tom Anderson and went to him when they wanted to get a deal done. They went to him as well when they wanted to spend themselves between the professional thighs of one of his gorgeous octoroons.

As for his standing with Chicken Dick, he learned something of it little more than a week after witnessing the murder on St. Claude. He'd been peddling papers down at the French Market one morning when he'd seen Dick standing in a crowd of roustabouts, his slouch hat pulled low and a cigarette stub bobbing from his lips while he talked. And before he could slip into the market's interior through a butcher's alcove Dick had spotted him, stared at him, and then summoned him with a slowly crooking index finger. Dumbly, helplessly, he'd signed back, "Me?" and Dick had nodded, "Yeah, you." And then he'd moved numbly towards Dick, who stood a head higher than any of the other burly men in their shapeless, sweat-stinking clothes. Reaching the group, he saw Dick disengage himself from its midst and go to his coat pocket. But what he produced wasn't what the boy had feared—that awful weapon—but a coin instead. Years later Tom Anderson could still vividly recall his thought at that moment: *"He wants a paper! That's all he wants, is a paper!"*

He handed Dick the paper and wouldn't have cared or even noticed maybe, if Dick hadn't handed him the coin. But Dick had and then had clapped him hard on the back. Then he had turned to the others in his group and said in a loud voice, "Any of you guys sees this kid around, he's okay. You remember that: this here kid is okay." Then Dick had looked down at him and winked one of those terrible eyes. So had begun what was to be a long and mutually beneficial association, one that endured even to the current day, though nowadays Dick was a bit long in the tooth for some of the rougher jobs Tom Anderson had once assigned him.

But the person who taught him most about angles, about percentages, was Edith Simms. In those days she worked out of a house on Gallatin, behind the French Market and where he was then peddling his *Picayunes*, steering, and running hop for the women. When he went to the local drugstore for Edith Simms, bringing the little packets of cocaine back to the house, he noted the difference in her behavior from that of her colleagues. She seemed not especially interested in the packets themselves, merely accepting them and carefully counting the change. He never saw her take the stuff, so that after a time he began to suspect that the tall, quiet woman with her heavy, upswept hair never took it at all and was procuring it for some favored customer. This among other things set her apart from the others and to the adolescent boy lent her an air of mystery that was compelling.

He only saw her outside the house a very few times and never in company with anyone else—another aspect to her mystery. Once when he was racing around a corner on Carondelet and almost ran into her. She had stopped short, glaring at him from out of the dim shadow of her hat. Then he saw recognition arrive in her eyes, but that was all: no glint or gleam of pleasure.

"Buster," she said firmly, "you wanna watch it," and then went on, he looking after her as she picked her tall way along the banquette raised a few inches above the gray mud of the late winter street where the air was still cold enough that year that the newest deposit of mule manure sent a thin snake of steam towards a sky that nearly matched the mud.

Another time he encountered her on Esplanade and she'd sent him to the drugstore for some hop. When he delivered it to her room and Edith had counted the change and given him his tip her windows were open on a soft spring afternoon, the drapes pulled aside so that the thin white curtains behind them bellied inward like girls' summer dresses, and the air was scented with bougainvillea and orange blossoms. Edith Simms herself seemed almost seduced by it all, seating herself on her divan and leaning back into its overstuffed cushions.

Suddenly, the sweet somnolence of spring was split by a high, short shout that was almost instantly followed by an answering one. Then there came another sound—dull, heavy, full of force—and then another shout, this one a word: *"Bitch!"* Then a rattle of windows along the row, a flinging open of doors, clatter of footsteps on the stairs of the house. Edith was off the divan, moving to the window in a few long strides, then out her door and down the stairs and he following. Out into the day he found a sudden crowd of whores and charwomen and men in their singlets, braces down, their white arms looking like strangers to the sun. But for a moment he couldn't make out the source of those sharp sounds that had drawn them and so was about to leap down the steps when she'd caught his out-flung arm with a swift, iron precision. She held him then in that amazing grip while he struggled to regain his balance, and then the crowd shifted, broke apart for a moment, and he saw what had drawn them all: two whores in the street, squared off for a battle that had already begun.

One of them he knew as Angie, a tall, rangy woman who wore her dingy hair screwed into a bun. The other was unknown to him, short, no-necked, and clenching a piece of stove wood that she had already used on Angie whose forehead flashed bright with new-brought blood. As he watched, Angie's assailant sprang at her again, delivering another clout that Angie was partly able to fend off with her forearm. She staggered sideways under it but drew a barber's razor, and he saw its severe nakedness sparkle as Angie's long arm brought it downward through the soft air. The other dropped the stove wood club in the dirt, grabbing at her upper arm and making a sound between a scream and a growl, staggering sideways herself, her slippers kicking up two tiny plumes of dust. With her other hand she reached for the club, and Angie's eyes were filled with running blood now, but she could still see enough to take another hack with the blade but missed. The no-necked woman moved inside then, making a low, scything swing that caught Angie in the ankle with the sound of something hard, resistless striking against something that wasn't—*chock!*—and Angie went down in the dirt with the other atop her and flailing away with the club.

That, however, was all he was to see of the fight, though later he heard all about it, how it ended. Because the iron grip that had never relaxed now hauled him back up the stairs like a tugboat, and Edith kept at it, pulling him up the hall stairs with their tacky carpeting and along the second-floor hall and then inside the room where she closed the door, not slamming it, and then closed the windows as well.

And there they stayed with the shouts of the fight and the crowd rising up to them, muffled a bit through the drapes she'd drawn. Until at last they heard the clang of the police wagon into Gallatin. But by that time Edith Simms had turned herself away from the whole commotion, using the same iron effort she had when stopping him on the steps and then bringing him back to the room. From a nightstand she produced a pack of playing cards, sat down at a little round table by the closed and curtained windows, and said simply, "Cotch. This is how you play it, and this"—making a deft hand movement he failed to follow—"is how you cheat." And dealt him his losing hand.

A few days thereafter, delivering for another woman in the house, he came upon Edith in the hallway running between the parlor and the pantry. She balanced some glasses and an ironstone pitcher of something on an oval tray, her dark hair down over the shoulders of her lavender shirtwaist. There was no particular expression on her face as with head and shoulders she motioned him to follow her upstairs.

In her room the streetward windows were curtained but the rearward one open to the noontime light, and he found her standing there holding the cord of the shade in one broad hand. Below in the yellow yard a couple of chickens pecked at the dust and pebbles and the pony turds from the stable. The roofs of the surrounding sheds were as gray and grained as weathered bone.

He had begun to repeat the gossip about the fight, the extent of the women's wounds, when she cut him short, flinging the cord back against the sash which it struck with a dry snap. She looked back at him over her shoulder with a mixture of pity and irritation, and in the long, hard silence he felt his throat tighten, the folklore of the fight suddenly leeched of its excitement.

"You see Harris out there?" she asked finally. Harris ran the house, bought his morning *Picayune* from him, and once in a while flipped him an extra coin.

"No. Was he—."

She cut him off again. "No, ya didn't, did ya. Cause he wasn't there." She turned to him, her hands empty now with the pitcher and tray on the table and the window cord still swinging lightly. "Smart guys are never around when the rough stuff starts, Buster. Never. They stay outta fights. They let other stiffs do the fightin, and when it's over they come along and *clean up*." She moved away from the yellow light of the window into the gray of the room. "Fightin's strictly for suckers. Remember that, why doncha."

So, there were only two times anyone could remember seeing Tom Anderson fighting.

Once was some months after the battle of the whores on Gallatin when Jimmie Enright cornered him on that same street. Enright wanted his stand because it was more lucrative than his own, what with steering and running hop for the women, and had been trying for some days to scare him off it. Now he made a direct challenge in front of three or four other kids.

"Come on, ya big sack a shit," Jimmie Enright said. "I'll fight ya for it fair and square." He edged toward Tommy Anderson with a pigeon-toed boxer's bob. One of Jimmie's older brothers had had a few bare-knuckles bouts and had taught Jimmie some moves. "Put up yer dukes, ya big shit."

Anderson backed up, his filthy newspaper sack held protectively before him. "I don't wanta fight you for it, Jimmie," he said, his voice strained, all right, but not quavering. "It's mine, and you got yours. Let's just—" But Jimmie Enright was having none of this, and just kept coming, his first punch hitting the sack but the next one landing on Anderson's collarbone. Enright's cannonball head began to weave like a snake looking to strike, and then he hammered home a left hook to the bigger boy's ear.

Anderson stumbled back against the wall that supported the steps of a raised cottage where he could retreat no farther. "C'mon, Jimmie," he tried again. "We been knowin each other a long time." Those were the last words Enright let him have, smashing him full in the face so that Anderson's knees buckled, and the sack slipped from his hands. The gush of blood from his nose released the blood lust of the others who now burst into raucous cheers, urging Jimmie to further carnage. Anderson stood there, his back to the bricks, with Jimmie Enright wading in for the kill.

"Kill the fucker, Jimmie!" one of the others yelled, and Jimmie Enright seemed set to do just that, slamming home two wicked blows to Anderson's body when suddenly in a move none of them truly saw Anderson's hands shot out, the first two fingers of each crossed for reinforcement, making them into pointed instruments that stabbed into Jimmie Enright's eyes. Instantly, Enright screamed in agony, his own hands transformed from fists to poor, probing paws that felt for his eyes and their grievous injuries. But Anderson wasn't through. With Enright now disabled and bent doubled, he brought back a long, heavy foot, then shot it deep into Jimmie Enright's crotch. Enright crumpled to the dirt, rolled onto his side, and retched, his hands pathetically quivering between his eyes and crotch and Anderson looming above him with his red fist raised like a hammer. He never let it fall, though, only picked up his sack, wiped his bleeding nose with it, and walked away.

The other instance came many years later when Anderson was famous, portly, and in a firm partnership with his mistress, Gertrude Dix. One night during Carnival a group of drunken college sports gathered outside the Annex, waggishly singing "I Wish I Was in Dixie." Anderson was inside, performing his genial duties, when someone reported what was going on out on Basin. Anderson excused himself from the table he was talking with, grabbed the sawed-off baseball bat Okey-Poke kept beneath the bar, and laid two of the collegians in the street. Then he shot his snowy cuffs and returned to his friends. Afterwards, some were ready to swear that he hadn't even been breathing hard when he'd come back into the Annex; you might have thought, they said, that he'd simply paid the lads a few bucks to move along.

So, they all knew he could fight and that lurking beneath that placid, genial exterior there was a dangerous man. But since he had men like Jimmie Enright and Okey-Poke working for him and even tougher specialists like Alto North and Chicken Dick the dangerous man, the quick and inventive fighter, never had to come out, was only there, in wait. And indeed, the dominant strain in his character actually was the placid, splendidly generous fellow he seemed to be, always ready to shake hands with tourists, visiting firemen, figures of the sporting world, politicians, and theatrical people. This was no act but the real thing. Dead-center above the bar of the Annex there hung a framed photograph of a smiling Tom Anderson shaking hands with T.R.—Teddy Roosevelt—the image a daily testimony to the fact of the man himself.

And it was this Tom Anderson who quietly, patiently listened to Muldoon's pedestrian report on the new beer garden at the Tuxedo. Privately, he accepted no man's assessment of anything as the last word. He believed himself to be the best and final judge of the affairs of his world. As for the women who had been his successive mistresses, he relied on them principally for their judgment of whores, which all of them had once been themselves, and he thought Gertrude Dix the most sagacious he'd come across yet. But with men and women both he carefully encouraged their belief that he highly valued their views, silently winnowing with his mind his wheat from their chaff.

In Fast-Mail Muldoon he felt he had at his service a thoroughly ordinary mind, one that with twelve years of training was reliable within its limitations. His man about town understood the working conditions of the District and what it took to be successful down here. Moreover, Muldoon had so little ambition for advancement and still less for any sort of fame that Anderson regarded him as constitutionally incapable of any embellishments other men might be tempted to in an effort to bring themselves forward in the estimation of their boss. On the contrary, Muldoon had been brought so low by life and then redeemed that there seemed nothing in this world that he would rather be than Tom Anderson's all-but-anonymous sub-altern, unremarkable even in his limp which might easily enough be taken as a souvenir of the Spanish-American War or the consequence of a mule's long-premeditated revenge.

So now Tom Anderson listened with his characteristically respectful attention, his blue eyes steadily on Muldoon and stroking his blond moustache with his four-and-a-half fingers. When Muldoon had come to the end of it—all but his embarrassing fall into the arms of the singer—he extracted a cheroot from his coat and offered it ceremoniously to his boss.

Tom Anderson smiled but shook his head. "Go right ahead," he said, giving Muldoon permission. He looked over at Okey-Poke. "Okey," he said, "an Irish here for Fast-Mail, if you would." When it was brought and Muldoon had raised it to Tom Anderson's good health, Anderson asked if the girl was any kind of singer.

"Not so much, no," Muldoon replied. "Course this musta been maybe only her first week or so, and the fellas was right rough on her." He glanced into his glass, seeing the girl's clasped hands, the way her gray eyes looked out and above the heads of her crude audience, as though she weren't thinking of them at all or even of the words she was singing but instead of something else altogether. He found himself wishing he knew what that might be.

"Well, it don't sound too serious, then," Tom Anderson said. "Maybe if they were to get a real ring-tailed roarer or some such back there, might be another thing...." He let the sentence trail away into the brilliant room. "Let's just keep an eye on it, shall we?" He tapped the bar's ebony surface with his hardened stub and was about to move off when he paused and turned on his heel. "Jimmie says she's a looker." Muldoon shrugged and wagged his head sideways, indicating this might be a matter of opinion.

On Canal Street the last day of February Tom Anderson had an opportunity to make up his own mind on that subject.

Ordinarily he tried to avoid luncheon engagements. He kept late hours at the Annex and liked to have his mornings and early afternoons free, arising late to a leisurely breakfast with the newspapers in his long, high house on Elysian Fields. Then a good soak in the bathtub, smoking a cigar and reading whatever items were left over from his hermeneutical examination of the news. When at last he emerged into the parlor, pink with health and pampering, he would hear Gertrude coughing in the kitchen, and then they would sit down over her breakfast to talk business.

Today, though, had been something of a state occasion, and he'd been at a long luncheon at Kolb's with four members of the city council, discussing his proposal to outfit the city's police force with a fleet of the new Jefferey sedans when they became available just after Easter.

"You're not going to find a finer auto for your force," he told his audience while they sat over Berlinerweisers in one of the restaurant's private rooms. He could guarantee a fine price for the fleet because he had been in a position to do several favors through the years for the man who was now the company's president, and it went without saying that Anderson's

Record Oil Refining Company would supply all necessary lubricants at a cost well below what the city could expect anywhere else. By the time they'd finished their Linzer tortes and cigars Tom Anderson had himself a deal and thought he might celebrate it by walking up Canal to Godchaux's to buy Gertrude something for Easter—a scarf or maybe that high-collared cape she'd admired in the window.

He settled for the cape. Out on Canal again with the box under his arm he was looking for a cab and thinking it was good to feel some satisfaction about business for a change. The deal was going to bring him some money, both in the commission he'd receive from the company's president and in the products and services his oil company would supply.

It was all welcome after what had begun as a vexing new year. He still didn't know quite what he was going to do about the Parker brothers over at the Tuxedo, but after hoping they would soon enough wreck themselves with their ham-handed efforts to make a show in the District, he now saw that they might cause some damage before they went to smash. His informants reported that just since Christmas they'd brought eight new men down from New York, all of them gunmen whose crude poses as barmen, waiters, cooks, and the like fooled nobody and actually seemed more designed *not* to fool anybody, to instead throw down the gauntlet to him. The man who ran them went by the name Gyp the Blood and was said to be an especially dangerous case with several killings to his credit. The Parkers were also employing a crew of teenagers as steerers, and these older boys were scaring off the kids who directed sporting men to the Annex and Anderson's other establishments. Just the other day Fast-Mail Muldoon had reported the tearful tale told by Timmy Moran whose pile of *Sporting Life* newsletters had been seized by one of the new teenagers who threatened to wallop Timmy good if he ever caught him again with that publication. And the day after that Billy Brundy had showed him a crudely put together pamphlet called *Spanish Fly,* a Parker brothers production meant to undercut *Sporting Life.*

So it was a real relief to be standing on Canal with the Jefferey deal done and the gift box under his arm. Amid the helter-skelter of the broad street's traffic—the trolleys lined up, the autos parked in angled ranks and those weaving through the horse-drawn carts and pedestrians—a cab chugged up to Godchaux's, and Tom Anderson signaled for it. But just then something made him raise his eyes, looking across Canal to where a woman was turning into the narrow course of Royal Street and the buildings of the Vieux Carré. While the hackie peered out impatiently Tom Anderson stood as if instantly frozen while inside him everything was already racing like a fire he'd witnessed once, sweeping with awesome speed over a prairie outside Carencro in Cajun country, consuming everything in its path with a huge roar that yet had something hollow at its center as though it had created a kind of tunnel out of its own heat and light and velocity.

It was her—he knew it. He had only that glance to go on before the fool cab had blundered up, obscuring his line of sight, but he felt he could not be mistaken, even after this many years—or a lifetime even: the erect carriage; the way the figure appeared to walk on the tips of her toes but with the head slightly cast down as if in thought; the shape of the face beneath the hat, though caught in something less than three-quarters view. So he stood there, his hand with its ruined finger motionless on his moustache, his light blue eyes staring after the figure even though now it had vanished from view, entering the narrow street and its warped old buildings with their moss-eaten cypress balconies and ornate railings.

The hackie continued to peer out at him, and with a start that was the sign of a major inward effort he dropped his hand from his mouth and climbed into the cab. In answer to the hackie's question, he merely said, "Royal. I'll tell you when," then removed his hat, ran the back of his hand across his wet, blazing brow, and edged over close to the window.

Into Royal after what felt to him like an interminable, inept delay he spotted her once again, still the erect carriage and the dancer's athletic poise, still the meditative attitude of the head. He could have cried out in relief that she hadn't turned into Customhouse or yet reached the Monteleone Hotel with its welcoming portico and vast lobby. But what he actually did when they had pulled past the figure was to say simply, "Here" in a voice that sounded as if it had suddenly grown fur somehow.

"You gettin out here?" the hackie asked, twisting his head sideways but not glancing back at his fare.

Anderson didn't answer, only swung out of the cab before it had really stopped, tossing a bill over the seat back and clutching both bowler and box in his left hand. He kept his balance though, and even had sufficient presence to avoid the swift onrush of an errand boy on a rusty gate of a bicycle, who now jumped the thing up from the street onto the banquette and careened on towards the Bienville corner.

Their eyes met, and he spoke her name.

"Adele," she answered. "It's Adele."

Telling Gertrude something of this chance sighting and what had followed, he rose from his chair in her office to fetch a cigar from the humidor. Evening had come, its grave fingers searching the handsome appointments of the room and turning all a monochromatic mauve. He inserted the cigar into the humidor's inbuilt clamp, then pushed down on the pitted nickel lever, neatly clipping the tip. Gertrude lit a cigarette, the match cutting into the gathering gloom, but Anderson made no move to follow suit, only sat down opposite her, smoothing the cigar's long black barrel. They might have been any middle-aged couple at the end of a day, trying together to sort through a family problem: the older, prosperous husband and the handsome, full-jawed wife whose red hair, dyed, helped disguise her true age, which even her husband had never learned.

"So, I guess she didn't tell you why she's come back," Gertrude said finally, seeing he wasn't ready yet to go on with his story. "I guess she didn't tell you that then."

"I don't know as she knows herself," he said, still smoothing the cigar.

"Well, it looks to me like if she wanted to hurt you bad— I mean, if she set out to do that—then this is what she'd do: come back here without letting you know and then take up with the Parkers." She turned on the desk lamp with its translucent green glass shade. In the light it cast she found Tom Anderson's face suddenly drawn and haggard as if he hadn't slept in a week. Behind him the Godchaux gift box sat unopened on a chair, her Easter present shelved for this urgent concern.

"She didn't know the score," he said and went on to tell her what the girl had told him. How the madam, Hattie Felton, scouting the hotels for likely looking recruits, had spied the girl sitting in a tea room three days running and had finally approached her with a proposition. The girl had told Felton it was true she was stranded but wanted her to understand that she was a singer who would happily accept that kind of position but not the sort Miss Felton apparently had in mind. Even so, this version left both Anderson and Gertrude with the bigger question of why the girl should have come back to this particular place, where she had to know he still was. Accident, happenstance, the uncertain fortunes of a performer's life—assuming she really was a singer—none of these would do. It did seem plausible, though, that Hattie Felton could in fact have offered to speak to a cabaret owner she knew who was looking for a female singer to open in his new beer garden. Also that the girl might well not have understood who the Harry Parker was who left a note at her hotel the day following, asking her to drop around to the Tuxedo the next afternoon. What was harder to swallow was the fact that she could have been working for the Parkers for almost three weeks and not have learned the score: that the brothers had in mind cutting up Tom Anderson's turf.

"Well, then, that would still leave us—me, anyways—with her wanting to hurt you some way, and finding it," Gertrude said. She started to light another cigarette but stopped short and folded her hands on the desktop.

Anderson had switched from stroking the cigar to twirling it. He shook his head and sighed. "I told her how it was," he replied heavily. "I told her how hard it was, me knowing she worked for those jaspers." He shifted the cigar to his left hand and raised both hands in a brief show of helplessness and resignation, leaving unexpressed but vividly present in mind that moment in his conversation with the girl when she had looked at him with that candid fearlessness that he could never forget and told him she had no intention of giving up her spot at the Tuxedo, that the brothers paid her better than she'd ever expected, and that she found herself rather pleased to have learned how to get along in what was after all a fairly difficult place. And after she'd told him that she'd smiled—but not with her eyes that looked flat and steely in the light of the Monteleone's tea room where they sat alone over their cold coffees.

"I can't *make* her quit," was all he said to Gertrude.

"You could double her pay, if you wanted."

He nodded his big head. "I told her I'd better whatever them jaspers paid."

Years before, when she'd first come down to the city from Philadelphia, Gertrude had heard the rumors about Tom Anderson and Kate Tidwell and about Kate Tidwell's beautiful daughter: how suddenly, mysteriously, both mother and daughter had disappeared from Anderson's house on Elysian Fields and then had turned up at his summer home in Biloxi. Later, when Gertrude had supplanted Hilma Burt as Anderson's mistress, she had lived with those old rumors, never asking about them. In her world as in his everyone had a past, and one of the tribal taboos was never to ask someone about the past. It was surprising to her then when one day Tom Anderson volunteered what she instantly understood to be a truncated, bowdlerized version of events in the Elysian Fields house, something or other about a misunderstanding between Kate and himself and obscurely involving the daughter. And he probably wouldn't have offered even that, she felt, had it not been that Kate had written him the news that the girl had abruptly left Biloxi for an unknown destination, asking him to send word if he knew anything. But he hadn't known anything—until now. Of that Gertrude felt certain.

"Well," she said, "if you can't get her to quit the Parkers, could you maybe get her to work inside for you over there?"

"I thought about that," he said, and indeed he had. "Not now, anyways, not the way she's talking now." He stroked his moustache, looking at his partner across the gloom and the lighted desk, but seeing instead the girl when she had concluded their conversation at the Monteleone by rising and giving him her hand, which he'd held in both of his as long as he dared. At that moment he'd asked, perhaps even a bit plaintively, if they would see each other, using once again that pet name, Cammie, and she with a smile, shaking her head and correcting him for the second time—"Adele." Then she'd said with a casualness that surprised him, "Well, it's a pretty small world after all, isn't it. I guess I found out today just how small. And so I expect we will see each other—we will have to."

There had been a hundred questions he wanted to put to her, but she'd already been in motion towards the tea room entrance, moving past him so closely he could smell her once again, and every bit of the past they had shared came over him. But all he could bring out was, "Isn't there something we could do?" But by then he was speaking to her back, and then she was gone.

"If you could do it—I mean, if you could do what you want here—what would that be, do you think?" Gertrude asked. It was the sort of cool question that had first brought her to his attention, the kind that so often in their partnership he'd found valuable. Yet now he found he didn't want to answer it, didn't welcome that cool, analytical probing.

So what he answered after finally lighting his cigar was only what he could answer under these circumstances. "I don't know about that, only that I got to get her out of there. I can't have her working for those jaspers." But what his partner heard out of her deep sagacity, her hard experience in a relentlessly hard world was, This is trouble, real trouble.

Almost from the very first, a year after he'd taken Kate Tidwell and her ten-year-old daughter into his home, Tom Anderson himself had seen the potential for real trouble, too, though gradually he was able to convince himself that he could handle whatever came along.

It began one night after a rare dinner party at his home, and filled with a glass more than he usually allowed himself he had slipped silently into the sleeping girl's room, run his hand up under the covers, and inserted a finger into the tight, enveloping heat of her untried vagina. She lay inert under his touch, no least flicker of alarmed movement. Later, he would wonder about that, but in the moment he was conscious only of an almost delirious sensation of pleasure far exceeding anything he'd ever known.

The next morning, lying in bed next to Kate, however, it was not that sweet delirium he thought of. Rather, it was a sickening awareness of his loss of control, a loss he knew to be potentially fatal to the man he had become: disgrace, pauperdom, madness, and death—they all lay waiting down this path he had set his foot on, he felt. Examples of the phenomenon were in almost stunning abundance in his world. And so, with a mighty effort he banished his desire to the dank basement of his being even while he helplessly took note of the girl's agonizing emergence into a pubescence about which she herself seemed blissfully casual.

There came, though, a day that he would mark as the true start of it, that place on the path from which there could be for him no turning back. In the late afternoon of that day he accidentally intersected with the girl, naked to the waist, as she came up the narrow corridor from her bedroom to the bath. The light came from behind her, finding her and settling on her as if it were not some neutral source that conferred depth and definition and hue on whatever happened to be in its path, but was instead possessed of a secret sort of volition in which it picked out certain objects to bestow itself upon, whether in beauty or pitiless revelation. And there in that narrow passageway, home to the single most powerful man in the city—string-puller, deal-maker, sub rosa, de facto mayor, whoremaster to half the nation—he saw the girl and how the light caught the tips of her upturned breasts and was awed by their instantaneous power over him; and simultaneously conscious, too, of the crucial necessity of somehow gaining control over that beauty if it were not to destroy him and the world he had painstakingly constructed. And so, speedily, he conceived a plot to accomplish that objective.

Thursdays were Kate Tidwell's day with her mama whom he had established in one of the old-time *placée* houses in the Marais: tidy, perfectly proportioned homes the pre-war Creole men had created for their colored concubines, complete down to the last detail—the uniformed maid who by careful design had to be a darker shade than the mistress. Every Thursday Kate left the house early for the French Market to pick out the freshest fish (pompano when it was available), which she usually prepared with prawns and roasted red peppers. She built her day around the preparation of the dish and generally waiting hand and foot on her mother, who God knew had done her best with her brood. That prematurely worn-out woman would sit gabbling in the kitchen while her daughter worked, cracking her work-roughened knuckles, spitting snuff juice into a cup, and exhibiting other slatternly habits acquired in that featureless, sodden stretch of country below Happy Jack, land that hardly deserved the designation but was more a sort of quaking green soup. Down there Kate had gone into the life early, to help out, and she felt a strong loyalty to Mama, manifesting itself in these ritual Thursdays that kept her in the Marais until early evening.

By the time Kate returned to the house on Elysian Fields the girl had been home for hours, fetched from Les Soeurs du Sacré Coeur by Criss the coachman. On this particular Thursday,

Tom Anderson dispatched the maid and Criss to the market and then sat down with the girl in the kitchen while she ate her bowl of rice pudding, still wearing her starched gray-and-white school smock. He chatted amiably with her, asking the latest news of her little world, of May-May, long her best friend but now apparently siding more with Corrine and making her feel the odd girl out. Also of Sister June, so pretty and so gay with the girls in French Composition that it was said some in the administration thought her lacking in appropriate sobriety and not the best influence on her young charges. And he sat there, smiling, smooth-faced, wholly attentive, and already half-tumescent, covertly catching glimpses of the demure rise and fall of her breast beneath the smock.

Then her departure for her room in the rearward section of the vast, dim house and he timing it, knowing almost to the instant how long it would take her to strip off the school smock and stand before the long mirror, assessing briefly the progress of her maturation, the emergence of the feminine form out of the chrysalis of childhood, before she would emerge again to walk the fourteen steps to the bath. So that when he saw the long brass handle of her door tilt downward, he was there, waiting to grasp it, pushing the door inward even as she was pulling it, as if she were really an accomplice, willing his entry, his powerful presence looming up in front of her, barring exit, breathing hard, the blond moustache in curious motion above what was almost a rictus reflex of the mouth, his powerful hands on her shoulders. And she looking up questioningly out of those gray eyes and heavy brows, asking, "Daddy, what is it?" And he responding, "Little gal, don't you know?" his hands sliding off her shoulders to grasp her buttocks.

And maybe at that point—or even before?—she did know as he maneuvered her in a crude, ancient dance across the carpet towards the bed, and then at the bed's edge shifting one hand from buttock to small of back—again like a dancer—pressing her into him, pressing her backwards and down onto the bed.

Later, he would tell himself that there was acquiescence then, that she willingly went down under him, that it was as nothing to lift the petticoat, to tear away the cotton bloomers, that during all this she made no outcry, no resistance, her eyes wide and staring into his. And that it was only after he'd turned her onto her stomach and entered her that way that she had at last cried out, and he'd put his hand over her mouth and she'd bitten his forefinger so fiercely that he himself had made a muffled outcry, jerking the hand away with a subsequent groan that might easily enough have been mistaken for the sound of profoundest pleasure. And maybe it was, partly at least, because he had long since been acquainted with the intimate connection between pain and exquisite pleasure, another thing he had learned from Edith Simms. It was she who had taken him to bed for the first time, and in doing so had commanded him to administer several lashes with a quirt to her bared buttocks; and then, at the moment of his own struggling, frantic climax she had given him a smart stroke with it. And so there the association was made, forged in his mind in the heat of sex.

The girl had said nothing when it was over, not when she'd watched him stripping the blood- and semen-stained sheets from her bed, taking them out to the small backyard between the house and stable, and burning them in the rust-red iron barrel. Nor later at sundown when the little family had supper and Kate reported to them that Mama was now insisting on wearing bright red knit gloves in this warm weather because she claimed they eased her arthritic fingers. Then Kate had playfully remarked that maybe T.A. himself might be in need of a little finger relief of some sort, considering what he'd done to his own when he'd ripped it on a nail in the stable. The girl had kept her eyes cast down on her plate while the mother had some further fun with this and Anderson had smiled ruefully, holding the crudely bandaged digit well away from his fork.

A week later the flame in his finger had deepened to a raging fever, and Anderson paid a visit to Dr. Molineux who took off the first joint and told Anderson he'd be lucky if that's all he lost. "I wouldn't take you for a fool—nobody would—but this was very foolish, Tom. Very foolish." The remark had another facet to it, Anderson well knew, and he doubted that Molineux had been at all hoodwinked about the alleged cause of the injury. And then a few weeks later Molineux thought still more needed to come off; the infection was still sullenly present. So that finally what Tom Anderson was left with was a functional stub that ended an inch below the big joint.

By this time his taking of the girl on Thursday afternoons had become a ritual, as regular a feature of that day as Kate's visits to Mama. These were solemn, silent occasions, the girl not so much passive as submissive and obedient beneath his heavy thrustings, the blood-pulsing explorations of his hands. Facing her on the bed, he found always the gray eyes staring at him under the heavy eyebrows with a candor he could only find wildly provocative. When he would turn her onto her stomach now, she would raise her posterior to his entry and clutch her fingers into the gathered sheets.

Only once did she ever cry out, and this after more than a year of what he thought of as their trystings. He was mounted behind her and had just shot his Jovian bolt—hot, white— when she screamed shortly and then herself had shuddered beneath him. Afterwards, she silently kissed his ruined finger and laid her cheek against it.

Who, he'd thought then, was to say that this wasn't a special sort of love? It was secret, yes, and it was forbidden, but what did that mean, really? Was he not himself in the very lucrative business of purveying things equally forbidden, curtained off from the censorious eye of the daylight world, that world that at sundown came calling for what he had to sell? And when he came to the trade as a boy it had been immemorially established, catering to some profound void in the human soul. No one in this city, certainly—none of the famous madams, whoremasters, courtesans, pimps, streetwalkers, sextrick artists—had ever invented any part of it, though there were to be sure some colorful local variations on ancient acts: there was a woman he recalled with a certain fondness who could suck up a platter of shucked oysters simply by the powerful contractions of what she called her Sweetie Pie. And Edith Simms, who had initiated him into so much—Edith, who he imagined had invented with her little goad the exciting nexus between smarting pain and genital release—had invented nothing. It had all been thought up long ago and far away from here. He had for a time worshipped Edith, and even after she had at last tired of his adolescent attentions and let him know that, he had continued to regard her as an original. But by then he was coming to understand what Edith's fate was likely to be: the very same as that of all the other women who nightly positioned themselves beneath the pulpy, sodden weight of their customers. And so, when he himself was in a position to rescue Edith from that and set her up on her own, he did it.

It was natural to him then that he should have wanted to save the girl from the depredations of other men: the first pimply pursuits of pubescent boys; the fiercer, more focused attentions of high schoolers and college sports; the lustful clutchings of the mature swains who would soon enough come calling with but one thing in mind. How different really would any of them be than the sports he catered to in the District or those horny-handed, fish-stinking men who had clambered aboard the girl's mother down in Happy Jack? All men wanted the same thing, entrance to the black box women had between their legs.

And so it was that he regarded himself not as the girl's violator, any more than he could have regarded Edith Simms as his, but instead as her rescuer and ultimate protector. Already he had given her his name, which he thought provided her with a protection probably unique in the city: for who would try to tamper with Tom Anderson's stepdaughter when it was well known that Anderson had any number of strong-armed men on his payroll? He had also given her a home in a good neighborhood as well as the classically rigid training of the sisters at Sacré Coeur. But more: she was now protected by the secret, seminal knowledge he had given her on Thursday afternoons and which he believed no subsequent aspirant could ever truly breech, so that he had transformed her from fair game into an eternal virgin of a special sort, wrapped in an inviolable, intimate knowledge of the primordial male need and her own need to satisfy it only in his paternal embrace.

He hadn't, it was true, worked out exactly how he could keep the girl his, especially in view of her mother's presence in the household. He saw her completing her studies at Sacré Coeur and then going on for further finishing at Newcomb College. Her mother was, he thought, a little better than average in intellect, and the late, shiftless father must have been considerably less than that. But the girl was unquestionably bright; he hardly needed the sisters to tell him that. But after Newcomb, what? Still further studies while he bought time?

He only knew his design must somehow be accomplished, that the girl must remain his as the kings of the olden time had reserved certain favored women to be theirs forever.

He spent some hours on this kind of forecasting without coming up with anything, highly unusual for a man who always looked ahead and was little short of brilliant in devising solutions to coming problems. What man working for him—pimp, thug, bartender, bookkeeper, cook—needed watching as he began to buckle beneath the accumulated weight of booze, dope, venereal disease? What madam, whore, cabaret girl was beginning to show the sure signs of dissolution and would need to be replaced? What rival businessman looked capable of making inroads on his domain? What upstart, reform-mouthed politician might possibly win office in the coming election and so needed courting? Did a man of middling consequence in his operations have a family problem that might be remedied easily enough with a small loan, a message to a creditor, landlord, loan shark, gambler? Then Tom Anderson might do what was necessary and in doing that endear himself to that fellow.

So it wasn't that he hadn't looked ahead in his obsessive love for the girl. It was if anything that in looking ahead he failed to pay attention to the present: he got her pregnant.

The girl said nothing to him, and he had no reason to suspect it. Then came Kate's blazing confrontation of him one morning, lighting up every detail of the dim parlor with its heavy velvet curtain that partitioned off the dining area; the fireplace festooned with cheap bric-a-brac; the heavy circular table with goldfish bowl and fat souvenir album of the Cotton Exposition. Here was a failure of concentration, a colossal mistake in judgment, the possible ruination of his plan. Because after a week of intense and failed discussions Criss had driven mother, daughter, and mama to the train station with their valises. Waiting behind in the long hallway to the street door were the trunks and heavy cypress boxes, stacked, that spoke of more permanent rearrangements. As the coach rattled away he'd stood there looking at these, then turned resignedly into the depleted parlor to find himself reflecting that he wouldn't much miss any of the vanished items that had cluttered the room and that he had long since ceased to see. They represented, he well knew, a whore's notion of opulent living. He didn't suppose he would miss Kate that much, either, especially since he was now getting involved with a new woman on the Line, Hilma Burt, who he thought might have potential as a business partner whereas Kate had been useless in that way. She had, however, made the household comfortable, which was to say that she'd made it predictable: that was what you wanted when you came back at dawn from a chronically unpredictable working environment and found your slippers exactly where you'd parked them yesterday and the day before that.

What he would miss—more profoundly than he wanted to face just then—was the girl. When Kate had accused him he hadn't denied it—what would be the point? But he hadn't told her he loved the girl and that he believed that love was returned. Instead, he'd passed his behavior off as just one of those things they both should understand. After all, both of them were thoroughly familiar with the practice of mothers putting their pubescent daughters to work in the houses, even using them as partners in ménage-à-trois tricks with customers who could afford that delicacy. Here, however, so he'd argued, there'd been no commercial usage of the girl but only a stepfather's private and pardonable sexual attraction. And so what was Kate's obdurate insistence on leaving him immediately, except jealousy?

He'd offered to get the girl to a reliable quadroon woman in the Marigny who catered exclusively to daughters of upper-crust families finding themselves in a similar fix. They could easily enough give it out, he'd said, that the girl was being temporarily withdrawn from Sacré Coeur and placed under the care of a specialist in problems of girls who were coming of age, and so forth... but Kate was having none of it, his blandishments all instantly flung aside and her anger unrelenting. She insisted he make arrangements for her, the girl, and her mother to go to Biloxi where he owned a summer home and establish them there in all appropriate comfort. Finally, he saw the futility of further argument and lifted his long, well-manicured hands in acquiescence and said he would attend to it.

Now they were gone to collect Mama, and in their absence the house suddenly assumed the cold, echoing vastness of a mausoleum into which he'd accidentally wandered. In the parlor he found himself staring down at the pointless dartings of the goldfish, their slim shadows flitting across the chalky pebbles at the bowl's bottom. Then he'd gone out of there and along the hall to the rear of the house and her room with its door ajar at an angle that made it appear as if she were just within, awaiting him. His mind veered quickly away from the possibility that she might not only have left the house but his life as well, instead flashing ahead to Biloxi, to some later date when he might hope to rescue her from what he had already begun to think of as her exile—perhaps when she'd come to full maturity and was capable of making her own decisions.

He pushed the door wider, entered, and was surrounded by the room's emptiness that came over him like the cold river mist that in winter crept up from the wharves and worked its way up the streets of the Quarter, draping itself over the branches of the oaks along Esplanade and Elysian Fields, and penetrating your home and everything in it. Except that where the snaky mist obliterated the smell of everything else, here he believed he could just detect some faint scent of her even as it was already vanishing. He drew in deeply, trying to fill himself with what there was left of it.

The bed had been stripped to its striped ticking. Here had been the seat of love, barren though it now appeared. Slowly, gently almost, he lowered himself onto it, burying his face in the cold rustle of the mattress naked of all but memory.

III. Mamie

He hated to think in such terms, but Tom Anderson had begun to wonder whether handling the Parker brothers' challenge might ultimately come down to so simple a matter as guns. Even with their recent imports Anderson knew he was still far deeper in manpower, and as a native he enjoyed the rewards of the sedulously cultivated connections he'd established at City Hall and police headquarters. Still, down on the streets, in the alleyways behind the bars, in the tonks and pool halls, numbers wouldn't count as much as expert gunmen might, and not that many of his men were true gunnies, whereas almost all of the Parkers' recruits seemed to be. Especially this Gyp the Blood character. On the very afternoon when he'd been feeling so good about the Jefferey car deal he'd put over, Gyp and another member of the Parker gang had gotten into it with four of his own out behind the Fairgrounds, and Gyp the Blood and his partner had pistols while none of his men did. Buster Daley had taken a slug in the kneecap, and another of his men had been winged running away. From the reports he'd gotten his losses could have been a lot worse.

He regarded Alto North as his coolest killer. Alto would draw and shoot without hesitation, he knew, but North was probably better with a knife than a pistol, most comfortable when he could close with an opponent and utilize his hand speed, his tensile strength, his nervelessness, to deal a disabling or deathly blow. Jimmie Enright was a street brawler who would take five blows to get in a good one of his own; but Jimmie wasn't much of a hand with a pistol. Okey-Poke was much the same. Anderson had seen him take on three drunks at once in the Annex and flatten them all. But Anderson couldn't recall the last time the barman had been called upon to shoot. Billy Brundy had put in his time on the boats and had a knuckle-knotted hand to show for some seaport scuffle. But Billy was an office guy nowadays and didn't carry any kind of weapon. As for Fast-Mail Muldoon, well, the Robert Charles thing had settled that issue long ago; he wouldn't want to have to count on Muldoon in any action requiring gunplay. Maybe only the Villalta brothers could be considered real gunmen. Both had been in the Spanish-American War, but Santos had manned a machine gun—hardly a weapon he'd be called upon to use in these streets.

That left his Negroes, most of them knife and razor types. When they used pistols, they were likely to be big, old-time black powder ones like a Navy Colt .44 that would put a sure-enough window in a man—if the .44 happened to be in working order. Chicken Dick was as rough-and-ready as they came, but how well old Dick would do against the New Yorkers was a question.

This Gyp the Blood was clearly of another sort, and so apparently was the man many thought was his brother and who went by the name of Toodoo, or something like that. These men could shoot and went armed at all times, so he'd learned, and whoever it was that had shot Buster Daley and the other man out at the Fairgrounds had known what they were doing.

On the other hand, if the Parkers were more savvy than headstrong, they might not actually have to pull their triggers. Because if the mere presence and reputations of their gunmen put fear into Anderson's operatives, causing them to reconsider their allegiances, it wouldn't have to come to any sort of Dodge City shoot-out. The turning of the tide could easily enough happen silently and fairly swiftly, too.

Tom Anderson had surrounded himself with men and women whose fealty he'd bought, a number of them rescued by him from disgrace, poverty, the threat of jail, as in the case of the now-crippled Buster Daley. But these same hirelings each had some inner weakness, and under the right circumstances Tom Anderson judged it would show itself again. If enough of them came to believe that the Parkers were bound to cut deeply into his turf, they would begin to look out for themselves, and some of them would go over to the opposition, to the outfit on the way up.

Everybody in the District knew the Parkers had had some success scaring off Anderson's kid steerers, and there were now several of the newly arrived tough guys hanging around corners in the District, discouraging sports from going to the Annex and other Anderson establishments. The forms of this discouragement were sometimes menacing enough to send the sports hurrying back where they came from, their thirst like their lust quenched by threats. Over at the 102 Billy Phillips was whining about business, and even the ever-loyal Jimmie Enright had fallen into a sullen sulk over there. And now he had a new problem to think about because Frank Huntz had just sold the Parkers the old Perdido.

It was a tonk on Robertson just opposite St. Louis Number

Two and had once belonged to Anderson and his partner, Ed Mochez: beer and wine, sawdust floors, a derelict upright piano: too rough for Ed Mochez's taste, and eventually he'd talked Anderson into selling it to Huntz. The profit was certainly modest enough, Mochez said, but worth the subtraction of the daily aggravation it took to run it. Why Huntz had suddenly and quietly sold it to the Parkers was something Anderson wanted to find out, but in any case the thing was done now.

It wasn't the Perdido, of course, that troubled him. By itself it was just another rough place, even rougher now, it seemed, than when Huntz had bought it. The piano player there, Mamie Desdoumes, Anderson had known of old, a lurching, disfigured woman missing the middle two fingers of her right hand. In her youth Mamie had been a passable cabaret singer. Nowadays, she didn't sing at all, and just about her only remaining virtue was stamina. She might have only ten or so tunes she could play, he thought, but she could play them continuously, from can't see to can, as the expression had it: crank her up with a few beers, and old Mamie could play on and on, the customers nodding off around her until finally she was the last one still awake in the stinking old joint. So, of course, the Perdido itself wasn't the point. It was that "those jaspers," as Tom Anderson now invariably referred to the Parkers, had gotten hold of another property in the District, *his* District.

But that wasn't all of it, not by half. The Parkers had the girl, too. And that was both insult and torment. She'd said she was proud of having learned how to get along at the Tuxedo, but Tom Anderson knew too well what lay in store for a woman in such a place, in any place in the District—he had only to cast his mind back on old Mamie as the nearest example. The girl was fearless, and he admired that, but to be fearless in her situation was in itself a cause for fear—his.

No, he would have to see to the Parkers and quickly. It wouldn't do, either, to simply out-maneuver them and ultimately defeat their designs on his turf. He would have to smash them, drive them clean out of the city, send them back to New York so crippled they wouldn't be able to operate even up there. Nothing short of this would give him the satisfaction, the peace of mind he craved. Then he would have his domain restored to its former integrity and proper order, and he would have the girl again. This time he meant to keep her forever.

As Muldoon approached the Annex a custard-colored sun dropped fast beyond St. Louis Number Two, the statues of Christ crucified even more sharply reliefed against it as though announcing the imminence of Easter. Inside, he'd told one of the waiters he'd have a cup of tomato bisque and a chop with his coffee, and while he waited for it Billy Brundy arrived with the envelope.

"Fast-Mail," Brundy said, handing it to him, "T.A. wants you to get this to the certain party. See you don't lose it, okay?" Muldoon took the square envelope whose flap always seemed so hard-sealed, and tucked it into his suit coat pocket where it rested against his shoulder holster, feeling it snug in there and heavy with a portent he couldn't imagine.

When he'd delivered the first one to the girl at The Frenchman's she'd asked him what it was, leaning into him to make herself heard through the ferocious din of the barn-like room and looking disinclined to accept what he was holding out while trying to be discreet about the nature of his errand. She'd kept her hands at her sides, the envelope suspended between them in the blue air, and all around them the moiling mass of the night people who would be drinking and dancing in here well up into the morning's broad hours. Finally, she'd accepted it with a shrug, and then he'd smiled, touched his hat brim, and begun the difficult passage to the street door. Out on Bienville at last, he'd run his hand around the back of his neck and found it wet with perspiration. It was always hot in The Frenchman's, but not quite that hot.

At that hour the place was always jammed to the walls: pimps and their played-out women; pool sharks and poker players; musicians and muscle men; bartenders, waiters, hostlers from the fire hall: all the District's professionals, so that it was impossible for a mere civilian sport to wedge his way in there. And on this morning with Tom Anderson's latest note still tucked in his breast pocket Muldoon found himself unable to move once he'd forced his way in the door and simply had to stand there, unable to advance a step in the dense heat and sound, immobilized like everybody else while Sammy Davis and Tony Jackson took turns on the piano, trying to cut each other with speed tunes and the crowd roaring when Jackson sat down on the bench and roaring again when it was Sammy's turn. Finally, something happened—somebody left or fell down or a man hoisted a woman up on the bar—and Muldoon found he could inch forward, encountering the familiar faces but not hers.

He kept moving when he could, darting his eyes about, and as he did so his anxiety mounted. Maybe she'd been there and gone, or maybe she'd left with somebody and he was too late with his delivery. But he knew well enough his anxiety was more than a mere matter of needing to fulfill his assignment, because there were other mornings now when he'd come in here messageless and had felt this same sensation, as if his stomach had ballooned upwards to touch the bottom of his throat.

On those occasions as on this one he looked through all the other faces, mentally discarding them, one after another, searching for some small glimpse of her: the back of her head, perhaps done up in a French roll; the shape of her neck as she leaned over to hear what someone was trying to say in that cauldron of sound; the soft curve of her cheek, youthfully full to his eye and as yet unmarked by this hazardous world she'd chosen to work in; the broad, womanly drape of her shoulder, caught briefly through the sweaty throng.

But whether bearing a message or empty-handed there was a telling similarity to his sensations as he slowly, determinedly forced his way into the room until he had arrived in her presence. Once there he felt he'd somehow entered a wholly different zone, one where the heat and smoke and the ripening odors of spent effort and simulated ardor—even the relentless, percussive playing of the professors—fell away, and he was alone in her company. And in that suddenly created solitude he was left with only the mute memory they shared, the accident in the dim, dingy hallway where his hobbled gait had intersected with a suddenly opened door and he'd fallen, headlong, into her bosom. He regarded this as their secret, the sole incident in their history—unless you could count the delivery of these notes from his boss—and imagined that the shadowed smile she showed him was her acknowledgement of that secret, that history.

Standing before her, or as near that as he could manage, he might be lucky enough to get out a few stammered, shouted words: "Hello there, again." "Hot in here, aint it." "Well, I see everybody's here again—you, too." Pathetic little rags of discourse, she accepted them with that shadowy smile to which she might add some grace note: "Yes, it certainly is close, isn't it?" And then there was nothing further he could think of, standing there in her light, perhaps holding a glass of beer so that he had at least something to do with his hands; or if it was impossible to get to the bar for a beer, then the last of his evening's allotment of cheroots, not smoking it, but only fussing with it. And she might be holding a glass of claret, keeping it close to her body to avoid spilling it if she were jostled. Then they'd simply look at each other a long moment, he trying to read what was in her face while trying not to seem to stare, until the high, roaring sea of bodies swept one or the other away, and it was over again for him.

This morning was no different except it took him longer to locate her and longer still to reach her beyond the piano because Game Kid had climbed atop the instrument to dance a jig while the guest professor, Louie Chauvin, took a turn. The crowd surged forward, cheering him on and blocking Muldoon's further advance. When Game Kid got down, the crowd eddied a bit, and he came on, seeing her in conversation with a cabaret girl he knew as Mabel who'd come into the District from Bogalusa a few years back and was beginning to show it.

"I gave him the straight shit on that, all right," he heard Mabel shouting in the ear of the girl who now saw him and half-turned in his direction. Then Mabel herself turned to find Tom Anderson's gimp and raised her head in a slight show of recognition, momentarily tightening the unhealthy looking fold of flesh she was adding under her chin. To her Muldoon was like a hundred other bloodsuckers down here who took advantage of the working women, indistinguishable except for his limp, which she'd heard he'd acquired when he'd taken a load of buckshot up his ass while running away from something—outraged husband, cop, or pursuing pimp whose woman had given him a free one.

Having the girl's eye now, Muldoon tapped his breast pocket. The girl nodded in acknowledgement, and then he was next to her and handing the heavy little square of paper to her while Mabel watched the exchange with only a vague show of curiosity, wondering what a looker like Adele could have to do with Tom Anderson's gimp.

Then it was over with once more, and under Mabel's baleful stare he turned about and bumped into the broad chest of Okey-Poke who grinned at him, holding his glass of beer high above the massed bodies. "Fast-Mail, my man!" Okey shouted. Behind Muldoon Mabel watched him work his way towards the door, then idly remarked to her companion, "I wonder how he shits with his ass all tore up like that? Must be like a goose."

Already by this time she had begun to filter into the jungle of his sleep and his awakenings, those terrible moments when he'd start up from his bed, not sure whether he was still dreaming or had crossed over the dark passageway into the waking world. Then he would be sure only that once again he'd been helplessly revisiting that night thirteen years before when his life had been changed, trying in dream to find a different, more honorable escape from that ancient peril. Now, though, he found that sometimes he awakened with an image of her merged with what he was sure must be the mob on Saratoga. There she was in a nightmare sea of faces that were pressing around him, staring at him, her face blanched, eyes wide, but whether in horror or fear for him he couldn't tell. Fully awake by that point, his thoughts shifted to her face as he saw it at The Frenchman's, wearing always an incongruous composure that was unreadable.

There was nothing to be gained, he knew, from lying in bed longer, though he dreaded to learn what the too-early hour was. But he'd reach anyway for the heavy railroad watch on his bedside table: he could read that face, all right and read its other side as well, though he didn't need to: on the smooth, worn back of the watch he could still make out the brief legend that summed up what his life had become:

From
TOM ANDERSON

Then, without shaving, he would dress roughly, pull on boots, and trudge down to the Stuyvesant Docks, past the dago's where the midday drinkers were by now sodden and sleepy while the afternoon newcomers were beginning to find their voices; past the ironmonger's and the dull, steady glint of the massed metal in the yard; across Tchoupitoulas and its iron-bright trolley tracks; through what traffic there might be of the dray horses or the mules and the carts they hauled. Then down the steps to the docks and their world of huge, blackened hulls and the straining hawsers of the moored ships and the workers moving more slowly now under the afternoon's light.

Then along the wharves, watching his step in the rude and heedless traffic that would make no allowance for his infirmity, the telltale *thump-ta-thump* of his footfalls, even though he was by now a familiar sight, the brick-faced fellow with the black moustache, stumping along with his hands plunged into the pockets of a suit coat that had seen better days. Upriver or down, it didn't seem to make any difference to the walker who would eventually come to a standstill, staring off across the river's mighty and almost motionless flow, as though he were waiting for some sign from the other side.

He wasn't looking anywhere, though, only brought to a halt by images that were well short of thoughts: Brundy, handing him one of those envelopes; the girl, a serenely beautiful and tranquil island in the ceaselessly roiling sea of The Frenchman's; the feel of the envelope when he handed it to her and the fact that in the last exchange he had contrived to fleetingly touch her hand in the act of delivery and felt a thrilling charge.

It was not, though, the thrill of desire, the sort he knew anyway, that he remembered experiencing first with Lou-Anne. In particular, he remembered a steamy night in the alley behind her family's cottage on Constantinople when he was within days of graduating from St. Alphonsus. A neighboring family had just moved, leaving behind their vacated home a pile of junk—boxes, a broken footstool, an antediluvian couch with one cushion missing and the other with a big black spring coiling out of it like a snake about to strike. Somehow, though, he and Lou-Anne had found a way to make use of it, she with her legs draped over his lap, and in the close darkness the kissing had progressed into more intimate touchings and he'd pushed her legs apart under her dress. And still she hadn't said quit until his hand had reached the center of her bloomers and he'd felt her wetness. Then she had said quit, or rather had panted, breathless in his ear, "We can't! We can't!" And he recalled also of those moments the surging pain in his own pants when she'd abruptly swung her legs from his lap.

That had been the closest they'd ever come, a few moments he'd lived on for years, including those months with Beverly when he had tried but failed to find her the romantic equal to the girl who had abandoned him to his limping, lopsided disgrace.

What he felt in the presence of this girl, however, was nothing like that. It was not that it was sexless exactly, nor was it truly devoid of desire. But it was as if the center of what he felt in her presence and in his subsequent contemplations of her was no longer located below his waist, in his crotch and loins—where it had been in those midnight moments in the alley with Lou-Anne: the customary locus of feeling for every man he knew. Where else *could* it be located? Where else for the sports whose dollars made possible the existence of the world that paid him a handsome living? Where else for those older men he'd grown up around, hearing their talk on the street corners of the Channel? Where for his peers, for himself, when they'd talked of girls, of certain young wives like Peg Younger who even with two brats in hand still turned heads on Magazine when she passed them with her glossy red-gold hair and that saucy swing of her ass? His brothers surely had known nothing but this locus of feeling, and until now neither had he, graduating with thoughtless ease from pubescent fantasies to his first whore, to a kind of unacknowledged disappointment that there really didn't seem to be more to the whole thing than that tightening in the thighs, thickening of the member, plunging assault, unutterable expenditure. And then that hollowed-out wonderment about it all.

Here, however, he found it was otherwise. The location of his feeling for the girl had mysteriously migrated upwards to settle around his chest where it formed a large, encompassing zone of warmth that reached all the way around to his back. The new location had, he felt, something deeper about it and was accompanied by a feeling of uneasy bewilderment. What man had felt what he was feeling now, and was this not a kind of betrayal of his manhood? He knew of no one he could possibly talk to about this upward shift—certainly not the priest at St. Alphonsus who, he was sure, regarded him as hopelessly lost. And when he compared it to what he felt on his visits to Octavia the exercise was pointless, because what he felt down in Bessie Browne's kitchen afterwards was pretty much akin to that cleaned-up, straightened-out, pinned-back feeling you had leaving the barbershop.

But if it wasn't sex—if that wasn't what he wanted when he saw the girl or thought about her, or anyway not the most of it—then what the hell else could it be? Moreover, what business had he walking around these docks with these mysterious feelings when the very man who sponsored his life clearly had feelings of his own about this same girl? Whenever he found himself beginning to speculate about the contents of the notes he so dutifully delivered he stopped abruptly and switched his mind to something else altogether: old habit here, learned first as a rookie cop who was told to look the other way when in the presence of things that didn't concern him. Even so, it wasn't possible to utterly avoid the knowledge that Tom Anderson had *some* sort of feelings for the girl, for surely he wasn't writing her about the weather or his uncle's lumbago.

On one of these solitary rambles along the wharves—this one at a particularly early hour—he allowed himself to think as far as the clear understanding that there was real danger here for him, harboring any sort of interest in the girl, let alone the kind he so clearly had developed. For swept along by the tide of such feelings wouldn't he almost inevitably come into some sort of conflicting contact with Anderson? Then what? Anderson could shut off his water any time he wanted.

So he stood there, smoking moodily at the very edge of the wharf. There had been heavy rains for several days up around Baton Rouge and northward, and the river was high with their evidence: drowned cattle as round as barrels, their tails standing straight up like Death's jack staffs; dogs with snouts pointing Gulfward; a sow with three shoats whirligigging about her. He'd meant to bring his pistol down for some target practice but had been so distracted he hadn't noticed he'd forgotten it until he was near the corner of Chippewa. Here were targets aplenty.

Behind him men moved about their heavy tasks, muttering, and one whistling the blues. A long, single-note boat horn cut through what wasn't even a reverie but only the foreboding that he had blundered out of the nightly trouble that was his work into trouble of another sort. It was one thing to deliver those notes as instructed and quite another to seek out the girl on other nights, if only to stand there in the doomed, hectic gaiety, bashful and tongue-tied before her.

He flipped the stub of the cheroot into the river and walked back the way he'd come, the light flat but a little dimmer as it began that fall towards late afternoon when normally he'd be going about those first, ritualistic preparations for work: sitting on the edge of his bed and assessing his condition, whether it had been an especially bad sleep; straightening and stretching his back; going into the streetward room for his calisthenics, the knee bends the doctor had prescribed years ago to give the game leg as much strength and tone as possible; then working up a good sweat with the pig iron dumbbells, lifting them straight out from his waist until he held them in a cruciform position for a count of ten; brewing a pot of coffee while he scrubbed himself in the tiny, claw-footed tub, his knees raised near his face like a jockey. If his sister Maureen had given him any leftovers, he might eat a couple of slices of cold ham, a dish of cabbage, a boiled potato from the ice box. All of this leading to that moment when he'd step out of his door to face his day while below him in the street the day of his neighbors was grinding to its weary end.

Some sort of commotion ahead drew his attention away from his murky cares—a loose group of loafers and roustabouts, hands on hips, and within them a tighter knot of boys, the tough ones who hung about the docks, learning to get even tougher, harder than their mean lives had already made them.

Inside them Muldoon saw a big box camera on its tripod, bellows extended, and next to it a tiny man lunging this way and that, his old-time frock coat swirling about him. It was the cameraman everybody in the District knew as Bellocq. As Muldoon drew up, peering through the laughing onlookers, he saw that the toughs were taunting Bellocq, that one had his slouch hat and another a wooden case that was obviously part of his equipment. As he made a grab for the latter, another kid would wave his hat at him, and Bellocq would turn in that direction, involuntarily raising a hand towards his uncovered head, a gleaming bulb like a huge, peeled Bermuda onion.

At the very moment when the hat was tossed across the circle and into the hands of the biggest of Bellocq's tormentors a gap opened in the group of onlookers, and Muldoon moved through it, swiftly snatching the big kid by the neck and spinning him about. The kid was caught off-balance, and Muldoon slapped his face hard in three quick movements—forehand, backhand, then a real open-handed crack again, meanwhile grabbing the hat from the kid's suddenly slack fingers. Then before any of the others could react, Muldoon lunged past Bellocq and grabbed the wooden case from a squat, freckled kid who stood there, his mouth open in surprise and alarm.

The case proved heavier than Muldoon had imagined, and his game-legged momentum carried him past the freckled kid and into the chest of one of the watchers who caught him, then shoved him away. Muldoon staggered sideways but set the case down to right himself, and as he did so he saw a short, thick billet of wood at his feet. He let go of the case for the billet, which was really too short to be an effective club but would have to do. Stepping into the midst of the circle, he handed the tiny man his hat, which he jammed on his head without a word, his eyes red with impotent rage.

And so there they stood, the crippled man and the misshapen one, the toughs recovered from their surprise, their fists balled and raised, their voices now raised as well—"Stay the fuck out of it, asshole!" "Y'all fixin to get killed long with him!"

They began to circle, feinting towards Muldoon from all directions, six of them. But Muldoon fastened his attention on the big kid he'd slapped, figuring it was he who would lead them in. He drew back his lips in a kind of grim smile and spoke through clenched teeth, "Come on then, my young friend, and I'll give you something to take home to Mama."

The big kid shot a glance at the club Muldoon was tapping his open palm with, calculating its usefulness. But he'd had enough, his face red and smarting. He wiped a grimy sleeve across it, smearing it with blood and snot, and spat a bloody clot at Muldoon's feet. The others waited.

"Go fuck yer own mama," he snarled, "you'n yer friend there, that dwarf or what!" The others joined in, still shifting about but not feinting a charge now. Muldoon could feel Bellocq just behind him and reached back to grab the man's frock coat, keeping him close. He kept his eyes riveted on those of the big kid and saw there was no real fight left there, and then the kid turned away and the others with him, still jeering, threatening. Then the audience broke apart as well with the fun over.

When the toughs were a safe distance away Muldoon let loose of Bellocq's coat and turned to him. The tiny man began furiously tugging at his clothes—vest, coat, waistband—his beardless face a blinding alabaster white and his eyes the color of garnets. "You okay?" Muldoon asked. "They hurt you any?"

"My plates."

Muldoon shook his head, signing he didn't understand.

"My plates." The tiny man snapped open the top of the wooden case and looked carefully within. Whatever he found, he said nothing to his rescuer, only snapped the case shut again and began to pack up the camera and tripod.

"Here, let me help you with that," offered Muldoon, but Bellocq only waved him off and continued swiftly and silently packing his gear. But when he began to hoist the heavy tripod Muldoon took it from him and grabbed the case as well, and then without a word exchanged the two trudged along the wharf and up the steps onto Tchoupitoulas and the trolley stop.

They waited there in Bellocq's furious silence, he refusing to so much as glance at Muldoon but facing upriver and tapping one foot impatiently. The longer they stood there, the warmer Muldoon's neck felt, and he became conscious, too, that his hand was stinging. He wondered whether he needed to have given the big kid that third and final crack, which, judging by his own hand must have hurt him a good deal. Then to their mutual relief they heard the trolley's approaching rattle and saw it sway and jerk around the shallow curve past Constantinople and Austerlitz, until it came to a screeching stop in front of them.

Muldoon watched the photographer clamber aboard, his long frock coat trailing after him like a little cloud. Muldoon handed up the case and tripod, its wooden legs yellowed and smoothed by long usage. As the car moved off he stared after it, searching for a glimpse of Bellocq, but the man was obscured by others on the rear platform. Yet he continued to stand there, looking after the car, even after it had made the turn at Celeste and disappeared from view. It wasn't, he told himself, that he'd been hoping right up to the last moment that Bellocq might wave one of his stubby arms in salute, gratitude, or simple farewell. That would have been a foolish expectation:

the man was far too angry and upset for anything like that. So maybe what kept him there was not the hope of any gesture from Bellocq but instead bemusement at his own gesture. Bellocq's trouble down on the docks hadn't been any of his business, and yet he had made it so. He couldn't imagine why.

That was the beginning of their odd acquaintance, one that could hardly be called a friendship since on those rare occasions when they passed each other in the street they never spoke, only nodded. Muldoon was never in the District in daylight, and that was when Bellocq was there most frequently. Still, on those early evening occasions when they did chance to meet and silently nodded Muldoon believed he could see something in the dark eyes of the other, some sort of response—flicker, flash—that passed beyond mere curt acknowledgement.

One evening after Jakey Ban-Ban, the head cook at the Annex, had coaxed him into having an Irish with him because it was Jakey's birthday, he was feeling so good that just for a few steps he had almost forgotten how when he took that left-legged step he had to pull along the right foot and allow for its first, toe-dropping failure. Then he spotted the photographer.

"Hey there, Bellocq!" he called out, cheerful in the gathering gloom, and was neither surprised nor especially disappointed when the other said nothing in return, only nodded, curt as ever, and kept on his way. But Muldoon felt better than ever for having said something at last, resolving to keep on saying something, even if there was never a return on his verbal investment.

On a subsequent evening, however, there actually was when he intersected with Bellocq at the corner of Conti and Franklin. "Hey there, Bellocq!" he said, stopping and looking the other squarely in the face. "I gotta see to something down to

Toro's. But then I'll meet you at the Annex, and I'll buy you one. Shouldn't take me that long—less than an hour, sure." Bellocq refused, but with that hesitation of a stray dog that really wants the chop bone but can't trust the strange hand that holds it towards him.

"Not tonight."

"Another time then," Muldoon came back, touching his hat and moving on to Toro's to see about customers' complaints that Frank Toro's wine had suddenly become all but undrinkable.

It was homemade stuff Toro's cousins made up, and Frank had talked Tom Anderson into letting him try it in the saloon. Muldoon knew nothing about wine but knew someone who did, and his mission tonight was to meet up with A Certain Sal, who in his long career as fence, waiter, cook, and bartender knew what could pass muster and what couldn't, even in so rough a place as Toro's. So, Sal would taste, and Muldoon would report his verdict.

Turning into Toro's, he felt his belly tighten and nudged his shoulder holster with his elbow. But inside everything was average: crowded, becoming boisterous, the near end of the bar beginning to clog up into a second row, mostly rough-looking screwmen who were talking prize fighting. Muldoon spotted the Toros and then found Alto North standing against a wall with one boot braced against it, apparently intent only on repairing a ragged thumbnail with a penknife. Occasionally, in the kitchen of the Annex Muldoon had walked past the meat locker when its man-sized door was opened and felt that invisible rush of icy air out into the hot buzz of the rest of the room with its stoves, its fry pans and griddles, its galvanized tubs of greasy dishwater. Passing through the gaze of the apparently indifferent and lounging North was a bit like that, he felt, and he still had a chilly spot between his shoulder blades as he sidled into a slot at the bar next to a man he recognized as a watchman somewhere in the neighborhood. He saw no sign of A Certain Sal and was wondering where he was when Frank Toro asked if he wanted coffee. Muldoon was about to answer when a voice at his elbow answered for him.

"He's gonna have yer wine, and me, too." And there suddenly beside him was Sal, small, slight of build, undistinguished of face and with a tired brown moustache beneath which his thin lips were drawn into a smile. Sal was some years older than he and showing a lot of gray hair beneath his cloth cap. Frank Toro had once told Muldoon that after the Black Hand's murder of police chief Hennessey, when all the city's Italians were in danger from mobs, Sal's grandmother had hidden the child in her root cellar for a week, and that after that dark experience Sal had been determined that whatever it took there would be no rough stuff in his life: he would be one of those guys who somehow managed always to get along. "It aint like I'm sayin he's yellow, like," Toro had said, "only I don know nobody he's hurt, you know?"

Now Frank Toro brought the wines—black, viscous-looking stuff that the two men lifted and sipped without preliminary ceremony.

"*Jesus!*" Sal gasped, making sure Frank Toro wasn't looking at him. "*Jesus!*" he coughed and wiped his mouth with his hand. "They gotta be cuttin this with cat spray." Muldoon almost never tasted wine of any sort. Once, Tom Anderson had insisted he have a glass of Veuve Cliquot and had chuckled good-naturedly when the champagne made Muldoon sneeze.

"That's okay," Tom Anderson had said, patting him paternally on the shoulder. "That's okay, lad: I done that way myself. You kinda have to sneak up on it, like."

There was no sneaking up on what the Toros were selling as wine; even Muldoon couldn't miss the strange aftertaste Sal was referring to with his pungent remark. And so, later, when he'd hoped that maybe Bellocq would have a drink with him, Muldoon dutifully made his report to Billy Brundy at the Annex, adding that Sal had said there probably wasn't any spot in the city low enough to get away with wine of that caliber.

Finally, there came an evening when Muldoon made another overture towards the photographer that was accepted. As he passed along St. Peter he saw Bellocq pulling shut a huge iron gate whose fan-shaped spokes splayed from a central hub that was the lock. The spokes reached so high that in being pulled to and pushed outward over the many decades since the place had been a Spanish tavern they had worn grooves in the stone archway. As Bellocq pulled, the gate screeched on its rust-roughened hinges, a keening kind of lamentation that reached to the center of Muldoon's spine and made him shiver.

Everybody in the District knew that Bellocq had for years now—some said even before the District officially opened—taken pictures of the girls. A few of the whores used his prints as business cards, and those who had seen samples found them straightforward, giving good, uncomplicated likenesses of the subjects. There wasn't anything "koo-koo" about them, Billy Brundy had reported to Tom Anderson years before, answering Anderson's not-quite-idle question. "He aint shootin snatch or other stuff," Brundy had said. "Some tits, if that's what they want. Mostly, it seems like it's the way they want to look, y'know—not like they'd maybe want to send back up to Baton Rouge or Breakaway or wherever the hell they came from—but not *salacious,* neither." Tom Anderson didn't know that word, but then there were a number of others Billy Brundy

used that Anderson overlooked and even, under certain circumstances, valued for the cachet they conferred on him for
having a man like Billy Brundy working under him. Here the
context was clear enough, anyway, and the rest of those fancy
syllables was window-dressing.

The subjects themselves, the girls, generally thought the misshapen little man took their photos because that was the way
he got his kicks—just looking. There were some johns like that
who came around, paid their money, but then didn't do anything up in the room, only asked the girl to take her clothes
off. Some of these types would masturbate while the girl just
sat there or lay motionless on her divan or even did her hair or
nails. But most of them were content to look and when their
time was up left peacefully enough. These customers—"Eye-
balls," the girls called them—were regarded as restful inter-
ludes in a long night's work, especially compared to the rough
stuff some of the younger sporting gents went in for. And there
were some girls who refused to believe Bellocq was anything
but one of these harmless types, that he was just another Eye-
ball who really didn't do anything under that black hood he
flipped over his head, except look. It was like his peephole or
keyhole, they claimed, even when some of the girls produced
the prints they used for business cards, complete with their
name and address on the back. "Oh, he don't make those himself," one girl scoffed. "I don't know who does it for him or
how they do it. But he don't do nothing under there but look
at yer titties, that I can tell ya."

Before she got lucky and struck it rich with a john who
actually married her and took her off to live with him in
Nashville, Geraldine Monette claimed she'd actually been up
to Bellocq's studio in the Quarter and posed for him there.
"He has these, like, oh, little boxes," she tried to explain, "and

when he puts these slabs of glass in there, there's nothing on them and he just leaves them in there a bit, and then, when you look at em, why there's your face. It's like some kinda magic trick, except those fellows—the ones that travel around with the shows?—they're all bunko guys, and this guy isn't. Either that, or he's the best there ever was, cause you can't tell how he's doing it, only there you are." She showed some of her skeptical colleagues a business card photo she said Bellocq had taken of her.

"That where you make them pictures?" Muldoon called out from the other side of St. Peter. The man turned around, a ring of keys held in both hands, the ponderous gate still just ajar.

"It's my studio, yes." He was still as frosty but no longer completely frozen.

"Like to come up and see it sometime," Muldoon came back with a smile and a touch of his forefinger to the brim of his bowler, and then limped onward. Ten steps beyond he heard the photographer's voice behind him.

"All right."

Muldoon turned to find him standing there in his unfashionably long coat, the key ring still held in both hands. Muldoon wasn't entirely sure he'd heard right and so said, "Ehh?" cupping a hand to an ear.

"I said, 'All right,' you may."

Muldoon's face split into his red Irish grin. "Grand!" he called out, returning a few steps along St. Peter. "Grand! Like to see how you do it. Have to be a Monday, though. Resta the nights I work." He nodded his head westward towards sunset and the District. The tiny fellow nodded himself.

"Monday next, then. Any time after two." He turned back to the gate, fitting a long key into the lock and turning it several times. Muldoon stood watching the process that seemed to him in keeping with so much else about the man—solitary, ponderously deliberate, out of some other era when men wore frock coats that reached below their knees, and French was the language used in these streets. He was on the point of turning away, seeing Bellocq pocket the key ring, but then Bellocq said, over his shoulder, "Come alone. This isn't some peep show."

And so that next Monday he was there shortly after two at the great black gate which he found locked, but there was a short scarf of much-faded red knotted about two of the bars, and he took this as a sign the photographer was somewhere inside. He rattled the gate and waited, then rattled it again, this time calling out, "Hey, there, Bellocq! It's me." St. Peter at this hour was quiet, and standing there in the post-luncheon lull, hand on the gate, Muldoon thought he heard sounds in a room somewhere above him, and waited patiently enough until there were unmistakable footfalls along the balcony and then descending towards the street. Then Bellocq was there inside the gate in his hat and his shirtsleeves furled above his elbows. The hairless skin of his surprisingly sinewy arms was a startling, bloodless white and recalled to Muldoon the sight of the huge onion dome of his head the toughs down at the Stuyvesant Docks had cruelly exposed when they'd snatched his hat.

When Bellocq had unlocked the gate and pulled it wide enough for Muldoon to sidle through, Muldoon said something in greeting and stuck out his hand. But the other merely motioned him in with a curt head gesture and turned the key again. He led Muldoon through the dank, narrow passageway and into a courtyard where a palm drooped its fronds over the broken cobbles. In the tree's ragged shadow a few large red carp floated in the inky depths of an ancient cistern faced with Spanish tiles. Doorways lined three sides of the courtyard, several of them missing their doors altogether and other doors listing dangerously on ruined frames. At the back there was a double set of doors that had once been glass-paneled, but now most of the glass lay scattered in shards on the stones that were moss-covered and slimy. Above where they stood ran the balcony on which the photographer's steps had sounded. A narrow, serpentine staircase wound up there, and Bellocq was on his way up it, calling back to Muldoon but without turning his head, "Mind the stairs: there's a tread missing." Indeed there was, about halfway up, and looking down through its empty space, Muldoon was startled to see the perfect image of himself in a large puddle that lay beneath the staircase. For just that instant up and down were lost to him, the mottled sky lay beneath him, the soles of his shoes, black and nail-studded, partially obscured his face, and he found himself holding hard to the spiraling railing to keep his balance. His guide kept on, however, and pulling his gaze away from the puddle so did he, hauling himself up to the narrow balcony with its wooden railing and more doorways matching the ones below, though these were in good condition and all firmly shut, two of them with stout padlocks.

At the far end a door stood open, and Bellocq went in. Following him, Muldoon found himself in a large room that was a jungle of alien objects, among which only the cameras and lenses made any sense to him. Shelving that ran around the walls was filled with dark brown bottles and cartons whose labels were meaningless. There were stacks of frames of various sizes, piles of heavy paper pressed down by bricks and cobblestones. Along one wall was what appeared to be a joined sequence of small vats on slim iron legs. In a corner beneath the shelving he recognized the case he'd rescued from the freckle-faced kid down at the docks. Festooned across an angle at the rear of the room were two wires from which photographs hung suspended by clothespins. They were all of ships, cranes, winches, warehouses, everything associated with the life of the great port. In a few of them dark and blurred human figures were caught going about their business, but plainly their presence was not the point of the shots but rather unavoidable and accidental.

The room was dominated by a table cobbled together out of two of the doors from downstairs. The joinery, he noted, was of almost professional grade, and if Bellocq himself had done it, the tiny man was something more than just a photographer. It was strewn with photographs, almost drifts of them, but at one of its corners there was a precise, neat stack, the edges and corners squared with a military precision and the whole held down by two bricks beneath which lay stretched a bit of soft pink cloth. Muldoon thought it might once have been a piece of a woman's undergarment.

He craned his head about, smiling somewhat vacantly, trying to signal his interest in it all. Bellocq stood behind the table scrutinizing him. Muldoon felt he wasn't going to get much help from his host but was going to have to come up with some explanation, justification for the enthusiasm he'd expressed a few days ago. His mind worked hard at this but without much success.

In fact, he had never been that much interested in photographs, either of cityscapes or family members, friends, even of himself. He could now recall only four of the last. There was the portrait taken at the time of his confirmation, his youthfully round face looking somewhat squeezed by the high starched collar whose cruel edge on his neck he could still remember. In his graduation class photo from St. Alphonsus, there he was right in the middle, "just where you belong," as Father Dyer had laughingly said, pulling him through the standing kids, and with his hands on both of Muldoon's shoulders forcefully placing him there. There was also the one that ran on the front page of the *Picayune* sports section; it showed him finishing the Crescent City Quarter-Mile, his head thrown back, arms raised in triumph as he broke the tape in record time. It was still a record, though just last year it had been threatened. For a long time the photo itself had hung in his parents' kitchen, steadily yellowing, the blacks turning to sepia, the whites to saffron and mustard, until some months after the riot the thing had disappeared from the wall, leaving behind it a shadow of itself, a beige-colored outline surrounded by walls that had themselves once been that color but had darkened through years of smoking pans, simmering kettles, the eruptions of un-tended coffeepots. He found himself wondering now who it had been who had at last removed it: his brokenhearted mother, maybe, who could no longer bear the accusing daily image of her once-heroic son, now reduced to a shuffle-gaited disgrace who did something for Mr. Anderson, himself no better than he ought to be. Or maybe it was his father who hadn't been able to stand his wife's grief and so had heavily removed it, putting it well out of the way, to lie face-up under some slowly settling stack of the sort of detritus you accumulated through the years, stuff that mounted like drifts of dust and that seemed, magically, to mount more quickly, more determinedly, as the years themselves mounted, until at last the stuff covered everything and you were dust yourself.

The other photograph hung where he could see it every working day of his life, if he wanted to, which he didn't. It had been taken a few years back at the bar of the Annex, where it still was, high up among the dozens of other framed shots that filled an entire wall: Edwin Booth in old age; Galli-Curci just starting out; Florenz Ziegfeld; John L. Sullivan, ponderous as an old Percheron in a vast, three-piece suit and shaking hands with Tom Anderson; President Roosevelt; Tommy's Lea, the chestnut gelding that had cleaned up everything here at the Fairgrounds and looked like a sure winner in the Derby until he broke down in the stretch; the martyred police chief, Hennessy. And high up, lost in this gallery of the forgotten and the famous, there was a group shot taken from the doorway of the Annex and showing those men who happened to be there that afternoon: two coppers in their tall helmets, some light-suited sporting gents, Okey-Poke behind the bar with towel in one hand and tumbler in the other. And there he was, Fast-Mail, in their midst, looking at the camera, his right foot raised and resting on the bar rail, his hat four-square, and wearing one of the heavy-cut suits Tom Anderson paid for. In order to get all of its details you had to stand on tiptoes almost, and he had never had anything like that sort of interest in it.

While his mind was grinding toward some kind of appropriate comment or response Bellocq regarded him with that same fixedness. "Aren't you really here to see the girls?" he said at last, his voice icy, accusatory. Oddly, this was a help to Muldoon because the one thing he was sure of was that it wasn't the girls.

"No," he said slowly, drawing the word out, "it aint the women, I guess." He shook his head and smiled a bit, as if to make the disclaimer look as true as he felt it was. "I get all the looks at em I need ever night of my life—cept Mondays, a course." His smile broadened just a bit more like an aperture opening, letting more light in. "It aint that. I get more looks at em than I can use, tell the truth.

"You know, sometimes I think I almost get sick of em, y'know. Oh, not all of em. But in the mornings? When they come to turn in their keys? Why some of em look so terrible it's hard to look at em." He had an instant image of some of the whores as they appeared at that awful hour, many of them drunk or hopped up; some of them marked by a rough customer or that even rougher customer, the pimp who had them on the string; almost all of them plainly exhausted and reeking of sweat, semen, the serial sex that was their work. "No, I get my share of looks at the girls, all right."

He hadn't meant to say this much and was surprised he had. He wondered why he had tried to explain himself to the photographer, who was at most merely a figure of faded derision in the District, one of those strange people who like himself had washed up there: Zozo La Brique; the fairy piano player, Tony Jackson; the twisted, three-fingered Mamie Desdoumes who never spoke; or the man they called Suicide Suzy who dressed as a woman and went about buttonholing passersby with his plans to kill himself. What in fact had brought him up here in the first place, since clearly he had no real interest in photography, in how it was that Bellocq did his work? Was he only seeking out another freak like himself?

Bellocq broke into his thoughts. "Well, you're quite wrong there," he said, and seeing the look on Muldoon's face added, "about the girls." His hands rested atop the bricks that held the neat pile of prints in place. "You're quite wrong there. You don't really see them. You can't." He glanced down briefly at the pile beneath his hands, then half-turned to the photos hanging from the wires behind him. "Are you interested then in photographs of shipping? Because these are the only other prints I have to show you. I doubt you'd find the more technical aspects of what I do very interesting. Anyway, I'm not sure I could do a good job of explaining them to you."

"Don't suppose I'd get it anyway," Muldoon answered with another of his smiles. "I wasn't too good at my studies back in school. Hadn't a been for the brothers I might still be there." He looked around the studio and its clutter once again, trying to evince interest in something, then asked the photographer what it was exactly that took him down to the docks so much.

"It's my work," Bellocq said simply, reaching to pick up a few prints from the table and handing them across to Muldoon. "I work for Merchants Marine and Salvage, as well as a few other concerns from time to time. And sometimes I take photographs for the city: they use them for promotional purposes." He shrugged, his small shoulders rising, then subsiding under his striped shirt and black suspenders. "It isn't very interesting work—as you can see for yourself." He held his hand out for the prints, and Muldoon gave them back. "But then, whose work really is interesting?" He looked hard at Muldoon as he asked this. "Is yours?"

Muldoon had never thought about it from this angle. He'd been so glad to get the work—and everything else that Tom Anderson provided along with it—that whether or not it was interesting was hardly a consideration. Just about the only things he had ever thought about his job were that it had its hazards and that he performed it faithfully. "Well, there's always somethin different most ever night," he said smilingly. "Some different kind of problem, seems like, just when you think you seen em all. I guess you could say that about it, anyways."

"Well, my work isn't interesting to me at all," Bellocq said. "But then, it's only what I get paid for." He had both hands back on the bricks now and patted them twice, lightly. "This is my real work. I don't get paid for it except if one of the girls wants multiples for business purposes. Then I charge for the materials." He lifted the bricks and the underlying cloth with a care that was almost ceremonial. "You can come around here and have a look, if you like."

Here then were the girls of whom rumor had so long spoken, the white working women of the District, portraits of them printed on heavy paper in tones ranging from delicate tan to rich chocolate, the faces most often looking directly at the camera and many posed before a white canvas backdrop, though here and there as Muldoon's hands moved down through the pile he found subjects posed in other attitudes.

There was one of a girl lying on her stomach atop a table, chin propped in her hands, face in profile. One leg in its dark stocking and high-heeled shoe was cocked skyward with a kind of gaiety that seemed almost demure, not suggestive. The shot conveyed the impression that here was a young lady taking her proper pleasure under heaven's bright sun, and except for a portion of a doorway visible to one side it might have been a scene from a country picnic and the girl herself an eligible object of any young man's attentions. Muldoon didn't recognize her, but from her looks he thought she might have been new to her work when she'd posed for Bellocq: she showed none of that telltale puffiness most of the girls came to acquire.

In another shot the subject was seated at a table, fully clothed but showing as much as possible of her legs, crossed at the knees and clad in the striped stockings the girls all loved, even though, as Octavia had told him, they ran so easily. She held a glass in one hand, regarding it with pleasant interest. On the table, label-out, was a fifth of Raleigh Rye, a big seller in the District.

Except for a few portraits that appeared to have been taken in the yards behind the houses, the rest had been shot within those places, some in parlors, but most in the rooms where the girls worked. On the walls of these Muldoon could make out the little decorations he knew so well. There were pennants of cities and colleges and tourist attractions—Atlanta, Tulane, Ole Miss, Lookout Mountain. There were cards with slogans and greetings—"O Babe Please Come," "Merry Xmas," "Honey Give Me Your Best." A few caught indistinct framed photographs of blurry faces out of the girls' pasts, the families they had left behind to come down here to work for a while.

He came to one of the famed sex-trick pony that performed at Emma Johnson's, only here the mother and daughter who appeared with the pony on stage merely stood smiling at either side of the animal's head. In another portrait you could just make out what looked like a goose in the act of penetrating a woman with his bill. Muldoon had never heard of that one.

For as long as he could remember the girls had liked to have little dogs around, and here in Bellocq's portraits they were shown, tense and quivering on the girls' laps or with the girls hugging them tightly: terriers, ratters, mutts, bug-eyed lap dogs on which the girls lavished attention so that the creatures were chronically overfed. Finding so many of them in the portraits, it occurred to him that the girls might like them so well because they were a good deal nicer than the average run of humans they had to deal with nightly.

Some of the girls posed entirely nude, some wearing only the long striped stockings, some with bared breasts, their shirtwaists shucked and gathered around their middles, simulating sudden, passionate abandon. Some stood at the doorways to their rooms. Some lay on their divans. A few were shown fixing their hair and staring into the mirror as they did so. Some simply sat, slump-shouldered at the edge of the bed.

But the more he looked at the portraits, the more he was struck by their sameness. It was true that there were different poses, different faces, differing states of undress. Still, there was a static, fixed quality to the portraits. It was almost as if they were all shots of the same woman gotten up in different costumes at different times. It was clear from some of the prints that the same little dog had appeared with different girls. Maybe, he thought, this was somehow like that, a technical trick. He'd heard the tales of Bellocq, the rumors of what he did—or didn't—when he put that black hood over his head, that he was some kind of wizard or conjure man. The girls said that. But he also knew that some of these same tale-tellers believed in voodoo and Marie Laveau—all that bosh. He also knew the old saw in the District—turn em upside down and all whores are the same—and he thought there was a kind of truth to it. After all, when a girl got you upstairs her bag of tricks was precisely the same as any other girl's, and you knew it couldn't be otherwise because they'd learned their trade from the older women of the house and sometimes from their mothers: "You want to ring his bell right off, you gotta press here, honey." Even Octavia, who took her time with him, was essentially like all the others he'd ever had, all those he ever would have.

He came to the portrait of a plumpish young woman, naked to the waist and with her post-pubescent breasts bared to Bellocq's lens. Her torso confronted the camera square-on, but her head was turned to the right and her eyes looked away in that direction. He was thinking of asking Bellocq whether this slight alteration in pose had been his idea or the girl's, but then, looking at those averted eyes, where they looked to, he was suddenly, powerfully reminded of his first glimpse of Adele, when he'd gone to report on her singing at the beer garden behind the Tuxedo, how when she'd begun her first number in front of her rough audience she too had looked away, over their heads, as if willing herself to be anywhere else.

At the same time it came to him the reason why all these portraits looked the same: it was in their eyes: they *all* looked away, even when they stared directly at the camera. And they all looked dead. Their eyes were dead—opaque, lusterless, filmed over by experiences unwillingly undergone, cumulatively endured, suffered, until finally—and quickly, too—the girl no longer really cared what things she had to do. And it was at that point, he now felt, that the life must have left the eyes.

And then? What happened then? How did they manage to go on when they saw Nothing. He stood there, gripping the plumpish girl's picture, trying to imagine what might have become of her, this particular and unexceptional one, where she had gone and to what, and thinking also for the first time that he worked among dead people who went through the motions of life but who were really dead inside. And this must be true for some of the higher-priced ones as well, the ones who gathered at The Frenchman's to laugh and drink and dance while the piano professors sped through their showy numbers and, later—as the sun climbed up into the day—when they changed tempo and mood, piling chorus on chorus of slow blues that seemed compounded of that dark, inky decay of graveyards and cypress swamps, the great river at dusk when it carried the swirling, sodden refuse that had been swept into it far away: blues that were black with the feeling of death itself. Well, *here* were the blues, all right, the images hidden in the lyrics he'd learned not to listen to.

He saw with sudden embarrassment that his thumbs and fingers were making indentations in the print and quickly turned the portrait face down on the growing stack of the discarded. Maybe he shouldn't have come up here to see this weird little man who took pictures of the great ships and the life of the wharves but whose real work, so he'd just confessed, was to take pictures of the dead people of a garishly lit world that underneath its lights, its paint, was dead itself. Wasn't this the ghoulish kind of thing you found in voodoo and such-like quackery where they worshipped the dead?

Beneath the picture of the plumpish girl was a full-length portrait of a strikingly beautiful young woman in formal attire, complete with hat, parasol, gloves, and a long dress that obscured all but the tips of her shoes. She stood outdoors, surrounded by the full-fledged shrubs of summer and a high hedge behind. Her face was slightly lifted, almost as if she might have been listening to something, a band, perhaps, playing popular tunes across a stretch of park. There was about the photograph and its figure an air of repose and even refinement utterly different from any of the others he'd so far seen, and he wondered whether it had somehow gotten in here among the whores by mistake.

He turned to Bellocq who hadn't been paying his guest any mind but had been busy with something on the shelf. "Who's this?" Muldoon asked, his hands along the edges of the print. Bellocq didn't respond right away, but finally he turned, came forward to the table, and picked up the print, squinting at it closely for something like a full minute.

"That's an old one," he said finally and turned it over in his hands. On its back was written "2201" in sharp, inky numerals like arrows that looked like whoever had written them had been in some haste and was numbering his way through a lengthy sequence. He returned it to the stack, casually and at a slant.

"Mamie," he said, turning back to his task at the shelf.

"Mamie?" Muldoon asked. He knew of only one Mamie, but clearly there had once been another, long ago, before he'd gone down to the District and had encountered there the silent, twisted blues player missing the middle two fingers of her right hand.

"Mamie." Bellocq's voice came back flat, declarative, and Muldoon turned about then to stare at the diminutive back with its black braces reinforced at the cross with a diamond-shaped bit of leather, much-polished with age and sweat and the wearing action of heavy, old-fashioned coats.

"Mamie who? Not the Mamie who plays at the Perdido. Used to be at the Sunset before that, I think."

"That Mamie," the voice still flat, even more inflectionless. It was like the pronouncement of a sentence.

Muldoon snatched the print off the stack, holding it as close to his face as the photographer had done moments ago, as though something had suddenly gone awry with his eyesight. He glared into its chocolate depths, searching for some thing, some clue, some old evidence there foreshadowing the appearance of the side-winding woman he knew, playing often with her right ear bent so close to the treble keys you wondered that her head didn't get in the way of her hand; the Mamie who at dawn might turn some of the slanted drunks weepy when she changed from the blues to a sentimental number that took you back a long way, not just in time and still less in musical taste, but rather to some other, earlier condition that obscurely reminded the drunks of something they'd once had and lost. But there was nothing there in the formal figure to suggest anything of some coming disaster that would transform this beauty into one of the District's freaks, no least hint of twisted spine and limping gait, that haggard face and hooded eyes that never looked directly at you, that refused to return your casual glance. As if the clue might be there on the back, he flipped the print over. But there was only that cipher—2201—and it meant nothing to him. He wondered what it meant to Bellocq, if he even remembered.

"But what in hell happened to her?" Muldoon asked, his voice rising into a plaintive range. "Something terrible must have happened to her—"

Bellocq cut him off, speaking still with his back turned but wearily, as if giving an answer worn with long and repeated usage: "What happens to all of them."

"But, *Jesus,* Bellocq!" Muldoon held the print out before him, wanting to hand it over to the man who'd made it, to make him take it back or admit he'd made a mistake here, that this wasn't the same Mamie, couldn't be. Bellocq faced about slowly and reached for the print and for that instant both men held different edges of the paper. Then Muldoon let it go, surrendered it, and the photographer glanced briefly at it, then up at Muldoon.

"Well, what is it?" he asked.

"I guess I want to know about what happened to Mamie. This here girl's a beauty, and Mamie—Mamie..." His voice trailed off and he simply shook his head. He tried again. "Mamie, she...." But that was all he could bring out, and in his stammering silence he heard for the first time something rustling in a corner of the studio. He turned quickly, trying to locate the source of the sound; in this clutter it might even be a rat, he thought. But he turned back to Bellocq, because the tiny man was telling him now that he didn't know what had happened.

"Nobody knows for certain," he said. "Anyway, it happened years ago, whatever it was. And what difference would it make? What difference could it make to you?"

"Well, I don't know," Muldoon brought out after a pause, "but a thing like this—" gesturing to the portrait that Bellocq had placed facedown in the stack of discards so that only its number showed. Muldoon stared at it, reminded of a section of a potter's field he'd been sent to with another officer when he'd been on the force: he no longer remembered the nature of that assignment, only those little slabs that marked where the bodies were, that could tell you nothing about how "158" had come to lie there or how "158" was any different from "159" or "166." "I don't know."

Bellocq was looking at him carefully now, noting that his characteristic ruddiness had paled, that Muldoon's face had become taut with some sort of emotion he was unable to express. He seemed ready to take a bleak kind of pity on his guest because he ventured a few syllables further than his severe sentence on the fate of all those who had posed for him up in the rooms where the quick, sordid deed was done and the money changed hands: lounging amidst the dusty plush of the pillows and sofas of the parlors where the madam and her coffle greeted the johns; standing in the trashy dust and chicken shit of the little yards behind the houses on Conti and Bienville, Iberville and Basin. "They all end up like that, sooner or later." He gestured to the numbered back of Mamie's image. "It happens quicker than you can imagine." He made another gesture, a more expansive one taking in the studio and its equipment. "That's what's kept me at it so long and why I have to work fast." The look on Muldoon's face told him his meaning was hardly grasped. He picked up another portrait of a girl, glanced at it, discarded it, then riffled down through several others.

"This girl, for example." He held up the full-length portrait of a girl lying on her side on a tasseled divan, her long fair hair partly but not completely covering her breasts. Her dark pubic triangle was fully in view yet she seemed oddly unconcerned with it or even connected with it. She stared straight into Bellocq's lens but, again, with those dead eyes Muldoon had just become so burningly aware of. "You wouldn't believe how beautiful this girl used to be, but you can still see some of that, even here." Muldoon heard the rustling sound once more and turned quickly to spot a parakeet in a tarnished cage that sat on the floor in a corner. "Now you can rent her for a dollar in that alley in back of Gipsy Shafer's—you know the one that runs between Iberville and Bienville?" Muldoon signed that he did. "Well, that's where you can find her if that's all you can afford. Of course, she doesn't look much like this anymore." He gazed at the girl in the photo, and for just the flicker of an instant his eyes seemed to soften. But the instant passed as he raised his face to Muldoon, the features hardened over, mask-like under the slouch hat.

"All of them are Mamie, if you like, all of them. And what I want to do is to catch something of that beauty they have before it's taken from them. Sometimes, I get it—when they're new, like this girl. Sometimes, I get just a shadow of it when it's already fading. Sometimes, by the point they pose for me it's gone, and then all you see are the ruins." He put the recumbent beauty facedown in the pile and shrugged his small shoulders again. "Sometimes, I simply miss what's there to see, for whatever reason. Those are the photographs I regret the most, my failures. Because if I don't get what's there to be gotten, what's left, it's lost."

He looked down at the dwindled stack of those Muldoon hadn't yet seen. "You're not a stupid man, Mr. Muldoon, only a thoughtless one. There isn't anything unusual about Mamie, not a thing. Unless it could be that she hasn't disappeared like most of them do. Not yet, anyway."

Muldoon had found out this much—and it was hardly anything: Mamie lived across the river in Algiers and took the ferry to work each evening, arriving at five at the Governor Nicholls wharf. So, he stood there now, in the small knot of waiting passengers, some of them with their umbrellas still spread—dull and black little moons against the bruised evening. The rain had stopped some minutes earlier, and the puddles in the cinders in front of the dock lay as smooth and untroubled as the surfaces of age-blackened coins.

The night before he'd tried casually to introduce the subject of Mamie Desdoumes to Okey-Poke at the Annex. It was late, the bar was sparsely attended, and what few were still hanging on seemed slumped within themselves, quiet over half-drunk glasses, and making no demands on Okey-Poke or his assistants.

"I guess the boss is a bit warm about Huntz and the Perdido," he began, making a bit more out of getting his cheroot going than was strictly necessary. Okey-Poke was polishing glasses and using them to reconstruct a depleted pyramid beneath one of the cherrywood arches that ran in their majestic sequence behind the bar. Okey-Poke grunted, tossed his head in silent affirmation, but said nothing. He seemed tired.

Muldoon tried again, more frontally. "What's in it for the Parkers, I wonder? I mean, it's a tonk with just Mamie there, playin them songs, same as she's played ever since I been down here, anyways. How do you figure it, Okey?"

Okey-Poke reached below the bar for another glass. The skin beneath his eyes looked dark and heavily creased, as if folded over and again like a letter an anxious passenger might keep compulsively rereading on a long journey. We're getting older, Muldoon thought, looking at him, by God, we're getting older. Okey-Poke was within a couple of years of him, he guessed, though he had been down here longer. Maybe it was the work.

Okey-Poke raised his eyes to Muldoon, another glass in hand. "Mamie aint in it. It's the spot, is all, another spot down here for them." He twirled his towel inside the rim of the glass. "The Tuxedo's bad enough, that and them guys they got spotted around, scarin off our customers. You see how it is yourself. This just ups the ante."

Muldoon flashed him a quick grin. "Remember our bet, Okey? You had T.A. eatin their lunch by Independence Day. What was that for now?—I forget. Twenty was it?" He winked broadly.

Okey-Poke wasn't in a joshing mood. "Tough guys," he muttered with a shake of his head. "When they come down, it was just some smart-asses from New York. Didn't know from nuthin. Now they got this Gyp the Blood guy, got him carryin guns in plain sight and just darin us to come at him. Nobody figured that." The talk would almost surely shoot into that channel if he didn't dam it off, and so Muldoon quickly tried again.

"What do you know about her—about Mamie?"

"What anybody else does, I guess."

"Musta been some kind of terrible accident to make her look like that—all twisted around like that, fingers tore off, and everything." He shook his head and took a large puff on the cheroot. Okey-Poke didn't look up when he grabbed another tumbler and began to massage it to a sparkling clarity; he only gave another head shake in a silent show of concurrence: yeah, musta been something terrible.

"Well, then," Muldoon blundered on after another puff on the now-blazing cheroot, tapping it unnecessarily in the small white ashtray that read around its rim, TOM ANDERSON'S ANNEX BASIN ST. AT IBERVILLE NEW ORLEANS. "What might have messed her up that bad, I wonder. You ever hear any story about that?" Okey-Poke stopped polishing now, the towel stilled in his hands, just like in the photograph that hung high on the wall behind Muldoon. His head came up slightly, and he stared at his old colleague with that level directness an experienced bartender used only when he saw a situation taking a turn into dangerous territory. The look lasted a full twenty seconds.

"Bad subject, Fast-Mail," he said flatly. "Bad subject." He swung his head down the bar to his left, where no summons was forthcoming. "Scuse me."

What he got from Jimmie Enright at the 102 the same night was only a little more, about as satisfying to a man long lost in the desert as a thimbleful of water might be, he thought.

"Nobody knows what happened to her," Jimmie Enright declared. He seemed vaguely annoyed at the question, old, trivial in comparison with his current problems. He was at his customary station at the far end of the bar, his small black eyes fixed on Billy Phillips up at the other end with his florid face, his full moustache wagging considerably as he argued something with a customer who kept jabbing his finger at his glass or at the bar. "Jesus, will ya look at him," Jimmie said under his breath. "Will ya just look at him, though." Muldoon, hoping to avert Jimmie from his obsession with how badly Phillips was running the 102, how impervious he was to Jimmie's advice, offered the observation that things looked like they'd picked up just a bit.

"Horseshit!" Jimmie snapped. "*Horseshit!* Great rollin road-apples, Fast-Mail! You know it, I know it. Only guy doesn't know it is T.A.—or if he does, he don't seem to want to do anything about it!" He looked fiercely at Muldoon as though Tom Anderson's troubleshooter ought to be doing something to correct the situation, which Jimmie said was sliding quickly from bad to disastrous.

"I been knowin him since we was newspaper squirts together," Jimmie said, lowering his voice once again and running his stubby-fingered hands through the bristles of his cannon-ball head. He puffed out his cheeks when he'd finished this exercise in self-control. "Long time. An this is the first time I seen him actin like this." He held out his hand palm up, then flipped it back and forth, regarding it as he did so with amazement, as if the hand were some detached witness to a staggeringly strange phenomenon. "He don't wanna listen to me, an he sure as shit don't seem to wanna do anything about them bastards," giving his head a vicious jerk in the direction of the Tuxedo. "Now, you know, Fast-Mail, that aint like him."

Muldoon rubbed his jaw with thumb and forefinger, feeling all the night's hours in the tough bristles that had sprouted since his early afternoon shave. "Course, I don't know him like you do, Jimmie." He wanted to add something that might close off the subject of the Tuxedo and bring it back to Mamie, but he couldn't think of anything more to say than that T.A. always had a plan, only sometimes you couldn't always see what it was until it was hatched.

"Well, this one's so—" Jimmie Enright broke off, searching for the word that would fit the baffled anger he lived with, the profound perplexity. "Well, *shit!* What's he waitin on is what I'd like to know." He leaned his head and shoulders close to Muldoon's chest. "We got to settle these fuckers' *hash,*" he growled in a low voice. "And quick, too. I seen the way things're headin. You seen it—people waitin around to see what he's gonna do. Lotsa loose talk startin. First that joint," jerking his head towards the Tuxedo whose outrageous, gilded light flooded through the doors of the 102, beguiling, bedazzling, beckoning customers to come across to where the real action was. "And now the Perdido, too. What's next?"

Mention of the Perdido gave Muldoon his chance again, and he took it. "Yeah, you have to wonder there. I mean, there's just Mamie, and what would they want with her, busted up the way she is? She aint even got all her fingers, and the way I hear it, she aint got all her marbles, either." He tapped his temple under its bowler. "Ever hear how she lost those fingers?"

Jimmie Enright shook his head. "Like I said, nobody knows nothin." He glared at Billy Phillips who was still in animated conversation with the customer who had quit pointing downward at his glass or the bar and had drawn back to place his hands on his hips. "Used to be a singer," Jimmie Enright said vaguely, his mind obviously elsewhere, "but then you already knew that. Only thing I ever heard was she mighta had some kinda fall or something out a window." He turned back to Muldoon and briefly mimed Mamie's side-winding gait, her twisted torso. "But the fingers, no." He stuck out his hand to grab a busboy passing close by. "Get us two Irish," he told the kid, and when the drinks were speedily produced Jimmie looked deeply into the light amber depths of his tumbler but didn't drink. "Lives over in Algiers," he said, "with all them hoodoo folks."

And that was why he found himself this evening at Governor Nicholls, surrounded by the now superfluous umbrellas, watching the ferry as it cut speed, a black belch blossoming from its smokestack, and the blunt prow beginning to waver just slightly as it made ready to nose to its berth. The dockhands were gathered, lines at the ready, and the passengers were beginning to shift about a bit, one or two leaning down to pick up bundles or satchels. And of all those who waited here none, he believed, could have done so with a greater anticipation or with more bizarre and impossible hopes: waiting here for *Mamie,* waiting to hear from those sealed, silent lips how she had come to be one of the District's sideshow people where once she would have stood out anywhere in her unspoiled beauty. When he phrased his quest to himself thus, it sounded ridiculous to his own ears, and he had no trouble at all imagining how it might sound to his colleagues and associates, to Frank Toro or Jimmie Enright or to his delivery driver, Santos Villalta, the laconic, spare-spoken ex-machine gunner who apparently wanted to know nothing more of the world he worked in than where to go and what to pick up and where to drop it off. And certainly his quest would fall on unsympathetic ears were he ever to express it to Okey-Poke who had tried to warn him away from the subject and whatever dark secret lay behind it.

In fact, everything he knew of his world and how it functioned, everything he knew of the District as a place thronged with secrets it was dangerous to pry into—everything told him to forget Mamie, to turn around right now and get away from here, leaving Mamie to carry her own secret up the rain-saturated streets to the stinking tonk and the battered instrument from which she had somehow to coax music for the night.

Yet he stayed, rooted to the cinders, stayed because he had come to feel that he must, that the secret history of Mamie Desdoumes made an obscure intersection with his own, in the turn it had taken in recent weeks.

In reaching down through the pile of prints to exhume the portrait of the youthful Mamie it had become for him suddenly, blazingly clear what it was that had brought him to the studio on St. Peter: it *was* the girls after all. Or rather it was *the* girl, Adele, whom he saw in that instant of exposure to the unmarried Mamie as just starting down the path that would lead—must lead—to the fate of all those pathetic, pasty-faced, dead-eyed women who had posed for Bellocq. He hadn't, he told himself, lied when Bellocq had made his initial accusation. Instead, it was that his mission hadn't begun to dawn on him until he'd reached that place in the pile where he saw the portrait of the plumpish girl with her post-pubescent breasts and then looked into those averted eyes. Then a light had come into the darkness of his own life, like those stabbing stilettos that reached into his shuttered bedroom—not much yet, but some anyway. And then beneath this nameless, doubtlessly dead girl he'd come at last to Mamie and had seen what Bellocq had seen, what Bellocq had been looking at all these years, what Bellocq had rightly said Muldoon had been blind to: the doom the District actually was, a prison that surrounded the girls, every one of them, including one so surpassingly beautiful as Mamie.

Once you stepped inside those walls, it didn't make any difference—Bellocq again—what you looked like: you weren't going to get out intact. The girls always said they hoped to—just a few years of this. In fact, their hope was hopeless, and for every Edith Simms and Bessie Browne who survived to run their own houses; for every Geraldine Monette who somehow got a john to marry her and take her away from all that, there were uncountable others who never escaped, who gave up hoping to escape, who worked through the mounting years, on their backs, on their knees, until they could no longer even command a dollar trick in an alley at the height of Carnival, like that once-beautiful girl Bellocq said worked the alley behind Gipsy Shafter's as a zombie-like dope fiend who took it any way the customers wanted. Geraldine Monette was a legend among the girls precisely because she had achieved the impossible.

And just as a girl's looks could not ultimately save her from the common fate, so it made no difference that a girl might begin work in the District as a singer, because even in that position she would be expected to provide other services for selected customers, and she would have to put out for the cabaret's manager or its owner or both.

Bellocq had asked him what difference the details of Mamie's story could possibly make, and he hadn't been able to answer. He still couldn't. But watching the first passengers descend onto the wharf, he knew he needed to hear at least some scrap, some remnant of the story of what the swift steps had been that had brought Mamie to the Perdido to play her wordless blues for customers so heedless the player herself might as well have been one of those wind-up contraptions you fed coins to. Only at the Perdido you fed the contraption a beer from time to time.

Then he saw her, putting one foot with a painful tentativeness on the gray plankings of the wharf, a shapeless bag of a woman, her head tightly bound in a blue turban. When she had finally gotten her other foot planted and squared herself about she began her slow, tortuous progress toward the wharf's gate behind which the new passengers waited, impatient with the woman's inconvenient handicap. And Muldoon found himself impatient as well, waiting, waiting, watching the approach of this woman who was not reminding him now of what a beauty she had been but instead of one of those street curs that at some point had been run over by a cart and so now trotted along the street at an angle, making you wonder how it actually made forward progress since it seemed more likely it ought to be going sideways until it ran itself into a fence.

But like the injured cur Mamie eventually did clear the gate and came through the waiting passengers with their bundles and their umbrellas that were mostly furled now, and he could hear the slow crunch of the cinders beneath her feet, the way she had to slither her right foot around to make another twisting advance. And he began to move, limping around a man and wife, both carrying small, twine-tied packages, intersecting with Mamie, speaking to her, saying her name. And she didn't respond, just kept on, her back hunched, her blue-turbaned head pointing westward, towards the District that crouched, invisible behind the Quarter, awaiting its own kind of passengers who would, soon now, arrive bearing other sorts of baggage—lust, loneliness, an unassuaged emptiness at heart, the simple, shallow gaiety of young men with some money in their pockets, time on their hands, and nothing much in mind. "Mamie," he croaked again, falling in with her easily enough, "Hey, Mamie." But she just kept on, reaching the railroad tracks which she began to negotiate with a single-minded caution, as if she were walking alone. So that finally, when they had reached the other side and the end of the French Market lay before them with its customary scraps and rinds lying in drifts about the base of the thick arcade, he dared to put out a hand and touch the sleeve of her shapeless dress.

"Hey, Mamie, I gotta talk to you." Then she did stop but not to face him, only stopped there under the sky's bruise, as though she were waiting for something, maybe only to hear the abashed retreat of this importunate stranger's footsteps. He repeated himself into what was suddenly to him a vast silence that had existed forever, that cancelled out the city's trivial sounds, that was now violated by the noise of his own wheedling voice and its pointless, impossible demand: "I gotta talk to you." His hands made vague gestures near her face. "I seen this photograph Bellocq made of you years back—you know the one." Again, his hands made motions that tried to describe the shape of the print. "What I mean is," he went on, his voice rising, "what I mean is you were just *beautiful* back then...." His voice trailed away into the violated silence, and as it did, Mamie slowly turned her head and looked at him, the first time he could ever recall her looking at anyone. "And what I want—what I need—" he rushed on, "is what happened?"

The eyes, a faded gray, looked back at him out of that deadness he had become aware of in the photographs: dead, depthless, unfathomable, unseeing. And then there came over the face the slow spread of a kind of smile so bleak Muldoon felt his heart shrivel in its pitiless presence. Then the mouth opened a bit and continued to open wider, revealing blackened gums, three worn molars, and a tiny stump of a tongue that while he gaped in horrified disbelief began to wag and pulse in a soundless ululation. She was laughing, the dead eyes above the blasted cavity of the mouth remaining exactly as they had been when she'd turned to look at him, completely divorced from the laughter. Here was the secret of Mamie's silence, of the transmogrification of the singer into sibyl whose prophetic utterance was this silence, whose mutilated tongue could never tell how it had come to be this way, what soul-deadening pain it had felt when it had been clipped or cut or whatever it was that had left only this stump that pulsed with a laughter that wasn't truly silent, that was to the man who leaned towards her a monstrous scream that tore the riverfront's crepuscular air, a scream that instantly vanquished that all-but-eternal silence he'd been so conscious of moments before; that filled all the available air and sucked the life-giving gas out of it; that told of desolation without surcease, of destruction, death; that made a mockery of spring; that left him gasping for air, breath, his empty hands clawing at the air, while Mamie turned away, closed her mouth and then with oblique determination began again her hopeless pilgrimage towards the Perdido.

IV. Adele

Passing up Bienville with his cousin Toodloo, Harry Parker saw the girl emerge from The Frenchman's into the blanched light of morning, a companion clearly more than merely tipsy clinging to her arm. He stopped short, shrinking cat-like, into the façade of Karro's Drugstore, watching Adele supporting her friend while looking anxiously up and down the street for a cab: once in a while you might be lucky enough to spot one, even at this hour, looking for a fare back to the Garden District, the Faubourg Marigny, or the Quarter. More commonly though what few cabs there were would be parked with their drowsing drivers along Basin, waiting for the last of the johns rolling out of the high-priced houses.

"Bring the car around," he said tensely. "I want to give them ladies a lift." He pointed to the women.

Toodloo squinted into the ambiguous light, his battle-battered face screwed up with the effort, upper lip lifting to expose his short, brown teeth. "Oh," he said then, identifying Adele. "Oh, yeah—there goes yer pussy. I see now why you want to give *her* a lift, anyways." He leered down at Harry

Parker from beneath his shabby cap. "What's that like, any-ways?" But then he quickly shut his mouth, seeing the look on his cousin's face. "I'll go get it," he said and went into a long-striding lope up Bienville to Marais, where he had the Over-land parked.

By the time the cousins had wheeled the heavy car up to The Frenchman's they found the women had been joined by two men, one of them rocking unsteadily on his heels, the other trying to engage Adele in conversation. Harry Parker stepped quickly from the Overland, a lithe, compact figure. In the dawn light his cheeks and upper lip were dark with stubble. "Looks like you ladies could use a lift," he said to Adele. She shot him a sharp glance, then looked at her tipsy friend and nodded once, then again, more decisively.

"Beat it, pal," Harry Parker said to the man who appeared to be taking the lead. "Toodloo, help these ladies in."

The lead man swung in Harry Parker's direction but made no move to step away from the women. His friend was too sodden to understand the direction developments had just taken and stood in the background, rocking, his hands stuffed in his pockets. But when he saw Toodloo's big frame interpose itself between him and the women, he slowly began to assemble a picture. "Say, there, you," he said. "Say, there."

Harry Parker grabbed his arm and pulled him close. "Say, there, yerself," he breathed. "Now, why don't you and your friend go someplace quiet and pull each other's pud, and leave these here ladies alone."

"Who's gonna make us?" the lead man asked. He looked from the car with its newly seated passengers back to Harry Parker.

"Only just this," Parker said quietly, squaring about and pulling back his leather coat to reveal the walnut handle of the pistol he had tucked into his waistband. "Just this here thirty-eight." The man recoiled into his friend, and in a moment Harry Parker was in the passenger's seat, the sedan's door had clanged shut, and Toodloo had it rolling up Bienville towards Claiborne. Then Harry Parker turned around to find Adele trying to adjust her friend who had already canted heavily against her.

"Well, well," he said, "yer girlfriend there is tight as a tick, looks like," his lips drawing back in a vulpine grin. "Least yer safe from those mugs, anyways." He jerked a thumb back in the direction of The Frenchman's.

"Yes," the girl said quietly from the shadow of the back seat. "That was lucky, you coming along that way."

"Wasn't it, though. Now where can we leave yer friend off at?" He kept his vulpine grin on her, even as she turned to see to the other woman, who slipped and swayed with every bump. She leaned close and asked her something Harry Parker couldn't hear over the motor's roar, and the woman mumbled a response that clearly was lost on Adele, too, who glanced back at Harry Parker, then asked again. The woman was quickly slipping into a drunken stupor even as Adele tried to pull her back from that to get her address. Watching the familiar drama, Harry Parker's mind had already moved smoothly ahead to when the drunk could be dumped at her cheap rooming house and the girl would be at his mercy, of which there was, he well knew, none, only a lust that burned the hotter for having been frustrated this long. Well, he thought grimly, today's the end of that: today's gonna be the day. He'd hired her in the first place because the moment she'd walked in for her audition he'd surmised how beautifully she must be built beneath her conventional clothes.

And then there'd been those candid gray eyes. That kind of look was all but unknown in his world, where women quailed when you looked at them a certain way. In his world a woman was asking for a beating if she returned your stare with one of her own. He'd known a whore once, up in Brooklyn, who did that. It had simultaneously angered and excited him. He wanted to learn where such a look came from, then wipe it off her face forever and so had put up with a great deal from her, including a time he knew for a certainty she'd held out on him. And, of course, the thing had ended badly, and he'd been forced to send her off with a mark on her face that she would have to carry forever, that would make her remember Harry Parker every time she looked in the mirror—or into the eyes of a prospective customer.

Here was another of that sort, only with an additional twist. This one carried herself as if the rules of his world didn't apply to her, as if she enjoyed some invisible exemption. Where that could have come from, he had no idea, though he had made efforts to find out: he knew where she lived; something of her daily habits—where she might walk, shop, have tea in the late afternoons of her off-days; knew she dropped in at The French-man's after hours, where she reluctantly accepted the little mash notes of Tom Anderson's gimp. But he could learn nothing of her background, where she came from, what the circumstances might be that had produced this haughty demeanor.

The drunken woman was slipping more steeply still towards sleep while Adele tried to hold her back from that, asking her again where she lived. But finally she raised her eyes to Harry Parker's and slowly shook her head. "It's hopeless, I guess," she said quietly, firmly. "I know she lives somewhere around Gayoso, but I'm afraid that isn't much help." She let her companion crumple over into her lap and placed a protective arm over her. Harry Parker's grin vanished. He hadn't counted on this.

"Where does she work, anyways?" he snarled. "Maybe we can take her back there and let her sleep it off—she belongs with them, let em take care of her."

The girl shook her head. "Groshell's. But they'll have locked up for certain. We can't just leave her out on the street." Toodloo had slowed the Overland as they crossed Derbigny, waiting for further instructions from his cousin. He heard the girl sigh deeply behind him and then say, resignedly, "I guess the only thing to do is to take her to my place." She leaned forward slightly, keeping a firm hold on the other woman. "Can you go over to Gravier?" she asked Toodloo. "I live just up from Tonti."

"Do it," Harry Parker told Toodloo, still facing back towards the girl. "Go on over to Gravier." When he turned around he muttered to himself, "Well, I'll be fucked for a fool."

Toodloo felt the edge of an impulse to laugh—but only the edge of it: the situation was funny, but he'd seen his cousin in action when provoked, and it was obvious that the frustration of his plans had put him in a dangerously ugly mood. He swung the Overland left toward Gravier and said nothing, and in that silence they arrived at the address the girl gave. Both men struggled to get the woman up the street steps of the rooming house and then up two more flights of stairs to the girl's room where they roughly dumped the body on the bed. Harry Parker looked at the unconscious form in naked disgust, making a sucking sound with his teeth. He had half a mind to get rid of his cousin and make a try at the girl in the front room, but Toodloo still stood there, grinning foolishly, his great hands hanging like hams at his sides, and behind him there was the girl, holding the door wide for their exit. It was simply no dice, Harry Parker saw, and there was nothing left to do but clamber down the darkened stairs to the street where they found a horse-drawn milk wagon had pulled up next to the Overland. The driver was nowhere in sight.

"Fuck me," Harry Parker spat. "*Fuck me!* What's next?" He climbed into the passenger seat while Toodloo stood behind him in the street, looking for the milkman and finally spotting him coming out of an alley with an empty crate in hand.

"Hey!" Toodloo hollered. "Get the hell over here and move this rig! We aint got all day!" Harry Parker had turned about to glare at the milkman when his eye fell on a square envelope in the back seat. Turning all the way around, he rose to his knees and retrieved it. Inside its heavy sheath was the letterhead sketch of the Annex's cupola.

Until that moment he'd thought it must have dropped out of the drunk woman's purse or pocket, but when he saw the artful brown lines of the sketch he knew it couldn't have been sent to her, that it was a note to the girl. And more than that, it became instantly clear that this was what Tom Anderson's gimp had been so bashfully handing over to her at The Frenchman's, not his own stammering mash notes. He felt his neck glow with private humiliation even before he read so much as a word. He could hardly believe he hadn't gotten it: the red-faced man with his limping badge of dishonor couldn't possibly have been his own agent; he'd been merely a go-between:

Cammie—my dear girl—

May I call on you—we have much to talk about I think—Or if you prefer I have a private suite @ the Monteleone where we could meet—My man Muldoon who brings this is thoroughly reliable & you may reply on back of this—

There was no signature, but there didn't need to be. The whole setup was now blazingly clear: how the girl had come to be here; how she had contrived to bring herself to his attention—but hadn't succumbed to his advances. She was

Anderson's plant, meant to dazzle him with the muted promise of her figure so that eventually in some moment of breathless passion he would whisper to her something of his plans. Looking through the heavy glass of the windshield at what was no longer dawn but morning he saw it all clearly now.

In Brooklyn he'd known men who'd become soft-brained with the syph, who'd done fool things, damaging things for worthless women. Not he. He'd always been careful about the women he bedded, choosing the young ones and the relatively untried. He'd inspected himself regularly, too. Yet here, he'd been mush-minded over Anderson's girl. He tucked the note inside his coat, watching while Toodloo exchanged words with the milkman who, coolly enough, tossed the crate in the bed of his wagon and climbed up into the seat.

Let her work for Anderson, Harry Parker thought, just let her. I'll feed her the garbage she wants, and I'll take my sweet time. And then, when the time's just right, I'll settle with that fat Mick fuck, and then I'll settle with her. When she carried *that* piece of information back to her sugar daddy, or whatever the hell he really was to her, it would be the straight goods and no mistake. Hell, Anderson was old enough to be her papa....

As they were for Muldoon, Mondays were an off-day for many of the night people, and when the weather took the turn towards sure-enough spring they would go in groups out to the lake, riding the old locomotive they called Smoky Mary to Milneburg. The trip cost fifteen cents roundtrip, and until late November when the skies casted over and the wind came walloping across the watery expanse from Mandeville, the bartenders and bouncers, the cotch and faro dealers, the pimps, madams, whores, and musicians carried their booze and picnic baskets to the squat town that hunkered by the lake, the line running straight through the town's center, past the Washington Hotel where politicians, touring authors, and theatrical troupes stayed in season, and on to the lighthouse and then the cavernous casino with its bandstand and broad dance floor and clusters of tables. Beyond this, a long wharf stretched out into the water, and off it like the legs of a centipede were the camps: two- and three-room cottages raised above the lake on indestructible cypress pilings that were connected to the wharf by splintering walkways. Most had boats tethered to them that in high season flew gay pennants, flags of city and state, family escutcheons.

In his early years as Tom Anderson's man about town Muldoon had made the trip a number of times, encouraged by Okey-Poke, who thought the recruit ought to make himself better known in the District, now that he no longer wore a uniform. But then Okey had gotten married and rarely went out himself anymore. Lacking his social sponsor, Muldoon had found himself awkward in that crowd and soon enough quit going. Instead, he spent his off-afternoons along the wharves where he might take some target practice; or visiting with his mother, who would take time away from her red-handed washing to cook him vast meals of cabbage, boiled potatoes, and ham hocks, speaking to him over her meaty shoulder of family obligations, about his very intermittent attendance at St. Alphonsus, and about how one mustn't let an accident spoil one's whole life.

Today, though, the season's first excursion, he'd decided to go out because he'd heard the girl was going with Mabel and some others of the group she met with at The Frenchman's.

As it happened, his trolley had stalled—some electrical problem—and he would have missed Smoky Mary had not Santos Villalta driven past, spotted him standing at the edge of a crowd beside the car, and called out through the snarl, asking if he needed a lift somewhere. Even so, the conductor had hollered, *"Board!"* when Villalta swung the Jefferey up to the station and slammed on the brakes. Villalta squeezed the claxon, and Pete Exnor, the conductor, signed that Muldoon would make it, and so he did, just.

He wouldn't risk walking the rocking aisles, looking for her, and settled into a seat next to Roscoe Grantham, who cooked at the Annex and was an inexhaustible talker on all matters, from those of obvious fact to the outermost limits of rumor. Roscoe was glad to have an audience, particularly one who listened a good deal more than he talked. By the time they'd come into Milneburg Muldoon had caught up on how so far form had been persistently upset out at the Fairgrounds races; about the spotty enforcement of the Tillinghast Law at the saloons and tonks; about the upcoming cocking main out in Crowley, where Roscoe's twin brother had his birds entered; but mostly about the Parker gang, about what had happened to Buster Daley out at the Fairgrounds and how he was likely to be crippled for life; and finally at some length about Gyp the Blood, who seemed like Billy the Kid himself. And what did he, Fast-Mail, think T.A. was going to do about all this, because talk was starting, even in the kitchen of the Annex.

Muldoon made a perfunctory reply to this last, telling Roscoe that Anderson wasn't called the "Mayor of Storyville" for nothing and that he was sure T.A. had a plan whose design they would all see soon enough. Then he stepped carefully down from the coach into the breezy afternoon with its slight overcast and the almost accidental air of abandonment that waterside resorts wore whenever they were in less than full use. Here, the tables had been set out around the dance floor but the chairs were still piled like racks of bones beneath the casino's high arches, and Quirella's Pier (always a summer hot spot) wore a settled aspect of neglect, as if the carefree revelers of another day had long ago fled some pestilence or other disaster.

The night people seemed not to care: the emptiness of the place meant it was all theirs, and they piled chattily off, carrying bundles and baskets while two burly men wrestled a beer keg down the steps of a coach. Roscoe Grantham remained anecdotally unconscious of all this, returning again to the subject of the Tillinghast Law, which he knew for an absolute fact had been an inside straight at City Hall. Muldoon watched the Negroes getting out of the last car, some of the women flamboyantly turned out like spring's first effulgent flowers. They had a string trio among them, and Muldoon recognized Charlie Totts, a mandolin player who had worked most of the District's spots, and his cousin, Fat Henry, a guitarist.

Muldoon had been reasonably grateful for Roscoe's company on the way out, but now, scanning the groups for sight of the girl, he began to foresee difficulties. There were some small parties already settling under the midnight boughs of the huge live oaks where the light was dim as dusk, and he caught a glimpse of the girl in the midst of one of these, Mabel from Bogalusa next to her, and was about to steer Roscoe in that direction. But just then Roscoe was hailed by some voices down near the wharf and quickly excused himself, leaving Muldoon without his voluble escort. He stopped, wondering how he might make his approach, when he himself was hailed and turned to find Bessie Browne and her girls, Octavia among them. He made his way over to them and sat carefully down in a position that allowed him to keep an eye on the girl.

"Ah, my andsome man," Octavia breathed, leaning towards him and lightly fingering his sleeve. In this unaccustomed light he noticed for the first time that her eyes were exactly the same tawny color as her skin. "Why you not come to Octavia these days, eh? I ask Bessie here. She say you around, but I don see you."

Muldoon colored and smiled, glad that Adele was well out of earshot and evidently listening to a story of Mabel's. "Oh, you know how it is," he said. "Sometimes you get busy with one thing and another." Octavia smiled a simulation of romantic resignation. There could be little doubt that she did indeed know how it was, how it must be.

"Francis," Bessie Browne said in her soft voice, "we've toted along a good deal of scrumptious food the girls fixed up. Lunch with us, why don't you." She undid the hasp of a large wicker hamper that must have taken two women to carry. Inside it he saw items wrapped in waxed paper neatly tied with twine and could make out the shapes of pieces of fried chicken, a ham hock, fish of some sort, and two ramekins that he thought probably contained some kind of salad. Lying on top of all this was a bottle of sherry that Bessie now brought out, asking one of the girls for some glasses. When they had been produced she poured a good two inches in his and handed it to him. "Here," she said, "you're looking a little peaked. You feeling all right these days, Francis?"

"Bout the same as ever," he said, clinking his glass against hers. "What about you there, Octavia?" looking over at the slender islander and thinking momentarily of her careful ministrations that he'd found both alluring and soothing. "You don't have a glass."

"Octavia have er rum," she replied, smiling her closed-lipped smile at him, the simulated romantic resignation replaced now by a professional familiarity: they were colleagues at least and probably even friends as well, if you could be friends without any obligations or expectations: that comforting you might require in an odd hour—some gray morning when the light offered neither comfort nor surprise and you realized you too had those blues the crib women sang of. Well, he and Octavia could hardly offer that to each other, not in the world they mutually moved in. He wondered how much the girls in the houses like Bessie's helped each other, and whether there had ever been anyone to help the plumpish girl whose portrait had lain atop that of Mamie Desdoumes in Bellocq's studio. Who if any had helped Mamie? To judge from her crippled appearance there had been no one. And no one to help the golden-haired girl who now scrounged for tricks in the alley behind Gipsy Shafer's.

He saw the girl arise from her group, her dark, voluminous skirt making the movement appear effortless as levitation. She said something to Mabel, who shook her head and made a declining motion with a piece of food she had in hand. The girl nodded and stepped through the shadows of the boughs and the wind-screwed old trunks, towards the docks, the boats, and the camps. Muldoon set down his untasted glass, knelt himself into position, and got up. "Scuse me a minute, will you?" he said to Bessie and Octavia, who looked over at Bessie with an expression that said, "So that's how it is now."

"He'll be back," Bessie Browne told her, watching as Muldoon limped after the girl whose large feathered hat flashed in the sun that had momentarily poked through the overcast.

He caught up with her just as she put her foot on the gray plankings of the wharf's central spine, and sensing the presence of someone behind her, she turned about. "Oh, it's you," she said, her tone a little more than merely neutral. "I was just going for a short stroll out here—to see the boats and all." She gestured outward, and her eyes warmed just a bit as she looked steadily at him. He was surprised to find that the eyes were gray, that her eyebrows were heavy, and that she had a faint down along her upper lip. He thought he had memorized everything about her looks but saw now how murky everything must be in The Frenchman's at dawn. He snatched off his bowler, feeling his face and neck ablaze in the breeze off the big lake.

"Mind some company?" he asked her.

She shook her head, smiled briefly at him, then set her face towards the choppy, gray-brown expanse, walking past the first of the camps that like so much else out here looked a bit battered after a season of disuse. Her pace was slow, almost languid, and she stepped with a dancer's long-striding grace, her head slightly inclined as if she were intent on watching the tips of her shoes peeking out from beneath her skirt's hem. Moving beside her but a step behind, he heard his foot fall with what seemed to him a thunderous report while the girl glided on with a silent effortlessness that made his own passage seem horrid to him. His mind leaped back for an instant to old Agee, demasted at the Wilderness and then in his helplessness shot from behind by the bandits outside the bag factory. If he hadn't been such a damned hero that day, he thought grimly, the chances were Tom Anderson might never have been reminded of the high school track star nor used a favor to get Fast-Mail Muldoon a spot on the force. In which case he might very well be living contentedly along, right there in the old neighborhood, taking his regular turn as watchman at the factory; providing security on Fridays when the payroll was brought down; married to Lou-Anne and with kids, bills to pay—all the familiar, shared concerns of his neighbors. And here came the heavy, helpless fall of his foot on the sounding boards, reminding him—and doubtless the girl as well—of what was, of what could never be otherwise.

That same sound—fate—yanked him back to the present, to the girl striding along almost next to him, the feathers of her hat in pinioned flight against the crown.

"Nice out here," he brought out. "Restful like."

She made a slight head turn, acknowledging the comment, but that was all, and they went on. They came to a boat, moored among others, and the girl paused at it, giving it a lingering look, then started on again. But then abruptly she stopped, turning back towards the boat, a long, high-sided one with a mast lying along its keelson and kelly-green lettering at its bow that spelled EVANGELINE.

"Would you like to go out—in the lake a little?" There was a faint flush on what he could see of her neck as she asked this. "I haven't been out since I can't remember when, and it would be nice to do it again." He pulled out his big, smooth watch, but before he could consult it she had looked at her own. "We have plenty of time," she said then. "Yes, plenty of time."

"This here yours?" he asked, nodding at the Evangeline, his own question suddenly sounding stupid to him.

"Well, no, it isn't. But I can use it when I like."

"Oh, a friend's, like."

"You might say that."

Out in the lake the water looked more brown than gray, the wind across from Mandeville sharper, the troughs between the chops steeper. He applied his brawny shoulders more strenuously to the thick-handled oars, pulling clear of the wharf's last, long reach. The boat leaped ahead into the lake, the water slapping hard against the slightly elevated prow.

Always, he'd been painfully aware of the poverty of his small talk with her, beginning with the time he'd blundered into her in the Tuxedo's hallway and had the mutually embarrassed exchange that followed. That poverty had been somewhat disguised in The Frenchman's by the constant, high noise—the laughter, the hollered salutations and insults; the percussive playing of the piano professors; a tray of glasses knocked from a waiter's hand; the bang of beer mugs on tabletops: *More! More!* Here there was none of that, nothing but the slugging of the lake against the invading hull, the metronomic protest of the oars in their locks, the wind whistling in his reddened ears. He tried not to stare at that face opposite his own, the one he'd thought he knew in such intimate detail but that now in daylight revealed new features that touched him more acutely.

"Nice out here," he helplessly repeated, glancing at the sky, the water, his hands curled about the oar handles. "I aint been out here that much lately myself." He pulled another stroke and then another, his neck swelling against his wilting collar, his shoulders bulging the seams of his coat. She looked at him with a sudden sharpness, as if she too were seeing him anew, and her lips parted slightly. Then she half-turned to look back at the shore.

"Don't you think we ought to turn around?" she asked, another measured, polite smile on her face, her eyes shadowed beneath her hat brim with the feathers of the sacrificed birds flattened against the crown.

"Right," he said between clenched teeth. "Right," and began to haul on the right oar, swinging the bow oblique to the wind, and then around with it. He rested just a moment then, feeling the boat rock uncertainly, then begin into a sideways drift. He dug in, pulling the bow shorewards again, back to the waiting groups under the oaks, back to what they knew.

The boat went easily before the wind, skipping over what had been the roughness of the chop with an oily ease that oddly angered him. In an instant, he felt, they'd be back at the wharf, and he'd have to surrender her to Mabel and the rest. "This night life," he found himself saying, digging more shallowly with the oars and lifting them a trifle higher in recovery. He sighed, showing his weariness with it all, and she inclined her head slightly, signifying that she was waiting for him to complete whatever it was he'd started to say.

"This night life," he began again. "Sometimes, it gets to me." He let go of the oars for a moment, lifting his hands, palms open to the wind. "Like out here, I mean: you get out here, and then you feel all that other stuff. Well, you know what I mean."

"How long have you been at it? Working down there, I mean."

He shrugged away the question as if it were irrelevant. But then he was aware of the seeming rudeness of the gesture and so supplied a number. "But it aint just that," he went on. "It aint the years so much that wears on a man. It's—oh—" He dropped the oars again to run a sleeve across his blazing brow, wet not only with the perspiration of effort but more with a feeling of urgency full upon him to express to the girl for once something he was only beginning to understand and to fear. "It's what it takes out of you, I guess."

"It can't be easy work, doing what you do," she offered.

There was some sort of difference here, he thought, that he wanted to make clear.

"No," he started, then stopped. He was again afraid of sounding rude. "No, not exactly that. I mean, there's guys been at it longer than me, and it seems like it don't get to em that much, from what I can tell." He had Okey-Poke and Jimmie Enright in mind, but even as he thought of them he saw again the tired skin beneath Okey's eyes and heard the rasp of Jimmie's anger about developments, an anger that was increasing by the night, as though even tough old Jimmie was getting ground right down to the nerves by the District's constant demands.

"What I mean is ... sometimes, when I leave there, and I'm goin home, and I see everbody else just goin to work—it makes me think this aint healthy. You ever feel that way?"

"I suppose I do," she said, trying to be helpful. Then for a minute or two there was nothing but the ambient sounds of water, wind, the heavy oars grinding in their locks. She looked to her left, then pointed, and he glanced over to find a fishing smack running quickly with the wind and four men in straw hats and salt-bleared clothing. One of them was looking over at them, making an ambiguous gesture, and shouting something across forty yards of water. Muldoon didn't catch it, but Adele quickly looked away.

"What would you do instead?" she asked.

In mid-stroke he let the oars fall slack. They dragged backwards as he shook his head. "Dunno."

A vision of himself in Charity Hospital came to him, lying helpless and swaddled in bandages like a baby; then taking those first steps away from his cot, not understanding until that moment that he was maimed and still less that he would remain so; feeling with a stunned wonderment the helpless drop of his foot; trying to pick it up again, to will its old, unconscious athletic compliance. And then realizing something of the import of what that doctor had said in his silvered way: that he was crippled now. But at least, so the doctor had cheerfully added, he could still have a "family life." Hearing that, he hadn't felt any cheer at all, nor any gratitude, either, only a heavy, in-bearing sense of himself as someone once, grotesquely, known as "Fast-Mail," now doomed to drag himself through the remainder of his days, leaving behind him a snail-like track of slime that was his disgrace.

Back with the groups sitting under the oaks, he excused himself from the girl's company and rejoined Bessie, Octavia, and the others. There wasn't much left in the hamper, and the girls had finished the sherry. He picked at a chicken thigh that tasted like sawdust, made himself take a desultory part in the conversation, and when Smoky Mary hooted twice he was glad enough to return to the cars, carrying the almost empty hamper but also the inner burden of the girl's question: what the hell *would* he do if he didn't work for Tom Anderson? What the hell would almost any of them do without Anderson and the District he controlled? He saw himself limping about behind some seedy bar, its floors filthy with sputum and sawdust, drawing growlers of beer for the foul-mouthed loungers on the porch: he supposed he might qualify for such a spot somewhere in the city. But even so, how much different would it actually be? The same basic environment, the same hazards, the same upside-down quality to his days. Only the pay and the perquisites would be different. He'd have to find a cheap room to rent, and so would Maureen and the girls, who would be hostages to his obscure, terribly belated misgivings about his work.

Or maybe he could find menial work back at the bag factory, wearing out his days until at last he would become one of those shuffling, stoop-shouldered dodderers, his moustache soiled with tobacco and forgotten bits of dinner; who'd been around so long and so inconspicuously that nobody knew exactly what he did—if he did anything—or even his right name: "Oh, that's old Mail-Sack. Don't know why they calls him that, cept I believe he once worked for the mails, or maybe it was the express office. Somebody said he was in the war, but nobody can figure out which one it was. Harmless old coot. Keeps to himself pretty much."

And the girl herself, what would she do other than sing in a beer garden? What were her alternatives as a performer? Muldoon knew little enough about singing, but he judged her current situation at the Tuxedo just about right for her talent.

Marriage, of course, was a possibility. And yet each night she went down to the District lessened by some small but actual increment her eligibility in the eyes of bachelors who would come to see her as merely a beer-hall hussie. And soon enough that was what she might very well become. What girl entering the District escaped unscarred, unscathed? As the rocking car chuffed back towards the city, he sat alone, thinking of Bellocq's words once again: "It happens quicker than you can imagine."

Smoky Mary arrived at the depot mere minutes ahead of the squall that had been threatening even before the picnickers had packed up and boarded her. Now as they climbed down the raindrops began to come in at a slant. There were a few cabs there but not nearly enough for the passengers and nearby pedestrians caught in what almost instantly became a raking, pellet-like onslaught. Muldoon was lucky, snagging a hack whose driver recognized him. The man was about to pull out for the Channel when Muldoon spotted the girl ducking back under the depot's overhang and grabbing at her hat.

"Hold on," Muldoon ordered. "Pull over and pick up that gal there under the archway." He pointed to the girl who had removed her hat and stood clutching it to her bosom. The hackie yanked his cab back into the ruck, muttering something under his breath as he inched forward towards the girl, and then Muldoon flung open the door, stepped into the rain, and waved to the girl who got in quickly enough.

"Goodness!" she exclaimed breathlessly, when she had seated herself and Muldoon had slammed the door shut. She dropped the once-glorious hat to the floor and pulled her skirt away from her thighs. "Goodness! When you come out without your umbrella—that's when it just *pours!* I certainly didn't see this coming." She smiled at him and cast a glance at the hat. "Neither did my hat." They both laughed.

"These are better, I guess," Muldoon smiled, tapping the all-but-impervious crown of the bowler he held in his lap. "I think I could start out swimming for Algiers and not make it. But this would." They laughed at that as well. "Don't suppose, though, it'd do for a lady." He leaned down and placed the bowler next to her hat as they swung away from the depot and towards the address the girl gave.

But when they turned into her street they found it blocked. From the looks of it a truck had broken down, mid-street, and a horse and cart had tried to squeeze past and gotten tangled up with another cart parked at the curb. The truck driver was nowhere to be seen, and the two carters were jawing at each other in the street and in between insults trying to disengage their ponderous wheels while the mule of the one and the horse of the other stood stolid, their ears aslant and dripping streams of hairy water. While the cab sat there the raking rain changed to a swirling, wind-whipped mist that all but blotted out the comic scene before them. The hackie squeezed his rubber claxon several times, then lifted his hands from the high steering wheel in a show of hopelessness.

"How far is it?" Muldoon asked Adele. He had no umbrella, either.

"It's just a few doors down from where that truck is," she told him, pointing through the gray swirl and the blurry outlines of the two carters.

"Well, then," he said, pulling off his coat, "you put this over your head, and I'll bring along your hat."

"But you—" she darted a glance downward, then quickly looked up again—"you'll just get *soaked*. Surely—"

"Oh, I can rate along quicker'n you think," he rejoined, his face and neck reddening.

The hackie saved them from further embarrassment, roughly

asking them what it was they were going to do. "Y'all's goin someplace else or what?"

"The lady's gonna run for it," Muldoon told him, opening the door for Adele while she pulled the coat close about her head and shoulders and stepped out into the pocked mud of the street. "And I'm gonna settle up with you here," he added, reaching for his purse. "This here looks like it'll get worse before it gets better." He gestured with his head towards the carters who had discarded business for pleasure and had begun to slug it out, doing as much slipping and falling as actual punching.

Then he was out in the swirl himself and making for the banquette with its surer footing. Once up on it he began to run, the good leg taking a long, sure stride, the right one making a hopping motion that once the gait was fairly achieved had about it something of the rocking regularity of a saddle horse in a canter. In this fashion he covered the distance smartly enough and found her waiting at the top of a short flight of steps that was partially protected by a stone arch.

Up in her sparsely decorated rooms he stood uncertainly just within the threshold, a circle of small puddles at his feet and still clutching her hat, which now resembled a song bird's nest violated by some predator. He saw her looking at it and saw now how much additional wreckage his care had caused. Their eyes met then, and when she began to laugh he joined in. When she stepped forward and relieved him of it he started to say something, but she raised a large, capable hand, palm out.

"It's quite all right," she assured him. "Couldn't be helped." Her laughter subsided into a broad, lingering smile as she dropped the disheveled thing heavily to the floor next to a chair. "And the day began so fair..." She shrugged, leaving the sentence incomplete. "What you need—what *we* need—is some good, hot tea."

By the time they'd begun their second cup they could see through the kitchen's two tiny windows that the rain had stopped, and the sun was poking through the clouds, gilding the edges of the buildings opposite. She was telling him for the second time that he needn't be concerned about her hat, that under the circumstances it could hardly be helped, hastening to amplify her meaning by referring to the lack of an umbrella. But that very haste, slight though it was, reminded him of the horribly loud and ponderous fall of his foot on the plankings of the wharf out at Milneburg; of his slow, ungainly clamber into the boat; and of that darting glance she'd thrown towards the floor of the cab, but really towards his foot, when she had predicted how soaked he would get if he were to lend her his coat, stumping along after her and crushing what little might be left of her hat and its brightness.

"I guess you might've been wondering how I come by this," he heard himself saying. He wagged his foot suddenly, looking down at it in its professionally thick brogan whose shiny wetness had now sunk into a dulled, lusterless gray-black. He wagged it once again in the room's sudden silence, then dared to glance up at her to catch her grave regard under her heavy eyebrows. She gave the slightest shrug, whether indicating she hadn't heard that bit of local lore or didn't wish to, he couldn't tell. He could hardly imagine she hadn't noticed, even in The Frenchman's where everybody was a bit lopsided.

"Anyways," he said with an effort at conversational diffidence, "it's a long story—you don't need to hear it. I do thank you, though, for the tea. Coffee's my drink, but, well, this tasted mighty good, I'll say."

"If you want to tell me how it happened, I'd be honored to listen. I know you were a famous runner once."

"I was," he came back quickly, surprised and cheered she

knew that much. "Still have some records, I think—one anyways. Course they don't amount to much." He wanted to smile
and tried, stroking his moustache and almost manually lifting
his lips.

"Well," she said, setting her cup and saucer on the tiny
table next to the potbellied coal stove, "it isn't everybody who
sets records. I mean, that *is* an accomplishment, isn't it?"

"I guess so. Anyways, at the time it seemed like it." He
placed his cup and saucer next to hers. "But then you learn
right quick it don't mean much." He raised both hands as if
opening up a much larger topic, one he now realized he both
ached to enter and dreaded doing so, one he had never fully
entered with another soul—not even his own in those ghastly,
twisted hours of dream and sudden, alarmed awakenings. "Who
cares what you did, right? It's what you can do as counts. I
had them trophies, medals and such—but then I get this." He
patted his damp thigh. "Hadn't a been for Tom Anderson,
don't rightly know what would've become of me."

"I understand he's very generous in that way," she said with
quiet measure. She seemed to be waiting. And maybe, he thought
now, he too had been waiting, waiting all these years for just
this moment when he might at last venture beyond where he'd
always stopped, unable always to supply the definitive answer
about Coakley, remembering that only once had he come even
this far and that many years ago with Maureen.

"What was I supposed to do then?" he'd said then to his
sister, asking the question instead of answering it, his voice
going up the scale, rising from his stomach where it customarily came from, up through his thorax, high into his throat, and
higher still until it sounded to him like a mere squeak, originating not even on his tongue but forward of that, as if it were
his teeth that were making the noise, grinding against each

other, making a sound compounded of spit and enamel and in-extinguishable anguish.

But now, for once, he had to go on and did.

Reciting for her the events of that night, he did so as they might have been retailed by witness, reporter, policeman, his-torian, until he had finally come to the place: the hellishly lighted chicken run and the dark, lumpish form sprawled just beyond safe reach: the hobnailed sole of the shoe, so motion-less, pointing at him, whether in beseechment or warning or absolution—"Go on, my man, I'm done."

"So, I get out there," he said, the words coming slowly now, almost singly, "and I grab for his foot, see—I grab for that foot—to feel something there—if I can tell something from the foot, like." He halted, his broad hands outstretched towards her as she sat, grave-eyed and waiting. "And so I grab it, like—I grab it and shake it—I shake it—shake it...." His hands came back in and cradled his head, covering the ears, al-most meeting at the top of his skull, bearing down, wanting to make certain, even now, that he had in fact given the foot the good, hard shake he was meant to give it. Or was even that enough? What could you tell from a foot, particularly one so thickly shod? Shouldn't he really have grabbed that foot and pulled the body under the slim overhang and determined there whether Coakley was alive or dead? But he hadn't. Exposed to the sniper fire out in the run, wanting to believe that Coakley was beyond rescue, he'd scuttled away.

He pulled his hands away from his head but didn't look up. "I didn't make it," he said. "Got shot. Good and shot."

"And the officer?"

"Well, they never figured that out exactly," he said, staring down at his feet, at his foot. "From what they could tell after-wards—I mean, when they finally did get him out—was he'd been hit twice in the back. But he was burned so bad they couldn't tell that much what killed him. They couldn't tell whether it was the bullets or the fire. So...." He looked up, his hands making futile gestures once more. He thought about adding that as far as the department was concerned, it made no difference what the cause of Coakley's death really was, but he didn't. Captain Porteous had testified he'd been ordered to rescue Coakley, which meant to bring him out, instead of which he'd left a fellow officer behind in attempting his own escape.

Afterwards, an enterprising reporter had sought out Coakley's family and had written up the unsparing details of how little was left of the heroic man who in his nine years on the force had won several decorations. But what was the point of adding these details to the story? The story's heart was *there,* in his moment of fright and indecision and flight. Always had been.

"So, you never knew."

He shook his head.

"Never to know. That must be very hard," the girl said in a soft voice. "You poor man." He felt she didn't understand, not quite: the not knowing was a torment, true enough. She had that right. But it was *before* that determination could have been made that was the story's heart, where its inmost meaning for him still lay.

But with her soft words, the sympathy they expressed, he heard a door closing. There was not to be some ultimate understanding, not here, not ever. He had come this far, had confessed to leaving Coakley before making absolutely certain he was dead. That was all he felt he had left in him. His mission into the chicken run had been a failure, all right.

But maybe a man was meant to have more than just that one, the one he'd failed at. A runner who lost a race or failed to hold a lead—hell, they didn't take him out behind the track and shoot him like a horse that had broken down. They let him line up again, in another event. And here before him in this kitchen was another chance, another event. He might still save this girl from what surely lay ahead for her, a life leading to degradation and ruin. Wouldn't that partly make up for Coakley—especially if Coakley had already been dead when he'd shaken his foot? Wasn't the saving of this precious young life equal to the saving of a body that might have had no least spark left in it? How heavy was that dark, still body, anyway, in the scales of justice?

"But surely you must have erased those doubts—about what you can do, you know—in your work for Mr. Anderson," she was saying now. "I mean, even if there might have been some doubt about that officer, you've worked in dangerous places all these years, and you must have done quite well, I should think. I hear Mr. Anderson is a generous fellow, but I don't think he would keep you more than twelve years if you hadn't been up to the challenges."

"Oh, I guess I've done all right," he said, dismissively flipping a hand upward. "Leastways, I haven't heard em complaining any. I do my job, haven't missed many nights." He didn't think it worth his while to tell her about the time he'd been slashed at the Perdido but had shown up for work after only a couple of days, his bandaged hand further protected by an outsized motorman's glove. What he wanted to impress upon her wasn't the quality of his courage in dangerous situations but the danger she herself was in by working where she did. "I guess I can take care of myself well as the next fellow when it comes to that." He sat bolt upright in his chair and looked directly into her face.

"But here's the thing, Miss: *you're* in danger now—being a woman down there and all. The District is just a real dangerous place for a woman."

She nodded. "Yes, of course it is. The poor women who have to work in some of those terrible places—" she broke off. He wanted to help her here, spare her having to mention the whores, the whole sordid business of which, so he thought, she must know little. She would know the general nature of the business; she couldn't avoid knowing that at least. But he thought she might not know the details—the sex-trick artists; the crib girls and how they looked when they turned in their keys to him; the gallery of dead-eyed zombies he'd seen in Bellocq's studio. So, he nodded vigorously at her words and added some of his own. "Yeah, and not only them. Not only them, Miss."

"Well, yes, I understand what you mean. There are others as well—the girls who work in some of the cabarets and so forth. I understand from my friend, Mabel, it can be pretty difficult working there, especially during Carnival." She glanced at their teacups, sitting side by side on the tiny table. The shafts of sun were coming lower and harder now, lighting up the two tiny windows and turning them from steely gray to washed gold. "Would you like some more tea, Mr. Muldoon? I think there's a spot left."

"No, no," he said, raising a hand. "Look, Miss, there's things you can't know." His neck bulged and reddened again, but he felt determined to press along. "Things I seen down there I can't tell you about. But I got to tell you this, anyways." He stopped, thinking once again of the stack of portraits in the studio and vainly wishing he could show them to her. *Then* she would have to understand his point.

"Do you happen to know Mamie Desdoumes?" he asked instead. "Plays piano over at the Perdido on Villere?"

"I don't believe I do. Does she come in The Frenchman's ever?"

"You'd remember her if you ever seen her—all hunched up and twisted. Got fingers missing from this hand." He held up his right hand, crooking its middle two fingers down. She looked at his hand with a questioning air. "Anyways, I happened to see this picture of her—photograph. It musta been taken when she was just startin out." He brought his hands together in his lap, twisting them into a nervous knot of fingers. "You wouldn't believe how good-looking she was."

"Did she have some kind of accident, then?" the girl asked.

"No. I don't believe it was an accident. She started out as a singer, in a cabaret."

"I'm afraid I'm not getting your meaning, Mr. Muldoon."

"What I mean, Miss—what I'm meaning to say—is these men, the ones that run the cabarets and such—like the Tuxedo. I mean, they expect you to do a lot more than just sing. A lot more." His face was a deep brick red now and his mouth working in ways that were beyond the enunciation of his words. "And you'll hafta do it, too, or they'll mark you, beat you up, and so forth. And when they get through with you, you won't be able to get that kind of work no more. You might not look bad as Mamie, but you won't ever look the same. That's a level fact, Miss."

The girl rose from her chair and took the cups and saucers to the little sink. When she turned about to face him, she placed her hands on the sideboard. "Oh, I see what you mean now. Yes, I do see. But you must understand Mr. Muldoon, that I have eyes—and ears, too. And I have some experience singing in other places, though not quite like this one, to be sure. I know what some of these men are like, what they might expect. And I've made it perfectly clear to the men at the Tuxedo that I am there to sing—and only to sing." She smiled a small smile that struck him as about as steely in its gray-eyed steadiness as the windowpanes had been before the sun had struck them in its downward glide.

"So you see, I'm grateful, truly, for your warning. But I don't really need to know your Mamie, though I can certainly sympathize with her, poor thing. I already know Mamie. I know dozens of Mamies."

Billy Brundy had taken the phone call in his office and told Jimmie Enright that T.A. was entertaining downstairs and had left strict instructions that he wasn't to be disturbed, not for anything. So Brundy didn't feel wonderful about descending the stairs to the bar where Anderson sat at a corner table with a party of eight that included Abe Attell and his manager, just in from New York for the races and fresh from the ex-champ's first comeback win, a third round K.O. of a hard-hitting kid. Looking at Attell, Brundy saw that the kid hadn't thrown the fight: Attell's face was pretty well marked up.

Tom Anderson saw him coming and knew this meant some sort of trouble. So, he rose, expressing his large-handed, rubicund apologies all around, and met Brundy near the kitchen door where Brundy told him Jimmie Enright was so enraged by tonight's developments at the 102 that he was absolutely insisting on seeing Anderson tonight.

"Well, what happened over there?" Tom Anderson asked, leaning close to Brundy who matched him in height though not in bulk. "What is it this time?" His tone was just this side of peevish, unusual, Brundy well knew, in this man of legendary equanimity. Hearing it, he thought for the first time, This business is beginning to get to him. It's really beginning to get under his hide. And right on the heels of that thought, he found himself thinking also that they had all—from Tom Anderson down—badly underestimated the quality of the Parkers' challenge, which at first seemed so ignorant, so ramshackled and ham-handed, that at worst it would be but a short-lived nuisance. There had been other challengers, too, but it was hard now even to recall their names.

Well, this was a good deal more than any nuisance, Brundy realized, whispering in Anderson's large red ear. It was a sure-enough threat. Partly, this was because of what he was telling Anderson about what had happened at the 102. But maybe even more because Jimmie Enright, who had seen them come and seen them go, clearly regarded it as a serious threat, one that some weeks back had sped past the nuisance stage like a runaway freight, and who had told Brundy that people were beginning to talk. Well, Jimmie Enright himself was talking now, even if he himself might not see it that way, would instead regard his phone call as a report, as intelligence.

Only an hour ago, Billy Brundy told Anderson, Charley Parker had surprised them by barging into the 102 with Gyp the Blood and another man they hadn't seen before. At first, they'd thought Charley was just drunk, talking loudly, bragging, plunking down a stack of silver dollars on the bar, telling Billy Phillips he was going to put his sorry ass in a sling, and that he was about to buy up Fewclothes Cabaret directly across Iberville and put up a sign even bigger than the one at the Tuxedo. Then Billy Phillips had pretended to ask Charley Parker something about the purchase, speaking in so low a voice that Charley leaned over the bar to have the question repeated. That was when Billy Phillips had sucker-punched him, knocking Parker flat. Instantly, Gyp the Blood had his pistol out and leveled at Phillips's forehead while the other man had jumped back and had his pistol covering the length of the bar with a cobra-like precision. And just there for a few seconds, Billy Brundy said, slipping into Jimmie Enright's voice, " 'It looked like it was gonna happen right there. An tell the truth, Billy, I almost wisht it had. I almost did—cept we'd a gotten it, too. This fuckin guy is such a fuckin *moron!* Why would he hit that guy? He's got to figure that Gyp is carryin. And the other guy, too. He's got to know what happened out at the Fairgrounds!'" Here Billy Brundy came back to his own voice and diction, telling Tom Anderson Jimmie couldn't figure out what the plan had really been with Parker and the others daring to come in the 102. Because if it had been to provoke just such a response from Phillips as they got, then that would have been the perfect pretext to drill him right there. But they hadn't, because Parker, picking himself up, had told them not to. And then the trio had left.

Tom Anderson looked searchingly into Billy Brundy's face, but all he got in return was a "search me" shrug of his broad, bony shoulders. Anderson pulled his gold watch from his checked vest and consulted its almost clock-sized face. "Tell him to come by at one," he said quietly, replacing the watch and glancing carefully about the room. He might well be bothered, Billy Brundy thought, admiringly, but he's still checking the crowd; he's still doing that.

"You be there, too," Anderson told him. "Up in Gertrude's office. Get hold of Muldoon. Tell him I want him down here to cover for you. He ought to be able to handle most anything that comes along down here."

But up in Gertrude's low-lit office it was Jimmie Enright who seemed unequal at the moment to handle what had come along at the 102. When Billy Brundy offered him an Ybor City cigar, Enright bit into it viciously and spit out the bits of its end, disregarding the expensive carpeting. He snorted high up in his oft-broken nose. "Ahhh, *fuck!*" he said at last, some rich smoke issuing on the words. Gertrude herself having long departed for the house on Elysian Fields, Jimmie Enright saw no need to mind his language or his manners in the company of these men: Anderson, Billy Brundy, and on Anderson's last-minute decision, Abe Attell. "Ahh, fuck, Tom. This thing's outta *hand,* man, outta *hand.* These Parker guys are goin for broke, an what we got on our hands is a fuckin four-alarm disaster—Billy Phillips.

"He coulda got us all killed tonight, an just for that minute, I wisht he had—not us, I mean, but him. But what I don't get is the set-up: if they come in there to get Phillips all heated up and then drill him, they done it, all right. It was perfect, Phillips bein what he is. But they don't do it, an I seen that Gyp guy, an he'd a done it right then. Instead of which he listens to Parker, who's still lyin there on the floor, an Parker yells, 'No!' Then he picks himself up and says, quiet-like, 'Not yet,' an they get outa there. Now, how do you figure that, anyways?" He looked at the others in turn, his cannonball head swiveling about in the sudden silence.

There was no answer, and so Enright went on. "But Phillips coulda got us all killed, like I told Billy here. And T.A., he's *killin us ever night.*" He measured out the final four words as deliberately as if he were pouring whiskey into a row of shot glasses. He clamped down on his cigar, speaking through it and looking straight at Tom Anderson, using the same, measured cadence though in a lower tone. "*We got to take care of that bunch, T.A., an we got to do it quick.*"

Tom Anderson ran his stub finger around the inner rim of his right ear, a habit of his when thinking. "I think he's bluffing about Fewclothes: George wouldn't do that without coming to me. And anyway, I don't think they have that kind of money." He glanced over at Abe Attell. "Do they? What do you know about these jaspers?"

The ex-champ folded his arms, his bruises looking darker in the office lighting. "First off, their name aint Parker. I don't know what it really is. Some guy I talked to thinks they're really kikes, but another guy says they're named Snell, Schnell— somethin like that. Whatever difference it makes. But I do know they go back somehow to the old Hudson Dusters, and so that must mean they got some of Big Tim's money behind em. So, yeah, I think they got money, all right; how much they got is what you got to figure."

"You think they'd bluff here with Fewclothes?" Anderson asked. "I've been knowin George Foucault and his father before him a long time," he added by way of explanation.

"Welll," Attell said slowly, drawing out the word and unfolding his arms, "that's a hard one to figure: you come in outa town, not knowing the track, how you gonna make yer bets?" He looked over at Jimmie Enright. "The man had been drinkin when he come in yer place, right?" Enright was about to say something, but Attell went right on. "Okay, okay, not as much, maybe, as he let on. But some. So that makes it a tougher call: coulda been the liquor talkin; coulda been the liquor doin part of the talkin. Coulda been, like you say, a bluff all along— wantin to see how you react—in which case having his man kill Phillips don't serve his purpose, if you see what I mean. Phillips probly aint important. It's like a feint in boxin: you try it out a couple times in the first few rounds, just to get yer man's reaction. What's he do each time?" He dabbed gently with his first two fingers at his upper lip, swollen from one of the kid's roundhouse rights.

"We know they got some money, anyways," Attell went on. "They bought them two places you mentioned," looking at Tom Anderson who nodded back. "Well, then," Attell concluded, "if they got that kinda dough, you gotta *assume* that aint the end of it." He spread his hands, fan-like, as though holding cards. "You gotta figure there's more where that come from. So, I think yer man here's right," nodding at Jimmie Enright. "You gotta go get em now. You wait and call their bluff and then they do buy, then they're *really* inside on you now, where they can bust you up pretty good." He shifted from pantomime card player to boxer, balling his fists and making soft, slow motions as if throwing body blows.

"And then, you wait for them to do something else after they buy, you're losin another round, and then the crowd begins to smell an upset. That aint good. You want my opinion, I say go get em." He paused to dab at his lip again. "You got anybody can work inside over there?" The others looked over at Tom Anderson, who silently shook his head.

Anderson had let his cigar go out, and while he got it going again he nodded to Jimmie Enright who began to outline the various ways they could go get the Parkers, every one of which Tom Anderson waved aside as too risky and certain to bring down the wrath of City Hall and then its desertion of him. It had to be, he said, something severe and dramatic but short of drastic. Maybe, he thought out loud, a good beating of a couple of those toughs who hung about the Southern terminal, scaring off his kid steerers and substituting copies of *Spanish Fly* for Billy Brundy's *Sporting Life*. It could, he said, be made to look like a simple robbery instead of a gang war—nobody traceable to any of his spots.

"What about Chicken Dick?" Billy Brundy asked. "He knows every tough nigger in town. They can break a few legs, for sure. The problem I see there is to make sure it stops with the legs."

Tom Anderson didn't say no to Billy Brundy's suggestion, and so the next evening Chicken Dick and two others waited around the sheds behind the Southern terminal whose high, arched windows were lamp-lit as night's veil dropped swiftly through a sunless sky. Out of the sheds' deeper gloom they watched as one of Parkers' steerers accosted exiting passengers, pressing copies of *Spanish Fly* into the hands of sporting gents.

"Man like that," Chicken Dick said slowly, almost meditatively, never taking his eyes off the figure on the corner with his armload of pamphlets, "need his laigs broke for him. You ready to go to work on him?" Black Benny Boyd was more than a head shorter than Dick but equally broad and with a mountainous set of shoulders. He nodded. "George?" Dick asked the third man who now wordlessly dropped a cigarette from his lips. Then the three moved forward, hugging the sheds until they had reached the end of the row where Chicken Dick stopped and pulled a length of iron rod from a sawed-off boot. The Parkers' man had just pressed a pamphlet on a potential customer and had half-turned away from the sheds to say something to the man's back, some bantering bit of advice. When he turned around he saw them coming, but too late. He dropped the pamphlets, whipped back the skirt of his coat to draw something, but Dick had the full momentum of his giant body in motion and was on him, the rod high-raised, invisible in the gloom, and when he swung it there was a whistling sound, the burning friction of air against iron wielded with a fearful force against the man's knee.

He would have screeched in agony except Black Benny arrived at the same instant as Dick's first blow, flinging a sweatered arm around the man's mouth, muffling his outcry while Benny's other hand came down on the nape of his neck with a sap. The Parkers' man crumpled like a sack of coal, and while Black Benny and George Robertson went to work on his head, Chicken Dick saw to his knees and legs. It was all over in two minutes, and then the little gang moved on to its next target, leaving at the corner a sprawled, inert body, one leg dangling off the banquette into the gutter.

By the time Chicken Dick had led them to an alley across from the St. Charles Hotel, where another Parker operative loitered just beyond the glow of the main entrance, he was feeling his years, all those blows he'd taken in battle, the scars and slashes of a lifetime that had known little else. But he thought he had one more job left in him tonight. "Him," he said hoarsely, pointing across toward the steerer who waited at the very edge of the penumbra made by the hotel's brightly lit entrance, its flashing front doors. "Him, and then we can quit." When the steerer had turned his back and walked a few steps further into shadow, importuning a man who'd refused the pamphlet, they ran at him.

But Dick was slower now and the others reluctant to take the lead, and the Parkers' man heard them coming, had time to let go of his pamphlets, and to drop to one knee with a pistol in hand. He got off two quick shots, sparks flying from the muzzle, and then they were on him, Dick flailing with the rod, no longer scrupulous now about where his blows landed. Tommy Nardico, the man who'd hired him, had specified there was to be no killing, and so far as Dick knew there hadn't been yet. But he was tired, and anyway this bastard had fired at them. As they mauled the man there came shouts behind them, and George Robertson was still kicking the downed figure when they heard a police whistle far up the street.

"Git his purse!" Chicken Dick hollered. "This sposed to be a robbry!" George Robertson flopped the man on his back, tore out his purse, tossed it to Dick, and then they were gone, Robertson hobbling a bit from where the man's second shot had nicked his thigh.

Back in the safety of the Astoria the action was reassuringly boisterous—the click of the pool balls; the shouts of the craps players and their audience; the blare of the cornet player and the thumping of his drummer from the tiny platform in the corner; and underneath all this the guttural, strophe-like commentary of the drinkers at the bar. Chicken Dick, his high forehead a blazing black with sweat and a major vein pulsing down the center of it, ordered beers for his colleagues of the evening, but George Robertson's thigh was throbbing, and he felt he needed something stronger and said so.

"My laig killin me, man. Git me two shots of Old Crow, why dontcha. Beer aint gonna touch this here pain, man."

Chicken Dick gave him a long, level look, then turned to the bartender. "Man here think he needs whiskey," he said. "Gimme two shots of Crow." When they were roughly plunked down, Chicken Dick pointed to George Robertson, then tossed the first one back with the briefest cock of his head. He pursed his lips, wiped them with the back of his hand, and handed the second glass to George Robertson. The bartender stood waiting, and Robertson dug for his purse.

"Mighty white of you, George," Dick said with a cold grin. "Night like this, man need a friend."

Chicken Dick stood them the next round, and when they were into the one following that Tommy Nardico arrived, and he and Dick went into the back room for the payoff: equal shares all around and an extra five for Dick that Tommy told him he could divide up as he pleased. So it was the hour of the false dawn when the three men came out onto South Rampart and Dick led them into an alley where he said they could divvy up without anyone nosing into their business. He pulled out the bills Tommy Nardico had given him, though the five stayed where he'd put it, and handed out the shares. Then he dug into his coat pocket for the few bills and coins they'd taken from their victims, telling George Robertson to give him a light.

At the instant of its sulfurous flare a shot sounded from across South Rampart. Chicken Dick straightened suddenly as if his back were bothering him, and then his hands moved as if to clutch the bills and coins to his chest. Then came another shot, the same, sharp-edged *crack* as the first, and with it the huge man let go of the money, the coins spilling, tumbling, some rolling on their edges; and the bills, suddenly only paper, robbed of their value, drifting weightlessly downward. And Dick followed, falling full into Black Benny's broad chest. Benny's instinct was to catch him in his arms, but then he jumped backward as if Dick had instantly become contagious, and Dick fell slantwise into the black dirt and cinders.

But Black Benny didn't see this, how the old outlaw he ran with and feared and looked up to had come to his end, because even before Dick had hit the dirt and displaced a little of it, Benny got his share as well, a bullet in the throat, a shot so superbly placed he never raised his hands to the spot of his mortal wound, only made a small, ambiguous waist-level gesture, as if he were saying with broad, calloused hands, "Okay, this was my run, and I almost made it, too."

And the third man, George Robertson, ran down the alley, suddenly limber-legged once again, to a low board fence which he scaled, dropping on the other side into someone's little garden patch with a moan of pain that he stifled with a mouthful of smoky sleeve.

V. Madame Papaloos

The suite at the Monteleone was tastefully done. Tom Anderson had learned a few things about taste on his way up the ladder, and had acquired vestiges of it himself. His clothes were the best, and the appointments of the Annex were equal to any in its class in New York or Boston or Chicago, which was why prominently placed sporting men felt at home there. Yet there clung to him traces of the Irish Channel, tricked out in its dearly bought finest: the ineradicable preference for some sort of *show*—kelly-green waistcoats; some flourish about the breast pocket; the over-bold pattern of some of his suits. He knew this about himself, could see it darkly mirrored in the style of his business partner, Ed Mochez, whose hundred suits were the garish garb of a pimp and gambler. When Ed Mochez walked into a spot, it was an *entrance,* which was Ed's point.

It wasn't Tom Anderson's point, though: he wanted to be known as a man of taste. That was why he'd had Gertrude supervise the decorating of the suite, its large sitting room, two adjoining bedrooms, and full bath: soft colors, soft lighting, deep carpeting, even a Childe Hassam painting above the sitting room's sofa. Here Anderson could hold his most sensitive sessions with the city's powerhouses, whose appearance at the Annex would be politically and socially impractical. Here they might meet for lengthy lunches in baronial privacy and no one the wiser—except the waiters who ceaselessly ferried the soups, the crab and redfish dishes, the pans of delicately fried Barataria Bay oysters, the chef's special preparation of sweetbreads (Anderson's favorite), the tarts and mince pies, and the house's famous Black Forest chocolate cake.

And here, too, from time to time, Tom Anderson would hold particularly sensitive sessions with young women who had come to his attention, or been brought to it by Billy Brundy, sessions that might last into evening and for which more than the sitting room would be required.

Gertrude understood this function of the suite, even while never making reference to it, and had seen to certain touches she knew would be flattering and soothing to these girls. They were no threat to her. Indeed, they had their limited function in the large, interlinked operation she and Tom Anderson were running. They came and they departed, and most of the time she never knew their faces, let alone the names they went by.

The girl was different. Gertrude had known that the moment Anderson told her of his encounter with her. He was by a long shot the most practical, farsighted man Gertrude had ever encountered in a world rife with those of addled or occluded vision, men and women who could be depended on for one thing only: that at some critical point they would make a judgment not based strictly on business. Not Tom Anderson, not yet. But the girl bore watching because she could see that he himself was troubled by the quality of his feelings for her. She didn't know when the girl would be invited to the suite, only that she would be, and Gertrude could easily visualize how it would go.

The girl would be spotted by Anderson's most trusted scout the instant she set her foot in the lobby, the man gliding quickly from behind the long front desk with its Tiffany lamps, meeting her, and with a slight inclination of the head beckoning her to follow him out of the lobby, up a hushed, burgundy-carpeted staircase with bright brass rods beneath its risers, the staircase narrowing as it circled to the second floor, until they had arrived at a door without a number.

And that was in fact precisely how the girl did arrive at what ought to have been Room 202 but wasn't: there was a 200 and a 203 but no 202. And then to the young man's single, sharp rap the door swung open and behind it stood Tom Anderson, tall, full-suited, and yet to the young man a Mr. Anderson who looked different, somehow. Was it the collar that looked a trifle awry? The flatness of the cravat as it folded into the waistcoat, as if it might have been readjusted too many times to keep plump its heavy silken folds? Or was it maybe the sheen off the man's forehead, a sheen made the more evident because the forehead itself wore an uncharacteristic pallor? Tom Anderson opened his mouth, but for a long instant no sound came out, and his servant saw only the dark hole of an older man's mouth under its carefully brushed moustache.

"Ah, August, there you are," Anderson's voice boomed, too loudly, and his hand fumbled into his pants pocket for a bill— which proved wondrously excessive when young August inspected it, walking away from the numberless door that had just closed behind him with a telltale quickness. Well, he thought, whoever the hell she is, she's sure enough the hot ticket.

August's silent assessment was no help to the girl, of course, standing just inside the entrance to the room that officially didn't exist, face to face with the man she'd known as Daddy when they'd shared the house on Elysian Fields and, in those last months, shared her bed as well—place of blinding, bewildering pain—the man she'd come to love as a small girl, suddenly transmogrified one afternoon into a frighteningly unfamiliar monster, thrusting with some horn up into her very soul. And thereafter on subsequent Thursday afternoons a ritual repetition of this act, which in its forbiddenness and her own silent acquiescence became a soul-altering experience that only intensified when she came not merely to expect it but actually to look forward to certain aspects of it: his first penetration of her innards; then his quick gasp of recognition and delight; his groan of climax; and at last, one afternoon, her own cry, which might not have been antiphonal but which surely could not have been autonomous, either. And still later that moment when, waiting for his vast seminal discharge, that molten river driven deep within her, she had found herself bucking hard beneath him while everything turned upside down within her with what she couldn't at that moment identify as pleasure but which thereafter she could and which she had never been able to reach again with any man other than the one who now stood before her.

And now she, too, noticed what the just-departed young man had: that Tom Anderson wasn't in sovereign possession of himself. It wasn't any discernible dishevelment of his person. There wasn't a hair out of place. The moustache was brushed and well-trimmed. And still she felt certain he was off-balance, even as he made the polite sounds of welcome, the gestures meant to reassure her that here she was in excellent hands, he the mayor of what was known as "Storyville," and whose reach extended to this holding in the very heart of the old aristocracy's quarter.

In answer to his preliminary question, she said she'd take tea. He rang down for it, and while they waited they talked about spring's slow, grudging arrival; about Carnival; about the front-page story of the Musica family, currently being held in the parish prison in connection with a giant swindle back in New York. But when the tea was brought and poured and she had taken her first sip she was determined to press what she felt was some obscure advantage she might not have again.

She leaned back in one of the chairs grouped about the sofa with the painting of flags and bunting hanging above it and said quietly, "I've come back here, and I've agreed to see you, for one reason. I've thought a lot about this over the years and in a number of places."

She saw that he was about to ask about those missing years. And for a few moments her own mind was diverted to those places—Florence in Alabama, Shreveport; and then for almost two years over in Galveston, a town whose palms and languorous Latin shapes whispered so seductively of her home that one Sunday when her husband was up in Mississippi on business she'd quickly, but without the least panic, packed what she regarded as her essentials and taken the train back here. Brant's face came to her now. He hadn't been a bad fellow at all and had done his best to love her and to let her know he found her both beautiful and talented. But he had never reached her. For that she had to come back here, to this place, this man, this moment. She did not want to miss the moment by cluttering it with fleeting, jumbled images of the past—though it was the past that had pulled her away from Biloxi and sent her on her travels to Alabama and the other stops. And in every one of these it had been the same: the past she had lived here with this man met her in the new locale, wherever it was. Again she recalled that Sunday when Brant had kissed her good-bye in Galveston and she'd felt afterwards something move deep within her, a prompting almost physical.

In her school days at Sacred Heart one of the sisters in the Nature Studies class had talked about what she called the "homing instinct," in geese, a thing so strong, she said, that it took over the birds, making them restless and unsettled where they were, until it lifted them from their bountiful marshlands, into the air, calling out to the others that were answering the same resistless thing.

"I've come back for the apology I'm owed—that you owe me," she said with a quiet finality.

He heard her words. But what he was thinking as she delivered them with her gray-eyed solemnity was not really the words, what they asked of him. What he was thinking of was what he beheld before him: this gorgeous creature, more stunning now in her early maturity than she had ever been in the first blush of her pubescence when he'd first had her. For here in his rooms was the broad-shouldered, full-bosomed beauty he had foreseen in that afternoon instant when he'd accidentally encountered her in the hallway of the house on Elysian Fields and had been hopelessly awed and humbled by her bright and budding breasts.

"How's that?" he asked, almost as a sleepwalker might. With the same somnambulistic slowness he placed his coffee cup and saucer on the low table and reached into his vest for a cigar. The girl waited, seeing she'd further tipped his balance and confident now she could wait as long as it would take for him to make some sort of response. Finally, when the blue-gray smoke plumed above his face he regarded at her steadily enough out of eyes that had regained at least something of their focus. Still, he didn't speak, only picked a tobacco flake from his tongue and flicked it away.

"An *apology*," he said then, drawing the word out slightly, giving the sense that he was turning it about in his mind and reflecting on its implications. "You know, where you're concerned, little gal, there's a lot of things I'm sorry for. You know I never wanted it to end like it did with your mama. I tried for days to talk her out of leaving that way—I swear, I never seen a woman get that mad and stay that mad, too. It could all have been worked out." He held his hands out to indicate the inclusive ease of the arrangements Kate wouldn't hear of.

A silence fell in the lush, low-lit room, and she let it gather, listening to its weight. "You stole my childhood from me," she said, staring at him in the careful light, the lifting cigar smoke, her voice level, grave. He put the cigar down and clasped his large hands together, leaning towards her. The attitude was vaguely prayerful.

"I never meant harm to you, my girl," he said softly, feeling he meant it: he hadn't.

"But you did harm. You made me a woman when I was still a child." Though she hadn't rehearsed the actual sentences, their sentiments had become deeply familiar through the years. "You took my virginity, and when you did that, you took my childhood along with it.

"Oh, I could still play with my friends, yes. I went to their birthday parties and such." She shrugged, suggesting the utterly trivial nature of such contacts, as she now saw them, as she had seen them even then. "And I went on with my studies at Sacred Heart. I even went to confession. But I was completely different inside. Completely. I was shut off from myself and everybody else. I couldn't even confide in you."

She had no trouble now reliving that time when, along with her schoolmates, she ripened towards womanhood but interiorly had already some time since arrived there, early brought to an intimate knowledge of her body's capacities to endure pain, provide pleasure, and to provide it for someone whose godlike stature was the major daily phenomenon of her childhood world. Other girls, she well knew, worshipped their papas. She could remember the devotions her friend May-May lavished on her papa, Mr. Cornelius; or those of Caroline Rideau on Colonel Rideau, who in those days was certainly distinguished-looking enough to justify them with his prematurely white and flowing moustache that Caroline would playfully and coquettishly stroke as he held still in majestic resignation in his easy chair. And all the while, how far removed she felt from these florid, unpremeditated demonstrations. For she knew what really went on between men and women; what as-yet unimaginable trials awaited her giggling, blushing peers as they preened and pampered their papas. Well, she'd felt what Papa had between his legs, knew its frightening, protean possibilities, how when Papa's breath came in gasps that were closer and closer together, how then he knew neither law, nor limit, nor at the final shuddering spasm maybe not love even, but only the primal urge to spend himself in whatever orifice he had chosen for that cleansing moment.

She knew, as they couldn't, the pain of those first penetrations when it felt to her that the god-beast must split her open, when she would grip anything—sheets, bedstead, the man himself—just to have hold of something in the engulfing sea of physical torment into which she'd been pitched. And, deeper in, she had come to know the beginnings of a feeling originating in herself, lying beyond pain, its farthest shore. Even if she had never wanted to name it, she could feel its resistless approach, could even chronicle its secret somatic history.

All of which knowledge, communicable to no one, immured her within invisible walls through the slits of which she looked out on the world the other girls inhabited with what too often seemed to her a mindless giddiness. Some of them, she felt sure, would never come to what she already knew, would go from virginal girlhood straight into the politely arranged marriages of their class and then suffer the appetites of their lawful masters. Some lucky few might eventually learn to enjoy it; others would simply endure it, comforted by grandmother's gently imparted experiences; and many would probably live by the ancestrally communicated mantra, "Remember, my dear, a lady never moves."

She began to look for secret signs that all fathers were made of the same stuff as Tom Anderson, and often enough she seemed to find these. When Caroline Rideau had them all over for her fourteenth birthday and the colonel toasted them three times with bumpers of iced champagne, he'd kissed them each in turn—"My dear little beauties" as he styled them in his best courtly fashion. When he came to her she could smell the wine on his breath and feel that handsome moustache as it just grazed her lips on its way to where it was supposed to go—her cheek. And she knew what it meant when the courtly hand lingered on her back, discretely but surely feeling for the edge of an undergarment that would tell the colonel of this dear little beauty's coming of age.

Later, up in Biloxi, she had learned, too, of the agony and shame of an abortion and felt that deepest cut of all in the back-street practitioner's remark to her mother afterwards: "Shouldn't think you'd be bothered with this here kind of problem again, not with this one, anyways."

"Surely," she resumed, "you must have known what you were doing to me—what it could do to me." But even as she said this, she saw that he hadn't considered much more—if anything—than how he was to possess her without getting caught. He'd given no thought to how she might be affected by his actions. Suddenly, she saw him as he really was, stripped for the moment of his power, his political connections, his wealth and influence, bending towards her in that prayerful attitude with his hands clasped. And there was a kind of *innocence* to him in this moment, his blue eyes as devoid of calculation as she could ever remember them. He was, after all, she thought, only a man and one who, like her, had been forced to grow up too fast, arriving at adulthood while still a child, with a child's primitive, unfledged understanding of inner complexities, of long-deferred but still inevitable consequences.

She had often wished to humble him, to extract from him a heart-rending confession of guilt and responsibility. Now what she felt was something closer to pity. She knew little of the specifics of his boyhood, of the homicidal junk dealer who had taught him life's first law, how not to get killed; nor of Edith Simms, who taught him that love always came with a price tag attached. But she knew enough to see that though he was capable of giving her the apology she'd come back here to get, he probably wasn't capable of giving her the understanding that would fill out that apology to its fullest dimension.

"Oh, my dear girl," he said, "I never meant no harm. I couldn't. Not to you, Cammie." She didn't bother to correct him here, and so he went on, telling her what was for him the sovereign truth: that he hadn't known that he had been slowly falling in love with her until that accidental meeting in the hallway when he'd been blinded by her beauty and by the simultaneous recognition of his love. What followed was not, he wanted her to understand, unnatural. It was instead entirely the opposite. It was love of the rarest sort, and had not Kate flared up like that he could have given her all the protection and privilege she could ever ask for.

He arose from his chair, the cigar long dead in the ashtray, and crossed to where she sat. And she watched, without any feeling of triumph and still less of hauteur, as he knelt by her chair and took her capable hands in his.

"Cammie—Adele, if you want it that way—I swear on my mother's grave I never meant any of this to come to you. I swear it." He was looking at her with a fierce, moist-eyed earnestness to which she returned a nod, all that she'd intended. "I swear to you, I'm sorry. I'm sorry, I am."

He added something else but she didn't catch it because he had buried his handsome, carefully coiffed head in her lap. When he had commenced that downward movement her hands had lifted in indecision. But now they descended, softly as doves sailing in at dusk, covering the smooth sandy curls of the man who in his own stronghold was abnegating himself. "Yes," she said, stroking his head, "yes, I can see now that you are," wondering why she felt as if she herself was being forgiven as well, at last.

Their hands were close but not quite touching as they sat side by side on the sofa. Evening had long since come, and with it Tom Anderson had turned off the electric lights in the suite and lit up the hurricane lamps he had an old fondness for. Before them on the low table were two half-filled wine glasses and a bottle slanted against an ice bucket on the low table. By now he had turned their talk from the past and the years of her life that he'd missed and was telling her how much it pained him that she continued to work for the Parker brothers. She said again, as she had when they had first encountered each other outside the Monteleone, that she had absolutely no idea who the Harry Parker was who had slipped a note under her door, asking her by the Tuxedo for an audition. All that, she told him again, had been the work of Hattie Rice.

Anderson ran the stub finger around his ear. "Yes, that's the way it would be," he almost mumbled. She looked at him questioningly. "Oh," he added, as if coming out a reverie, "Hattie is Charley Parker's old lady—I mean, she goes with him. So, naturally...." He knew he didn't need to finish that sentence.

So, by the time she learned the brothers had set themselves up in New Orleans to challenge Anderson, she went on, she had already been singing at the Tuxedo for some weeks. "I don't know how much you know about me," she said with characteristic solemnity, not looking at him but instead down at her hands in her lap. "I mean, about the person I've become, the person I've *had* to become.

"Anyway, I found that I enjoyed the work there. Oh, not everything about it, of course. But I mean the challenge of it, of getting those men to listen to me—after their fashion. That and the money they were willing to pay me. I don't mind telling you I've worked for less in other places, and some of them were a lot—oh—rougher than the Tuxedo."

"But, my dear girl, you do understand now how things are." It wasn't a question, and she didn't take it as one. He took one of her hands from her lap, enveloping it in both of his, the maimed finger covered but there nonetheless, talisman of their secret history, its dark and lawless character. "And you do understand, I know, that it's a real dangerous place over there, for lots of reasons. Like to get more dangerous yet before it's done."

"Oh, I know that well enough," she said. "Yes, I know some of the risks. I know that Gyp fellow, but he's not as bad as Harry Parker." Suddenly her lips parted in an ironic smile. "Did you know it was Harry Parker who introduced me to your man, Muldoon?" Tom Anderson's eyes widened and he let go of her hand. "Not in any way you could have imagined," she went on.

"It was after I'd been singing one night, and I'd gone down the hall to this kind of office where I freshen up a bit. I was feeling a bit nervous and wondering whether I was up to the work, when who should come bursting in but Harry Parker. And he—oh, well, you can imagine what he wanted. So, natually, I ran right out of there, quick as I could—and that's when I met your man. I mean, I almost knocked him over when I threw open the door." She smiled again, but Tom Anderson didn't.

"Next time you might not be so lucky," he said. "Them jaspers play for keeps."

"I must say, your Mr. Muldoon is a very earnest fellow," she said, apparently ignoring his remark. "I don't exactly know what's on his mind, but whatever it is, he seems to have a lot of trouble getting it out, at least around me. Do you find him that way?"

"Muldoon don't have much of a mind," Anderson answered. "He's kinda like a clock or a watch, maybe—something you wind up. That's why he's useful to me—because he don't have anything on his mind, except what ever man down there does, and I don't even know if Muldoon even thinks much about that. He goes to Bessie Browne's most ever night and visits one of her women. But that don't take too much thought."

Adele shook her head. "I don't think that's what's on his mind when he's around me," she said. "There's something else." She looked over at him, and again that ironic smile played about her lips. "There's a way you two sound alike: he tells me how dangerous it is for a woman to work down in the District, and you tell me the same thing." She came to a stop, the smile gone. "You know what I think? I think the whole area, the whole situation, is more dangerous just now for *you* than it is for me."

Tom Anderson stared steadily at her, and if at the beginning of their interview she had found him something less than his customarily composed self, the man now seemed fully restored: alert and ready to evaluate any new piece of information that might come to him: the Tom Anderson who had risen to become the single most powerful person in the city. Even the fit and fold of his suit and cravat now struck her as more crisp and correct, as if magically he'd grown back into their dimensions.

"They're out to destroy you, if they can," she said with a flat declarative tone. "What I hear—not from them—but what others are saying, is that they want to drive you out. From what I can see, they are that sort."

He already knew this, of course, though lately it had occurred to him that he had come to this assessment in sluggardly fashion and well after Jimmie Enright and even the rash Billy Phillips had pointed it out to him. Maybe, he fleetingly thought, it was partly because Billy Phillips had become so hysterically insistent about it that he hadn't taken it seriously enough, soon enough. So he hardly needed this remark from the girl, or if he did, he needed it only as confirmation of how widespread this sort of talk had actually become. What he really needed from her were vital details. "Can you help me, then?" he asked.

"Well, I only know what I hear—the talk," she answered. "After all, I'm only the singer and not even the only one now. But there's been all this talk the last few nights about those murders over on Rampart, and I heard Gyp the Blood did them. But people are saying they had something or other to do with you." She took a decorous sip of her wine.

He shook his head and shrugged. "What would those niggers way over there have to do with me, I wonder?" He thought briefly but without too much regret of old Chicken Dick, doubtless by now dumped in a potter's field, the soggy clods flung down atop the coffin's cheap boards and within its eternal midnight the eyes of the outlaw open and staring and not even the grace note of slugs to weight their lids on the Forever. Well, he'd taken a shot at the Parkers with that plan, and it hadn't worked out well; it wasn't even a standoff, as the thing out at the Fairgrounds hadn't been, either: Buster Daley out of commission and the other fellow so scared of the Parker gang he was useless for further action. And in this latest skirmish it wasn't even the loss of Dick and Black Benny that was troubling. It was how the Parkers had so swiftly traced them: *that* was the really impressive thing, suggesting how wide a network of informants and allies they must have developed.

"Did you hear anything about them buying up Fewclothes Cabaret?" he asked, already knowing what her answer would be. She hadn't. But he well knew that the girl's close encounter with Harry Parker in that office wouldn't be Parker's last try at her, that he would rape her if he had to; in which case he wouldn't have to divulge anything of his plans: it would be simple force, the savage entry, and that would be that. No, for Parker to tell her anything of value she would have to go to bed with him with a seeming willingness, and even in that case—ghastly to contemplate—Parker might not let anything slip, might even feed her some misinformation. He wondered whether she could possibly promise Parker something, make some sort of flirtatious move—something short of actual sex that might tease information from him—and decided he couldn't ask that of her. Not now, at least. Instead, he asked her if they could see each other again soon, thinking as he asked this that he had never in his life seen anything so beautiful. And he was so close to her once again that it seemed impossible he was not to have her once more and finally, as of old he had dreamed he must.

She sighed, dropped her eyes to her hands folded in her lap. There was a silent, short stasis, and then her nod was so spare only they could have noted it.

Mamie wouldn't let go of him, even after he'd watched her wordlessly limp off into what wasn't so much sundown as it was the day's death. Nor on subsequent days when he pondered who else he might safely ask about her and had come up empty. Either they knew just enough to discourage his inquiry, as Okey-Poke had, or else they hadn't been around long enough to know more than a vague, useless fragment of rumor. He thought that if Bellocq didn't know, then maybe no one left alive knew—except Mamie herself, and she couldn't tell. In any case, there was danger for him in pursuing this further, that he knew: the District was a hive of dark secrets; everyone had them, and you just didn't go around prying.

And yet, Mamie held him, because of the girl and because of what he saw behind the girl, the dark, predatory shapes of Harry Parker, his brother, and Gyp the Blood who everybody had already fingered as the killer of Chicken Dick and Black Benny Boyd. Those killings and the muggings of the Parkers' steerers had brought matters close to the boiling point, making it even riskier for him to try to rake up murky matters of the past. So, he held his tongue, until the night when he saw Mamie again.

It was outside the Perdido, and she was standing in a sliver of an alley running between the warped old tonk and Mendoza's oyster saloon, buying a small sack of brick dust from Zozo La Brique, two silhouettes hunched in a bargaining posture. Zozo. Why hadn't he thought of her? She had worked these streets before there even was such a thing as the District and must know more than Bellocq or Jimmie Enright, or any of them.

He went past the alley, then waited for Zozo at the corner, running a toothpick around his mouth. When he heard her shuffling up behind him he turned to her. "Evenin, Zozo," he said, casually. "Workin late, aint you?"

"Ahh, Monsieur Fast-Mail, you ave to work when they want." She smiled a weary smile. *"Mais, mes chiens, mes chiens."* She glanced at her feet and shook her turbaned head with its tie-knot winging out from behind her left ear. Muldoon had only a handful of French words, but her meaning was clear: her feet hurt.

"I bet," he replied in sympathy. He knew how feet could hurt and her an old woman burdened by age and the buckets she balanced on her age-polished stave. "Say," he went on with a smile, "wasn't that Mamie I seen you with back there— the piano player?" Zozo had already begun to work her way across the street, and she kept on, speaking to him over her shoulder.

"Ah, *oui*, yes. Mamie, she one of my old customers, long time." On the opposite corner she turned to face him, a white man in a brown suit and bowler, waiting for whatever it was he wanted from her, her "dogs" killing her and the way long to her cottage out in the marsh along Bayou St. John.

"So, you've known her a long time then." She nodded, looking up at him through the gloomy glare of the lights from the tonks, saloons, and restaurants. "I always wondered," Muldoon went on, trying to keep that casual tone he'd adopted as his emotional disguise, "about her—Mamie, that is. Real busted up. But here's the thing: I seen this picture of her when she was young—oh, way back, like." The face looking up at him through the red and black glare and gloom betrayed nothing, only that patience it had been forced to learn in a white man's world. "And what I'd like to know," Muldoon went on, the casual tone beginning to wear thin now, the urgency behind it forcing its way to the surface, "is just this: what happened there? I mean, what got her busted up like that? Must have been something terrible, I'd say." He felt himself breathing harder here, as if in the bent, burdened person of the old woman he was close to something, if not the truth, then *a* truth, anyway, and not only about Mamie but about the world through which he nightly moved in a sort of supervisory capacity.

"No, no," Zozo muttered. She shook her head, and her buckets rattled in agreement. "That one too much for me." She shook her head again. "That one go too deep, Monsieur." She made a move to get around the white man, but he put his good foot in her way and held out an arm, feeling at once the injustice of his act, the imponderable advantage he was taking of this colored woman who dabbled in mystery, in mysteries, who sold an utterly worthless item as a specific against the ill fortune that hung over the women of the District like a sword.

"But you know something, Zozo. You been around these streets forever, right?" He continued to bar her way. "Or you know someone who does know."

"*S'il vous plaît*, Monsieur Fast-Mail. Let me pass."

He hesitated only an instant, then with his own show of weariness let his arm drop to his side. Zozo shifted beneath her sacking and began to move past him.

"I don't know nothing bout that business, please." He fell into step with her, the two of them walking in silence towards the lights of Canal. When they had almost reached it, she stopped, shifted again beneath her burden and looked both ways before stepping off the banquette. Muldoon watched her closely, thinking she might be mulling something over in her mind, but she stepped into the street still within her silence. Then without so much as a nod or turn of her head she muttered something, and he stepped into the street with her.

"Maybe Madame Papaloos—maybe she help you."

"Madame Papaloos? The hoodoo woman?" he asked quickly, lowering his own voice into the conspiratorial range. Zozo La Brique just kept going, finally gaining the broad street's farther side that defined the boundary between the District and the rest of the world.

"Madame Papaloos," she simply repeated as she turned in the direction of the lake. "Madame Papaloos, she know some of these tings, but I don't say she know this one. I don't say that, Monsieur."

"But where does she live? How can I get a message to her?" he asked. He reached into his pants pocket for his purse and snapped it open with his thumb and forefinger, pulling out some coins that he tried to hand Zozo. She wouldn't take them, only kept up that slow, relentless shuffle, so that after a few steps he dropped them in the sagging pocket of the coarse apron she wore. "Can you tell her I need to see her?"

"She live out West End way. Way out. If I see her, I tell her for you. When you come?"

"Tomorrow," he said to her back. "Tell her I'll come out tomorrow—say around three." She was fading away now, into the night, as he called to her. "You mean out there where them cabins and such are, right?" Zozo made no reply, leaving him standing in the glow of one of the street's high, goosenecked lights. He heard the muffled clankings of her buckets even after he could no longer distinguish the figure that carried them. Then he turned back into the District.

———

He rode the streetcar in a fine drizzle as far as Metairie Cemetery. When the wind gusted from off the lake it blew the mist against the car windows, turning them a sickly white and reminding him of the one other time he'd been out this way. It was many years back when he'd accompanied his father to see a fisherman about some business, and while the two men had talked he'd taken a long stick out to the narrow dock. Lying on his belly, he'd poked about in waters inky with mud and tree rot and been startled to find against the spindly pilings a nest of cottonmouths whose jaws yawned wide, stringy, gray-white against the thoughtless probings of his stick.

When the car jerked to a stop at the cemetery, rocking back on its metallic haunches, he grasped his umbrella and swung off into the misty swirl that quickly blanketed his shoulders before he could get the umbrella unfurled. Before him stretched Metairie's entrance—arches, cupolas, the equestrian figure of some Confederate hero. He followed its wall along the extension of Esplanade, beyond the cemetery and past the last of the raw, unfinished streets that marked out in mud and a few battered board houses the city's boundless ambitions.

Here the solid ground began to give way to marshland. He stopped, looking through the grayness towards where low trees rose above the marsh and beyond these to giant oaks and cypresses and a faint density of the gray that he thought must be smoke. He cast one way, then another for a path through the marsh and then found it, a narrow walkway of joined cypress planks raised a few inches above the water and the tough reeds and grasses. Leading with his good foot, he stepped out onto its drizzle-darkened and slippery sections, his umbrella held low for better balance.

In twenty minutes his careful progress brought him to higher ground and a clearing that proved to be a charcoal burner's operation, announced by a stump field and haphazard piles of cut wood, bucked up to fit the kiln that smoked profusely in the mist. A black man under a broad straw hat stopped his raking of smoldering sticks to silently regard the sober-suited stranger gingerly making his way cross the clearing to where the cypress walkway took up once more on the clearing's farther side. Here the way was darker, the waters higher and more extensive, the reeds taller and thicker. Above were oaks and patriarchal cypresses bearded with moss that swung slightly like the goatees of those old soldiers Muldoon recalled from his boyhood, mustered for some ancient commemorative event.

He arrived at the first of the fishermen's shacks with their wharfing, nets, and boats, and beyond these the solemn, warped shacks of hunters, trappers, tramps, and outlaws living in lean-to's. Beneath three soaring oaks were two cabins linked by docking, and as he neared these a boil of dogs came from one of them, causing him to tighten his grip on the umbrella and nudge his chest with the inside of his left elbow, feeling the pistol there in its holster. The dogs came down towards the walkway, following the lead of a heavy-headed cur that had some mastiff in it. To shoot a man's dog out here would have consequences, he knew, but he felt that if the lead dog came for him, the others would follow. Then the consequences might be more serious yet if they should drag him down. While he was wondering whether he needed to draw the pistol, two turbaned, bulky mulatto women emerged, one from each cabin, and raised their high voices at the pack. The part-mastiff swung his ponderous head around towards them, then gave a valedictory *huff* and made his way back through his followers towards the women. When the others had gone back and the last of the barkings had ceased, he called out, asking where

Madame Papaloos lived. This started the dogs again but over them both women pointed him onward, into the bigger trees, and he was able to gather that he must look for a palmetto house.

He soon found it, shaggy with the thatching that covered the pitch of the roof and all but one corner of the cottage where there was an open door. Above the door a bit of red calico swung slightly in the wind. But for all its shagginess and shapelessness there was a muted air of tidiness about the place. A wide board walkway ran to it over the mud, reeds, and puddles. He went down it until he came to a tiny porch by the door, and pausing there at the bottom step he saw movement within. He was in the act of closing the umbrella and furling it when Madame Papaloos filled the doorway above him, tall, broad, her West Indian features polished like expensive, well-cared-for leather beneath a straw hat that sported a band of the same red calico that fluttered above her.

"You the white man Zozo said was coming," she said. He said he was. She regarded him with impassive silence and then made a vague gesture with her head and at the same time made a kind of clicking sound with her tongue and teeth. "And you come about the woman." He nodded and thought to add, "Yes, I have." Again there was that head gesture that wasn't quite invitation and the clicking sound. She turned in the doorway and went in, and he went up the two steps behind her and was about to stoop under the bit of calico when her voice boomed out of the dimness. "Leave that outside." He saw her pointing to his umbrella.

Inside, the room was barren except for a table and two chairs. Its single window looked out on the cypress walkway by which he'd come, its frame blurred by the heavy thatching so that it was more pyramidal than rectangular. She motioned him to the chair nearest the door, then turned her back on him, sweeping aside a heavy crimson curtain and disappearing behind it. It fell back into place so swiftly Muldoon couldn't catch a glimpse of anything behind it. But he could hear her in there, moving about and making that odd clicking sound now and again.

Waiting at the empty table for the hoodoo woman, his mind skipped back helplessly to his ingrained disbelief in precisely the sort of mumbo-jumbo Madame Papaloos so clearly dealt in. He remembered an older kid at St. Alphonsus, Turk Seavoy, who had once wryly observed to a bunch of his cronies that just about the only thing hoodoo had going for it was that all the brothers at the school were so set against it. "Wasn't for that," Turk had said, "you'd be bound to take it for the crock of shit it is," drawing a large laugh from his street corner audience. Then he'd gone on to blaspheme against Brother Paul, claiming over the rising tide of laughter that "if Brother Paul told you your ass was red and blue like them monkeys they got in the zoo, then you'd know for sure it wasn't without checking in the mirror." Well, the old Turk had died under mysterious circumstances some years thereafter, and at the wake someone had muttered that maybe it didn't pay to go around making jokes about hoodoo and all that stuff; and then somebody else had spoken up and told the first guy to shut up, that what they were gathered for was to give old Turk a good sendoff. Which, as he recalled it, they had.

But the old prejudice was with him yet, and waiting for Madame Papaloos to materialize again from beyond the curtain, he told himself that he wasn't out here to have her work her mumbo-jumbo but simply because he'd run out of leads on the mystery of Mamie and that Zozo had said that maybe Madame Papaloos knew something. Knowing something meant you had some sort of knowledge, some evidence of a thing; it didn't mean working with spirits and the like.

But when the curtain moved and Madame Papaloos came back in the room bearing a tall candle and a glass of water, his heart sank. He wasn't going to hear the truth about Mamie—or anything else—from this woman. It had been a fool's errand he'd been on. And why, he asked himself now as Madame Papaloos set the spare paraphernalia on the table between them, should he have expected anything more? Zozo was his source, and she sold brick dust to ward off bad luck. He was going to get the old mumbo-jumbo, pay for it, and then walk the long way back towards town through the marsh and the mist. He watched her light the candle, shake out the match and look at it intently as its head changed from tiny glow to dead black, then carefully put it in her apron pocket.

She was hatless now and wearing a turban of the same color as her hatband and the bit of rag above the doorway. Beneath the turban's tight fit he could see a few strands of white hair, slightly surprising to him: her face was lined and there were deep pouches beneath her eyes, but her bearing and movements were limber and forceful enough to have been those of a person of middle years only.

"This woman," she said, her eyes looking down at the table.

"Yeah."

"She have her own story, same as you."

He gaped at her, trying to catch her eyes as if to surmise her meaning and follow her. But he couldn't. Her lids were as heavy and flat as an Oriental's. He couldn't peer under them to see where they looked. In the silence he wondered if he waited long enough, she might look up at him, and then he might possibly catch a hint of something—anything. But she kept her eyes on the table, and he believed in the utter silence that he could hear the muffled ticking of the big watch Tom Anderson had given him, marking off the moments in his vest pocket.

The longer they sat there, the more distant he felt from his original intent, which was to do what he could to save the girl by way of Mamie's awful example. The girl herself had pointedly said that she already knew Mamie, her story. He didn't believe that: she hadn't seen that photograph in the stack on Bellocq's table, nor had she seen the grotesque figure Mamie had become. But sitting in this silence, this séance, it was as if he'd come all this way to talk about Mamie herself and not what Mamie represented.

He had to say something, to jog her onward. "Well," he said, "yes. That's what I come out here to get—her story. To find out what it is."

"She have her story, yes." Madame Papaloos might have flicked her eyes sideways at the water glass, but he couldn't be sure. "But you, you must want that—"

"Oh, *yeah!*" he broke in. "I do! That's what I want, all right!"

She shook her head slowly, decisively. "No," she softly breathed, looking down at the table. "You must want it. Only it."

He felt his neck bulging inside his damp collar, wondering what she meant, what he could reply to get her going. "Well, I do, I do," he repeated, feeling lost and foolish. "That's what I come for, all right."

"No," she said again with that negative headshake. "No, Monsieur. For love, if you want that, then you must want the story. You must want it because it belong to her." She lifted her eyes to his for the first time since she'd looked at him from the doorway of the cottage. "Only this way can Madame Papaloos help." She slowly lifted one hand from her lap and placed it palm up on the table, its fingers long and almost white on their undersides. She studied it a long moment. Then she took the hand back.

"You want Madame Papaloos to help with love, you must help, too. You got to love, truly, her story."

He was lost, he knew, having already said at least twice that he had come just for that. But how was he to love what he didn't know? Was it a matter of making clear to her that he was sincere in his interest? Or was she herself confused here and thinking he wanted her help in getting Mamie to love him?

"Look," he said, placing both of his broad hands on the table. "What I want, what I got to have, is what happened to Mamie, how she got all twisted, like. See, I seen this picture of when she was young, and she was beautiful, just beautiful. It aint a question of love—that aint in it." His words began to tumble into each other as he leaned across towards her, gripping the table with his hands. "Zozo said you knew the story." He reached into his pocket for his purse and flung down a rumpled bill on the table. "That's yours," he said, "if you can tell me who did that to Mamie."

But even as he said this Madame Papaloos was in the act of rising from her chair. She didn't even look at the bill but only at him. "Madame Papaloos don't work that matter." She shook her head in time with her words, which he heard as a sentence. "Madame Papaloos work for love. She can make people fall in love. She can make em fall out. Maybe sometime she do other matters. She can maybe make people be silent when they go to the judge. She can make things happen, yes.

"But aint nobody can unmake what already happen, what happen before. You asking too much." Still not looking at it, she pushed the bill across the table with a long forefinger. "You got to go now."

He lurched up from the table and snatched the bill, feeling its shabby worthlessness in his clutching fingers, staring at the polished, impassive features of the hoodoo woman. She knows! She knows something! he thought.

"Give me a name!" he cried out. "Just a name—that's all!"

Madame Papaloos leaned forward and with quick precision pinched out the candle. The smoke wavered uncertainly above the twisted wick, then began its wispy ascent toward the dark ridge pole that ran under the palmetto thatching. She picked up the water glass and, placing one hand over it, shook her head at him one more time.

"Who was it?" he demanded, struggling to get the words out through a throat that felt as if it were lined with old husks. "Who was it? You know. I know you know."

Madame Papaloos moved to the crimson curtain, took hold of its edge, then turned about. "You have the same story she have," she said, "but she know it." The last syllables were muffled by the curtain's quick fall, leaving him alone with the tarry smell of the dead candle, the suddenly stilled curtain, and then the sound of someone shutting something—a door, maybe.

There was nothing left for him here, nothing but the walkway that went back the same way it had come, though it seemed longer now. The rain had stopped while he was with Madame Papaloos, and so he didn't miss his umbrella until he saw the city's spires across the dismal marsh. The sky hung low over all like a sooty cerement.

VI. Toodloo

"Well, shit! I hadta see it to believe it!" Jimmie Enright was saying to Muldoon and Okey-Poke at the bar of the Annex. It was a few minutes before six. The bar's surface was gleaming darkly; Okey-Poke's pyramids of glasses were in sparkling order; the towels for the evening trade hung fresh from their brass rings; and the other bartenders stood in the classic pose of readiness, their hands braced on the bar's inner edge. But there were only five customers spread out along the bar and two tables occupied beneath the welcoming blaze of the ceiling's celebrated lights. Smoke bellied up from one of the tables where two portly men puffed at cigars while examining a sheaf of papers between them.

"I didn't but half believe it before, but I sure as hell got to now!" Jimmie Enright continued. "I had to wade through all that shit just to get in here." He waved in the general direction of the catercornered front doors. Beyond them on Iberville lay haphazard heaps of boards, lathing, bricks, and a wheelbarrow overflowing with chunks of plaster and glass and lengths of broken framing. "No wonder nobody's in here," Enright said.

"I wouldna come in here myself, except only to say hello to you guys."

"Glad to have you with us again, Jimmie," Okey-Poke said. Beneath his black vest his shirt sparkled in its adamantine sheath of starch.

Since early that morning when a crew of black laborers had arrived at Fewclothes Cabaret there had been an invasive din of ripping, smashing, and rending from across Iberville and clouds of brick and plaster dust wafting over to the Annex and entering it with every swing of the double doors. The workers had knocked off for the day, but the debris remained just where they'd left it.

Here in rubble, disruption, and a sparse house was rumor verified: the Parkers had bought out Tom Anderson's friend, George Foucault. So now Anderson's three hirelings were trying, each in his own way, to assimilate the new fact and its implications: Okey-Poke behind his studiously professional bartender's aplomb; Muldoon with his red face a bit longer than usual and trifling with a cup of coffee already gone tepid; and Jimmie Enright who had wanted to see for himself and had and now was trying to digest the fact by reminding his colleagues of what they already knew, the history of Tom Anderson and the Foucaults, father and son. Nanny had been T.A.'s first business partner when they'd dealt in coal and stove wood before T.A. had gotten into oil. They'd also owned race horses together, Jimmie recalled. "Could hardly be called a stable, cept they had that stud Nanny used the money from to buy that fuckin joint—and now just look at it, would you?"

If the District had its scop, it was this slope-shouldered man within whose cannonball head lay the history and the legends of the place and much that had preceded its creation, too—the bleak, blackened tales of who had done what to whom and when and how that deal had turned out. Now En-right felt compelled to recite to Okey-Poke and Fast-Mail of the time when Nanny had run to T.A. to beg him to do something to rescue his son.

"George had a few nigger whores on the string," Jimmie Enright said. "Nothin wrong with that, long's you understand what yer into there. Competition's full of rough dudes who don't take too good to your workin their own kind. Macbeth, Sore Dick, Yellow Galvez—remember that bastard? Cut yer fuckin throat for you if you crossed him? Didn't mean nothin that you was a white man. Plus which, it's one thing runnin Matilda and Noreen from out there in the western parishes, what come in here from Indian Village or Edna or What-the-Fuck, and they're so happy to get the steady work you could tell em to take it from the circus elephant, and they'd ask you what time you wanted this done.

"But the nigger whores, they're somethin else—savages, really. Got no souls. Hopped up. And so what does young George do but fuckin *fall in love* with one of his jungle bunnies. And then he *kills* her. Kills her in a crib, right down there," jerking his thumb in a vaguely westward direction down Iberville. "And there was witnesses.

"So, here comes Nanny, all lathered up. 'T.A., you gotta help me! My son! My son!' And so, by God, he does, too. He gets Nanny calmed down, and he gets George outta town, up to New York and then clear up to Canada somewheres where he goes to work for a French guy who learns him the cabaret business. And meanwhile, he finds out who the witnesses are—all niggers—an he takes care of them, gets em outta town, gives em money, gets one a pretty good job as a maid. All except this one, Bang-Zang—never will forget that name—who don't wanta play along. Which is why, like I say, you gotta understand the trade here: they aint like Matilda and Noreen. Anyways, her he takes care of in another way such that, ah, old Bang-Zang aint a problem no more."

He paused long enough to whip down the last of his Jameson's, wiping his mouth with the back of his scarred, stubby hand. He pulled out his watch, shoved it back into the pocket of his checked pants, and belched, blowing out his cheeks. "So, this is his reward, you might say. George sells to them pricks, and we don't even get a chance to bid." Jimmie turned his head to the entrance where a couple of college kids stood irresolute, looking about the almost deserted saloon and speaking closely to one another. Then they turned and left.

"There!" Jimmie Enright said, glaring at the others. "See that? George never could forgive T.A. for all he done for him. So, here's the payback at last. Took long enough, but then, sometimes that's the way it works." He slammed his hat on that perfect sphere of a head with its bristles like iron filings and shook hands with Okey-Poke and then Muldoon.

"Gotta be goin," he said, not moving yet, as if once back inside what had been his bailiwick he was loathe to leave it for the 102 where nothing but trouble could await him. "Sometimes," he said after a moment's silence, "I really think it's a shame I aint got tits. That way I could give Billy-Boy what he needs ever night."

When he had gone, Okey-Poke began to give his length of the bar a very superfluous going-over, using long, meditative strokes with his rag, looking down at his hand as though it were doing the work on its own. Muldoon recognized the response for what it was and almost wished Okey would give him a rag of his own to occupy his mind, instead of which he was forced to confront the old image of a woman, strapped to a creosote pole on Robertson and two police officers looking on while some young sports made a broad show of lighting the fire-crackers they'd shoved up her most private place. Bang-Zang.

He'd been a rookie cop back then, but he knew better than to try on the threadbare excuse that his veteran partner had found the scene comic and had encouraged him to do so as well, that you had to laugh in order to be considered a regular fellow in the department. Such an excuse, if it ever fit, didn't now. Nor was there any comfort to be found in the fact that after all Bang-Zang was a nigger whore and a particularly depraved one at that. Jimmie Enright said the nigger women in the District were different from the white ones, and he supposed there must be some sort of truth to this, especially if you were comparing the blues-singing crib girls to the whites and the octoroons who worked in the high-priced houses along Basin. But whatever the difference—and he couldn't work it out himself—he knew it couldn't be absolute. In the eyes of the law Octavia was a nigger, too, the same as Bang-Zang, who had been several shades darker, but he was forced to acknowledge that he had never felt any racial difference when he was within her warm, wet cave and they were separated by nothing but tissue. Moreover, he now knew, as he could not have when he'd come upon Bang-Zang, that all of the women of the District, whatever their shade of color, were captives, every one of them.

And standing high above the District was the man he worked for and in whose castle he now stood. He knew very well that this man himself had done nothing to the vanished Bang-Zang. Probably he'd never even seen her. He could also appreciate the expression of loyalty that had prompted Tom Anderson's rescue of his friend's son. He himself had been a recipient of that loyalty, as had so many others. At the time of the incident on Robertson he'd thought nothing of it when

Bang-Zang wasn't around anymore: they came and went with such frequency you couldn't possibly keep track of them, even if you had wanted to. Probably, she'd been scared out of the District to some other location, he'd thought then—if he'd thought anything. Now, however, Jimmie Enright's story raised another possibility. He looked up from his coffee cup at Okey-Poke who was still moving that rag back and forth, wondering if he was ever visited with troubling thoughts such as these that seemed to be clustering more and more closely about him in these gray, rainy days of spring, and if he was, what he did about them.

A hearty, fraternal voice sounded at his elbow, the kind he knew of old. Then a meaty hand slapped him smartly between the shoulder blades and he turned to find an unfamiliar face grinning at him from the midst of a quartet of sporting men who had come up to the bar. "Fast-Mail Muldoon, by God!" the voice said, booming out of the grinning, faintly freckled face. A few sprigs of sandy hair peeked out from beneath the hat, and Muldoon thought he might possibly have seen the man somewhere before. "Fast-Mail Muldoon," the voice repeated, this time with something almost reverent in its tone. "I saw you run the Crescent City Quarter Mile when you set the record!" He turned to his comrades, the hand that had clapped Muldoon on the back still there while he invited the others to behold the old hero.

"Boys," he said, but they were already bantering with Okey-Poke, and he had to repeat himself a couple of times. "Boys, I want you to meet Fast-Mail Muldoon, personal friend of mine." Now he had their attention, and they looked at Muldoon, head to toe, with an almost esthetic appreciation, as if he'd been a thoroughbred out at the Fairgrounds. "Set the record for the quarter-mile a ways back, and it still stands.

And he anchored the mile relay when they took the state." The man paused for dramatic effect, and Muldoon could see Okey-Poke out of the corner of his eye, patiently waiting for the men to place their orders. In the pause, Muldoon turned to the man and made a smile. The man placed his hands on Muldoon's shoulders. "Sic em, Fast-Mail," he said.

When he cut into the chop and found it badly overdone, Tom Anderson shoved the plate away with a quick flick of his hand. The boiled egg had been just the opposite, so runny he couldn't spoon it from his cup. He was tempted to speak to Caroline in the kitchen but didn't, merely wiped his mouth and moustache and arose from the table. Caroline was Gertrude's cook, prized more for her long, loyal service than for the actual quality of her cooking. What Tom Anderson prized most was a tranquil, orderly household and never more so than these days. So, he said nothing about the egg or the chop. Later when he went to the Annex he could easily enough remedy what hunger he had, though lately he'd been off his feed; just yesterday Gertrude had remarked that he was looking a trifle pinched around the gills, as she put it. It would have been superfluous if she'd asked him whether he was feeling all right: she knew well enough what the Parker gang had been up to, including the latest problem of the construction trash allowed to collect in the street outside the Annex so that a stranger down there might well imagine he'd strayed into an abandoned section of town.

Anderson entered his study and eyed the telephone, tempted to call Billy Brundy to ask if there had been any response from City Hall to Brundy's repeated requests for some action on the construction debris. Instead, he reached for a cigar. It wouldn't do, he told himself, to give even Billy Brundy the idea that he was anything more than mildly perturbed about the whole matter, though by now the debris had reached sizeable proportions and still not so much as a peep from the mayor.

He was smoking and trying to concentrate on the morning papers when the phone rang and then his servant Criss came in to report that Mr. Brundy was on the phone. In his study he put the receiver to his ear and listened to the glottal stop as Criss hung up the other phone in the hall alcove.

The news was not reassuring, because what Billy Brundy now told him was that he'd been unable to reach the mayor himself and had talked instead with Gaston. The second he heard Gaston's name Anderson knew what it meant. The mayor used the annoyingly correct college man to deal with citizens whose complaints were little more than nuisances but who were themselves too prominent to brush off. But the brush-off was in fact just what you were getting when you got Gaston.

It got worse as Billy Brundy went on, doing a fair imitation of the Baton Rouge man's starchy diction. The chief, Gaston had said, was very upset about street violence near some of the downtown hotels and in particular a terrible assault outside the Southern terminal witnessed by Dr. and Mrs. Garneault of Lafayette that so upset Mrs. Garneault that she was confined to her hotel room for her entire stay in the city. Then there had been the murders on South Rampart that same night, and these had besmirched the city's reputation all over the South and doubtless far beyond as well. When Billy Brundy protested that these affairs had nothing to do with Mr. Anderson, Gaston had cut him short. The chief, he said, wished to remind all interested parties that the District existed on the sufferance of the citizenry and that it was a very thin sufferance at that—one that could not possibly bear the weight of tribal warfare. The chief, he continued, was a very tolerant man, as he was certain

Mr. Brundy appreciated. But tolerance had its limitations, and the chief wanted to remind the interested parties that all previous understandings were conditional on the maintenance of strict order in the District.

Brundy paused a moment, and when he resumed it was to tell Anderson that Charley Parker had been to see the mayor. The mayor had found Parker rough of manner, Brundy said, like so many Yankees were. But he thought that underneath that the newcomer seemed reasonable enough and might some day prove to be a genuine community asset.

"What about the trash on Iberville?" Anderson asked, his voice smooth, level as ever.

"He said he'd look into it directly," Brundy said. "I guess he probably will, now that we've had our little chat."

Later that morning when he kept Gertrude company at her breakfast Tom Anderson reported all this. She heard him out as she ate, then lit a cigarette and asked what he would do if the mayor didn't see to the trash—and keep on seeing to it each day. Would he have the Parkers cited?

"Wouldn't do," he said, inspecting the nails of his mutilated hand.

"I don't think so, either," she said. "It would only bring more attention to where you don't want it. But then, so would some other stuff—more direct stuff, I mean." She looked sharply his way. "I hope you aint thinking of anything like that."

He shook his head, still inspecting his nails and picking at a ragged bit of skin below a cuticle. "No, no," he reassured her. "That wouldn't do, either." Privately, he had briefly considered having Fewclothes torched some night but had dismissed the idea as too risky on several counts. Suspicion would immediately fall on him and infuriate the mayor. Then, the cabaret was physically joined to a property he owned and was scant yards away from the Annex itself; if the fire should get out of control, it would be a disaster. Finally, if he did have the building torched, the cleanup would further clog the intersection, even more, probably, than the current construction did. So, as far as Fewclothes was concerned, he felt his hands were tied.

What, Gertrude was asking him now, did he hear from the girl about the Parkers' plans for Fewclothes? His mind flashed back to a hushed moment in the suite at the Monteleone when he'd asked her just that question, a moment that for him had the quality of velvet about it somehow—soft, cushy, deep, dusky—when he had looked down into those gray eyes and she'd said she'd heard nothing more than that the brothers planned to make it much like the Tuxedo but with more emphasis on dancing.

"She don't hear that much," he answered. "Probably no more than one of our cooks might. They're going to put a bigger bandstand in there, that and another one of them signs." Gertrude was looking at him as she lit another cigarette, the smoke drifting towards him, almost white as it left her mouth, then turning blue as it crossed the window's light.

"Too bad she's useless that way," she said.

He shrugged. "New and all, you know."

Gertrude let the subject drop for the moment, going on to talk of her upcoming trip to Chicago to visit her only living kin, a half-sister some years younger who lived outside the city in Pullman, where her husband was assistant town manager under a relative of Mr. Pullman himself. From the first, Gertrude had never asked him to account for his dealings with other women, nor had he asked her about other men—and women, for that matter. Away from each other, involved in affairs of the night that took them to strange places, they conducted themselves as they saw fit and asked each other no needlessly troublesome questions. Their work brought them enough trouble as it was. When they were together as in this morning moment they were fully comfortable in each other's company. And there were other moments as well—fewer than before, it was true—when they met in bed and Tom Anderson found satisfaction in her body and what it could do. Gertrude, he reflected now, was built for pleasure, not speed, and at his age he had developed an appreciation of that. This was a good thing he had here, he knew, and he didn't want to upset it if he could help it. So, hearing her talk of Chicago, he was grateful the subject of the girl was behind them for the time being.

Gertrude was no prattler, but as she talked on about State Street, the tall buildings, the grand white showplaces left over from the World's Fair, it was clear she was enthusiastic about the trip and eager to see Marion, whom she hadn't visited in more than two years. "It's not the same for you," she said, tapping her cigarette into a silver ashtray with its tiny upraised figure of a riderless racehorse. "You live here with kin all around you. Marion's all I got." He nodded agreeably, half-listening now and the other half of his attention shuttling uneasily between the Parkers and the girl.

"No, no," he said. "Can't be the same. I'd miss em if they lived way off like Marion." Marion had never visited New Orleans, and he was certain she had no idea what her half-sister did down here. She knew only that Mr. Anderson was a highly placed man in civic affairs and that Gertrude helped him. He had wondered, though, whether her husband, Broderick, might have gotten wind of matters a bit more specific. Men traveled, and men talked. It was as simple as that. And in fact a good portion of Tom Anderson's trade depended on the talk of traveling men who had been to New Orleans and had had their own good times at one or another of Tom Anderson's establishments.

"I just love walking down State Street and looking in all those windows," Gertrude was saying with a small smile on her face. She still had lovely skin, he thought, with a natural bit of rose color to her cheeks. "It's not as broad as Canal, but somehow it seems like it because the buildings are so high for blocks and blocks. It's like you're at the bottom of a canyon or something." She broke off, hearing her own voice sounding like a newcomer from Plaquemines where Kate had come from with her brown gums and slatternly ways.

She forcefully pulled herself away from thoughts of Chicago, coming back to the pressing business of the Parker gang. "Do you think you made a mistake using those Negroes?" she asked. "How come you didn't use Nonnie and Bert instead?"

Nonnie and Bert Pickett were Channel boys, tough, game—but not too bright, especially Nonnie. Anderson had in fact thought of using them but hadn't, because the last time he had he'd been forced to do some fancy footwork and spend some money to clean up a mess the Picketts made when they'd gotten carried away with some routine "maintenance work"— a code term he and Billy Brundy used. He hadn't wanted to risk a repetition of that just now and had turned to Chicken Dick instead.

"Actually, I think Chicken Dick was a bit brighter than the Picketts," he said. Caroline poked her head in from the kitchen, asking if he wanted to join the Missus in a cup of chicory. But he signed "No" with a single shake of his head. "Maybe I was wrong...." His voice trailed off, thinking about what had happened to Dick and the others on South Rampart.

Most likely it was drink that had betrayed his men and led to their deaths. So often in his world it was, but he was far too clear-sighted to curse it. Drink was the sovereign oil that made all his enterprises work and without which they would be un-thinkable. Still, the stuff that made them work also made them unpredictable and volatile. Early on he had seen its effects on adults and except for a single, sponsored experience had never over-indulged.

It was Edith—again—who had insisted he needed to un-derstand what liquor did to you, and under her expert guid-ance he'd gotten good and drunk up in her room. Once was plenty, and for many years now when he played host at the Annex or elsewhere all the bartenders had standing orders to water his drinks heavily, or else, on well-rehearsed, covert in-structions, to serve him colored water with distracting gar-nishes of fruit.

But Dick and that crowd drank hard, and he had little trouble imagining that they might have done some loud brag-ging at the Astoria or one of the other Negro tonks, maybe flashed some bills, made outlandish, flashy bets on a cotch game. It remained impressive though that the newly arrived Parkers had been able to establish lines of informants who got word to them of the telltale behavior of Dick and his cohorts. And once they had Dick and the others lined up in their sights they hadn't missed a shot, either: Dick and Black Benny dropped on the spot and the other fellow wounded.

Gertrude had returned to the prospect of her trip and was talking of the things she wanted to do again, but she would not be going to the stockyards, she said, where Broderick had taken them on her last visit. Once was enough of that. "Actu-ally," she amended, "it was interesting. I mean, the amount of meat they can turn out of there in a single day!" Her business-woman's mind had clearly been energized and engaged by that aspect of the yards. "It wasn't even all the blood," she went on, explaining why she wouldn't be going back, "but what it was was the *smell*. I think I must have told you I couldn't wear those clothes again on that visit, even though Marion hung them out behind the house for days—till it rained anyways." She took a final deep pull on her cigarette and stubbed it out in the ashtray, meanwhile turning up her nose as she scented once more those gutters flowing with arterial blood. "That I couldn't take again."

There was another thing she couldn't take, either, she said now. She paused while Caroline cleared the last of the breakfast dishes and then could be heard rattling at the kitchen sink. "And I think you know well enough, Tom, what it is." He had been picking again at the ragged cuticle while she went on about Chicago, but now raised his eyebrows to meet her direct gaze. "What you do with that girl is your own business. I don't ask, though, like I say, I do wish she was good for something, working where she does.

"But what I won't stand for is being made a fool of. If you want to meet up with her, do it in private, please, not in public. That, and I don't want her in this house."

"Fair enough," Tom Anderson replied. He reached across and patted Gertrude's hand. "Couldn't be fairer, for sure."

Muldoon sat on the edge of the narrow, rustling bed at the foot of which the thin orange coverlet lay folded neatly back, out of the way of business. Octavia had turned from him, hanging up his suit coat on the back of the door and purring in that languorous Caribbean cadence he used to find simultaneously soothing and arousing. "What Octavia done to cost er this andsome man's most pleasant company, eh?" She faced him with an arch smile. The words were meant to remind him of what they had shared here: her easy, unhurried advances; her hands at his collar and tie; the slipping of his braces from his shoulders—no fumbling uncertainty anywhere. And after the ceremonial disrobing, the tender washing of his awakened member in the warm medicinal fluid. Then the inner art, her movements like a tropical breeze: warm, steady, until at last he shudderingly came, and it was over again. Afterwards, down in the kitchen Bessie Browne's slightly grave talk was a kind of conversational cosmetic like Octavia's, helping him get over the old emptiness, that hollowed-out feeling that you wanted to believe was a kind of cleansing but that you suspected wasn't, was only the way a bathtub might feel—if a bathtub could—when it had been drained of water scaly with bodily excrescences.

But none of this tonight, Octavia's words sounding transparent in intent and pathetic, too: threadbare from serial nightly employment—an act, not entirely unlike those circus acts they put on at Emma Johnson's Studio. So, instead of being enkindled, knowledge suspended, or, better, temporarily obliterated by desire and release, he looked down at the rug beneath his brogans and saw its threads, its nappy tufts that made him think of pubic hair, of this woman's vagina, worn and nappy as the rug. And for what felt to him like the very first time he wondered at the room's shabby appointments: the rug, the faded stripe of the wallpaper, the dangerous sag of the cane-seated chair, the very rustle of the lumpy mattress on which he slumped and atop which for some years he had lain with the woman who now stood off to the side, giving him a silent, professional appraisal, wondering what state of the male mind was going to make more difficult the efficient dispatch of her well-tried goods.

Clearly, it was going to take a special effort. His member, she could see, lay entombed within the folds of his heavy twill pants, while his shoulders were slumped and his braces lay in flaccid loops at his waist. Here, her experience said, was a tough case, a sad sack, a limp fish. She had patience, though, and as these fellows went she liked this one well enough: he was sober, quiet, clean, and unfailingly polite. When she was in his embrace and felt his biceps tighten as he mounted what she had for some forgotten reason long visualized as a hill with a flat summit, she was able to accept with a certain pleasure what he was climbing towards and assist him with moans and thrusting hips.

She spoke his name softly. "Fast-Mail, you don got it for Octavia," she said, her head cocked to the side and her lips parted in a slight smile. "Not tonight. What trouble my andsome man ave when he come in ere and no ave it for what he know Octavia got?" She was pretty sure she knew what it was and why Muldoon hadn't been topping off his nights with a visit between her legs. She and Bessie had both witnessed the little lakeside drama, the way Muldoon, seeing the strange girl arise to walk out on the central dock, had himself arisen with uncharacteristic rudeness to stump after her and then take her out in the boat. Bessie had said then that he'd be back, and so he was now. But that girl was with him, a palpable presence in the room, making herself felt in the slump of the man's shoulders, the droop of his braces, the uselessness of his member.

She thought of a number of expediencies—tricks—she might use to get him going: straddling his leg and rubbing her crotch bewitchingly along it; or, standing over him, her legs spread, and lifting the hem of her dress to slowly finger herself; or, kneeling there, fishing his member from his rumpled fly and putting it into her mouth, moaning the while with her pleasure. But she decided none of these would work, at least not now. Besides, they knew each other so well that maybe some solicitous talk might be best.

"My andsome man," she began, sitting down next to him and taking one of his hands in hers, "ave they blues for that little puta what sings at they Tuxedo, no?" She stroked the top of his head as Muldoon turned his head to regard her dully. He shook his head, coloring slightly.

"It aint like that," he said at last.

"Even worse, then," she smiled back, still stroking his hand. "Even worse, cause if you just got they pussy blues, you maybe can get some elp, no? There is always ways to get in er pussy—I know some—." She stopped short as Muldoon pulled his hand from between those long, limber fingers that knew their ways so well about his body, where to touch, where to barely linger, where to hold fast.

"It aint like that," he repeated hoarsely, wondering whether he should even try to describe how in fact it was. How when he thought of the girl he wasn't thinking below the waist—hers or his, either—but somewhere higher, up around his own chest where a warmth suffused him that reached into his throat and made it thick with unfamiliar feeling. He tried fleetingly to recall what relationship this feeling bore to what he'd had for Lou-Anne but failed. And anyway, how could he hope to articulate any of this to a woman coarsened by dealings with hundreds of men pretty much like himself—and some far worse? He glanced over at her, her handsome, high-cheeked face with its single dark mole just on the prominence of one cheek, her skin almost oriental looking under the tinted light, her eyes narrowed in appraisal. No, no attempt at explanation was possible. Besides, what kind of gentleman would it be who would clumsily confess to one woman what he felt for another? Or to tell her why he had never in his life felt less inclined to have sex?

He was no great lover, he knew, just a john like all the others. *This* was what he knew of sex, this kind of room, this kind of woman, a numbing, blurred succession of them, and in which his lawful wife, Beverly, hardly even figured as an integer. He knew nothing, really, of this other feeling, and so now, answering her comment about the girl and the kind of blues she thought he had he only ran his hands through his bristly black hair and shook his head in apology and admission that here lay a matter too deep for either of them.

She thought otherwise. "Much worse," she repeated, this time with a slow shake of her head. "Pussy they easiest thing to get," she said, still looking steadily at him, though he had returned to his surveillance of the rug between his shoes. "A woman, she can sell it to you for money; she can sell it for a bag of beans, if she need that. You know these things, Fast-Mail.

"But if what you want is something more, that is way up there—*way* up there—and for that you don pay. For that there is no pay you can give." She took his hand once again, turning its palm up in hers, tracing its horizontal lines, its vertical ones, the long, livid white scar of the old knife wound. He himself now looked down at it in a kind of wonderment. Once, back at St. Alphonsus, he'd seen a map of the state's watercourses, the creeks falling into the rivers—the Red, the Calcasieu, the Tensas—and then the big river, pulsing into the warm wash of the Gulf and lost there.

"What do the lines mean?" he asked. "You read palms?"

She shook her head. Had he been anonymous, she might have pretended to occult knowledge, but now she merely shook her head and smiled at him. "No," she said through the smile, "Octavia, she work other thins, what you come for, Fast-Mail. What you come for before.

"She read her man, and that man"—she let loose of his hand and tapped it twice—"he don come for me. He got no come for Octavia tonight."

She arose slowly from the bed, turned to look down at him, and held out her own hand, the limber fingers long, steady. "But this still my room, no? Still my bed." He looked at the unwavering hand held in front of his face. "And for these, my andsome man, you still got to pay."

Down in the hum of the kitchen he sat at the corner table, waiting for Bessie Browne to join him for their ritual breakfast, two veteran workers at the fag end of another night in a demanding trade. But Bessie was late, and so he sat there, huddled almost, while the clatter of the cleanup rose around him. He was so unobtrusive by himself that nobody so much as offered him a cup of coffee until Bessie came in, glanced quickly into the corner, then snapped her fingers, the sharp sound cutting through the girls' voices, the clatter of china and glassware tumbled into the sink with its glistening pile of suds. And presently she was across from him, sitting down quickly and replacing a strand of hair, her face bearing a faint sheen about its cheeks and forehead so that he wondered whether her late arrival meant that she herself had been entertaining some particularly favored customer. Then as she continued to make small, tidying gestures, straightening her blouse, pulling the shawl closer about her shoulders, he felt sure of it and turned his head away to find a girl—new, he thought—advancing towards them with a coffee pitcher in one hand and two cups and saucers stacked in the other. She put the cups and saucers down, left the pitcher, and returned with a smaller pitcher of cream.

"Bread or what, ma'am?" she asked, her roughened hands clasped before her.

"Madge, this is Mr. Muldoon," Bessie said. "When you see him in here, you make sure he's got his cup of coffee and whatever else he wants." She nodded in Muldoon's direction. The girl looked at Muldoon fixedly as though trying to memorize his features, then nodded and turned away to other chores. Bessie mumbled something under her breath as she poured the coffee, the smoke from the cups rising around them, joining the sweaty steam from the suds-dancing sink. Muldoon's reserve, painfully acquired after the riot and cutting him off forever from the natural effervescence of his youthful years of triumph, now kept him busy with his coffee and cheroot, his eyes everywhere else than on Bessie who continued making minor adjustments and dabbing at her short, heavy neck with a scented handkerchief. She muttered something again, and this time he got it, a comment on the quality of help available in the District these days. Still, he kept busy with his coffee and cigar, waiting for Bessie to take up her part. Meanwhile, his puzzling failure upstairs sat about him like a cloud, and he thought it possible that when Bessie had finally gotten herself rearranged she would spot it easily.

"Breakfast?" she asked him finally, the handkerchief held between her hands and her elbows propped on the table. He shook his head. The idea of food at this moment was vaguely nauseating, though he could recall many a morning when he'd come down here from Octavia feeling ravenous and as if what Bessie's girls served up—steak with sautéed onions, hot bread, grits—couldn't fill up that empty feeling in his stomach. More often than not, she'd join him, though never heartily: a couple of slices off a baguette from Madame Beguet's down on Decatur, dabbed with Brewster's salted butter, and that was about it. Once, he remembered, she'd had a beignet covered with powdered sugar and had laughed a bit self-consciously afterwards, licking her fingers. "I was a fat girl," she said then by way of explanation. "When I turned twelve I found out you could have a more interesting time if you laid off stuff like this." She nodded to the empty saucer with its remnant white drifts. "I allow myself one or two of these a year. Sometimes, I think it's only so I can remember being fat." And she'd laughed again.

But there would be no nostalgic, memory-inducing beignet this morning for Bessie, nor even a slice of buttered baguette. Like him, she was for some reason too disordered to eat. "Nothing then," she said to the rough-handed girl who had stood waiting for orders. "Just bring us some more coffee." When the girl had turned back Bessie followed her with her eyes.

"Don't believe that one'll make it," she said quietly to Muldoon. "Work doesn't take too much, you know, but even that little seems like it's too much for that one. The few that come down here looking to clear and such, most of em really want to work upstairs where they've heard the money is. But truth is, the ones that come in that way, well, for some reason more than a few don't seem to have what it takes to work down here, even at such work as this." She made a head gesture at the girl at the sideboard.

Muldoon nodded in acknowledgement. The housekeeping here and in the other houses along Basin couldn't take that much brain work, he thought. But it called for other traits, and maybe this girl lacked them, hadn't yet acquired that toughness that would enable her to shrug off what nightly she would see even in so menial a position: dusting, carrying, clearing, sweeping, and along with the inevitable detritus from the street there would be, under and around the beds, toilets, and wash basins the casual leavings of the sexual transactions—bits of body lint, pubic hairs, wadded handkerchiefs. There would be as well the stiffened sheets to wash with their yellow-gray seminal stains and the washrags and little towels the girls used on the customers' members. There would be the enigmatic blots on the carpets of the rooms and stairs and hallways—blurred hieroglyphics spelling out narratives of lust and endurance, pitiable loneliness, desperate opportunism. And then such a girl would have to trundle down the back stairs to the kitchen with trays of the smeared plates and the glasses numbed lips had slobbered into.

There would be a lot to learn, working in such a place and even more to learn to tolerate, to overlook. And so it was no wonder some weren't up to it, and maybe that might ultimately prove to be the luck of just such a girl as this Madge with her reddish, untidy hair held partially in place with bobby pins, her soiled apron, her hands roughened by harsh detergents. From her looks Muldoon didn't think she'd come to Bessie aspiring to work upstairs, and so maybe failing to satisfy Bessie would be her ticket out of the District with something of her spirit intact. Yet watching now as she came back towards their corner table, bearing the coffeepot as though it contained gunpowder, he found himself wondering whether she had any spirit to be robbed of, whether it had been taken from her some time ago in Indian Village or Edna, those western towns Jimmie Enright had invoked a few nights back, trying to describe where such girls came from.

"Francis," Bessie Browne said when the girl had poured more coffee and they were alone again, "you got trouble. You didn't pick it up here; you brought it in with you." This sounded to him as if she and Octavia had been talking, and he was about to say that when she held up a small, plump hand like a cop directing noontime traffic on Canal. "Come on," she said, "we been knowin each other a long time—too long for that." In the act of shrugging he became instantly aware he was missing something—he'd left his shoulder holster and pistol hanging on the hook of Octavia's door. His eyes widened in surprise and confusion while his inner elbow went quickly to his ribcage like a man flashingly feeling for his wallet and already knowing it wouldn't be there.

"I left something—up there," he began, putting his hands on the table to rise from it.

Again the small, plump hand went up in a staying motion. "I got it," she told him in a reassuring tone. "It's in the office."

"Oh," he said, relieved and embarrassed both. "Thanks."

She shook her head slowly. "Francis, Francis," she said. "Some gunman you are." Her accompanying smile was less mocking than her words, conveying instead her concern. "Better not let those Tuxedo boys catch you goin round buck like that."

"Fewclothes now, too."

"Aint that somethin, though." He nodded, looking at his dead cheroot and deciding it wasn't worth it to go through the charade again of lighting it. He might as well be buck naked in front of Bessie, who could see right through him, straight to that trouble she said he'd picked up elsewhere, like it was a dose, that Octavia had spotted, that was filtering into his daytime dreams, mingling there with ancient dishonor.

"That girl, that's your trouble. And I can tell you she is trouble, too."

"What do you know about her?" he began, but again she cut him off.

"The question is, what do you?"

"I know what I see," he came back, hearing the lameness of the response.

"Come on, Francis," she said flatly. "You been down here long enough to know better than that. This whole thing—" she opened her hands in an expansive movement, one of them still clutching the handkerchief, "is all show. Right? The customers—*they're* the ones supposed to believe what they see, not us. We show em what we want em to believe."

"Well," he said, wagging his head, "yeah. I know, I know." He studied his hands open on the table. "But I've talked to her, you haven't. And I know she's a class girl." He interlaced his fingers, still not looking up. "I just don't want to see her get banged up, is all. Can't a fellow——."

"No he can't," she cut in shortly. "Not down here, and you know it. You can't protect any of these women, Francis." She leaned towards him, her right hand poised to tick off the reasons on her left one. "First thing is most of em were wrong when they came down here. That's for starters. People—the ones always pointing the finger at us—say they're good girls gone astray, that we corrupted them. You know better, or ought to, anyways. *I* know better. There isn't a one of them, hardly, that comes to me and wants to work that hasn't been had: some by boyfriends, but most in the family—brother, father, uncle, whoever." Her voice had risen slightly but less in exasperation than in incredulity, that she should find herself explaining to this veteran the plainest facts of the life they both lived.

She took a breath, looked into her still-full cup. She seemed to be meditating something further. When she raised her eyes to his she said, "You know how I came to be here?" He shook his head. "I was sold."

Now it was his turn to look incredulous.

"Yeah, sold. My parents were from somewhere up in Ohio, near Kentucky. They worked their way southeast. He was a sharecropper. My mother took in washing, and she took on the boss, whoever he happened to be. Had to be that way to get along: there were five of us kids, but one died.

"But I remember her pretty well, and I remember the nights when there'd be another man in the house, and I'd hear them, sweating, tossing. And, oh, I'd know even then what it was, and I knew why, too."

Bessie had always seemed different to him, almost demure in this world where that kind of comportment was so rare it appeared to be a kind of bizarre pose when you met up with it. But her polite and quietly refined manner was so consistent you came to believe in it, that it wasn't a pose, that it was just the way she was. Now here she was giving him another view altogether, a glimpse of the life she'd lived, something of what she'd gone through to become the woman she seemed—unfailingly—to be. He thought back on her appearance a few minutes before when she'd come into the kitchen. Was that the real Bessie, the hustling gal behind the mask of the refined madam? Was Bessie even her real name, he wondered with an inward start?

"I won't say they out-and-out sold me," Bessie continued, speaking of her folks. "I won't put it quite that way. What they did was they kind of leased me to a woman here—name of Gambrell—who ran a boarding house and said she'd see to me, see I learned to keep house. Some money changed hands there, probably not much, but enough to get them going again. And they—my folks—said they'd come back for me when they could." She smiled a small, sad smile. "Well, you know the rest. They never did.

"Pretty soon—I was thirteen, I think—Mrs. G.—that's what I called her—had me going down for a few of the boarders. They were mostly okay fellows. Mrs. G. didn't take in any river riff-raff; a lot of them were drummers. Anyways, at first it was rough; I won't say it wasn't. But you know what? After a while I got to *like* it. A fact.

"And you know how men are: they go for a girl with hot pants, and they'll call for her all night long." She patted her breast lightly and while she was at it took another touch at her hair, as though even in the midst of her life story it still didn't feel quite right. "Mrs. G. knew she had a good thing here," she added.

"I stayed with her fourteen years and took care of her at the end. She left me money, and that's how I got my start.

"Does this make sense to you, Francis? I hope so, anyways, because I'm not telling it to you so you can go home and sleep tight. But suppose you'd met me back then. I was a trim little number, I can tell you. Would you think I was a nice girl and try to save me? Huh?" Her question was sharp as a jab in the chest, and having to make some sort of response, he shrugged his shoulders.

"For God sake, man!" she exclaimed. "I'm telling you I got so I *liked* my work, and I don't mind saying I was good at it, too: I gave those fellows their money's worth. But if you'd met up with me back then and tried to save me from getting all 'banged up,' why, I'd have laughed in your face—if I didn't spit in it."

She waved the hesitant Madge forward with the coffeepot. "You can't save a whore, Francis. Truth is, a good two-thirds of em don't want to be saved, and the other third don't know how to be saved and can't learn—too late for em." He started to say something but she was still directing the traffic of this conversation, holding up that little hand. "I know, I know, you're going to tell me she isn't turning tricks, and maybe she isn't. But if she isn't yet—*if*—she soon will be. Why else do you think she's down there, anyways, if not to get into that part of it? I haven't seen her myself, but I hear she's a looker, and for a girl like that there's some good money to be made. She sure as hell isn't at the Tuxedo to further her singing career. I hear she's no good."

"You don't know her like I do," he came back stubbornly. "She's no whore, that I can tell you. She's a singer, maybe not the best, but good enough to have sung in other spots. She knows the ropes, too—some of em, anyways." His face reddened in embarrassment at having to defend her character as well as his own assessment of it. There was so much more to her, he felt, than he could ever hope to convey, even to Bessie, who he thought was probably a lot smarter and more sympathetic than Octavia.

"So you know her, do you?" Bessie's tone had an edge to it now. He said he did, somewhat. "Well then, what does she tell you about Tom Anderson? Everybody knows you're a go-between. Doesn't that make you wonder just a little, Francis?"

"They're friends—from some time ago, I guess. She's some kind of distant relation through her mother's people back in Galveston." Bessie said nothing to this, only waited. "You don't think I opened them letters?" he asked, suddenly aghast at what might be an oblique suspicion of hers.

She shook her head. "No. That wouldn't be like you, Francis." She appeared to be considering which tack to take here, and there was a moment when the noises of the kitchen rushed between them. "Friends," she said then, repeating his characterization neutrally enough. "Well, he's got lots of those, that's sure. Friendliest man you'd ever want to meet. Did I ever tell you he owned a part of this?" She tapped the tabletop.

"I guess I musta heard that."

"Well, he did. I bought a share from him and Mochez with the money Mrs. G. left me. Then after a while Mochez sold his share to me, so then it was me and Tom Anderson. But I wanted my own place: if you don't have to answer to anybody, that's best. Avoids complications. Then you don't—." She didn't finish her observation because just then the back door was flung wide and they saw, against the black sheet of what wasn't yet dawn, the whiteness of the kitchen's steam reliefed against it as

Brewster the milkman barged in with his wire cases in either hand, adding his clanking to the general noise, making his hearty, perfunctory, mindlessly unvarying remarks about bringing nothing but the best for Bessie. His ankle-length tan slicker glistened and dripped in his quick errand: it was raining again. Then he was gone, slamming the door behind him in the way that Bessie had long ago given up asking him not to do.

"Anyways, he sold to me," she continued. "I think he liked me some—saw I had a head for business. His terms were hard, but I have to admit they were fair. Now, like I say, I'm mighty glad it's all mine, because I wouldn't want to have to answer to Tom Anderson, especially these days. What about you, Francis? In case anything should happen, you have anything of your own put by?"

He thought of his suits and shoes, darkly ranked in the closet of the Washington Street cottage; of his tidy bank balance, those shares he had in the Record Refinery; of his frugal, almost monkish style of living.

"Yeah, I got some put by," he said. "Course it wouldn't take me that far, I don't suppose, if it come to that."

She raised her penciled eyebrows. "Might come to that," she said at last. "Might just."

"We both know things're changing down here, right? You *do* see that, right, Francis?" There was something so neutral to her tone it was almost cold, and he looked across at his familiar breakfast partner to find a lone businesswoman, calculating what she might have to do if the balance of power in the District should shift and who was advising him to do some forecasting himself.

"Oh, I see it, all right," he said, a bit defensively. "Who don't? But what's it mean, anyways? What's it add up to, tell me that."

"I was going to ask you that," she smiled briefly. Then her face once again assumed its slightly grave, unreadable composure. "You're out and about a lot more than I am. I hardly ever get out of this place." Privately, though, she thought she was in a better position to assess the drift of events than he was, despite the wide range of his nightly movements: in the District there was probably no one who was more thoroughly Tom Anderson's man than Francis Muldoon, except possibly Billy Brundy or that Enright fellow. Muldoon was so far inside the Anderson empire he couldn't see it from the outside. Or maybe he didn't want to.

She placed her small hands palms down on either side of her coffee cup, as if playing cards. "Well, we know who the new players are in town," she said. "At least, we know what they call themselves. We know now they have some money, but we don't know how much. And we don't know, either, what they plan to do. I mean, are they gonna stop at Fewclothes, or do they want the whole shebang? If they do—if they want it all—what I say to you, Francis, is you need to keep track of that pistol, that and watch your back."

"I never claimed I was a gunman," he said. "Never. Not even when I worked for Mente. I never hit one of them bandits. I *ran* after em."

"I know that, Francis. I know you never claimed that. But what I'm saying is if real trouble starts like what went on with the Parkers' steerers and those niggers on South Rampart, then you'll have to *act* like a gunman, because the Parkers will sure enough take you for one. To them, you'll just be one of Tom Anderson's men and fair game. Now, it might not come to that—I hope it doesn't. Because if it does, City Hall will come down on all of us like a wagonload of bricks and close us all up.

"Anderson's a smart man, and he knows what would happen if there was a sure-enough war. But it might not be up to him, you know? They might force his hand, make him go to war. They look kind of reckless to me, and they wouldn't be the first ones to underestimate him with those easygoing ways of his—smile, soft voice, soft hands, all that. But you don't build what he has by being soft. He can play plenty rough when he has to, and, like I say, they might make him play that way."

Muldoon nodded slowly. He had lately come to suspect more than he had wanted about how rough his boss could play. When Tom Anderson had rescued him from the dump heap of disgrace he'd made it clear he wasn't hiring him to be one of his strong-armed men. There were already plenty of such fellows on the payroll, Anderson had said with a genial smile. Muldoon would have other kinds of duties, gentler, more mannerly, the sort that called for a suit and tie, not a red flannel undershirt and cloth cap. But now it wasn't that simple— maybe it never had been—and it wasn't just men like Alto North, the Pickett brothers, and Buster Daley who did the dirty work. Everybody, it seemed, got their hands dirty down here, including the woman sitting across from him who had done business with Tom Anderson, whose house profited by its proximity to the Annex, and who would be put out of business if Tom Anderson went down in a war between rival outfits. Scant weeks ago it seemed to him that he understood pretty accurately the demands and hazards of his job and was satisfied these were substantially outweighed by its rewards: the cottage he shared with his sister, his bank balance and stock shares, and suits finer than anyone else in his old neighborhood. Now, though, when he totted the thing up, the demands appeared to outweigh the old rewards, and Bessie Browne had just raised for him the possibility that he might be called upon to use his pistol in the service of his boss and redeemer. The hoary thing in his past that had so long stalked him in his sleep was suddenly vividly present in this waking moment, and his neck felt wet and wobbly in his collar.

"Well, anyways," he brought out at last, "this aint Tombstone City yet, and if I have to, I reckon I can shoot that thing good enough."

"Francis," Bessie Browne came back in a quiet tone that said she'd spoken her piece, "I'm glad to hear that. I really am."

Toodloo Chapter leaned his heavy-boned arms on the bar at the Tuxedo and took another mighty suck at his beer. He glanced down at his hand, dipped his other hand into his mug, and rubbed out a long smear of blood on his left thumb and forefinger. Any minute now she'd be finished out in the garden and would be coming along the passageway into the weltering noise of the bar, moving with that graceful side-to-side gait he'd come to know and appreciate, where her bottom half did all the moving while the top stayed steady somehow and she looked at you with those unblinking eyes. And he'd be waiting for her. Waiting because she'd asked him to. His bull neck bulged and reddened against his flannel collar as he thought of it, and not only because she was so mysterious, so seductive yet unreachable, but because cousin Harry had been trying to get in her pants for weeks now and hadn't. And here she'd come up to him offstage in the beer garden and whispered slowly to him, "Why don't you wait up for me at the bar? I'm almost finished back here."

What had happened was that he'd gotten a report of some roughnecks in the beer garden giving her an especially hard time and had gone to the end of the passageway to see what was up. They were there, all right, a quartet of screwmen up from the docks, all of them skunked and three of them having trouble holding their heads up. The fourth was a guy he recognized from other nights here, a stocky, red-thatched man, his nose bulbous and blotched with some disfiguring disease. He'd had some trouble with Red before. It hadn't come to blows, but they knew each other the way street dogs did whose daily beats overlapped. Tonight looked like it was going to be different: Red was ugly drunk, and his flung remarks were like incendiary bombs exploding over Adele as she and Johnnie Staultz, the mandolin player, tried to perform through shouts of "cunt," and "pussy," and offers of five dollars for a fuck—as though these insults were all in a night's work, were part of the performer's life, like the smoke clouds from the cigars, pipes, and cigarettes; the spilled pitchers of beer; or the men, singly and in small huddles, who lurched up in the middle of a number and clumped out, their nailed, muddy boots registering gritty sounds of disapproval.

Toodloo watched this for three or four minutes. Red's companions appeared too drunk to be much of a problem, but just in case he went back to the bar and told Chance Henderson to bring his club back to the lookout station at the entrance to the garden. "Hend," he said then, "see that there table, the one with the red hair and loud mouth?"

"Yeah," Chance Henderson said after a moment's inspection, "that's Red Armbruster. Can be a mean customer. Me and him went around and around one time—I think it was just after you opened here."

"Okay. I'll handle Red. Them others are too drunk to be any trouble, but what I want is you to take care of my ass while I see to Red."

Chance Henderson fingered the club, an eighteen-inch billet well-oiled by the kind of handling that had made him useful to the Parkers up in Brooklyn. He spun it in his hands, his eyes on the table. "Don't worry none about them," he said softly, nodding at the three screwmen who only now and then jerked their sodden heads upward when Red let go with another bomb: "Oh, come on, babe! Give it to me, an ah'll sho nuff give it to you where you like it!"

"All the rest of em look okay to me," Chance Henderson said, sweeping his eyes over the crowd, the men sprawled on their seats, a few whores clinging to their dark-sleeved arms, most of the men engaged in drink or muttered conversation and without more than passing interest in the singer and still less in Red who kept hurling his bombs. Toodloo grunted, a guttural noise seeming to arise from some region lower than his belly, as if from his bowels, like an old lion coughing. Then he was in motion, big-bodied, his hands hanging far below his shirt cuffs, taking a route through the tables that brought him up behind Red and his slumping comrades, grabbing Red's hair with both hands, jerking his head back, then slamming it down on the table with a sound that was like a man striking a bass drum with his boot—hollow, resonant, deep, unforgiving. The victim himself made no sound, either at the moment of stunning impact or when Toodloo jerked him off his chair and swiftly hauled him through the tables and out to a back gate that he unlatched, flinging the body into the alleyway.

"*Jesus!* Toodloo!" Chance Henderson breathed when Toodloo had turned around to see whether there'd been any trouble with Red's comrades. Chance Henderson was thinking of the very bad look on the victim's face as Toodloo dragged him away. There might have been blood coming from Red's eyes, never a good sign, he knew. So now he repeated it, "*Jesus!*"

"*What?*" Toodloo snarled, turning on him, his small eyes flashing and snapping between their heavily creased lids. He'd smelled blood, even had a long smear of it along the top of one hand, and Chance Henderson knew the big man was doubly dangerous in these circumstances. So the two Jesuses were all he ventured. In a minute or two, after Toodloo had left, he'd have someone else see what was out there in the alley. Now he merely shook his head, watching the others at Red's table who didn't appear to have noticed that Red had gone off somewhere. Their whole concentration was in keeping their heads off the table, their eyes blindly swinging in the general direction of the little stage where the singer had paused between numbers to whisper something in the passing Toodloo's ear and to place a hand, briefly, deftly on his back as he moved into the stark single-lighted passageway.

Which was why he now waited in the bar, tense, hunched over his mug, surrounded by gabbling customers whose whiskered jaws flapped in high, hard exchanges, in equally hard laughter, while the cabaret girls worked the booths, some of them with their quick hands probing the men's sweaty flies while with their backs they tried to shield this aspect of their trade. Toodloo paid them no mind: it hadn't taken him many days down here with his cousins to see the cabaret girls for the poor pickings they were. When he wanted a flop he went to Emma Johnson's, where they knew a number of tricks he'd never been exposed to up in Brooklyn's Williamsburg section.

Along with his younger brother, Toodlum, he'd been raised up there with Harry and Charley, whose last name then was Perkosky, in that neighborhood where the shadows of the Williamsburg Bridge lay athwart the jammed, clogged streets— streets hardly more than lanes between tenements whose vertical lines imposed virtually the only regularity on the haphazard, helter-skelter life eked out by the immigrant populace. On every street corner metal barrels belched poisonous flames and smoke, winter and summer; hogsheads were high-heaped with refuse or saleable food or rags; carts and draft horses and then, later, the first primitive trucks stood at impassable angles while in between and all around them boiled peddlers, rag pickers, tradesmen, mothers trailing their ragamuffin children, policemen, and purse-snatchers. And over all this lay the somber shadows of the bridge, spidery where its suspension cables caught the changing light, heavy and imprisoning where its massive superstructure fell on the waterfront streets.

The bridge shaped the four cousins in ways they could scarcely comprehend except randomly, like the time they were playing in its barred shadows on a summer's afternoon, and looking at the other three Toodlum had laughed and shouted, "You're all zebras! You're all fuckin zebras!" Toodloo had never crossed it into Manhattan. But Toodlum once did, and, wandering into the wrong East Side neighborhood had returned to Williamsburg with a badly bleeding left ear—it was a rock, delivered at fairly close range, he reported—and pronounced the fabled island a lump of shit, as far as he was concerned. His Manhattan souvenir was a permanent deafness in the wounded ear. Still, he wanted them all to go back there in style someday and told them they would, too. In the meantime, they would have to make their own breaks; they could not expect any from their own hand-to-mouth parents or from anyone else they knew of.

When Toodloo had just turned thirteen and Toodlum was twelve they were hawking newspapers mornings and evenings and four days a week working in a fish stall: scraping scales; cutting off fins, tails, heads; digging their fingers into intestines; sweeping; pushing the slush of melted ice into the gutter. Across the narrow street they marked the comings and goings of an old Jewish peddler whose horse rang its weary shoes on the cobbles while from his high seat the iron-bearded driver cried his wares, his needs to the bricks and blackened metal balconies of all of Brooklyn. They'd heard a rumor the old man was rich, which they believed because he was a Jew and because he betrayed no least trace of wealth, living in what appeared to them to be a conspicuous poverty: stabling his horse directly behind his building; entering his dungeon-like door across from the fish stall at evening, silent and solitary as a condemned man. There wasn't so much as a candle gleam from those dark rooms or the glimmer of a cook stove, so that the boys were left to imagine the old man went to sleep in a supperless darkness, clutching bundles of ragged bills to his famished chest.

When they'd heard the rumor Toodlum had thought of robbing the old man, but after weeks of watching for some least telltale sign of treasure buried in those dark rooms, they were about to dismiss the story when on an end-of-the-month Friday Toodlum saw the old man return home three hours early. Passing his brother outside the stall he muttered that something was up. He was certain of it minutes later, when he spotted the ochre flare of an oil lamp from the rooms. Still later the first of the tenement's lodgers trudged home and descended the three steps to the old man's rooms as though going to judgment. At his knock the door opened to the stingy gleam of the lamp and then closed again after the lodger climbed the steps and went to his room. When Toodlum saw the same routine repeated twice more, he gripped his brother's elbow tightly. "There!" he said in a low, tense whisper. "We was right!" Toodloo merely shrugged; sometimes it was hard for him to follow his younger brother's enthusiasms. He'd all but forgotten the old Jew. "He *owns* the fucker!" Toodlum spat out, pushing his broom but glaring across the street. "They're payin him rent money!"

Harry Perkosky thought of his younger cousin as a kind of genius, possessed of a rare combination of daring, cunning, and physical dexterity. The kid had already made several purse and parcel snatchings in broad daylight and had also found a way into a clothier's apartment. He'd let the other three in and they'd made off with a rug that brought them an extraordinary thirty dollars from a fence. Now when Toodlum brought the Perkoskys the idea of using the stable behind the old man's tenement as a way into his rooms, Harry felt his assessment of the kid once again confirmed. "A regular fuckin criminal genius!" he exclaimed to Charley. "A fuckin genius! He's gonna make us rich!"

Toodlum's scheme called for him to get part-time work at the stable behind the tenement, mucking out stalls, feeding and watering the horses, and all the while assessing what he coolly told the others were the "obstacles." When he'd satisfied himself that the job could be done, they'd wait for the day the rent was due, break in, beat up the old man, and make off with what Toodlum was certain was a huge store of cash. "These old fuckers don't trust no banks," he said. "They keep it all in mattresses or grips or under the floor or somethin like that. We have Charley here watchin from across the way, and when we sees the last guy—Angelo, that wop what runs the fruit stand off Eighth and is *always* the last one home—pay up, then's when we make our move. The old fucker won't have time to stash it, and we'll beat the shit outta him and take it. Must be thousands there, but even if we can't find it all, we'll make off with plenty for our trouble. And if we're real lucky, if we hit it just right, he might have his hiding hole or whatever opened to put the rent money in, which, if he does, we get the whole of it." He grinned at the others. "I always said we'd go back over the bridge in style someday, and if things break like I figure, we'll do that real soon." Toodlum had paused, feeling his lumpy left ear gingerly. "There's a score I'd like to settle over there..."

The chief of the obstacles to the job was that the only entrance from the stable to the peddler's rooms was a heavily boarded window seven feet above a corral in which two dispirited horses stood hock-high in ancient manure. No one ever went in there except the new kid who filled the water trough and dumped feed into the small corner basket from which the horses nibbled: they had once belonged to the owner's father who had made his son promise to care for them after his death. So they waited for their own deaths and barely glanced at the little kid who brought them food and water.

At noontime the owner went down the street for his dinner, leaving his hunchbacked kinsman in charge, an occasion that Howard, known as Hump, improved twice weekly by going in the opposite direction to visit a whore who was impervious to his disfigurement. That was when Toodlum brought a ladder into the corral from the stable's moldy recesses and carefully loosened the window's heavy boards, widening the nail holes with his penknife until the nails themselves slid smoothly, easily in and out at the mere touch of a hammer's claw. By the time Hump returned, scant minutes before the boss, the kid was industriously at work, mucking out the stalls and whistling tunelessly. "I can have those boards off and be inside in less than a minute," he told the others. "He'll never know what hit him."

The appointed night came and with it Charley Perkosky's signal when he saw Angelo the fruit vendor deliver his rent and enter the building. Toodloo, by far the biggest and maybe the least bothered by considerations, moved quickly out of the alley across from the stable and was upon Hump before the man ever heard him. At the last, too-late second, the man had sensed something and half-turned to catch Toodloo's stunning blow with a blackjack fashioned from horsehide and buckshot. Hump sagged sideways, one hand flung instinctively out to catch himself, but Toodloo cracked him again before he hit the floor, then dragged the body into a stall and summoned the others.

They ran with the ladder, spooking the nags in the corral. Toodlum prized off the boards, flung them aside, and then vaulted into inky blackness. He knew as soon as his feet hit the floor that something was wrong: the peddler's light that Charley saw had been extinguished. It was his young mind's next-to-last perception, because then he heard the measured, metallic back-click of a heavy pistol's hammer and the final click as the invisible cylinder revolved upward into its appointed slot. Then he knew he was going to die, which he instantly did, the ball from the peddler's pistol tearing into his deaf ear and angling out below the base of his skull, bearing along with it brain matter in a spray of blood.

In the numbed aftermath the survivors never understood how the peddler had outsmarted them, getting no further in their ruminations than Harry Perkosky's blunt-edged guess that all the while they'd been marking him, the peddler had had them in his sights, too, and had even discovered Toodlum's work on the window boards. He'd been expecting them on rent day, Harry guessed—either that or the old bastard had been expecting them every night for a month and had lain there in the dark with his horse pistol cocked.

Toodloo wanted to ambush the old kike and compulsively repeated this for months. He'd been attached to his brother and missed his guidance and his flair. Life was duller somehow; nothing much happened now that Toodlum was gone, he said. Finally, Harry had enough of this, saying savagely to Toodloo one evening, "Shut up about that, ya dumb cluck! If that old kike was smart enough to kill Toodlum, he'd plug *you* before ya knew what hit ya!" And Toodloo had shut up then, though harboring a grudge about the insult. As for Harry, he too missed the "regular fuckin criminal genius," and had to admit to himself that life was indeed less exciting with Toodlum gone. And he was still missing Toodlum in the years of his steady progress through the Brooklyn underworld, feeling certain he would be rising faster with Toodlum's help and imagination. "They got the wrong guy," Harry would say to Charley, now and then. "They shoulda plugged old Toodloo, cept if they'd a hit him where they hit Toodlum, it wouldn't a hurt him none."

That one got back to Toodloo as well, who bore it as well as he could. And he had to admit that down here in New Orleans he was doing a damn sight better than he would be on his own back in Brooklyn: the pay was good and the fucking was terrific. Some of the things these whores down here knew and would let you do to them—well, there wasn't anything like it back home. And now, too, there was this dame they'd all been circling around for weeks and who had Harry creaming his shorts. But Harry hadn't been able to get anywhere with her, and now he himself had—or was about to.

"Aw, for Christ sake, Harry," Charley had said one afternoon when Harry was talking about what he was going to do to her when the moment was just right. "Aw, for Christ sake! You got that cunt on the brain—it's like she give you the syph without you even gettin in her. Pretty soon, you're gonna give it to the rest of us. Get it over with, fer Christ sake: grab her when she comes in, take her back there to the office, and fuck her! It'll be a real relief to the rest of us, I can tell ya that. You want me to hold her down while you do it? I got no problem with that. Christ! We did that to Jackie Gamble up on top of Lester's garage when we was eleven, for Christ sake!"

But Harry was thinking with a grim and settled satisfaction of the double fucking he had in mind: to fuck the snotty look off the girl's face while at the same time giving old Tom Anderson himself a good ass-reaming, because since his accidental discovery of Anderson's note, he was certain the girl was his mistress. But the conditions had to be right, and they weren't yet.

"I don't want to do that strong-arm stuff, if I don't have to," Harry smiled through bared teeth. "That's for you and Toodloo, with them whores that got holes big around as a baseball bat. This one's got class all over her, and probably tight as a ten-year-old." He sneered at Charley and Toodloo. "Besides, if I did that, we'd have to kill her before she went to the cops, and right now I don't want to do that. There's too much satisfaction I'll get when the time's just right.

"No, the way it's got to be with her is she's got to want it, y'know? Really *want* it." His long-slabbed face cracked into its vulpine grin, his nose almost touching the snarling curl of his upper lip. He wondered for a moment which part of his plan would give him the greater satisfaction, the fucking of the girl or the mortal insult that would be to Tom Anderson, and decided he didn't have to choose. Both would be equally delicious. The former would in fact signal his conquest of Anderson's territory. There'd be nothing left for the old duffer to do but to crawl off to some hole in the sticks and live on lard. "If I wait," he said to his kinsman, "if I'm patient and choose the right time, when she's got so she wants it, I'll give it to her where she aint had nothin except maybe bum wad." He spat on the floor of the raw, dim-lit room they used as an office and where some weeks ago he'd made a grab for the girl, had gotten one hand on her tit, and felt to his savage satisfaction that there was fully as much there as he'd imagined. But then she'd ripped herself out of his grasp somehow, and bolted the room—and into the arms of that fool gimp that worked for Tom Anderson, which then had sent the gimp to mooning about the girl at The Frenchman's and carrying Tom Anderson's messages to her. What, Harry wondered, could the gimp possibly have thought was in those notes he so dutifully delivered?

Toodloo knew nothing of the notes. What he did know was that the girl had never whispered in Harry's ear, asking him to meet her in the bar, and as he turned his heavy head in the direction of the passageway he saw her. He wasn't sure what Harry had meant when he said she had class all over her, but watching her move, he thought that must be what it was. She seemed untouched by the drinkers, the drunks, the grabbers and gropers, the gamblers taking a stretch from some table down the street where the oil lamp still smoked in the center of the scarred table and its cluster of emptied glasses; the cabaret girls with their wet pantaloons; the newcomer johns, just off the line with their telltale feathers waving jauntily from hatbands or buttonholes. She seemed utterly impervious to any of this, her eyes steadily on him and then her hand touching his elbow so lightly and briefly he had to wonder whether it had actually happened or he'd only imagined it.

But it had, because now she leaned into him and said breathily, "This place is so awfully noisy, and I want to be able to thank you for what you did back there. I can hardly do that here." He looked down into her steady gray eyes, couldn't think what to say, and so simply gestured with his head back in the direction of the passageway from which she'd just come. He didn't wait for a response but grabbed her elbow and shouldered back through the crowd, making for the raw office he knew would be empty. Harry and Charley both were down at Fewclothes with the electrical people who hadn't thus far been able to produce a satisfactory brilliance in the unfinished rooms. The brothers were absolutely determined Fewclothes must out-dazzle the Annex.

"I don't want to go in there," she said as he put his hand on the office's doorknob. "That place gives me the fantods—it doesn't have any windows." He gawked at her, his face lined and coarsened by experience and weather so that it was already deeply grooved, though he was just over thirty.

"Whatever you say," he muttered, drawing her farther along the passageway towards the entrance to the dance hall, mostly empty now that the band was taking one of the two ten-minute breaks they were allowed per night. There was a tiny room, almost a cell, off the bandstand where King Keppard and his boys gathered to toss down drinks. It had a pallet rolled up against the wall and one chair. The only light came from the hall, and in it Keppard and the others were passing around a bottle, flecks and moving glints of yellow light catching their arms, shoulders, backs, but most of their figures in dark shadow.

"Gimme another whacka that suckah, man," growled Keppard, glancing but briefly at the big white man who now blocked most of what light got in there. Keppard grabbed the bottle, tossed his head back, and took an enormous hit of the whiskey. When he pulled the bottle down at last he laughed and coughed all at once, then turned his oriental eyes on Toodloo, wiping his mouth with his free hand. "Whatcha want in here, white man?" He took out his pocket watch and glanced at it with a showy frown. "Aint time to hit yet." Keppard took his orders from Harry and Charley, not from this goon he'd never spoken a word to before. "This is our place to hang out, man. Harry, he give it to us."

Toodloo was in no mood for backtalk from a nigger. Keppard was big, a strong-looking guy, and with liquor in him might well fight back if Toodloo should grab hold of him and attempt to shove him out. The others waited to see what their leader would do. Toodloo felt the girl there just behind him and quelled his instinct to tangle with the cornetist. Later, maybe, he might have a better opportunity to even this score. So now, his Adam's apple bobbed, his eyes widened and narrowed, and all he said was, "Yeah, yeah. Right. It's your place. But right now, see, I need it. You guys can take an extra few minutes if you'll move it on out there—" he gestured with his head towards the hall. "I'll make it up to ya at closing, give ya a little sweetener." He patted his pocket.

"Let's take it, King," the clarinet player said, rubbing his mouth. "My chops busted, man."

"Okay, boss," Keppard said with a shrug of his heavy shoulders. He looked past Toodloo to the girl standing behind him. "Jack, bring the jug." Toodloo stepped aside, the girl close to him, and the men filed past, moving to a corner of the bandstand where they turned their backs on the hall and began to pass the bottle again, its barrel glinting against the high ceiling's few lights.

"Please don't pull that door to," the girl said when she and Toodloo had entered the little room and he'd half-turned as if that was what he meant to do. "I can't stand closed spaces." Her chest was heaving as she said this, and he stared frankly at it, noting its deep movement. Well, hell, he thought, Harry said this one had class, and maybe this is part of what that means.

"Why—" he began, but she checked him by reaching forward and putting her light fingers on his lips.

"Because," she said. She took her fingers quickly away. "I wonder whether you can understand how hard it is for a singer to concentrate when there's a man like *that*—" she allowed a look of disgust to travel swiftly across her face, "right in front of you." She shook her head. "Well, I guess you can, because you surely took the situation—I mean, you got him out of there in a hurry, and I—I—wanted to thank you, truly, for doing that." She smiled in so lingering a fashion that Toodloo thought he had never in his life been smiled upon with such steady and genuine radiance. He felt himself invaded by a feeling unknown to him, a sort of warmth that both softened him and hardened him at the same instant, and brought to mind some vague longing impossible to identify.

"Nuthin," is what he finally said. "He's nuthin. Just another of them rats from the sewer. I could handle three of em at a time, if I had to." He checked himself with another obscure impulse. "Unless they had gats, maybe."

She raised her heavy eyebrows in question. "Gats?"

"Gats. Guns, pistols, like."

"Oh, I see."

"But down here them types mostly don't. Razors, maybe, or knives. Up north—Brooklyn, Hackensack, like that—they might." He shrugged. "It was nuthin to take care a him." He heard a burst of laughter from just beyond the doorway: the Keppard bunch, evidently fully enjoying the longer break he'd granted them. For the second time in the last few minutes he was glad his cousins were over at Fewclothes, watching the electrical man turn the lights on and off.

"Well," she said then, "that's really what I wanted to say to you. I don't mean to keep you from your work." With this she straightened as if to leave, their little moment together over with.

"Ah," he said, "I do pretty much what I like, long's things run regular. Course you get mugs like that, an then you gotta take care of business. I don't have to be nowheres special just now."

Again, she gave him that radiant expression and leaned back against the splintery yellow boards, clasping her hands in front of her as she did when singing. "I see a good deal of your relatives," she said after a pause. "They're your cousins, right?" He nodded. "Well, as I say, I see a good deal of them in here, but I don't see that much of you, that is—" she laughed shortly—"I mean, I *see* you, of course, but we never talk."

"I aint much a one for that, I guess."

She saw him mostly in outline, the light behind him and his frame looking huge, solid, immovable, as if somehow a barge had been hauled up into the hall. His bitter, beery breath blasted into her face, completely filling the air of the tawdry stall where the Negro men drank and spat. "But I *can* talk," he went on with a different tone. When he leaned slightly sideways on these words she could see a portion of his face twist into a smile as bitter as his breath. "I can talk, and I can understand, too, what they got in mind, even if they don't think I do." He moved towards her, and she braced herself. But he only leaned against the wall next to her. Beneath the beer she smelled a cheap toilet water and hair oil instead of the unmediated and bestial body odor so pervasive in the rooms of the Tuxedo.

"Of course, they never tell any of us anything," she said, glancing over at him, then out into the hall where she could see dancers standing about, looking into the corner where King Keppard and his boys stood at their ease, talking more loudly now, the last of the bottle going around and Keppard doing what she knew was a mock field hand's delivery: "White man, he say 'git!' and we git. But he don't say 'hit,' so we aint gonna hit." They all chuckled, the clarinet player's chuckle traveling up into a falsetto. She thought Toodloo must have heard the joke, too, and seen the dancers waiting for Keppard to hit: to stomp his fancy black shoe with its high cork sole and heel and play the blues or the latest popular number. She thought Toodloo was about to go out there and get them started and so hastened to complete her thought. "We're just workers in here—the staff, I mean: the singers, the musicians, and so forth. So, naturally, they wouldn't tell us anything about what's going on. About the new place they're opening up. Fewclothes, isn't it? But people say, we're all going to move over there once they get it finished.

"But they must tell you things, since you're family. Otherwise, how could you help them?" She allowed herself a girlish giggle that carried a nervous note right in the middle of it. But he seemed not to notice, and it was hard to tell whether he was even listening to her words. She hurried on. "Another thing everybody says—here, down at The Frenchman's—is that whatever your cousins have in mind, Tom Anderson isn't the man to stand by and let them take all his trade away."

At last he made a response. "They say that, eh?"

She nodded. "They do."

"Well, they don't know Harry. They don't know Charley. And they don't know Gyp, that's for sure." His square, broad hands made a short, emphatic chopping gesture in the air. There was a man up in Brooklyn, he told her now, who made the mistake of not taking Harry and Charley seriously, a Guinea guy named Roderigo who paraded around his turf in a white hat and a long, black cape that had ivory buttons down both sides of its front. Roderigo was a pimp and a loans guy, he told her, "A very big deal in them days, and I aint ashamed to say I shined his shoes a time or two myself, when I was a kid." But what was important, he wanted the girl to understand, was that this is how this bunch did business. "Quick, like," he said, repeating again that decisive, chopping movement with both hands. "These guys, they don't fuck around. Harry and Charley, they get a plan, they *move* it, I'll tell ya. Old Roderigo, they fixed his ass, all right." He made a sardonic grimace. "Big man in his day, like this here Anderson, but he made a mistake. He figured them for punks. I'll tell ya, Harry and Charley wasn't punks even when they was punks, ya know? These old guys, they move too slow." He stared down at her as if wondering whether he'd made his meaning clear and seemed about to add something by way of emphasis but then changed his mind.

"I gotta get those jigs goin," he said, stepping to the doorway.

"And I have to get back to the garden myself," she said. "I'm about to be late."

"No!" he said forcefully, turning back and blocking the door. "You wait here. I got somethin ta tell ya."

He went into the hall and said something to Keppard she couldn't hear. But then she heard Keppard reminding the white man he'd promised them a little sweetener at the end of the night.

"Yeah, yeah, yeah," Toodloo tossed off. "You come ta me then, you'll get it, like I say." Then he was back inside the stall where she waited. He himself seemed to be listening for something, his head turned slightly to one side, his hands tensed and held away from his sides. From the hall there came the heavy, emphatic sound of a foot stomping twice, and then Keppard and his bunch jumped into a fast number she'd heard many times before but whose title she'd never learned. They all sounded pretty much the same to her. When the band's brassy blare completely filled the hall and some of the dancers had begun to step to the raggy rhythm, Toodloo turned towards her and grabbed her arm so roughly she almost cried out.

"Listen!" he said under the sound of the band, his face almost touching the top of her head. "Listen, good! This bunch moves quick. They aint gonna play around an wait on Anderson. Saturday night, Sunday morning, you don't come *near* here, understand? You make a phone call to here. You tell em yer sick, you got mumps, measles, somethin. You just stay the hell away from here cause it aint gonna be safe anywhere inside here, understand me?" She nodded, looking up, holding her breath. "Anywheres in here, even back there." He gestured with his thumb towards the beer garden. "An fer Chrissake, don't say nothin to nobody about what I been tellin ya. Otherwise, we'll both be dead for Easter." He pulled her into him with a sudden, resistless force, and the hand that had held her arm now grabbed her head, forcing it back, while the other hand completely enveloped her breast. He kissed her hard, his rough-shaven muzzle rasping across her mouth like a hacksaw. She looked into his eyes that even in the shadowed stall seemed to take on a feral glow. He pumped her breast twice, and then he was gone.

She'd taken one hell of a chance for him. It made his heart thump and his member stir in his shorts, thinking about what she'd dared just now, slipping out the back of the Tuxedo to make a phone call from Anstedt's Saloon. "Oh, my darling girl," he'd said with almost a sob after she'd quickly given her report. "Oh, my darling girl!" Then he told her to ring off quick.

Now he stood in the dead center of his spacious office, his maimed hand stroking his moustache quickly, his eyes fixed and unseeing on a patch of the flowered carpet Gertrude had picked out for him. He was having trouble forcing from his orderly mind the image of that ape—Torkum or Tookey, some crazy name the man went by—running his great, simian paws over Cammie's flawless body, grabbing off great chunks of its tenderest parts as if they were bananas on a tree. The ape would have to pay and quickly, before he could spew his vile story into the streets of the District.

He tried to swing his thoughts to the import of the information she had risked everything to give him: that something really big was going to happen Saturday night or Easter morning at the Tuxedo. But for the moment all he could focus on were those hateful hands moving over the soft-skinned terrain he'd known since even before its first signs of ripening, that he believed belonged to him alone, even though he well knew other men had touched it—the fellow in Galveston.... But they hadn't really possessed it, surely had never known it in its every curve and declivity, its tiny, endearing nicks, lines, stipples, modulations of coloring. Looking up out of this reverent contemplation of her body, he saw himself reflected, darkly, in the window, both hands to his face, his torso hunched. It was a shocking, pitiable pose he found himself in, and he instantly dropped his hands and straightened up, though he continued to stare at the negative apparition in the night-filled pane.

He'd seen men run out of their wits for women, plenty of them down here. George Foucault came quickly to mind. Men who had debased themselves for what some woman—*the* woman—had between her legs. The existence and import of such a pervasive, manhood-stripping spectacle was yet another thing he had to thank Edith for. When she'd seen him becoming besotted with her, she'd cut it off short: no more languorous free ones of a late afternoon, she guiding him, silently, firmly; no more friendly games of cotch; no more friendly anything. He was made instantly aware of the change one afternoon when he'd come up the back steps to her room and rapped on it in their agreed-upon *ratta-ratta* code. After a time, she had appeared, her hair down, chemise partly opened—and her hand on the crotch of a john.

"I'm busy, sonny," she said icily, "as maybe even you can see." She gave the man's crotch a backhanded tickle and closed the door on a phase of his life.

At this moment, he remembered how he'd stood there, immobile outside Edith's closed door, hunched, just as he'd seen himself in the window's reflection. And he remembered as well his long, moping walk afterwards that had ended out at Chalmette Cemetery: past Algiers Point across the river where a barge puffed white smoke against a blue sky as unconcernedly as if nothing extraordinary, let alone tragic, had just happened or could ever happen. Life went on regardless as white smoke lifting inevitably skyward. Past the desolate wharf at the end of Tennessee. Past Lizardy, Flood, Tupelo, out to where the pitted, time-tarnished angels spread their immovable wings and the Christs spread their lifeless arms over the ranks of the oven tombs raised only a little against the river's ravening suck.

Inside the cemetery he'd flung himself down on a nameless, dateless slab and surrendered to an adolescent sobbing that was the more anguished for its gross singularity: Edith, his love...and her *hand*....And what made that youthful moment the more indelible for him, like a scar on his brain, was the caretaker, a rigid elderly man of military bearing, who had materialized out of the settling gloom with what Tom Anderson remembered as a rake or some other long-handled tool, and seeing the big blond kid there, heaving on the slab, had ordered him to get the hell off that and get the hell out—it was past closing time. He'd looked up into that spare, bone-hard face topped by wisps of gray hair that stirred slightly in a breeze up from the river, the eyes like scratched shooters rolled for ages over the gravel of schoolyards until their original brightness had become opaque, dull. Looking into them out of his own reddened and swollen eyes, he'd known there was no help to be had there, no appeal that was even thinkable. There was nothing—nothing to do but what the man had ordered: get the hell out.

Much later, after he'd begun to get established, after he and Edith were speaking again and she was satisfied that he would never again be trouble, he'd felt an impulse late one afternoon to take a hack out to the cemetery, where he made inquiries about a man who might have worked there twelve or so years ago. He'd felt obscurely that he owed this man something, some expression that wasn't quite gratitude but that came up close to that. It was almost as if the man had been placed there to drive home the interior, continuing significance of the lesson Edith had so graphically given him hours back: the worst sin a man could be guilty of was to get cunt-struck. But nobody at Chalmette could recall a man matching Tom Anderson's recollection. Old Pierce, they said, would have been there about that time, but Pierce was a wingy—a one-armed man—and so surely Anderson would have remembered so singular a detail. Well, it probably didn't make any difference who the all-but-apparitional figure had been—his name, one arm or two. The thing was, the figure had told him what he most needed at that moment to hear: to get out and to get on with it.

Straightening his back still more, coming out of that recollection, he went to the humidor on the sideboard, its dark

Brazilwood glistening under its daily polishings, and the pewter plaque on its front side reading:

To Mr Thos Anderson
With Admiration
From Arturo Pastrano
New Orleans Light-Heavyweight Champion, 1909

He clamped off the end of a black Havana and got it going quickly, the stogie puffing like a locomotive as he began to pace.

The clear need was to discriminate here. The ape was a danger, true enough, both because of who he was and, more particularly, because of what he'd just told the girl. He knew nothing more about the man than that he was a bouncer at the Tuxedo and a chauffeur for his relative, Harry Parker. As that sort of man, the chances were he was a drinker, and that was the problem: he could easily enough get loose-lipped tonight and brag about what he'd done with the girl, along with the usual exaggerations. And that might lead to a further and more dangerous brag about something big that was to happen at the Tuxedo in a matter of hours. This could place the girl in mortal jeopardy. Moreover, if it got back to the Parkers, as it likely would, the first thing they would do was to call off whatever it was they had planned, thus canceling the value of the information the girl had risked so much to give him, and that had conferred on him and his people an incalculable tactical advantage—the knowledge of the time and the place. By quickly shutting up the single source of this vital information he could formulate an effective response to it and at the same time take the girl out of harm's way. So, first the ape must go.

He heard Billy Brundy's light, long-legged step on the stairs. "Say, Billy," he called out, his voice slow, steady as ever, "is Fast-Mail downstairs?" Billy Brundy had reached the top step, where he could either enter his small closet of an office or else, turning hard right, enter that of his boss.

"He aint just now," he said. The electric light from the ceiling shone directly over Brundy's thinning brown hair and cast shadows under the high, brief cheekbones and the hollow below the lower lip. It made his yellowish skin look positively Chinese. "He's down on Decatur with Santos."

Tom Anderson thought a moment. "Danny down on the door?" Billy Brundy came along to the door of Tom Anderson's office but didn't enter. He nodded. "Well, then, you tell Danny to get down to Toro's and bring Alto North back here; tell him to tell Alto to use the back way up." He turned away to his desk, speaking over his shoulder. "Here," he said, handing Billy Brundy a key. "Give Danny this for Alto."

"Right," Billy Brundy said, pocketing the key and turning away to the stairs he'd just climbed. But then Anderson called him back.

"Wait a second, can you, Billy?" He stood there in the middle of the room, tall, fashionably portly in an outfit with matching coat and vest and contrasting fawn-colored trousers with spats. Billy Brundy took it all in, from the blond curls that were beginning to show silver, down to the gleaming tips of his shoes, and he had to think, once again, Hell of a show— hell of a turnout. But something else crossed his mind at the same instant as he beheld his boss in his handsome turnout, a shadow that came and went, that was not central to his vision but only on the edge: has this man slipped, or are all these hesitations the parts of a careful reconnoiter?

The man himself stood where Billy Brundy had first seen him when he'd gained the landing, his four-and-a-half-fingered hand holding the Havana near his mouth, as though he had almost said something but had decided to call it back. "Wait a second," Tom Anderson repeated after a longish pause. "Where's Muldoon going with the load?"

"Astoria." Brundy checked his watch. "My guess is he should be back here within half an hour." He stood there, just outside the door, the light behind him now, outlining his high-shouldered, thin frame. He waited while Tom Anderson silently wondered about the wisdom of sending Danny. Why involve yet another man, another set of eyes, when in something like half an hour he could send a man as steady and reliable as a clock?

"Billy, let's forget Danny, shall we?" Tom Anderson said quietly, moving the cigar away from his mouth. "When Fast-Mail comes back, you send him down to Toro's for Alto. When you see Santos roll up, you hold him and tell Fast-Mail what I said." He held out his hand, and Billy Brundy gave him back the key. He took a mighty pull on the Havana, its end turning from a dull to a full-flavored red and, as Billy Brundy watched, erupting into an angry, volcanic orange showering sparks onto the expensive, high-pile carpet Gertrude had picked up at a private auction in the Garden District—an estate of one of the old Creole families, broken up at last by everything that had transpired since the War Between the States. Tom Anderson glanced down at the fiery shower he'd created, but that was all. He turned his back on Billy and moved with a heavy deliberation back to his desk, where he would wait for Alto North to be delivered.

"Something's up here," Muldoon muttered to Santos Villalta as the driver eased the Jefferey to the raised banquette on the Iberville side of the Annex. They saw Billy Brundy on the top step, talking with two customers. Despite his social graces—stories, vocabulary, languages, mimicry—Brundy had never been particularly easy with casual customers and never stood out in front like a greeter. Yet there he was, his black and gray-striped alpaca vest opened to the chilly dark. Santos said nothing, merely pulled the long brake lever upwards with a ratcheting, oily sound, and glanced calmly at his passenger, the hectic glow of the hundred ceiling lights within catching the scar beneath his left eye. It was a war souvenir, he'd once told Muldoon: a gun had jammed, ejecting a shell casing into his face. It was just about the only personal comment Muldoon could recall the man ever making—if you discounted the occasional remarks Santos might make as they rolled on their nightly errands past some streetwalker swinging her rear in a way that caught the solemn driver's eye. Or those mumbled bits of Spanish Santos made as he maneuvered the long car in traffic. But then, of course, Muldoon had no way of understanding these and rather regarded them as just another noise the Jefferey itself made.

He swung his legs in tandem onto the running board, his eyes on Billy Brundy, who was pretending to be engaged with the two customers but who was returning Muldoon's look. Muldoon pulled on his hat and tugged at his vest, coming around the glare of the big headlamps and almost colliding with Chris Burwell of the force, who was prodding a sulky streetwalker with the end of his billy. "Git-git-git-git!" Burwell was saying, poking at the woman's rear end with every "git." "Ya'll doan come back to this yere corner, or ah'll run your sorry ass straight to the calabosso, sure." On the other side of Iberville the woman's pimp stood in the lights from Few-clothes, mouthing silent obscenities. As Muldoon stepped up on the banquette the lights across the way flickered, went out, then came back on, full force. Muldoon glanced over at Few-clothes and saw figures within, but already Billy Brundy had his arm, holding him where he was while he stooped down to speak to Santos.

"Don't go anywhere with this," he said in an undertone. "T.A. wants you to take Fast-Mail down the Line to Toro's and bring Alto North back here, pronto, *comprende?*" Santos nodded once. It was all the same to him. Then Billy Brundy turned to Muldoon, still holding his arm lightly and leaning into him. "Send him up the back way." Then he turned to the two sporting men at the door.

"Gentlemen!" he said heartily, clapping them both on the shoulder simultaneously. "Gentlemen, step in and have a drink on Tom Anderson."

"You heard what he said," Muldoon said, taking off his hat and settling himself once more in the stiff seat. Santos released the brake lever and jammed the Jefferey into gear, taking it around onto Basin that at this hour still had its complement of precariously ambulatory figures, black, lurching cutouts against the red wink of the house lamps, the oily ochre clouds of the saloons.

Then there were three silent men on the way back from Toro's, Santos taking the route up Bienville, then down Franklin, where they were obliged to run through the insolent brilliance of the Tuxedo, Santos and Muldoon staring straight before them, Alto North motionless in back, sitting on an empty whiskey crate. Whether he turned to notice the place at all, Muldoon couldn't have said. He thought North missed nothing that had to do with his job—but missed almost everything else in the world.

Behind the Annex, as he swung his legs out of the Jefferey, Muldoon wondered yet again what could be inside the man who now noiselessly moved into position slightly behind him, waiting while he fumbled in the alley's gloom for the key that fit the barred gate to the steep steps within. How did you arrive at the point where nothing touched you, where you never had an attack of nerves, and you moved through life like a machine with wires, chain-pulleys, and cogwheels? Would life be easier that way instead of being the ill-assorted heap of emotions he felt he'd become since meeting the girl? Had the man at his back ever felt his heart racing, slamming against its breastbone as if it wanted to leap through and explode in air? Santos with his flat gunner's eyes that had sighted on advancing soldiers and mowed them down in the grasses, who had kept his hands working the gun until it had seared his flesh through his heavy gloves—even Santos had blood, guts, feelings and seemed positively joyful next to Alto North. And Chicken Dick, who they claimed was so tough he could chew razor blades and spit them out pig iron—even Chicken Dick was a man, a human, and Muldoon had no doubt that when the Parker bunch had ambushed him, Old Dick had felt the heavy smack of the bullets that had spilled his smoking blood into the street, or wherever it was they'd drilled him down. What would come out of Alto North when he got his, machine oil, an ooze of ice shavings?

Watching the slim, straight figure mount the steps within the gate that so easily swung on its hinges, Muldoon found himself seized by the sudden and complete conviction that he was in the act of watching the beginning of a murder, its first, calculating phase. Not up in those rooms, of course, with their noiseless carpeting, their lampshades and curtains, the desk, sideboard, humidor, sumptuous chairs, coffee table; the walls covered with prints and photographs of pugilists, politicians, businessmen from Baton Rouge and Boston. But the first steps would be taken up there—had, in fact, already been taken when he'd opened the gate for Alto North. There could be no other reason for North's presence here. Muldoon felt certain the man had never before set foot in the Annex.

He stood in the oyster shells of the narrow alley that had

been carved out before there were autos, staring up into the darkness, thinking that the victim's—whoever it was—remaining moments on earth now had a number to them, one that dwindled even as he, the gatekeeper, stood there. And there was nothing to be done, the coming event inexorable, unstoppable as the second hand of a clock that ran around the face forever—or did at any rate until Time itself had a stop on Judgment Day, as the brothers at St. Alphonsus tirelessly reminded the boys. "Even you, young Muldoon," he recalled Brother Cosgrove telling him one afternoon as his own time in high school was running out, "even you will come to a stop, fast as you now are, my lad. How brief, lad—think on it now—your little race." And he remembered as well the smiles in that classroom, the ones he could see around him and the ones he couldn't, because this was a favorite theme for Brother Cosgrove, and he was the brother's favorite student, which explained why Brother Cosgrove (not that much older than he) often chose him for illustrative purposes. So, he'd known he wasn't really risking anything when he'd replied, smilingly, "But, Brother Cosgrove, sir, I aint a distance man, anyhow, sir. I'm built for speed."

"Indeed you are, my handsome lad," Brother Cosgrove replied, his regular features with his dark, Northern beard held perfectly straight against the laughter that rippled against the walls and the bright squares of the window. "And so are we all." He swept his black, cassock-clad arm over the warm, restless bunch of them. "Not a one of us is built for distance. None." Certainly not Brother Cosgrove himself who not many years thereafter died a horrid death, of lockjaw he contracted from a barber's carelessly cleaned razor.

Behind him he heard the heavy, concentrated fall of urine onto the oyster shells: Santos pissing in the alley. He waited until it stopped and even a few moments after that because he knew Santos always gave himself a vigorous shaking and occasionally even a fairly thorough inspection before buttoning up. When he did turn back he found Santos looking at him from the other side of the car. "Where you want him now?" Santos asked, nodding at the Jefferey.

"Oh, here will be all right, I guess. Least till we get some other run to make."

When at last the Parker brothers called it a night and told Chance Henderson, the bookkeeper Bluto Gerstner, and Gyp the Blood to close up, Toodloo Chapter was wearily grateful. It had been a bitch of a night all around.

The business with Red hadn't turned out that well after all, because Chance Henderson reported to him that they couldn't wake Red up. And so after a while Toodloo and Chance had gone into the alley where they wrapped Red in some burlap sacking and a horse blanket, tumbled him into the back seat of Harry Parker's car, and taken him up to the Claiborne gate of St. Louis Number 1. Inside, they'd propped Red against an oven tomb. "He's still breathin, anyways," Chance reported. Toodloo slapped his palms together, dusting off the fiber of the burlap and said maybe the sun would wake Red in the morning.

"Harry and them don't need to know nothin bout old Red," Toodloo said as they drove back to the Toledo. "They won't miss his business." Chance said nothing. He wasn't looking to cross Toodloo over one drunk, or two even.

Then there'd been the business of the girl, which, when he thought about it, made him sweaty, both with the anticipation of what he felt sure his payoff must be and what he'd told her to get it. To cool himself he'd put away a stupendous amount of beer, enough so that when King Keppard approached him for that sweetener Toodloo had promised he had no idea what the nigger was talking about and merely glared at him redly while Keppard began to raise his voice. Then a dim recollection swam to the surface of Toodloo's brain, and he pulled five rumpled bills from his coat pocket, handed them to Keppard, and told him to divvy them up as he chose. "Two-to-one he keeps three," he slurred to Chance Henderson, who only nodded.

So he was truly ready when Harry Parker came up to him at the bar pushing his hat back. "Okay, Toodloo. I guess you can bring it around now," he sighed, muttering something else as he turned away, his narrow shoulders sagging under his own fatigue. But Toodloo couldn't remember where they'd parked after depositing Red and had to ask Chance, who told him the car was over on Marais, a few doors this side of Canal. He noticed Chance looking at him closely and made an effort to walk straight as he left the Tuxedo, the great sign's lights flooding down on his shoulders, his grimy, whiskered face shrouded beneath his cap. Across the street there was only a single figure outside the entrance to the 102 Ranch, but he was too fagged even to take any satisfaction from that, walking stiff-legged and listing up Iberville to Marais and turning past Rice's Café, which was quiet now. A man was sweeping at the entrance and didn't look up as Toodloo went past.

Finally, after a couple of passes, he found the car, and when he had cranked the motor over and listened to its regular chugs, he settled himself wearily in the driver's seat. He pulled off his cap and took a deep lungful of the dank river air, his eyes closed for a long instant as he held the air in his chest.

A hand flashed silently out of the all-but-complete obscurity of the back seat, seizing the driver's hair and yanking the head back against the seat. And in that same split-second the assassin's other hand, bone-white, disembodied, came forward, drawing the long arc of a blade across the driver's neck that, too late, had tightened in a reflexive, creaturely apprehension of mortal peril. A great *whoosh* of air exploded from Toodloo Chapter's neck, his last lungful arrested on its upward passage, followed by a geyser of blood, the initial burst of it hitting the wheel and steering column and spraying off in all directions as if it had been shot from a great height.

The hand that held the hair kept its grip among the oily roots as the last of the air escaped the wound with a soft, sighing sound like the victim's own gratitude that it was over, quickly and almost painlessly. After all, life had been a struggle from the first, and now it was not. The back door opened and then was softly, carefully shut. Up Marais dawn fell on the man with the broom outside of Rice's, who continued his metronomic movements.

VII. Evangeline

Something awakened him. But it wasn't with the old violence where the stalking beast would pounce, its hot breath instantly slathering him with sweat. This felt different. So, he lay there, silently searching for its source: the cry of the crab seller, chant of the praline woman, cough of the bulldog in the next yard, wearing deeper with each day the trench that ran beneath his wire tether. But he heard nothing except the sounds of the cottage itself, expanding under the midday light, the clinched wood groaning against the tyranny of the round-headed nails and those older square-heads pounded home twenty years after Appomattox. But these were always the small, interior noises he heard *after* he'd been awakened, not what so often yanked him straight up from slumber.

Maybe it was the image of the girl. He tried searching backward in his mind for some trace of her, her scent, maybe, which he believed he could still recall from that moment in the passageway of the Tuxedo when blundering into her bosom was like falling into a bed of flowers. But it didn't seem to have been her, either; or if it was, it was as though she'd been there, reflected in the mirror of his mind but now vanished from it, leaving behind only the tarnished and reversed images of an empty room. Working backwards from this present moment in his tousled bed, he came unexpectedly across old Hamilton, last name only, a man he'd known at the bag factory: old Hamilton, riffling through the yellow tabs of accounts in the company office and he, idly watching Hamilton's dirty, calloused thumb and forefinger searching, hunting some name— Ga, Ge, Go—and wondering then in his whole and youthful vigor, his invincible innocence, what it would take to spend your life so, hunting down debit. He'd left old Hamilton behind when he'd left the factory for the force, but now he wondered whether he really had. Because here he lay, riffling just like Hamilton back through memory and dream fragments for something—anything—that might explain what had awakened him and instantly filled him with a deep, premonitory unease.

And then in the interior of the silence he had it. This was Holy Saturday, the day before Easter when by long custom not even church bells were suffered to ring, when the Church itself denied consolation to its children, and in the city's streets only a few godless laborers were to be seen; or else, bent, black-clad figures, hurrying on inescapable errands, anxious to escape the sacrilegious light. Here was the moment in the year, so he'd been catechized, when creation itself stood still, poised on that ancient event, when redemption was possible through simple assent to the truth of Christ's sacrifice. So it was this that had awakened him, this strange, unnatural silence, that had seeped from Good Friday into Holy Saturday, into his cottage, under his doorsill, and into his very bed and bedding. Lying in it felt like being buried alive.

He knew better than to try to fight against it, trying to struggle back into sleep, however early the hour might prove to be. He swung his legs free of the sheets, feeling the cold of the floorboards on his naked soles. Then Bessie Browne's well-meant remarks came back to him, about how he'd better not let those Tuxedo boys catch him, buck naked (as he now was) without his pistol. Did he really know how to use that thing, she'd asked?

Target practice on Holy Saturday, he thought grimly: you couldn't get any more sacrilegious than that. Why, on the Holy Saturdays of his boyhood you couldn't even get a meal, and most families he knew fasted until after midnight mass when they might have a spare, somber supper. He recalled his paternal grandparents having nothing but bread and water on this day. Still, he now found himself throwing on some rough clothing, splashing icy water over his unshaven jaws, then getting out the pistol and a box of cartridges from the shelf above his dark, ranked suits in the closet. Then he almost slammed out of the cottage, as if wanting to take some oblique vengeance on the silent day that had invaded his sleep.

There was nothing to be seen on Washington as far down as Tchoupitoulas, not a figure anywhere, not even a cur on its private errands. The sky was an hourless sheet of hammered metal, though even so he knew the hour must be awfully early. The saloon on Chippewa was tight-shuttered, its battle-scarred door chained and padlocked, the scrap metal yard across from it also chained shut, though as he passed it his eye caught movement behind the high board gates. It was the spotted guard dog that never barked, only regarded you from within a baleful silence. He was almost grateful to find it there, so sepulchral did the city seem.

You couldn't chain up the docks, though. They operated every day of the year, though on this day they were doing so at something less than half-speed. Below the Louisiana entrance a group of Negroes stood about in slouch hats, suspenders, and flannel shirts. In their midst was a rusted barrel into which they were feeding sheets of newspaper and holding their horny hands above the brief flare of the flames. One of them was singing a blues, drawing out the last syllables of the lines into suspended moans. When the smallest of them turned to look at the crippled passage of the hatless white man, Muldoon recognized the café-au-lait face. It was Half-Hand, a veteran pool-shooter along the Saratoga halls. Half-Hand tossed his head briefly upward in recognition, then spat. It wasn't personal, Muldoon knew.

Aline, Antonine, Amelia, Austerlitz—the farther along he went, the more he could see how high the relentless rains had raised the river. More, he could hear it, a steady, hurrying sound, lower than a roar but deeper, more insistent and with the timbre of half a continent to it and carrying all manner of things past at such a rate that Muldoon had to turn his head fairly quickly to mark their down-river passage. There were large lengths of timber, some standing almost upright for an instant; hogsheads moving past so quickly they didn't have time to describe a full revolution before they were gone; a section of what once had been a shed, the nails still holding the slats together somehow. In the great, roiled rush he could spot portions of dead things—paws, tails, a bloated belly—but couldn't tell what they once had been. When, forty yards out, what looked like a mule or horse came by he recalled his ostensible mission down here, drew his pistol and fired at it. He saw no small spout raised up near the thing, and the noise was too full for him to hear the thud of a hit. But then, a moment later a three-foot-long earthen jar came rolling past, its reddish sides glazed and greasy-looking, and he shot at that and saw his bullet blow a piece out of its upper edge. The vessel went quickly under as if it had never been, and as he looked after where he judged it must now be, he heard a sound behind him and spun about, suddenly tensed, though he had the presence not to point the pistol.

It was a round-shouldered, pot-bellied man who'd come up behind him, a derby hat pushed far back above his pale face, black vest over a soiled and collarless shirt, and his fallen chops covered with gray stubble. Muldoon took him for an out-of-work clerk or bookkeeper who'd come down here simply because he had nothing better to do. In the fellow's soft air of long-sunken melancholy Muldoon saw he had nothing to fear—except the state of his own nerves that had caused him to overreact. But the man seemed not to have noticed that. He sucked at his molars, looking after the disappeared jug. "Pretty fair shot there," he said after a moment, nodding at the pistol Muldoon held. "Y'all do much of this sort of thing?"

Muldoon hesitated, looking down himself at the pistol, as if he'd never particularly noticed it before. "Not really," he brought out finally. "Come down here of an afternoon sometimes, just for the practice of it, you might say." He paused. "That there was a lucky one, anyways."

The man made a sound, a sort of muffled snort that Muldoon took as a kind of agreement. Then he sucked at his teeth again and moved off. When he was a few yards away Muldoon heard him fart briefly.

A dead dog came whirling past, close to the wharf, big, fawn-colored, and wearing a collar. Somewhere upriver someone would be missing that dog about now, he judged. He wondered how it had gotten sucked into the flood, and raised his pistol for a shot just as the body rolled belly-up, the forelegs folded like prayer, and he could see the dark row of tits: a bitch, recently pregnant. He lowered the pistol, his own stomach suddenly turning with the idea of putting a slug in there, and with this what little heart there had ever been for his mission now vanished like the jar and the dog.

He returned the pistol to his coat pocket and trudged back along the wharf. His gaseous, tooth-sucking audience-of-one had disappeared, and so had the group of Negroes gathered about the barrel below the Louisiana entrance. The fire had gone out, and there were only a few scattered pages of the newspapers they'd been using as fuel, shifting uneasily in the gusts of wind off the river. A sheet of these, vagrant, discarded, suddenly lifted, sailed, and wrapped itself around his leg, and he reached down to snatch it away. As he did so his eye caught the date—the twenty-first, today—and he held it up, scanning it with a mixture of boredom and distraction. It was an inside page—metropolitan items and police reports—of interest only to those who like himself at this moment had time on their hands: a report of vandalism at a parochial grade school; the sighting of what was said to be the season's first rabid dog, up on Eighth Street. And then this: *"Saloon Employee Found Murdered,"* the item read, the agate jumping at him many times magnified.

Police discovered a body in a parked automobile in the fourteen-hundred block of Marais this morning. Details are incomplete but papers on the man identify him as Arthur Chapter thought to have been an employee of the Tuxedo Saloon on Franklin at Bienville. Foul play is certain but robbery is discounted as the man's wallet was yet on his person. Tensions in the Red Light District have been high of late leading officers to fear the man's murder may be part of a larger problem.

He dropped the page. Perversely, as if it had volition, it reattached itself to his leg once again, then fell away. But by that time he was already in motion towards the steps to the Tchoupitoulas trolley stop. Here, he instantly understood, was the meaning of Alto North's appearance at the Annex last night, and this was the latest action in what now clearly was a war.

He waited at the stop with an impatience that was silently blasphemous, cursing the trolley's infernal delay, taking the Lord's name in vain, and shifting his weight from one foot to the other like a man on hell's hot coals. Except that the coals weren't underfoot; they were in his chest, for he couldn't escape the knowledge that he'd been the gatekeeper to murder when he'd unlocked that door behind the Annex, then stood aside to watch the steady, nerveless ascent of the murderer who mounted to receive his instructions. That made him some sort of accessory, he thought; he remembered that much from his days on the force. And what the hell difference could it make just what sort of accessory he was in the eyes of the law and what penalty there would be to pay for it. Even more, he now was forced to ponder, as he had never wanted to in all the previous years, how many other times, running his errands, he had been an accessory to crimes ranging from forced, ticketless passages to oblivion, to assault, to murders like this one of the Chapter fellow, whoever he had been.

Nor was this all of it. He knew now, as he probably had when Bessie Browne said it, that soon—perhaps this very day, Holy Saturday or no—when the shooting started, Tom Anderson would require him to take his part.

As he saw the trolley trundling towards him through the metallic glare of the afternoon his mind flashed yet again to the stack of photographs in Bellocq's studio. Those women. He, Francis Muldoon, had hardly forced them to take up the desperate lives they lived in the District. In different ways both Jimmie Enright and Bessie Browne had said such women came looking for this work and were glad when they got it. Most, Bessie claimed, had already been ruined before they arrived at her doorstep. And as far as that went, hell, he hardly knew any of them, their names or what they did after they'd handed him their keys. But where did a man's responsibility end, anyways? Was he supposed to shepherd them home, for Christ's sake? And even in this present matter, what could he have done about Alto North and the man whose very name had already slipped from his memory as the trolley rattled to a stop, clanking like a skeleton in its Holy Saturday emptiness?

There proved at least a corporeal driver at the controls of the spectral vehicle, though Muldoon thought he'd never before seen the lean, handsome young man who wore his brass-banded cap with what might have seemed a touching, jaunty pride. But the red-faced man who hauled himself into the empty car was in no mood for another's callow airs. So they rode voicelessly onward, the metal of the car ferociously loud in its barren passage to Canal, where Muldoon changed for the cemetery line as far as Galvez, where he got off and began the same long-striding, hopping gait he'd used when he'd seen the girl home in the pelting rain following the picnic. And thinking of that, hopping high in his necessitous improvisation, he recalled what the girl had asked him when they'd been together on the lake's wide, choppy water: "What else would you do?" But he couldn't recall what he'd said in answer, only that he was certain it couldn't have been a satisfactory one because now, under the same unforgiving, metallic cover—minus the rain—he still didn't have one. What *would* he do, marked by what he'd done—or hadn't—in the crucible of the chicken run on Saratoga as well as by what he might very well be called upon to do in the next hours or days? Old Hamilton came again to mind, as he hadn't in so many years until this morning. Mean and boring though he'd found old Hamilton's work, the man could find employment somewhere, could keep books, whereas he himself couldn't. He most likely couldn't even operate the pedals of the trolley as had the lean youngster who'd jerked the car to a stop on Tchoupitoulas.

Then, before he expected it he found himself there, at the street door to the girl's building on Gravier. He rang the bell, and without waiting for an answer, flung the heavy door back with a slam and climbed quickly to the second floor. Outside her flat, his chest heaving, he stared at the dulled brass numerals glued to a bit of cheap pasteboard. Then he rapped hard on the door, feeling it rattle in its frame, hearing the answering silence. The only sound he was aware of in the entire building was the thunderous pulsing in his own eardrums.

He rapped again, using a little less force this time. Still nothing. Then a door opened down the hall, and a woman of about his age peered around it, her hair done up in paper curlers and her face greasy with ointment. She stared narrowly at him a long moment while he felt the flush mount from the collarless neck of his shirt. Then the head withdrew and the door closed softly. Alone again, his hand rose towards her door, then paused, hesitant, embarrassed, until the urgency of his errand took over once more, and he rapped twice. Then he stood there in the silence, rubbing his knuckles, reflecting that it would hardly do to wait here where with his whiskers and rough clothes and a loaded pistol in his pocket he might easily be mistaken for a criminal. The presence of the weapon suddenly felt huge and heavy at his waist. Better to wait across the street than here.

Yet with more than an hour gone and pacing a tight oval across from her building, he thought how foolish his vigil likely was: she might be anywhere, might be at a friend's, might go directly from there to the Tuxedo, which he was now convinced would be the most dangerous place in the city tonight—if the Annex wasn't.

A few doors down Gravier, a butcher's boy came out onto the banquette, spat into the street, and scratched himself under his blood-smeared apron. Muldoon walked past him into the shop where he asked one of the men behind the chest-high counter for a scrap of paper and a pencil. The man nodded, silently holding up one finger while he finished tying up a roast. He tore off a strip of butcher's paper from a roll, rummaged about a moment, and then handed the paper and a square, thick-leaded pencil across the counter. Muldoon was still in the act of thanking him when the man turned back to his tasks.

In a corner by the street-front door there was a high stool, and Muldoon used it as his desk, turning the heavy sheet on its other side when he spotted the butcher's broad, blood-marked thumbprint in a corner. There was blood on the other side as well but not nearly so much, and in any case it would have to do. He looked at the otherwise blank surface and then over his shoulder at the big wall clock behind the counter. He licked the lead and held the pencil above the waiting sheet.

"*Sat—5.12 p.m.,*" he wrote blackly. He moved the pencil down below this entry and licked the lead again, moving it in tiny, preparatory jerks above the paper as if afraid to commit something to the sheet that would be irrefragable, graven as a tombstone inscription.

> *My Miss—*
> *Sure you did not see item in to-days paper—about the murder on Marais—but am certain it means plenty trouble down there soon.*

He paused and decided to underline the word "soon."

Would kindly advise you not to go to yr work until
this blows by, as I have great care for yr person.
                    Always yr friend,
                    Francis Muldoon.

He folded the paper into a square, the two edges slightly jagged where they'd been ripped from the roller but then stopped himself, unfolded it, and added a postscript:

"<u>*Very Dangerous,*</u>" underlining it twice before pocketing the note and placing the pencil atop the counter.

Tom Anderson sat behind his desk, which was crowded with keepsakes, mementos, gifts ceremonial and fraternal, pebbles, odd bits of wood and tile that only he could possibly have understood and valued for their histories and provenances. All this atop and around the edges of a kelly-green blotter sumptuously bordered with gilt-ruled, padded leather. The curtains were drawn against the quick-fading light of the sunless sunset that oozed wetly beyond the westerly reaches of the silent, bell-less city, stilled on the edge of Easter. He looked across at Jimmie Enright and Billy Brundy, who sat awaiting his word, his construction of a newly arisen situation only he as yet understood.

"Jimmie," he said presently, nodding in the direction of the sideboard, where the humidor sat with its load of Havanas, "have one, and don't forget your friends." He smiled through the low light of the strategically placed electric lights and the big hurricane lamp on the desk about whose broad base clustered some of the household icons. Jimmie nodded, rising in response to the quiet voice and its careful mixture of the friendly and the regal.

Jimmie clamped off the cigars' ends and distributed them, beginning with Tom Anderson. In a minute there arose a blue cloud of conspiratorial smoke, Billy Brundy and Jimmie Enright puffing industriously but Tom Anderson's one mighty puff sufficient to set his cigar instantly aflame. He leaned back in his high leather throne, his coat draped over its back. When he saw that his lieutenants had their cigars going he leaned forward, elbows on desk, his maimed hand holding the cigar, his other one clasping it at the wrist, and told them he had information that something big was to happen tonight at the Tuxedo, something that was meant to be a surprise from the Parkers. But, he said, quietly, glancing casually at his cigar and lowering his voice as if in afterthought, "It aint exactly a surprise now, is it? And that's why I have you boys here—to help me spring the real surprise." He nodded at them in turn, beginning with Billy Brundy.

"So, I asked myself when I got wind of this," Tom Anderson continued deliberately, "what could this thing be from them jaspers, something that has to happen over there?" He let go of his maimed hand long enough to take a shallow, ceremonial puff of the cigar. "And the answer I come up with is it's gotta be a lure, some kind of bait, a trap, where they get us over there, shoot us, and then claim self-defense." Jimmie Enright nodded quickly, squinting at his boss through the blued air, but Billy Brundy made no motion except to look down at his cigar a second and give it a half turn.

"They're gonna do something—we don't know exactly what—to bring us over to their place," Anderson went on. He slowly set the cigar in a deep brass ashtray and brought his hands together. The gestures and the delay during which they occurred were silently impressive. "And we have to take the bait. We have to walk into their trap." He looked at Billy Brundy. "The difference is we know it's a trap and we go in there prepared. Like the man said, 'Forewarned is forearmed.'

And we go forearmed. That way, it don't really make a difference what the trap is. But I can pretty well guess, can't you, Billy?"

Billy Brundy looked up from his cigar and raised his eyebrows. "My guess would be some kind of sweet deal, some kind of peace offering, or like that."

Tom Anderson smiled and nodded. "My thought, too. What they want is to get me over there, and they want you two fellows. After that, well, I think they aint that particular. They'll take who they can get. If they could get me and you fellows, why then they'd pretty much have the run of the place— could do what they like." He started to reach for the cigar in the ashtray but changed his mind.

"Whatever it is, I doubt they'd risk coming over here to the Annex," Billy Brundy said. "But they might come across to the 102 and say they wanted to talk turkey with you, don't you think, T.A.? That would be how I'd go about it."

Tom Anderson smiled again. "My thought, again, Billy." He swung his gaze to Jimmie Enright. "And what I want you to do, Jimmie, is tell em, 'Okay, we'll hear you out: we'll come on over to hear what y'all got to say, and then we'll report that to Tom Anderson.' And then we'll send some of us over there, walking right straight into their little trap, sweet as can be, lambs to the slaughter. Only we'll have our hammers back, and we'll get the drop on them jaspers. And *then* we'll talk business with them, all right. We'll finish with them, and we'll finish it tonight.

"Jimmie here had it right a while back, didn't you, Jimmie. Remember, you told us how we had to finish with these birds?" Jimmie nodded his cannonball head vigorously and started to say something, but Tom Anderson's question was only rhetorical, and he went right on. "Only I didn't see that just then. Didn't see it until South Rampart, really." He shook his head. Jimmie Enright felt warm all over, once again involved in the inner workings of the outfit.

"I didn't want it to come to this," Tom Anderson said. "It's bad for business. And this'll be bad for business, too—real bad—in the short run." He leaned back in the high chair that creaked under his substantial, prosperous weight. "They might close us up for a spell," he said, "the whole District. So, short run, it's bad for business. This kind of thing always is. But I've seen it happen that you can lose a race and still come out winners at the end of the day. I've seen that many a time."

"Who're you thinking of, T.A.?" Billy Brundy asked. "I mean, who're you thinking of sending over there?"

"Jimmie." Tom Anderson looked steadily at Jimmie a long moment, knowing that just now Jimmie would willingly take on the whole Parker gang by himself. "Jimmie. Then, Alto. Okey. Santos outside in the car." There was a pause and Anderson ran the stub finger around the rim of his ear. "Fast-Mail," he said then. He looked at them in turn. "He might be a coward, but I think if he's put in the right situation, you can maybe get him to pull the trigger. What do you figure, Jimmie?"

"He's okay," said Jimmie. "I feel like he's okay. When we're all there around him, covering his ass, like, I don't think Fast-Mail'll run or nothin." He looked over at Billy Brundy, waiting for the kind of qualification Brundy so often came up with. But Brundy only looked down at his long-fingered hands and the steadily upward wisping smoke of the cigar that slanted out of the tangle of fingers. "No, I think Fast-Mail'll be okay with all of us there," Jimmie Enright repeated. "When we're over there in their joint numbers is important. Fast-Mail's a number, so he counts, right? I wouldn't want him exactly covering my ass, but a guy what's got a gun—well, you gotta account for him with someone else. So, whatever Fast-Mail does, he like uses up one of them, right?"

Tom Anderson nodded. He trusted Jimmie Enright as he trusted no other, except Gertrude, of course. He wished fleetingly she were in town so he could talk this through with her, but in her absence, he'd found another use for the house, and on this night of all nights he was grateful the place was completely available to him. He'd even sent Mammy Callie down to visit with her sons near Deer Range, and so of the normal household that left only old Criss, who had grown so deaf he rarely spoke these days, even when his boss spoke to him directly.

"Well, what's your idea here, Billy?" he asked. "You think Fast-Mail'll shoot if he has to, or will he run again?"

"Likely he's been askin himself that question every day of his life," Billy Brundy said quietly. "Don't know what answer he's come up with, but I go with Jimmie here: numbers is numbers, and Fast-Mail is a number with a pistol in his hand. Who else you got in mind, T.A.?"

"Let's see," Tom Anderson said, recollecting those he'd already mentioned. "I said Jimmie here. Then, Alto, Okey, Fast-Mail. Santos out front." He noticed that Billy Brundy's cigar had gone out and pulled a match from one of the green ceramic holders they used downstairs in the restaurant. "And Billy," he added, striking the match against the desk's underside and reaching it across to Billy, the flame shielded by his cupped fingers. He saw the startled look on Billy Brundy's face and motioned him to put the cigar back in his mouth, but it was too late. The match winked out. Anderson shoved the match holder across the cluttered desktop towards Billy Brundy, shaking his head once.

"Not you, Billy. *Billy*."

"Ahh," breathed Billy Brundy, reaching now for the little green holder. *"Billy."*

"Billy."

"Son-of-a-bitch!" exploded Jimmie Enright. "I'll be a son-of-a-bitch!" He strained his bull neck towards his boss, his jaw jutting in a kind of fierce vindication. "You gonna let me take him, T.A.? I been wantin to settle that little bastard's hash ever since you sent me down there—to help him, I mean."

"If they don't do it themselves, straightaway, which would surprise me no end, then I want you to see to it," Tom Anderson replied, casual, quiet, conversational, as if discussing the merciful, long-delayed dispatch of an old mule that had outlived its usefulness and had existed on a sufferance that at last had run its course. "Either way, the thing is, we don't want Billy coming out of the Tuxedo. That fellow has caused us plenty trouble as it is. When we finish with the Parkers, we finish with him, too."

He leaned back in the big chair and crossed his legs, taking a long, judicial puff at the Havana. "I can't say I didn't offer the fellow—twice now—a handsome price for his share; the second time much more than the place was really worth." He shook his great, sandy-haired head. "Wouldn't hear of it." He looked at Jimmie and smiled again. "You were right there again, Jimmie, my old friend: fellow is just a hard-headed fool, quite different than his pa, who was a very level fellow—sat low in the water, kept his head steady, good fellow to do business with."

"Business first," Billy Brundy said. "I had to learn that the hard way when I was still a kid. Happened down in Veracruz, which is one sweet town." He had the cigar going again. "Only," he went on, his diction a bit muffled by the cigar, "there were years after that where I didn't want to think about Veracruz."

"Why was that, Billy?" Tom Anderson asked in his quiet, conversational tone, the tone that through the years had invited all sorts of confidences: stray references with no discernible substance or shape; accounts by strangers of encounters with obscure family members that Anderson's tone and manner encouraged and even coached for further oblique details; autobiographical excursions that often ended in sodden sloughs; recitations of long-dead, hopeless love affairs with nameless women. It was all okay, Tom Anderson's confidential voice told you, all of it. "Tell us about this Veracruz business, why don't you, Billy," he said. "I've never been down that way, and I don't think Jimmie has, either."

And Billy Brundy did just that, taking on the voices and accents of the various characters, spinning out the tale at a leisurely length. After all, there was yet plenty of time before the Parker bunch could be expected, either here, or, more likely, around the corner.

The Parker Brothers stood in the yellow rawness of their little office at the Tuxedo, waiting for Gyp the Blood. "Gyp says Anderson aint goin for it," Charley said. He had his back to Harry and was feeding slugs from his coat pocket into a .41. "He said he wouldn't come over here to talk if it was high noon on Easter." He pushed the last of the slugs home, snapped the cylinder into the frame, and turned to his brother. "I don't, either. Even a fat mick can smell a rat if it's big enough."

Harry Parker leaned back against the opposite wall. He seemed not to be listening to his brother but was concerned instead to see that Charley had pushed Bluto Gerstner's ledgers into disarray, and he knew Gerstner would be unhappy about that. Gerstner already had plenty of complaints about keeping the brothers' books and was a fanatic about neatness. Harry would straighten them in a minute, but first he wanted to set his brother straight about his plan, one he thought would have made old Toodlum envious in its intricacy, its devious misdirection.

In a few minutes, he told Charley, they'd go across to the 102 and tell Enright and Phillips that things had gone far enough, and they were ready to talk peace with Anderson before the whole situation got out of hand and the police came down on all of them. He knew well enough, he said now, that Anderson was far too wily to come across to the Tuxedo tonight or probably ever. So the bait they were dropping wasn't a real bait meant to hook the big fish. Instead it was a lure for the smaller fry who would take it, he felt pretty sure. They would come over because Anderson would order them to do so.

"And when they come in," Harry Parker said, crossing the tiny space to straighten Bluto Gerstner's books, centering them on the rough shelf and realigning their edges, "then—*bam*." He didn't pronounce the word with any special emphasis nor even a quiet drama. It was just a word, a sound, like the wind, perhaps, flinging a shutter against a wall. But as he made it a very small smile flickered quickly across his parted lips, more like a momentary grimace, the false facial gesture an animal might make when it was cornered and about to attack. He was thinking now of a further strategic intricacy he had devised, and for an instant he thought of divulging it to Charley but then quickly changed his mind: its dramatic charge might be defused if anyone else knew of it until the very moment he decided to set it off. "The thing is," he said, standing beside his brother, his hands yet on Bluto's precious books, "I don't really need Anderson. Fact is, I don't *want* him to come over here." Charley gaped at him in surprise. "I mean, he's better off alive for us." He kept his hands on the books while his brother continued his slightly incredulous stare: after all, hadn't they been scheming towards just this moment, when Anderson would step right into their trap?

"See, Charley, this way, when we pop Phillips and Enright, then Anderson's *got* to come to us. Maybe not right away. But he's got to come to us—or we go to him—because with Phillips and Enright dead he'll see how it is: we got this place, we got Fewclothes, and we've knocked off his partner and his toughest guy. What's he got left? He's *got* to make a deal, and we'll put those old Irish balls in a vice." He let go of the books to pick up the .41, hefting it with both hands.

"Think about it a minute." He cocked his head at Charley. "Just think along with me for a minute. We get Anderson in here and pop him, that what we got, eh? What we got?" He shrugged.

"Here's what we got to deal with. We got that guy what writes up Anderson's whorehouses; we got all them loose guys we don't even know who they are. And none of these guys knows enough to make a deal. They don't know shit—which is just the way Anderson wants it." He put the .41 carefully back on the shelf next to the ledgers and looked at it a long moment before turning his eyes back to Charley. "Which leaves us exactly one person who can make a deal—Anderson's whore, Gertie." His lips curled back over the long canines in another of those smiles that weren't smiles. "Now, wouldn't *that* be neat, us havin to try to make a deal with an old, wore-out whore? I mean, they're so *reliable,* like."

Now it was Charley who had to smile, both in response to his brother's ironic characterization of whores in general and in admiration of the cleverness of a plan that comprehended and foresaw all the contingencies. Harry, he felt, wasn't at all overplaying his hand here, as sometimes he had up in Brooklyn. He was playing it close, and he was playing it tough. Spontaneously he reached out to shake his brother's hand, but Harry just shrugged again. He wasn't through yet and wanted Charley's attention more than his premature admiration. There would be time for that later when they'd gotten everything they wanted.

"Enright and that fool, Phillips, will follow us over here to hear our offer," Harry Parker said. "And they might send another guy, too—maybe even two guys. You and me and Chance'll be behind the bar with our guns down there, ready. We got Gyp back here with Karst. When they come in and get to the bar to talk, then here comes Gyp and Karst, businesslike—broom, tray—and when Gyp gets to Phillips, he pops him, and you and Chance and me go to work on Enright and anybody else they bring. They'll have guns on em, sure—which is necessary—but we got the element of surprise, which in a thing like this is everything. We do our job right, we can drop em all in a crossfire."

He dug into his molars after a troublesome bit of beef he'd had for dinner, got it, and pulled it out, inspecting it on the end of his thin index finger. "How do I know we'll get at least Enright and Phillips over here? Because of Toodloo, is how." He ate the white bit of beef gristle from his fingertip, mincing it with his front teeth. "A man who did that to Toodloo is a panicked man, brother, just panicked. Aint no reason to take care of old Toodloo like that—what's he get for that? No, he's panicked and he'll want to hear our deal, that I can promise you."

Charley raised his eyebrows slightly. Maybe Toodloo's killing was a sign of panic, but the manner and execution of it certainly weren't. It had been done as neatly, as cleanly as could be. If Tom Anderson was panicked, he had somebody working for him who wasn't. Charley had seen the body; Harry hadn't. Old Toodloo's eyes were wide open, and his throat looked like it had mysteriously grown a mouth, one that oddly appeared to be wearing a wide, fixed grin. This was no amateur job, but a cool, thoroughly professional piece of work.

Harry hadn't seemed the least upset by the killing, had said no when Charley had asked if he wanted to go to the morgue to claim the body. But then Harry had never, he thought, gotten over the loss of Toodlum, and for some obscure reason blamed Toodloo for it. It was as if Harry thought Toodloo ought to have been the first one through the window, when in fact the plan—all of it—had been Toodlum's from the start, and it was he who had insisted on being the first one in. At the very least, he thought now, they'd miss old Toodloo's muscle and nerve. Not that bright, to be sure, but tough and game as they came.

Charley began adjusting his pants and tucking the .41 into his waistband. Now they had this kid Karst who could do some of the things Toodloo had: drive, heft kegs, keep order in the Tuxedo, and, if need be, shoot. He was a big, broad-shouldered guy from somewhere out there—Iowa, Indiana—and had been along when he and Gyp had dropped the niggers on South Rampart, though Charley couldn't tell where Karst's shots had actually gone. But he did know that Karst had pulled the trigger, several times, and so maybe that was the essential fact: that he was at least willing if not exceptionally able. It didn't take a marksman to shoot an unsuspecting man when you were standing next to him at the bar. It took nerve, and Charley thought Karst had it.

Gyp thrust himself into the dingy room, pulling the door closed behind him so quickly it clicked against his heel. His hawk's features were so tightly stretched over his skull that his face gave off a cadaverous glare that sent an inward wince through Charley. At this stage in the war Gyp's entire body seemed to have become a weapon, a blade turned against everything outside itself. Charley found himself wondering, not for the first time but with a greater urgency than ever, just what this man *wouldn't* do. Good man to have on your side, he thought. Wouldn't want it the other way around.

Gyp took them in swiftly, his eyes unreadable, shrouded beneath their hoods. "Well," he said with a soft, measured outbreath that was almost a hiss, "we went by there, like you said to. But that kid Karst, he don't know the players and all, and what I seen was Phillips, workin his jaw like always, and Enright, and the gimp, the one moves around from place to place. So when do *we* move?" He looked at Harry and made a motion with his elbows, hitching the skirts of his coat back a bit and showing just a flash of the brace of .32 five-shots he had tucked into his waistband. Harry turned his back on him as if he had something important to attend to on the little desk. Charley had to admire the maneuver. Under the circumstances he wouldn't turn his back on Gyp just now.

"We'll go over in a second," Harry said over his shoulder. "Me, Charley, and Chance. We'll go unarmed. Charley, leave that thing with Karst on your way out." He turned then to face Gyp. "I want you and Karst waitin around just inside the door and watchin the 102. Ten minutes or so, you don't see Chance come out and spit, then you figure somethins gone off, and you and Karst come on. Have Karst pack Charley's number with him. But if you do see Chance come out, you just stay here and wait for us to show. If we come out of there lookin easy, everything's jake." He looked steadily at Gyp, whose hands had been hitched close to his sides but who now slowly raised them, running them through his short-cropped auburn hair. Under their raptorial hoods his eyes blinked twice, then stayed steady on Harry, who then began to outline the plan once they'd lured Anderson's men into the Tuxedo.

When he'd finished there was a sudden silence in the little room, and then the noises from the bar and dance hall rushed in, and in that instant Charley Parker knew the noises had been there all along, that it had been the pressure of the situation that had temporarily blotted everything else out.

"Sounds okay to me," Gyp said, "but you'll never get Anderson in here. Never. I said that right off." He nodded at Charley but without taking his eyes off Harry.

"I was just explainin to Charley here that I don't have to have him," Harry said. "Better if I don't. What we want is Enright and Phillips. If the gimp comes along, well, fine. This way Anderson's left to make a deal, see? Without him we got nobody we can deal with and things'll be real messy. When Anderson hears how we dropped his boys, that'll get his flag up."

"He used to be a cop, I heard," Gyp said, standing, spread-legged and on the balls of his feet. "The gimp."

"Right, he was," Harry came back. "Badge, billy, brass buttons, the works. But he got shot in the asshole runnin away from a nigger, and they canned him. Some copper, eh?"

"He carries a gun," Gyp said flatly.

"Right," Charley said. "Shoulder holster."

"Must be able to shoot it, then."

"Nobody's seen that," Charley said. "Like you just said, he mostly moves around to where they need him, fixin stuff, bringin booze. Mornings, he collects the crib keys." He shrugged, indicating that the gimp was probably of little consequence in the impending action. Gyp sniffed and hitched at his waistband with his inner elbows.

"Okay," Harry said then with a deep breath. "Charley, you and me are gonna have a drink with Chance—only a taste. I want us to smell like liquor. Then we'll go across to talk business." He didn't ask Gyp to join them, knowing he didn't drink.

"Billy," Jimmie Enright said into the telephone's mouthpiece, "tell Okey to come on, pronto. Tell im to come in through the kitchen and wait there with Alto. I can see em standin across the street lookin this way."

"How many and who?" Billy Brundy asked, his voice tense and up a little.

"The brothers and that Chance guy that tends bar." Jimmie Enright paused, peering through the small, square window at the knot of figures across Franklin, the loungers with their mugs and growlers, smoking, spitting; and the three figures that stood slightly apart from them, staring across at the 102. "I don't spot the Gypsy guy. Tell Okey to move it." He hung the receiver back on its box and watched the three men as they stepped slowly off the banquette onto the cobbled street, their figures etched now by the outrageous lights of the sign, faceless cutouts the color of night as they marched toward the 102. He turned from the window, rolling back down the bar, passing one of the bartenders and then coming to Billy Phillips who stood in his white shirt, four-in-hand tie, and long white apron with the words "The 102 Ranch" running across its left breast in the wavy script of the same kelly green Tom Anderson used at the Annex.

Phillips was making an impressive show of shaking up an aniseed ratafia cocktail—his specialty—the ice chips clattering against the shaker he held head-high, his heavy young face smiling at the waiting customer. Jimmie Enright knew the fellow, a maker of industrial belts who came in here at this hour because, so he was now telling his neighbor, there wasn't anybody else left in the whole town who could make this traditional drink the way Billy Phillips could. Billy had made himself into a first-rate bartender; Jimmie Enright had to give him that. When he wasn't jawing about the Parkers and the Tuxedo or about City Hall he could be an honest-to-God asset to the place. Too bad he had to have so hard a head, Jimmie thought grimly, and it wasn't as if they hadn't given him his chances. Well, he'd squandered them all like a sailor ashore. Now his leave was up.

"Brace yourself, Billy," Jimmie Enright muttered out of the side of his mouth as he passed behind Phillips. "Company comin from across the street."

Billy Phillips whipped his head about to look after the retreating Enright, then back again in time to catch the entrance of the Parkers and just behind them the balding, broad-shouldered man he knew tended bar at the Tuxedo. The shaker stopped in midair, and Billy Phillips's jaw dropped, then instantly clamped shut. The belt manufacturer had just started explaining to his neighbor that the cow leather he now had to use in his factory was inferior to the old-time buffalo belts, both in durability and elasticity, but when he glanced back at Billy Phillips he beheld an astonishing transformation of the genial host and expert bartender into an empurpled, mad-eyed stranger, the sort of man you would go out of your way to avoid on a city street.

As the three newcomers shouldered their way to a spot at the bar's upper end Jimmie Enright continued on to Muldoon's station near the kitchen doors and repeated what he'd just said to Billy Phillips. "Steady now, Fast-Mail. We got company." He flicked his piggish eyes at Muldoon who stood with his game leg on the rail, cradling a cup of coffee, and then he was past him. An aproned kid came out of the kitchen with a rag in hand, and Jimmie Enright quickly grabbed the half-door on its backward swing. Watching him move through it and into the kitchen, Muldoon caught sight of Alto North standing easily at a counter, a coffee mug held in his slender hand. In the doors' brief aperture North's eyes met Muldoon's, North marking him with a swift inventory that Muldoon felt took in everything except who he was. Then the doors whanged shut once more, and Muldoon could see nothing except the disembodied feet of others in the kitchen, going about their repetitive chores.

He stepped back carefully from the bar to see who the "company" was and spotted them. So now it was all in place, all the pieces gathered, and he was one of the pieces. He nudged his pistol, tugged at the skirts of his coat, and stepped back to the bar, touching his saucer, waiting, thinking of the girl, glad he'd slipped the note beneath her door, but worried that she might not have returned to get it. While he was wondering whether he might possibly have time to slip out, get across Franklin, and enter the beer garden from the alley, there came a sound like a pistol shot.

He had two simultaneous sensations—that the room had all the while been revolving very slowly; and that now it had jerked to a sudden, jarring stop. For what felt like an endless moment without depth or definition, a total disruption of duration, the figures of bartenders, waiters, customers were frozen in the attitudes they'd had when the shot sounded, as though caught in a photograph; and the bar, its ranked bottles and glasses, the low canopy of smoke and the paddlewheel fans above it were similarly suspended. Muldoon's heart, too, seemed to have stopped between beats, stilled within his breast and even the racing blood caught up, held solid within the veins.

Then the world moved once more, slowly, hesitantly, the

waiters shifting their trays, the bartenders looking about, the smoke eddying lazily once again under the turning blades of the fans, and the customers running numbed hands over coats and vests, feeling for leaks. But when his eye fell on Billy Phillips, Muldoon saw it hadn't been a pistol shot after all, only Phillips slamming the shining shaker down on the bar with such violence that the cap had come off and sailed high into the air to glance off a row of glasses behind him.

"*Christ!* Billy," the belt man breathed. "Jesus Christ! What was that for?" Phillips said nothing in response, pouring the drink into the waiting glass, roughly, heedlessly, a good portion of it slopping over onto the bar. Then he turned up the bar with a stiff-legged stride like a fighting cock.

"I'll take these guys, Gibby," he said to Lew Gibson, the bartender who had just asked the Parkers what they were drinking. "Y'all can take my spot down there." He jerked his head backwards to where the belt man stood with his mouth an almost perfect O, staring at Phillips as if he were an escaped madman.

"Sure thing, Billy," Lew Gibson said. He'd recognized the three men the instant they'd come through the doors and was happy to let his boss handle what he knew would be at best a ticklish situation, at worst a violent one. He handed Billy Phillips his towel as if surrendering a flag and walked quickly away. But Phillips held the towel/flag only an instant, flinging it heedlessly aside. Behind him Gibby heard Phillips's voice, tense and raw as an over-strained hawser, asking the three men what it would be, while ahead of him he saw the red, reassuring face of Fast-Mail Muldoon who had stepped away from the bar to assess the action at the other end.

Muldoon saw the men make their order, watched as Billy Phillips reached quickly back for a bottle of I.W. Harper and a clutch of glasses. But now Gibby was there directly in front of him, staring at him, and so reluctantly he had to turn his attention to him.

"What in hell is up?" Gibby finally managed to bring out. "Look here, Fast-Mail, I signed on here when Billy opened this place because I thought it was a good spot to be. You and me," he gestured with his hands fluttering upward like startled birds, "we go back a ways. And you damn well know I been in a lot worse places than this." He tapped the bar with two fingers. "A lot worse, so we don't got to kid ourselves here. But this damn thing—it's gettin way outta hand, Fast-Mail. You know it, I know it. Only guy who doesn't is Billy. I'm tellin you something awful big is gonna bust loose in here, maybe tonight. And I don't wanta be around for it." He leaned across into Muldoon's face, slightly lowering his voice. "Money's good—we both know that. But it aint worth your goddam *life!* I got a wife and kiddies!"

"I know, I know," Muldoon said. "But wait a minute, can't you, Gibby. We need to watch out just here." He nodded quickly towards the bar's other end, where Billy Phillips was slopping the whiskey into the three glasses and glaring at the Parkers and Chance Henderson. Harry Parker reached into his pocket then, and brought out some coins, but Billy Phillips had the drop on him, saying hoarsely, "Your money's no good in this spot, mister. Just this one is on me."

"Well," Harry Parker said with an obvious false cheer, "that's a nice surprise, for sure. Mighty white of you, Phillips." He raised his glass and nodded, indicating his companions should do likewise. "We'll drink your health, then."

"My health's fine," Phillips said, "and it'd be one hell of a lot better yet if certain folks would stay outta other folks' business—and outta their place of business, for that matter. Now, just what in the hell brings you in here, anyways?"

"Well, that's just it, Phillips," Harry Parker came back, still keeping up that almost mockingly false cheer. He hadn't taken a sip of the whiskey he held, though both Charley and Chance had done so. "That's just what we come about—business. And what we've been thinkin is that this here whole thing has kinda got off on the wrong track like, and we'd like to get it set right again.

"See—" he leaned forward and set the untasted glass on the bar—"way I figure it, there's plenty of business down here for everybody; don't need any of this pushin and crowdin. It's bad for both of us."

"You can't talk no business with me," Bill Phillips said roughly, putting both hands on the bar and only inches away from Harry Parker's glass. "It's way too late for that—you foreigners shoulda thought about that before you started in musclin about, goin behind folks' backs, that sort of stuff you must do up north there. Well, here it don't go, that I can tell ya." Charley Parker leaned over to say something into Chance Henderson's ear, and Henderson nodded, and stepped out the front doors, returning only seconds later, just as Jimmie Enright was making his way out of the kitchen and up the bar, nodding at Muldoon as he passed. Harry Parker now turned to his brother and made an elaborate, ceremonial bow, clinking his glass with Charley's and whipping the whiskey down. Phillips's face was now the color of an old Mexican saddle, and the big vein in his neck was standing out against the high starched white of his collar.

Harry Parker swallowed his whiskey and wiped his mouth with his hand. "What I was gonna say," he began again, "was I think your boss ought to hear our proposition before you say no to it. He might wanta make that kind of decision himself."

"First off, he aint my boss," Billy Phillips snarled. "We're partners. Second, there aint a thing you could say that could

interest him in the slightest—lessen it would be that you foreigners had finally decided it was time to pack it up before
more folks get hurt."

"Here, here," Jimmie Enright cut in, looking from Billy
Phillips to the three men across the bar, their postures upright,
tense, and their hands showing. "What's all this?"

"Man here don't want to listen to a business proposition
we got to make Tom Anderson," Charley said. "Maybe we
can talk to you about it, and you can talk to Tom Anderson."
He looked at Billy Phillips and said, "Your pal here don't seem
in a reasonable mood tonight." He started to say something
more, but Harry Parker laid a quick hand on his arm.

Jimmie Enright glanced quickly at Billy Phillips, then back at
the visitors, Chance Henderson hanging well in the background.
"This aint a good time to talk business," Enright said. "Late and
all. Now, what I say is this: why don't you fellas drink up before
trouble starts, and then, if you want, I'll speak personal to Mr.
Anderson Monday." He placed his arms akimbo and stared
hard at Harry Parker, then Charley. Just for the flicker of an instant Harry Parker's face looked indecisive, as if he were mulling
his choices. Then the old sardonic look came back and he swallowed the last of his whiskey and reached slowly into his pants
pocket, pulling out a couple of silver dollars.

"I guess this'll buy us one more, won't it, even at your
prices?" He showed Jimmie Enright the coins, but even as he
was doing so Billy Phillips shot his hand across the bar and
flipped the dollars out of Harry Parker's hand. Like small
moons suddenly out of orbit, they spun to the floor, and a man
standing behind Harry skipped sideways as if the coins might
be molten.

"No, by Christ!" roared Phillips. "Y'all aint havin another
in here, not now, not ever!" He reached beneath the bar and

came up clenching an age-blackened belaying pin. "By Christ!" he repeated through gritted teeth, "I've had enough now."

Chance Henderson turned to scoop up the scattered coins while Harry Parker slowly raised his hands from the bar, carefully pulling aside the skirts of his coat. "We aint armed," he said to Jimmie Enright, holding the coat wide.

"Y'all don't follow my advice and get outta here pretty quick, you'll wish you was," Jimmie Enright said. "Now, I done already said you oughta leave before trouble started, and now it has started, sure enough."

The man who had skipped away from the spilled silver now stepped farther away as Chance Henderson retrieved the last refractory coin. The belt man still stood with his cocktail untasted before him, staring pop-eyed at Billy Phillips, though he had closed his mouth a little. And up the bar Francis Muldoon had nudged his holster yet again and stepped away from the bar to the middle of the room, waiting for what would come.

But nothing did come, or so it seemed. The Parkers said something to each other while Chance Henderson waited, and then the three of them turned and walked to the street doors, Harry Parker lagging behind but still moving. At the last moment, though, with his hand on the door and the incident evidently over, he spun about, his wolfish face split into a grin, the long canines gleaming yellowly.

"*Hey!*" he yelled back at Billy Phillips and Jimmie Enright. "*Hey!* All of you!" He swung his head to survey the entire room. Then Harry Parker leaned forward from the waist and his thin torso gathered into the convulsive effort of a scream. "*Tom Anderson fucks his own! You hear me? Tom Anderson fucks his own!*" Then he turned and was quickly through the doors, following the others.

Behind in the room he had left there were still the words, final, awful in their obscure implications, lethally defamatory, explosive in the response they demanded.

Harry Parker caught up with the other two before they'd reached the banquette on Franklin's other side. Charley Parker and Chance Henderson turned to see if there was pursuit, but Harry merely barged through the Tuxedo's doors, almost slamming into big Karst, who stood just within. Gyp the Blood stood off to one side, both hands a little out from his sides.

"Well," Gyp said, "Anderson aint comin, is he."

"No, he aint," Harry Parker said, heading for the office and his gun. "But you can bet yer ass Phillips and Enright will be along any minute now. I want you and Karst back here before they come in."

In the office Charley began to laugh about what his brother had yelled as they left the 102, playfully punching Harry's arm. "How in hell did you come up with that one?" he asked. "I didn't think they was gonna go for nothin tonight till you made that one up. I wish I'd seen their faces!"

"I didn't make nothin up," Harry said, reaching into the box beneath the little shelf and bringing up a .44. "That's what he does."

"What the hell are you talking about?"

"I mean, that's what he does: he fucks his own." Harry sounded a little annoyed as he checked the pistol's load. "That Adele—which I know aint her real name—she's his niece or his cousin or somethin. Anyway, they're related somehow, and he fucks her regular, has been right along."

"How do you know that?"

"Never mind how. I know it, is all—have for some time. By the way, is she back there?" He jerked his head in the direction of the beer garden.

"She's sick. A friend of hers is takin care of her and called in this afternoon."

Harry grunted as he tucked the .44 into his waistband and snugged his coat up around his shoulders. "No matter," he said, more to himself than either Charley or Gyp or Karst, who was just coming through the office door. "I'll be takin care of that lyin little pussy later. Right now we got business to handle." Then he quickly went through the plan with them again. "It's gotta be *fast!*" he said, snapping his fingers. "I mean *fast*. Soon's they get up to the bar you two"—pointing to Karst and Gyp the Blood—"come on out. Then we let em have it. I want Enright."

In the 102 Jimmie Enright and Billy Phillips stared at each other in a silence almost perfect, Phillips still holding the pin and all the patrons staring at them, too, wondering what they were going to do about the terrible thing that had just been uttered. Muldoon stood in the center of the room wondering the same thing and wondering at the same time what Harry Parker had meant by it. If he'd meant that Tom Anderson went to bed with some of the whores and the cabaret girls, the insult was almost pointless. Everybody down here knew that the men who ran women commonly went to bed with them. They all fucked their own, if you wanted to put it that way. Both Ed Mochez and Clarke Wade, the biggest pimps in the District, were well-known for this, and Muldoon knew that Wade had twice been stabbed—once nearly fatally in the groin—by women he'd had on the string. And not many weeks ago in this very place Muldoon had been chatting with Horace Gentry, a pimp and poker player, who had told him soberly that the only way you could keep women productive and reasonably reliable was to bed them and beat them every once in a while. "They's the only things they really understand," Gentry claimed, blowing a spew of cigar smoke across the bar. "You got to dick em ever once in a while, even if you don't really feel like it no more. Same as you got to crack em in the teeth, just for nothin in particular. You don't do them things, they begin to think you've plumb forgot about em. Next thing you know, they've either quit you for somebody else, or you got em holdin out on you: 'How many tricks you turn tonight, babe?' 'Oh, honey, such a tough night I had. I only turn three.' When, shit, you been spottin em right along, and you know they done five, maybe six even." Gentry had rapped the bar three times, emphasizing his point.

But this was such an obvious fact of life that Muldoon was having trouble imagining this was all Harry Parker had meant because Parker had looked too satisfied with himself when he'd yelled it and also because of its powerhouse impact on both Jimmie Enright and Billy Phillips. Now he saw Billy Phillips practically trotting down the bar towards the kitchen with Jimmie Enright right behind him. When Jimmie overtook Phillips, he pulled him forcefully through the kitchen's double doors that were flung wide, then flapped back and forth. Then Muldoon found himself staring once again into the amazed face of Lew Gibson, who was saying something about this being a "nut house," not a saloon, and he was trying to think of something to say back to Gibby when Jimmie Enright stuck his reddened face through the doors and motioned Muldoon in. "Scuse me, Gibby," Muldoon said. "Be back in a minute," knowing it was hardly going to be so simple a meeting as that, that the big trouble Gibby had fearfully predicted was already upon them all, and it was too late to wish you were elsewhere.

Inside the kitchen and partially obscured by a few hanging, long-handled skillets stood Okey-Poke and Alto North and just behind them Billy Phillips still with the belaying pin in one hand and smacking it into the palm of his other with a compulsive and mindless violence.

"Now, I don't know what these fuckers was really in my joint for just now," he was saying to Alto North's back but to nobody in particular as far as Muldoon could make out, "but since they did come in and said what they said, me and Jimmie are agreed: we gotta clean up that shit across the street—and we gotta do it tonight! They wanta talk business with T.A.? Well, *I'm* in charge here, and by Christ, they'll talk business with me!"

Standing on the other side of the hanging skillets, Jimmie Enright cut in. "He's right, boys. Tonight has got to be it. We've waited and we've waited, and we've watched this shit get piled up real high. T.A. don't know yet what just happened in here, and I don't want to have to be the one to tell him tomorrow, without we have gone over there and taken care of this shit once and for all." He swung his cannonball head in a vicious half-circle. "I'm too old to look for other work," he continued but now in a more measured cadence. "But that's what I am lookin at if I have to go to T.A. tomorrow after what was said in front of everybody in here tonight—and that those bastards are still in business. Somehow—don't ask me how, cause I don't have the answer—T.A. found out—the way he always does—there was gonna be trouble tonight. That's why we're all here. And so now we're gonna go over there and take care of it."

"Well, what're we talkin about here?" Okey-Poke asked. "We gonna break some legs, bust heads?" He looked at Jimmie, but Billy Phillips started to answer before Jimmie cut him off.

"We're gonna put them outta business," Jimmie said. "Whatever that takes. You bring that pistol like I told ya?"

Okey-Poke nodded. "I brought it, all right. And I brought

this." He pulled up a pants leg to show them the much-polished hilt of the short club he kept in his boot. These days, though there were still occasions when he had to use it, the fact was that the Annex had become a pretty tame place, one where politicians, sports, and theatrical figures felt safe while all around the outside of its brilliant premises swirled the dark dangers of the District. Okey-Poke was still a tough guy, but he wasn't the rough-and-ready kid who'd learned the art of keeping order from the legendary Shot Johnston. Muldoon found himself exchanging a long look with Okey-Poke whose face under the kitchen lights looked not so much hard as haggard.

"When yer fightin clubs, it's always good to bring a gun," Jimmie Enright said. "It's good you got that club with you, Okey, cause I know you know how to use it. But fact is, when we go across, we're gonna be ready to shoot first. We aint goin over there to just jaw."

"You mean *kill* em?" Okey asked Jimmie, shooting Muldoon another swift glance.

"Kill em," Billy Phillips said. "Kill the brothers—or anyway cripple em up so bad they're outta business and outta town. It's the only way we got left."

"Well, what about this Gyp guy?" Okey continued. "From what I understood about Buster Daley this guy aint gonna just be standin around with his thumb up his ass."

"I have him," Alto North said quietly.

"What T.A. learned," Jimmie Enright said, taking them all in, "is that they plan to knock him off. Now, that may not be tonight, but if it aint, it's Monday; and if not Monday, then the one after that. And boys, the day the Parkers drop Tom Anderson is the day we're all outta work, sure. And not only that, cause they'll come for us, ever one.

"Me, I got no choice, got no place to go. Where'm I gonna

go at my age and bein what I've always been? Bogalusa? Shit! I *gotta* stay here! Maybe you guys aint. You got plans for where to go, how to live?" He took them all in once more, his piggish eyes flashing. "Cause if yer like me, this here is it. So. I aint goin nowheres—except over to the Tuxedo."

Nobody said anything for a moment. A waiter came in with a tray of glasses and unloaded them at the sink where the Chinaman in his inevitable skull cap was up to his thin elbows in hot suds. When the waiter had cleared out, Jimmie Enright turned to Muldoon.

"What about you, Fast-Mail?" Jimmie said. "You got that fancy cottage with yer sister and all, am I right? Well sir, this here's part of the work that pays for that." He hunched his bullish shoulders and leaned forward, balancing on his pigeon toes. "We aint askin you to kill nobody—nor you, either, Okey. But you gotta be there for me and Alto and Billy here. Can you do it? Can you?" He glared at Muldoon, who was simultaneously aware that Alto North was staring at him so steadily that he felt he must turn his glance away from Enright to return that stare. Even as he did so he felt the muscles in his neck quiver inside a collar that seemed suddenly very loose, as though somehow he had shrunk within it since putting it on yesterday afternoon. North made a motion with his tight, scarred mouth, as though tasting something bad and wanting to spit it out, twisting his lips to the side so that the long scar was furled. His eyes never left Muldoon, who was making every effort to look steadily back but felt as if his head might be visibly wobbling on his quivering neck. Then North spoke to him for the first time, ever, making a very slight motion of his head but his eyes never leaving Muldoon's face.

"I know how you come by that," North said. "But I always wondered, is it wood or what?"

"Which?" Muldoon asked, knowing, his neck and face instantly ablaze with anger and humiliation.

"That," North came back, flicking his icehouse eyes down at Muldoon's game leg.

Billy Phillips started again to say something, but out of the corner of his eye Muldoon saw Jimmie Enright lay a restraining hand on Phillips: Enright wanted to hear—and see—how Muldoon was going to respond to this challenge, this dress rehearsal for what he would be asked to do across the street.

A jumble of images filled his head as he stared back at North standing coolly there in front of him, waiting. North had put his mug on the counter and had both hands free. He thought once again of the note he'd tried to get to the girl; of Maureen and her little girls and what would become of them if things went wrong right here or across the street; or, if somehow he survived both Alto North and the impending action at the Tuxedo, what would happen to all of them if Tom Anderson should go down to the Parkers. He thought Jimmie Enright was right about that part of it, anyway: the city would be a very unsafe place for any man who'd worked for Anderson, especially someone who'd been at it as long as he had.

There was another thing he felt sure of as well: that Alto North could know nothing really about how he'd "come by" his disfiguring gait: this remorseless creature who was oblivious to anyone else except as a potential target: what could such a person know of the boy who'd once flashed heroically over the cinders of the city's tracks, flying towards that string that always broke against his chest with the slightest, dry snap of triumph? And what could he know of the life Muldoon had had to put together and to live in the long years since the Robert Charles riot, limping through these hellishly lit streets as Tom Anderson's mechanical man? And now it had all come down to just this: he had to go on being the mechanical man, even if it meant drawing his pistol on another man and if need be pulling the trigger.

They were all looking at him: Alto North with his feral fixity; Okey-Poke, who Muldoon felt wasn't a killer but probably would shoot if he had to; Billy Phillips, now cholerically useless for anything other than mayhem; and Jimmie Enright with those bright little eyes that were boring into him, waiting to learn if he was in or out.

He didn't want to run the risk of doing anything with his hands that Alto North might want to misinterpret. Instead, he lifted his right foot and shook it, once. "It aint wood," he said as steadily as he was able. "You can feel of it yourself if you like."

Again Alto North made the little gesture of distaste, furling his scar, but he said nothing.

"You got that gun?" Jimmie Enright asked him now. Muldoon nodded and nudged it with the inside of his elbow. "And you can work it and all?"

"Took some target practice just this afternoon—before coming to work," Muldoon answered. "Works fine."

Jimmie Enright took a deep breath. "Okay," he said then on the exhale. "Billy, I want you to leave that thing right where it's at." He pointed to the pin in Phillips's hand. Phillips was about to object, but he saw the look on Jimmie Enright's face with his upper lip curled back like a bulldog about to bite and tossed the pin on the counter in disgust. "Me and Alto will do what fightin needs doin," Jimmie Enright said. "Okey and Fast-Mail'll be cover in case somethin goes wrong. And then we got Santos out front in the auto: anybody but us comes through that door is a dead man."

Nobody said anything on the way across; as Jimmie had put it, they weren't going over to jaw. Jimmie and Billy Phillips led the way, then Alto North by himself with Okey-Poke and

Muldoon just behind. When he spotted them Santos Villalta rolled the Jefferey just past the entrance to the Tuxedo and parked it with the engine running.

To Muldoon, Franklin felt miles wide, the Tuxedo's lights winking on the other side like those of a city glimpsed from afar by a lone traveler. He blinked his eyes hard, trying for focus, while underfoot his game leg kept clanging awkwardly off the cobblestones that seemed purposely placed to trip him up. So they went onward toward the closed doors behind which they knew the Parkers and Gyp the Blood would be waiting. The doors looked like they'd never been opened, and all the loungers had mysteriously vanished as if to a sudden summons.

Then they were through the doors and into the big room that like the banquette outside seemed strangely deserted, only a few men hanging about just inside and the middle of it occupied by a quartet of drinkers who had their heads so close together they might have been whispering. The booths were all empty except for two. In one a man slumped, far in his cups, one hand held to his forehead in apparent self-commiseration. In the other, the last one, a woman had her arm draped around an older man whose Stetson was canted at an almost impossible angle. The whole place looked as if it had closed an hour before, and these were just the dregs the management hadn't gotten around to yet. But the Parkers weren't themselves in the process of cleaning up. They stood wide-spaced behind the bar and the Henderson fellow with them. When Muldoon glanced at him the man seemed to have undergone a profound transformation, his face ashen and glistening. For just an instant Muldoon wondered whether it was in fact the same man who'd been in the 102 only a few minutes ago.

As Jimmie Enright and Billy Phillips reached the bar, Jimmie with his arm around Phillips's shoulders, Muldoon saw

Gyp the Blood and another man come through the far doorway that Muldoon knew led into the hallway where a lifetime ago he'd fallen into the arms of the girl. Again, his attention skipped away from the mortally fraught situation, wondering whether she was back there or if his note had warned her away. Having at least tried to save her seemed now no consolation whatever. She was either elsewhere or in a position where she might well be shot.

Gyp the Blood came halfway down the bar with a tray in hand, then deposited it on the bar. Right behind him came the man who'd followed him in, a broom in hand and making sloppy swipes with it under the railing. Gyp came slowly on. Just before he reached Billy Phillips, Phillips reached into his pocket and brought out some dollars that he dropped on the bar with a careless bravado. He seemed completely oblivious of the silent, hawk-faced man who had come up to his elbow, almost touching him.

"I don't expect you to buy a man a drink," Billy Phillips said, "so I'll buy me and my friends one." Harry Parker shook his head, telling him they were closed. A loud noise at the room's far end drew Muldoon's attention from the cluster at the bar, and he saw two other men lurch into the room from the hallway, one of them the cornetist, King Keppard, hollering and laughing; both of them were clearly drunk. And as he watched them, in that same second there was a flash and an explosion, and Muldoon saw Billy Phillips's head on fire and his body already beginning its sideways sag into Jimmie Enright. Behind the bar Harry Parker was clawing at his face and eyes with both hands, trying to clear something that had been splashed in it. Then he dropped one hand and had his pistol pointed at Jimmie Enright. Jimmie fired first, but Harry Parker's shot was hardly a split second later, hitting Jimmie just below his collar. Muldoon couldn't tell where Jimmie's shot had gone, only that it had hit home because Harry Parker gave a kind of gasp, made a half-turn, then dropped from sight with a two-stage thud, as though his head or trunk had bounced off a cabinet before the rest of him hit the floor. There was a scream rising like a siren's wail from somewhere in the room, and Alto North was ducking behind the collapsing Jimmie, bracing his gun hand on the bar's edge and firing at Gyp the Blood who had retreated to the end of the bar and now had both pistols drawn. He fired once at Alto North, but the other pistol flew out of his hand, crashing into a mirror behind the bar where it created large, concentric cracks. Charley Parker stood his ground, firing twice at Alto North, then swinging his pistol at Muldoon.

Through the blue haze Muldoon beheld the muzzle of Charley Parker's pistol swing blackly his way and found he had his own pistol out and was raising it at Charley Parker, knowing even in the act that he was too late, that Parker would hit him first. He tensed, drawing himself together in anticipation of the impact, but the other man's gun clicked dully, harmlessly, and before Charley Parker could get off another shot Alto North had bobbed up right in front of him and hit him twice. Parker reeled back into a row of glasses, spilling them sideways, but he still had enough in him to make a kind of shuffling, doubled-over run down the bar and into the hallway. Muldoon heard Okey-Poke yelling something and saw him pointing. He turned that way to find Henderson's blanched and glistening face staring at him, his pistol showing but pointed upwards at the ceiling. Then Henderson ducked out of sight behind the bar.

The wide man with the broom had dropped it the instant Gyp the Blood had shot Billy Phillips and scuttled away towards the hall, where he'd collided with Keppard and his com-

panion, and the three big bodies were still disentangling themselves when Alto North dropped into a panther-like crouch
and raced the length of the bar, his pistol in one hand, knife in
the other. Keppard rolled away from the other two men, and
Alto North hardly broke stride, firing a shot into the body of
the man who'd held the broom. But North's business was
elsewhere, around the corner of the bar where Gyp the Blood
lay. Muldoon saw North come up from his crouch, saw his
knife hand rise over Gyp, and then the blade plunge downward once, rise again, then plunge downward once more, and
Muldoon heard North grunt with the effort of that finishing
stroke.

He found himself at the bar now, bending over Jimmie Enright who lay open-eyed and still grasping the rail with one
hand while yet holding his pistol though the fingers had fallen
away from the grip. Sidestepping Jimmie, he pulled himself
onto the bar and across it to find himself staring wildly down
into the face of the man Henderson, who was crouched below
on the dirty plankings, as much of him underneath the sinks as
he could manage. He was still holding his pistol but holding
it only as a child might a stuffed animal or toy. Henderson
looked up into Muldoon's blazing face, his eyes riveted on the
pistol Muldoon held, his lips drawn back from his teeth in a
silent screech. Leaning over the bar's inner edge Muldoon kept
the pistol on Henderson and was going to tell him to drop
his gun but never got the chance. Stepping lithely over the
sprawled body of Harry Parker, Alto North stamped on Henderson's gun hand, then fired a bullet between those blind,
beseeching eyes. Henderson's head jerked backwards, hitting
the planking with a loud thud, the grimace still in place, only
a little wider. Muldoon tore his eyes away from this to find
Alto North looking at him.

"Why?" Muldoon started to ask. The man had so clearly been useless, harmless. But North only made that sour little expression with his lips and turned back, running upright now as he entered the hallway leading past the dance hall to the beer garden beyond.

Muldoon ran too, after North, past the crouching figures of King Keppard and his friend, past Gyp the Blood, who lay on his back just at the bar's end, his arms flung out from his sides, the palms of his hands facing up and looking white as marble. The single dingy light still shone on the mud-tracked boards of the hallway floor, the office door hung ajar, and when he shot a glance into the dance hall Muldoon saw it was empty also, the little bandstand with its wooden railing, the three chairs and empty bottle and leather megaphone just as Keppard and his bunch had left them only minutes ago.

He lunged past, gun at the ready. If the girl was on the premises, she would be back in the beer garden, perhaps cowering under some chairs in the corner where they stacked the kegs. And maybe Charley Parker and Alto North would be there as well. But there was no one he could see, not so much as a terrified waiter, flattened against the fence, or a drunk asleep in his boots at one of the gray, splintered tables. The gate was open, though, and he hopped through the tables and chairs to the alley's edge.

There in the dull, wet cinders lay a body on its stomach with one knee flexed as if it had fallen in full flight: it was the big fellow who'd held the broom when he'd trailed Gyp the Blood into the bar. So he simply stood there above the body, his chest heaving, his gun hand slowly lowering in that utter emptiness, until at last the .32 hung harmless at his side. Down at one end of the alley a single bulb burned harmlessly on towards morning. His face tickled, and he reached slowly up to find it running with sweat. Wiping it roughly with his coat sleeve, he knocked his derby off, started to pick it up, but then went abruptly back the way he'd come, limping slowly enough into the bar.

The four men who'd stood in the middle of the room had gone. So had those at the door. There was a man under the table of one of the booths; Muldoon could see his eyes staring at the .32 Muldoon still held, and Muldoon himself now looked down at it, then jammed it carelessly into his shoulder holster. The high, siren-like wailing continued like something mechanical that had broken. It was the older man in the last booth. He was holding his head with both hands, his Stetson still somehow on, though crushed by its owner's clutching fingers. The girl next to him had both her arms around the man and was shaking with silent sobs. Then the wailing stopped, and the only sound Muldoon heard in the room was coming from Jimmie Enright, who was blowing bloody bubbles from his opened lips; when they reached their maximum diameter they popped and dissolved into frothy rivulets that ran from both sides of his mouth. Muldoon stepped over to him and bent down. "Jimmie," he breathed. His hand hovered indecisively inches above Jimmie's face. The eyes that had been wide open were now shut and slightly squinted, as if Jimmie might be concentrating on producing those bubbles. What was left of Billy Phillips's head was touching one of Jimmie's feet. In that instant when Muldoon had been distracted by the entrance of the loud-talking Keppard and his companion, Gyp the Blood must have put his pistol flush with the back of Billy Phillips's head and fired. Some of Billy's hair had caught fire, and there was still an acrid taper of smoke standing almost straight up from the head and rising towards the stamped metal of the ceiling where it joined the old smoke of cigarettes and cigars and pipes and that lower, heavier layer of gun smoke that hung in a heavy, motionless scarf over the long room.

The older man in the far booth sank slowly into the girl's arms, relinquishing his hold on his head. The Stetson dropped onto the table. At Muldoon's feet Jimmie Enright produced one final bubble, a big one that trembled on his parted lips, glistening dully, then blew apart. The sudden silence lasted only seconds, though, and then a chunk of the mirror, broken by Gyp the Blood's flying pistol, fell off and crashed among the bottles and glasses, making what Muldoon thought was a tremendous and impossible clatter.

He became aware that there was someone else in the room besides the man under the table and the sobbing couple. King Keppard and his friend had scrambled off somewhere. He wheeled about on his good leg. Santos Villalta stood in the entrance, holding both doors wide, drawing the smoke languidly towards him. For the first time in memory Muldoon saw emotion in the ex-machine gunner's face, his mouth open, his eyes wide and dark as he took in the bodies of Billy Phillips and Jimmie Enright. *"Nombre de Dios,"* he said softly, then let go of the doors and advanced into the room. "They dead?" he asked without looking at Muldoon.

"Anderson," Muldoon muttered. He wasn't answering Santos. Instead, he was looking around the room at the bodies that Santos Villalta could see and those he couldn't—the ones behind the bar and out in the alley. He took in once again the cowering figure beneath the table, and the couple in the last booth who had all but slid out of sight. He looked at the smashed mirror with its missing chunk now in small shards among the glassware and bottles. In the middle of the floor he saw what he guessed must be evidence of the four men who'd been standing with their heads so close together when the Anderson bunch had walked in on their errand of death: a pipe with the dottle spilled from its bowl, gray and lifeless and fine as powdered bone. And above all this was the heavy scarf of gun smoke that had been stirred by the opening and shutting of the Tuxedo's doors, so that now it took on a sort of life, transmogrified from scarf to snake, a huge boa that coiled slowly over this desolation, seeking out what life might remain.

"Anderson," Muldoon said again, now not muttering but pronouncing. Santos Villalta was still staring about, assessing the carnage, what it meant. Muldoon gripped his elbow. "Get me up to Anderson's house," he said into the driver's ear, as if there were anyone left in here capable of caring where they went.

Under the blaze of the Tuxedo's sign the big Jefferey was there, chugging obediently in place; Santos had mastered all the new techniques and kept the car in perfect condition. As the two men jumped into it, slamming the doors simultaneously, they heard the sound of a siren, a police wagon tearing up Basin. Santos Villalta jammed the Jefferey forward, careening around Bienville, away from the river, and on through the Sabbath-silenced streets to Claiborne. When he'd swung onto Claiborne towards Elysian Fields he finally spoke, asking Muldoon where Okey-Poke had gone. "I see him ron this way," he said. Muldoon didn't answer. He'd forgotten about Okey, and now, reminded of him, he didn't care. Okey would have to take care of himself. They all would. And he had something he himself must take care of right now, at the house on Elysian Fields.

As they neared it Santos suddenly swerved violently, narrowly missing a spectral black vendor in matching ministerial frock coat, pulling his cart across the street. It was loaded with Easter blooms—white, pink, jasmine—and it was these Santos had seen at the last second. As it was, Muldoon was flung so hard against the door that he ricocheted back against the gear-shift, and the Jefferey made a screeching protest as Santos swung the wheel back and slammed on the brakes. The car came to a shuddering stop fifty yards from the house that was a half-block deep, a high, white vault with a flight of steps rising steeply from the street to a narrow porch. Muldoon had never been inside it but had made a couple of calls at the back door on business and knew it had been built in the '70s by a cousin of the scalawag governor, Warmoth. There was an old tale of someone buried out back by the stable the Negroes said, a haunt that was seen standing motionless by the stable doors on certain moonless nights.

"You best get the hell outta here," Muldoon told Santos as he righted himself and swung out onto the running board. "If I was you, I'd find a place to park this thing somewhere and then find a place to park yourself a while." In the all-but-opaque interior of the cab he thought he saw Santos make a curt nod, and then he was out on the banquette, listening to the Jefferey roaring up Elysian Fields. He thought Santos might have family who lived in that direction. When the roar had begun to die he heard soft sounds behind him and turned about. It was the black flower vendor, wheeling his cart about and picking up the spilled Easter bouquets that had saved his life. Muldoon stood there a moment, then went across and began to help the man gather them and put them back in the cart. The other said nothing but made short, smoothing gestures over the blooms, cradling them in his arms before putting them in the cart. When they were finished the vendor crossed himself and took up the cart's polished handles again, pulling it down the street towards the river.

He was alone then. He could not recall ever feeling so utterly alone, not even in those interminable hours when he'd lain bandaged in his bed in the convalescent ward through the remainder of that awful summer, the heat relentless even in the middle of the night, his only company confused, disconnected images of what might have happened on Saratoga.

The flower vendor vanished into the obscurity of dawning, and he turned back towards the house and its inhospitably steep steps up which he now hauled himself, gripping the iron rail Tom Anderson had ordered to replace the original wooden one. Up on the porch he could see a light somewhere within, but the streetward rooms were dark behind the louvered shutters that hung inside the ponderous exterior ones hooked to the outside boards.

His knocking at the door must be thundering through all these rooms, he thought, awakening not only the entire household but everyone else on the street. But he didn't care, thundering on, the stretched skin of his knuckles beginning to break, abrade. His mission here might as well be public since he had no least care for its consequences. And as he continued to pound at the unforgiving, iron-grained cypress, he saw before him the interior of the Tuxedo, the suspended smoke, the smashed mirror with its black, missing chunk, the final, suspiring bubble on Jimmie Enright's lips—Jimmie, loyal to the last.

He only realized—and then dazedly—when his fist missed its mark and fell into empty air that the door had opened and that inside it, dimly outlined against the obscure, rearward light there stood the tall, full figure of Tom Anderson. He was holding the doorknob with his maimed right hand, his left hand held behind the waist and sash of the Chinese smoking jacket he wore with its broad, stiff lapels. Muldoon thought it probable Anderson held a pistol in that hidden hand. Beneath the smoking jacket Muldoon could see he was still in a dress shirt with gold studs, though he had taken the collar off. He might well have been an inveterate opera-goer who had come home late after a post-performance dinner and then stayed up to replay in his mind the night's most stirring arias.

"Oh, it's you," Anderson said, casual even now.

"Yeah, it's me," Muldoon rasped. "Just me."

"Well, I guess you better come in, then." He swung the door wider and turned in front of Muldoon, leading him down a narrow, darkened hall. At its far end a door was cracked a few inches and out of it shone the bit of light he'd spied from the porch, slanting its sliver along the hallway and the figured runner. "Couldn't you have phoned?" Anderson asked over his shoulder.

"There wasn't time." Muldoon could see now the pistol in Anderson's hand, and he was holding it with a casualness, an ease that Muldoon was bound to find remarkable, even though he'd witnessed just these traits so many times down through the years. Passing the alcove beneath the stairs, Anderson laid the gun on a small table next to a tablet of paper and a couple of pencils. It might as well have been just a third pencil the way he put it there. Above the table hung the telephone box. His slippered feet were soundless on the runner as they glided on towards the light, whereas Muldoon clumped along behind him, seeing only what light got past Anderson's high, broad frame.

Even before Anderson reached the door and swung it open, Muldoon knew, somehow, whether it was by scent or the vaguest prefiguration of what wasn't even a shadow, a faint stirring, the sound of a silken sleeve brushing a tabletop, the tinkle of a piece of jewelry, or the slow, expectant parting of lips. So that when Anderson led him into the yellow light of the kitchen he was not completely surprised, was even at that moment beginning to make the internal adjustment: finding her there at the table in a gray silk wrapper even he could see was both new and very expensive, the large domed overhead light falling on her erect, broad shoulders, catching the swell of her breasts and creating shadows beneath them, and her gray eyes as fearless and candid as ever.

Still, he stopped there at the threshold, while Anderson in all his regal ease, his casual sovereignty, crossed to the stove on which there sat a lidded pot. His back still turned on Muldoon, he took a towel from the sideboard and lifted the lid, speaking as he did.

"Coffee?"

"*You,*" Muldoon breathed, his black eyes on the girl. She returned their blaze with that same even candor that had so captivated him from the first, when he'd sought her out in the hurly-burly of the Frenchman's; or that time out on the lake, when she'd sat facing him, occasionally holding onto her feathered hat in the wide, windy expanse: in all those places this same unruffled gaze, which he had numbly interpreted as the expression of a deep equipoise but that now, here in Anderson's house, suddenly seemed monstrous, soulless, a gaze that could look on anything and not be moved because behind it there was nothing that could be moved; or, if there was, it must be something so peculiarly personal that it had nothing at all to do with the world he thought he lived in. He knew that Anderson regarded him as a kind of human watch or clock—reliable, steady, utterly predictable. Jimmie Enright had told him that once, years ago when Jimmie was running the Annex; he apparently thought it was a compliment. Now he found himself wondering if the being before him at the table was really a lot closer to a watch or clock than he'd ever been. Or were her torments like his own—deeply hidden phantoms of the dark hours between days?

His mind skipped suddenly from the girl to that other machine, Alto North, going about his work in the Tuxedo, cutting men down as if they were so much pork; and from North to Santos Villalta, who had driven him here—invariably emotionless, unreachable. Were these the kind of people Tom Anderson sedulously surrounded himself with as tractable, useful to his many purposes, just as he'd reached into the hospital to rescue him from his obloquy? Earlier, when he'd noticed the dead eyes of all the women who'd sat for Bellocq, it had occurred to him, and for the first time, too, that he worked among dead people, and that the District itself was a kind of giant charnel house, bordered by its formal cemeteries, St. Louis Number 1 and 2. Now it came to him, staring at the girl who was staring right back, that those who weren't dead were instead machines. How could he have missed these things over all these years, unless he himself really had become part watch or clock, as Anderson believed?

Anderson had seated himself at the table with a thick white mug of coffee from which steam arose in a cheerful curl. He crossed his long legs, one slippered foot swinging twice, then stopping. "Well, my good man," he said presently, "let's hear about your night. What have you got for me?"

"They're all dead," Muldoon rasped, tearing his eyes from the girl to face his boss. Anderson's eyebrows lifted and he cocked his head slightly in a silent question. "They're all dead in there," Muldoon repeated. "Jimmie, Billy Phillips, Harry Parker, Gyp the Blood, two guys I don't know their names...." While he was saying this Anderson was stroking his moustache yet keeping his eyes on Muldoon. Now he replied in his quiet tone that he'd been expecting trouble.

"Been expecting it for some time, really. Had to happen, sooner or later, I guess. Them jaspers never knew when enough was enough. Well, now they do. But, this is bad, no question of it. It'll bring plenty trouble—for you, too, Fast-Mail. Who saw what went on, do you reckon? Anybody we know?"

"*You* did this!" Muldoon roared suddenly, startled by the volume, the unbidden violence of his own voice. "*You* did this! How you worked it all out, I don't know. But I know you done it. You got old Jimmie to lead us over there, and Billy without even a club." Until blurting this out he hadn't realized that somewhere over the last hour or so he'd come to understand the significance of the exchange between Jimmie and Billy in the 102 kitchen: it was a piece of the big set-up. He still stood where he had been, at the threshold, but now he took a step into the room and leaned from the waist forward, jutting his unshaven jaw at Anderson.

"You know who saw what went on? *I* saw it. That's all. I'm the only one left who saw it all."

Anderson nodded, still stroking his moustache. "Good, good," he said behind his hand. "That'll be some help, any-ways." He was already thinking ahead, beginning to formu-late a strategy in which his man about town, his clock-like functionary, could serve yet another purpose. But when he looked up he found Muldoon with the .32 drawn and held up-right in his shaking hand. The girl glanced quickly at Ander-son and half-rose, but Anderson motioned her back into her chair.

"Excited, man—you're excited." He merely glanced at the pistol searching Muldoon's face some long moments. He un-crossed his legs, clasped his hands, and when he finally spoke it was in a different tone, one that carried a burden of wearied condescension.

"You're excited. But let me guess here. Let me guess you didn't do anything in there, didn't do any shooting with that thing." He nodded at the pistol Muldoon still held in his shaking hand, its muzzle aimed at the ceiling.

"You're damned right I didn't!" he answered, his voice loud yet but no longer a roar. "I didn't shoot nobody, but I'm gonna shoot you, Tom Anderson. That I am."

Anderson shook his big, blond head slowly, sadly, as if here was but another burden he had to carry as a man of the world running enterprises fraught with the congenital weaknesses of hirelings he'd rescued, befriended, counseled, paid handsomely, protected. He allowed himself a histrionic sigh. "No, no," he said. "No, you aint going to use that thing to shoot anybody. Not tonight, not ever.

"Fast-Mail," he continued after another, effective pause, "you're a cowardly son-of-a-buck. I kind of misjudged you there. But then, I wasn't paying you to be a brave fellow, was I? Now, Jimmie—Jimmie was brave as a bulldog. We're gonna miss Jimmie, all right. But we won't miss you, Fast-Mail." He unclasped his hands and made a brief, dismissive backhanded gesture at the .32. "I don't guess you'll be doing any shooting in here. The only thing you was ever any good for was running: you ran those races when you was a kid, and you ran em good, too, I'll give you that much. And you ran them bandits down. But then you didn't stop running. You ran off from old Coakley. And now, by God, you've run over here, run away from the Tuxedo and left your friends for dead, just like you did old Coakley." He kept his blue eyes steadily on Muldoon as he delivered this judgment, but then he glanced meaningfully down at Muldoon's game leg.

"Prob'ly don't move too fast on that thing," he drawled, "but if I was in your shoes right now, why, I'd keep on running. Best thing you can do."

The girl was looking at Anderson, and now he returned

her gaze. "Cammie," he said, his voice softening but still filled with casual authority, "be a good gal, will you, and call down to Billy Brundy. Ask him to find a way to get in touch with Alto North. Might be he's back at Toro's. Our man here don't tell us he's dead. Anyways, I got one more job for him to finish up over here." He looked back at Muldoon. "I'd make the call myself, only I don't feel comfortable leaving you in here with this...*desperado.*"

The girl rose to go to the phone box down the hall, but as she did so Muldoon brought the .32 level on Anderson. She stopped, her hand on the table, looking at Muldoon with her gray eyes that so nearly matched her wrapper.

"Go on, gal," Anderson said, still in that altered, softened tone. "Go on, now. He aint gonna hurt anybody." He smiled at her, and as he did Muldoon was cast back to that moment in the 102 when Harry Parker had wheeled about at the door, yelling back at the whole room that Tom Anderson fucked his own. Standing at the bar, he'd thought about it briefly, wondering what the hell Harry Parker could have meant by that—if anything. At best it had seemed a dumb, viciously worded challenge. Now, though, he saw that it had been he himself who'd been too dumb to get it. Here, in this room, these two people—that had been Harry Parker's real point, a literal one, though in what specific way the girl was Anderson's "own" he couldn't guess.

And maybe it didn't really matter, anyway. Because there was a bigger thing here than whatever the truth was about Anderson and the girl, whose true name, it was clear, he had never known. Tom Anderson did indeed fuck his own, every one of them, and he, Francis Muldoon, was one of those Tom Anderson fucked. It wasn't only the nameless and now forgotten whores Anderson had run and fucked and discarded. It wasn't only those women obscurely memorialized in that stack of chocolate-hued prints up in Bellocq's studio. It wasn't even Mamie Desdoumes, whose story had so gripped him and the riddling truth of which Madame Papaloos had pronounced in the dim emptiness of her hut outside the city. It was all of them, all the women and all the men Anderson paid for and who nightly did his bidding. Especially those who at the last had resolutely walked across Franklin, their heels ringing on the cobbles, towards the death that lay waiting within. That had been the final fucking, he thought, the final, ultimate violation, the last service Anderson could extract from them. And tomorrow, which was already today, Anderson would doubtless set about finding suitable replacement parts for them. And the only thing that could put an end to this ghastly process, this solemn, serial, remorseless violation of other women, other men was himself, the former Fast-Mail Muldoon, and the .32 revolver he kept leveled on Anderson's prosperous, calmly breathing breast.

Except he couldn't.

The girl moved gracefully past him with her dancer's long stride, going to the phone where she would make the call that would bring Alto North out here to put a bullet in Muldoon's back or brain—if not today, then the day after, or the one after that. He could already envision the newspaper squib that wouldn't make Easter's edition but would the Monday one. It would read much like that reporting the death of the man found in the auto on Marais: *"The fugitive Francis Muldoon, suspect in the murders at the Tuxedo that profaned the Holy Sabbath and stank in the nostrils of the Most High...."*

And it was this same stench—forever to be in his own nostrils—that made him know he couldn't execute Anderson. He already had it on him as it was: the stench of the burned powder and hair, of the blood and brain matter blown into Harry Parker's face at the Tuxedo. He'd carried it in here with him, embedded in the closely woven fibers of the suit Tom Anderson had paid for. He could smell it on himself, the ineradicable reek of a corruption beyond crime. And it was this, he now realized, that had stayed his finger on the trigger inside the Tuxedo. He had realized, glaring down into the face of that man crouched behind the bar, that if he pulled the trigger, he would have to live with this reek forever, in his nostrils, in his soul. Stalked through the years by the beast of old disgrace, he knew something of penalty and penance, too. This was enough. He probably couldn't escape Alto North who might even now be climbing into an auto and speeding this way to deliver Tom Anderson's own special brand of justice—the bullet to the back or the head and then his body dumped in the Mississippi and heading seaward in the river's dark rush, to fetch up at last near Mozambique Point or Cat Island. But he could, at least, at last, escape disgrace, wipe clean his slate in sparing Tom Anderson.

He put the pistol back in its holster.

"Ahh," Tom Anderson breathed. "I thought not. Haven't misjudged you after all, Fast-Mail. Except only tonight. You wasn't even good for being a number over there, was you. No sir, not even a number." He jerked his thumb over his shoulder. "Back way's there." Muldoon knew that way, had been up and down its steps. Instead, he went the way he'd come in, along the hallway now, past the girl standing in the alcove, her hands held lightly before her, as though on the stage at the Tuxedo's beer garden and about to sing. Whether she had already made the call to Billy Brundy, he couldn't tell, her attitude ambiguous, her eyes as unreadable as ever. The pistol lay just where Anderson had placed it.

"You poor fool," she whispered to him as he came abreast of her.

"Maybe," he said, wanting, as always, to say something more. But this time it was she who wanted to add something.

"The boat," she said to his broad back. "Get to the boat if you can."

He came out of the doorway and down the inhospitable steps, clutching the iron railing. It was dawn in the streets. A man and a boy came past where he stood, both in their modest Easter best, and swaying riverward on the high seat of a cart, the horse at a swinging, mile-eating clip-clop that told Muldoon they had been on the road more than a few minutes. The man touched his hat, and Muldoon was about to touch his own when he remembered he'd knocked it off in the beer garden. He'd bought it less than a year ago on Canal, and the haberdasher had stamped his name into the band, "F. Muldoon"—just one of the little extra services the concern provided for their good customers. When they had gone, their forms diminishing to his gaze, he pulled out his watch from his vest pocket and found it had stopped some hours back. As he was about to replace it he was seized by a sudden, resistless impulse and threw it into the street.

Even before it hit he'd begun to run towards the lake, but less than a block onward he felt the insistent slam of the .32 in its holster. He stopped, pulled off his coat, ripped the pistol from its holster, and then he flung that away, too, sending it in a high, lightless arc over a flowered hedge whose buds were pinched and immature in this late spring. He heard it thud into the sodden earth of the garden bed beyond the hedge, and then he unbuckled the harness of the holster, letting it drop where he stood. Then he began to run again: Genius, Johnson, Force, Virtue, Law, Hope, his feet passing over the names of the streets and their blue-tiled insets in the pavings of the intersections.

He had achieved by now that peculiar, high-hopping kind of canter he had when he'd run through the rain towards the girl's flat on Gravier. Yet what it brought to mind now was not that signal experience, so long precious to him in its intimacy, its confessional quality, but instead learning to skip when he'd been a small boy back in the Channel. How high he had hopped then! What freedom from earth he'd felt at the apex of his leap! Really, it was almost like flying. And it hadn't been long after that when on three consecutive nights he'd had dreams of flying just above the mule manure and bottles and wads of newspaper that were the landscape he knew, his knotty little legs in their short pants making long, floating, shadowless strides above all that. Maybe that was when it had first come to him that he could be a real runner, someone special. And once, a few years thereafter, he'd been on the verge of telling this to one of the brothers at St. Alphonsus—that his career as a runner might just have begun in the dreams that had been inspired by skipping. But he hadn't told the brother anything after all; it seemed silly somehow. And so he'd just gone on, collecting trophies, medals with their cloth appendages like tiny bits of bunting, all those stories in the sports pages.

But here he found himself once more, hopping along the city's streets, a long way from that time and place and purpose, taking his long, left-footed stride, then bringing the flopping right foot after it, the toes dropping forward, volitionless, before he could put weight on them and force the foot to at least bear some balance. Even so, he could see now that he was leaving Tom Anderson's neighborhood behind, the named streets beginning to peter out—Industry, Agriculture, Abundance—and the land rising ever so slightly towards Metairie Ridge.

Ahead of him a bicyclist labored slowly, a cane pole held in one hand while with the other he steered a wobbly course toward the lake. After a block Muldoon came even with him, startling the man as he drew up on his shoulder. Their eyes met for an instant as the man turned his head to find the shining, red-faced runner hanging there. Then Muldoon inched past, the left foot pounding and his runner's heart pounding, too, within his breast.

"By God! Fast-Mail," he gasped to himself, hearing through his pounding the bicycle's tires crunching deliberately over the shells of long-dead crustaceans, "you may not be half the man you was, but you can still make better time than some that's whole." So he ran on, believing this.